REIGN

K.T. HOLDER

For my Wife

AUTHOR'S NOTE

This book is a work of fantasy fiction, and while it contains magical elements and imaginary settings, it also includes themes that may be distressing to some readers.

I believe stories should be immersive, but also that you deserve to make informed choices about the content you engage with. If you'd like to see a list of content warnings for this and my other books, you can find one linked on my website:

www.ktholder.com

Please be aware that some content warnings may be minor spoilers.

Thank you for reading,
KT Holder

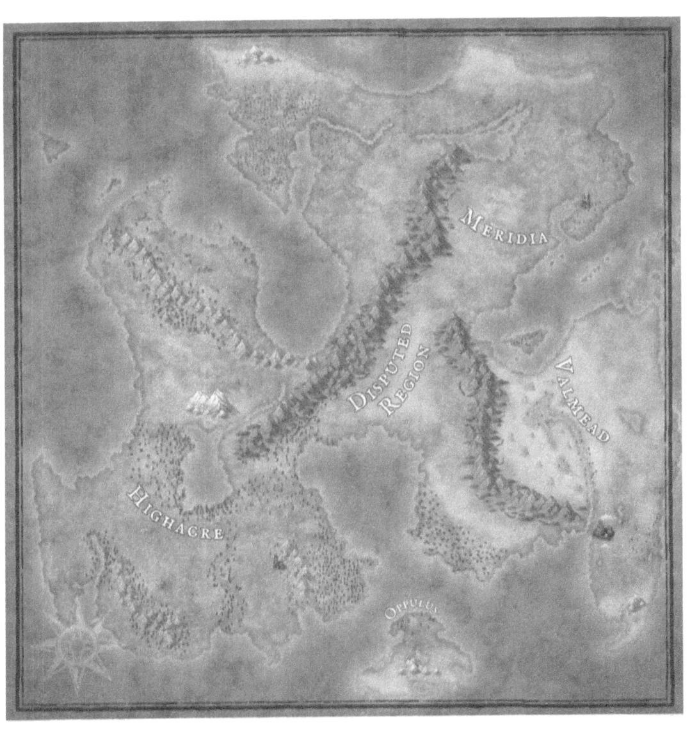

Meridia
Valmead
Disputed Region
Highacre
Oppulus

PROLOGUE

THE WIND BLEW through her hair as she stood on the hill, watching the battle preparation below.

How did it come to this?

So many lives had been lost. So many friends.

Had it all been worth it?

She turned her face to the sun, closed her eyes, and took a deep breath.

It was time.

She had a war to win.

1

Claire tried to open her eyes. She couldn't tell if they were caked closed with sleep, or if it was the bruising and swelling. She managed to open them enough for thin lines of light to pierce through before she gave up, exhausted.

What day is it?

She lifted her head slowly, cracking her neck to either side, and took a deep breath. Pain exploded in her ribs, reminding her of the beating she took yesterday. Or was it the day before? Everything was bleeding together. She had lost all concept of time. Some days she was beaten and physically tortured, others she was left in the cell with different sounds playing at painfully high volumes. Recently, they had taken her to a new room, where they strapped her to a chair, forcing her to watch and listen to the repetitive information blasted at her for hours. Trying to rewire her brain.

Claire tried to rub her eyes and found her hands were tied behind her back. She sighed.

Torture today then.

It was easier for her to process time when she assumed it was one type of torture per day. But in reality, she may have been experiencing only one type for a couple of hours before being transferred to the next. Being in a place where time had no meaning, Claire was trying to attach meaning where she could. Though if one type of torture a day was the correct measurement, then Claire had been here for a depressingly long time.

She heard the door open and tensed up automatically. Claire flinched when hands touched her face, but then relief and gratitude washed over her as the fingers guided a straw into her mouth. She took as much water as she dared, not wanting to drink too much only to lose it later.

He's taking care of me. Just like the prime minister and Ezra are taking care of Highacre.

As the door closed again, Claire shook her head, trying to clear the echo of the propaganda. Was it propaganda? Claire was almost sure it was. Hadn't she been arrested by the prime minister's personal police force? And she was sure Ezra had personally tortured her. Almost sure. Or had she dreamed it?

She hadn't seen Ezra since that first time he visited. If that had been real, surely he would have been back. But maybe she wasn't important enough to warrant his time. Maybe she had dreamed it, and he hadn't visited at all. She thought she had been gathering evidence against Ezra before she was brought here. Maybe that was influencing her dreams.

Claire tried to shift her weight, but all that managed to achieve was to remind her of her injuries and aching muscles. Her foot cramped painfully as her lower back spasmed. She cried out and was instantly embarrassed by the show of weakness. She lowered her head and hoped the cameras couldn't see her tears.

Why hadn't they rescued her?

The princess is weak and ran away at the first sign of trouble. She has abandoned you.

Claire shook her head clear again, instantly regretting the movement. What was real and what was false? She felt like her mind was underwater. She couldn't find the space to think clearly. Claire was sure if she just found the space, she could figure this out. Her foot cramped again, and Claire focussed on the pain this time. That was real. The pain was real; the torture was real. Someone was holding her against her will. She needed to escape. But that seemed laughably impossible.

She flinched as the door opened again.

"Oh dear, what have they done to you?"

Claire struggled to open her eyes. She needed to open them. If she could see, she could tell what was real and what was a trick.

"Here now, let me help you."

Claire flinched as a soft, warm cloth gently dabbed at her face, washing away the blood and grime. It felt so good. A small part of her mind said she should fight it. Not accept any kindness. It was a trick. The rest of her mind told that part to shut up, and she relaxed into the tiny luxury.

"I'm just going to dab a little of this balm on your face to help with your wounds. It won't hurt you, but it is a little cold. I'm sorry."

Claire tried to find the lie in the voice. It couldn't be him. Were they using a vocal distorter? They could have copied his voice patterns by now.

She flinched instinctively despite the man's warning. He cooed and apologised in a soft, warm voice as he tended to her face and then moved on to her other injuries. Her face tingled where he'd applied the balm. Whether it was that, or simply him cleaning her face, Claire found she could finally open her eyes.

She blanched as her eyes told the same story as her ears. Her mentor was sitting on a chair across from her, cleaning blood off her arm and applying antiseptic to her cuts.

"Are you here to get me out?" Claire whispered, her voice cracking from lack of use.

"Now, now. Let's just focus on getting you cleaned up," he replied.

"We need to get out of here. Now."

"I know it may not seem like it, but you're safe here."

She stared at him in disbelief. For a time, they were silent as he cleaned and dressed her wounds. Finally, he put his bucket to the side and looked at her, a kind smile lighting his eyes.

"You've been through an ordeal."

Claire considered that the understatement of the century and didn't feel it required a response.

"I don't expect you remember it all, but you were taken by Meridian forces. They tried to turn you against Highacre, but you're too strong for that. You fought them, just like I taught you." He smiled again. Claire remained silent. That was a lie. Wasn't it?

"We got you back a couple of days ago, but you were fighting us. They did a real job brainwashing you." He leant in conspiratorially. "I've heard that they might have developed a way to implant false memories, but that's highly classified."

Claire searched his face. A small wave of panic grew in her chest. She was almost certain it was her mentor and not an imposter. But last time she saw him, they had been looking to fight against whatever power was interfering in Highacren politics. That didn't include investigating the latest technological developments from Meridia. So how would he know if they had developed a way to implant false memories? And he no longer had access to anything highly classified. He'd been fired.

Implanted memories would be a convenient way to explain everything. Well, to explain everything in a way to suit his own narrative. But then, how would she know what memories were real?

"We've spent the last couple of days trying to see if they did any actual damage to your brain, and also playing you some news clips to bring you back. Show you what's real."

News clips? The bombardment of messages about the prime minister and Ezra was nothing like news clips. All they kept saying was that the two men were great—saving Highacre, helping the people. Modern-day heroes.

Seeing her face, her mentor looked slightly abashed. "Okay, I know. They were a little more full-on. That's my fault. I authorised them to turn it up a notch. I wanted you back and operational quickly."

"What's going on?"

"Last time we met, I was pretty negative. I had just been fired from the Highacren Intelligence Agency, and I was bitter. I'll admit it."

So at least that memory was real.

"But I was blaming the wrong side. The prime minister wasn't trying to get rid of the agency completely. He was trying to cut away the dead wood and build something worthwhile in its place. The old regime had become lax. Highacre was lazy in our victory, and we were ignoring the signs that Meridia was gearing up for round two." He sighed. "The PM saw the warning signs, but no one would listen. Change is uncomfortable, and everyone was comfortable in their ignorance, thinking we'd won peace for good. We saw the PM's actions as a grab for power. But what he was really trying to do was bring Highacre into a state of readiness to counter the inevitable Meridian invasion."

Had Meridia invaded? Claire tried to force her brain to work. She remembered an attack on the arena, but that had been terrorists. Or at least, she thought that was terrorists. And they'd been condemned by Meridia, right? But Meridia *had* pressed into the Disputed Region between Highacre and Meridia. They had taken some mines, maybe? The felixium mines! But that was it. They hadn't declared war. At least, she didn't think they had. But her mentor was telling her that Meridia were the ones who had taken her. Tortured her. She didn't think that was real, but it did seem to fit.

"Look, I was like you. I thought the PM was out for himself. Grabbing power after the royal family was assassinated by Meridia. But he was thrust into a leadership position he never wanted because of the power vacuum. And of course, others saw the opportunity too late, and they used the tragic deaths of the royal family to try to unseat him and take the power for themselves. I'm ashamed that I didn't see it at first. But he needed to get rid of those who wanted to destabilise Highacre for their own gain. Destabilise us while the wolves were at our door. That's why he shut the HIA down. But he was looking to build something better in its place. Something free from self-interested vermin. Something free of bureaucratic power magnets."

He sounded like her mentor had sounded before he was fired. Energised, passionate. Like he had a purpose, a mission. Claire felt the familiar urge to be a part of the mission. To join a team and work together for a common goal.

"I get your skepticism," he said with a chuckle. "And while I admit that I misjudged the PM, I still don't like the guy. He's still a politician."

Claire let a laugh escape her lips. Her throat was still fairly dry, and it sounded like a cough. Her mentor stood and shuffled to the door, talking softly to someone outside. He returned with another glass of water and a straw. She drank gratefully.

"Ezra though," he continued, "he's the one that's really in charge, and he is all about preventing another war. He'll be able to ensure that the new agency is not overly politicised, or used for political purposes. He really knows his craft."

"Yeah, which he learned in Meridia by spying on High-acre." Claire tried to gesture, and was reminded that she was restrained. She looked accusingly at her mentor.

"Oh, yes." He chuckled again, looking embarrassed, then got up and shuffled around behind her. "When we got you back, you were a little, er, animated and enthusiastic about escaping."

Claire felt a tug, and then her arms were free. Blood returned to her hands painfully as she rubbed her wrists.

"Which we don't blame you for, of course. Anyone who goes through what you went through would be looking to escape at the first opportunity. But after you knocked out the third guard, we had to put you in some restraints."

Claire couldn't remember that at all. She frowned as she looked at the marks on her wrists. Did they have to restrain her so tightly?

"Look, Ezra was all for Meridia, but then they screwed him. He's not loyal to them. He became a businessman. What he really wants is peace to enable positive trade across the world so he can be rich and live on a yacht, or whatever rich people do. The PM's asked him to get our new intelligence agency up and running, and he's agreed. It's a win-win for him, and it's great for us. We get the inside scoop on the tactics the Meridians use, and a new effective agency. So, no, I don't like the PM. But I get what he is doing now, and I'm sorry for some of the things I said about him. He and Ezra are the real deal."

Real deal. The phrase from the footage that had been repeatedly blasted at Claire resonated, echoing in her mind.

"They want to help. They're the good guys."

Good guys.

"I know it's hard, especially after the brainwashing job those Meridians did on you." Her mentor looked sympathetically at Claire. "But we can trust them. Especially Ezra. I'd trust the bloke with my life. And you should too."

Claire could vaguely remember thinking that she *couldn't* trust Ezra. But for the life of her, she couldn't remember why. It was just out of reach, like a name forgotten, but on the tip of your tongue. Maybe she was wrong. Maybe that was a false memory, and there was no reason not to trust Ezra.

Maybe she dreamed it.

2

*H*IGHACRE IS AT WAR.

Everything froze. A high-pitched ringing began in Lily's ears.

I'm too late.

Lily could hear her own heartbeat as she moved forwards, her mind stuck in the slow-motion sludge of wanting to go back. Wanting it not to be true. Needing another chance.

With a snap, everything came back into focus. People were moving urgently, talking loudly about what had just happened. Those who supported the prime minister were cheering, gleefully congratulating themselves on sending their country to war with Meridia. A war they would not personally fight.

Not all were with the prime minister. Lily could see some politicians looking sombre, shaking their heads, disappointment on their faces. Some even looked scared, and she thought she saw a couple wiping tears hurriedly away. But no one was loudly protesting. No one wanted to stand out in opposition. Lily could feel the fear.

"What do we do now?"

Lily looked at Ava. Her Meridian friend looked as stunned as Lily felt. They had hoped to get to the Tower in time to prevent the declaration of war. But in the rush, no one had thought about what would happen if they failed.

Lily had never been at war before. Would Ava be okay? She was a Meridian, but as ambassador to court, surely she would be treated well. Lily chastised herself. Surely every Meridian currently in Highacre would be treated well, regardless of status.

But would they? From what Giles and Naomi had told her, the HSP was oppressing the Highacren population. If that was how the citizens were being treated, what would happen to any Meridians living in Highacre?

They will *be treated respectfully.* Lily swore it to herself. She would make sure the Meridians within her borders were treated well, just as she would end the oppression of the HSP. And if she could negate the declaration of war, then maybe she wouldn't need to worry so much about the Meridians in Highacre at all.

She needed to do something. She *was* queen now, after all. Sure, they had performed the ceremony in the back of a van as they sped their way to the Tower. And yes, the prime minister was still claiming that Lily had not successfully completed the Trials and therefore had not been confirmed as the rightful ruler of Highacre. But she had been assured that the experts agreed he was wrong, and her coronation was legitimate.

Lily went to approach the parliamentary floor, but the politicians were already dispersing.

Hurry. Speak up and call them all back.

But it was like Lily's feet were stuck. What if they didn't listen? What if she couldn't take back the declaration for some reason? Irrational social anxiety gripped her, and the idea of asserting herself in this room full of important people had a paralysing effect.

It doesn't matter! You have to try.

Lily took a deep breath and stepped in the direction of the podium. She saw several large, heavily armed police walking with purpose towards her and her friends.

"Naomi?" Lily called, making sure her bodyguard had seen the men too.

"I see them," Naomi responded darkly.

"HSP," gasped Giles in alarm, spotting what the two women were looking at.

"The prime minister's new police force?" asked Ava, now looking at the men too.

"The prime minister's personal militia, more like," muttered Alexei. Naomi gave him a look, and he shrugged. "My father has a similar group back home."

Alexei's father was the Valmeadian dictator, and Lily vaguely wondered if that was where the prime minister got the idea in the first place.

"Alexei, you must come with me at once."

So focussed on the approaching HSP officers, the group startled at the sudden arrival of Sergei Romanovich, the Valmeadian ambassador. His normally jovial face was dark and his eyes darted around the room, identifying exits and scanning for threats.

"Sergei, what's going on?" Alexei asked, feet firmly planted.

"We have to get out of here. It is not safe for us. Quickly, before they stop us."

"Why would they stop you?" Lily asked, confused. The declaration was against Meridia. The Valmeadian diplomats should be fine.

Sergei glared at Lily. "I must get the Great Leader's son home. I will not ask where you have kept him these last months, only that you let us go, and go now."

"Sergei, what's wrong?" asked Alexei. Lily could hear the concern in his voice. Something was clearly off for Sergei to be this upset.

"It's your father," Sergei said urgently, his face softening as he looked at Alexei. "He's been taken ill—"

"Ava! You're back, thank goodness," Ezra Brown, the ex-Meridian ambassador, appeared and swept Ava into a tight embrace. The group stared in surprise at the unexpected familiarity.

"It's okay, I'm fine," Ava reassured him, gently disentangling herself. Lily watched, stunned. Ava didn't seem surprised by the affection, nor was she overly embarrassed by the public display. In fact, she seemed pleased by Ezra's concern.

"I've been so worried," Ezra said, relinquishing his hold, but keeping his grip on her arms.

The little alarm in Lily's mind that had been ringing softly to let her know that something was wrong started blaring.

What was going on here?

Ezra and Ava had both been Meridian ambassadors, before Ava was pushed through the interdimensional portal with Lily. But she had never seen them as particularly close. In fact, Ezra was currently topping Lily's list of people likely involved in, if not behind everything, that had gone wrong in Highacre. In particular, the murder of the entire royal family. Her family.

Surely if Ava was this close to him, she would have mentioned it. Especially since they had become... What were they? Lily refocussed. Now was not the time to worry about her love life.

"Sirs, ma'ams."

While distracted, the group had been surrounded by the HSP officers. They stood in a loose circle around Lily and her friends, their weapons displayed threateningly, barring anyone from leaving. The leader ignored Lily, instead addressing the ambassadors.

"I'm under orders to bring you into custody and confine you to your quarters."

"What? No," Lily protested.

"They're my orders, ma'am, and you'd be best advised not to interfere."

Lily bristled at the dismissal. The prime minister had seen her arrive. He was the one who sent the HSP over to them. This officer knew exactly who she was.

"Surely there's some mistake," Ezra pleaded. "I've only just got my daughter back. You can't mean to detain her."

What?

"Daughter?" Lily addressed the question to Ava, who was now the focus of everyone's attention and stunned looks. She had the grace to look embarrassed, though she didn't seem to have an immediate answer. And she certainly wasn't denying it.

"Yes, Ava is my daughter. Didn't she tell you?" Ezra asked, looking surprised at Lily's confusion.

Ava glanced over at Lily, apology in her eyes, but Lily was fuming, the pain of Ava's deception fueling her anger. She had confided in Ava, and Ava had been her best friend before becoming something more. Lily groaned internally.

Tell me I haven't fallen into a honey trap.

Mixed with the sting of betrayal was frustration with herself. How could she have been so stupid?

"Sorry sir, they are my orders. Direct from the prime minister. I'm sure you can take it up with him. We'll make sure she's comfortable in her rooms." The officer's tone was deferential to Ezra, in stark contrast to the tone he'd used when addressing Lily.

Ezra hesitated and looked at Ava. Something of an unspoken message appeared to pass between them, and then Ezra nodded. HSP officers stepped forwards behind each ambassador and began marching them away.

Lily could hear Sergei protesting as they left, and Alexei was trying to regain the man's attention, asking about his father. Lily could feel Ava's eyes on her, but studiously avoided looking her way.

She heard boots moving behind her and turned to see the remaining HSP officers standing near Naomi, Giles, and herself in a way that indicated they were not free to leave. Ezra stood unencumbered to the side of their little group, watching with interested amusement.

"Your Majesty, I am to escort you back to the palace and secure you in your rooms. For your own safety," the HSP officer said.

"Like hell."

The HSP officer blinked, but quickly resumed his rigid demeanour.

"Ma'am, the prime minister is concerned for your safety. We are at war, and you could be the target of assassination attempts. We have not yet accounted for all the foreigners within our borders. I assess the risk to your safety as very high."

"If I am to be escorted anywhere, it'll be by my Royal Guards."

"They're not here."

"I am." Naomi stepped in front of Lily protectively. "I am Her Majesty's personal bodyguard."

The HSP officer considered Naomi, looking her up and down. He then looked pointedly around at the lack of other Royal Guards.

"Excellent. Ma'am, you will accompany Her Majesty and account for her personal safety. We will provide an escort for you both to ensure you arrive at the palace safely."

Lily looked for a way out and found none. She could argue the point, of course. She was fairly certain the prime minister didn't have the power to detain the sovereign, even for her own safety. However, the HSP officers were heavily armed and significantly outnumbered Lily and her advisors. Arguing the point with the officer in charge wouldn't help, either. He had his orders and was solely focussed on following them, whether or not they were lawful. All she would gain from protesting was to cause a scene, and she had no doubt that would play to the prime minister's favour. In fact, that was probably what he wanted.

What she needed to do was talk to the prime minister now, while he was surrounded by politicians. Once she told him publicly that the coronation had occurred and she was queen, he'd be limited in his actions, even if he continued to dispute her claim.

Lily scanned the room, looking for the man she had come to hate. She found him holding court with a group of old men who were laughing sycophantically at whatever he'd just said.

Their eyes met, and the prime minister's narrowed, a wicked grin tickling his lips. Then he broke contact, returning to his friends, telling Lily she wasn't worth his time.

"I must speak with the prime minister," Lily told the HSP officer with a confidence she didn't feel.

"I'm afraid we must leave now, ma'am."

"I'm not going anywhere until I speak with Reginald Toth. You can take me to him, or bring him to me, but I'm not leaving without talking to him."

The officer shook his head. "Sorry ma'am. My orders are—"

Before he could stop her, Lily darted around him and began striding towards the prime minister. Toth didn't look up, but he did break off his conversation with his cronies and turn to head for the door. He didn't want to hear what Lily had to say.

Lily's cheeks flamed with anger at this man who was destroying Highacre, but unwilling to speak with her. Who was choosing the easy way out, the adult version of clamping one's hands over one's ears and singing "la la la".

"Toth!" she called before she had time to consider what she might say, or the ramifications of him publicly ignoring her.

She sensed his hesitation, as he took a moment to consider his own options. Curiosity won out and Toth turned slowly, an eyebrow raised, his expression one of being addressed by an unruly citizen, not his queen.

She felt the presence of the HSP officers behind her, waiting to grab her should Toth give the signal. She gripped her confidence, which was quickly liquifying and threatening to drain away.

"I am the Queen of Highacre," Lily said loudly, speaking to Toth, but addressing the room. "I was coronated by Lord Philipe less than an hour ago, and as rightful leader of this nation, I nullify your declaration of war."

Murmuring broke out around the room; some curious and some hopeful, but most, it seemed to Lily, was speculation of how Toth would react.

He peered down at her now, as if trying to place her.

"Your Majesty," he said eventually. "You've returned. Welcome back."

Toth spoke as if Lily had impulsively taken a holiday,

leaving him in charge, and was now trying to reassert herself.

"I'll be happy to brief you on the matters I have managed in your absence. But for now, and until we confirm that the proper protocol was followed, and you have been *correctly* coronated, leaving aside the small matter of whether you were, in fact, confirmed," he muttered loudly as an aside to his fellow politicians, who tittered and scoffed, "I'm afraid the emergency powers remain in place and I still have the helm. It would be irresponsible, under the circumstances—which I will brief you on—for Highacre to fail to respond to Meridia."

Toth made a show of looking over Lily's shoulder at Giles.

"I'll have my people reach out to make an appointment for me to bring you up to speed... *Your Majesty*." His tone dripped sarcasm. "In the meantime, your safety is of utmost concern. I've asked my HSP officers to escort you to the palace and keep you safe. I'm sure you understand."

And having delivered the equivalent of "be a good dear and run along", Toth turned and strode triumphantly from the room. All eyes swung back to Lily, who was left standing in the public gallery with HSP officers on either side, like a girl who had shoplifted a lipstick but been told by the benevolent owner that if she left now, he wouldn't press charges.

"Ma'am," said the HSP officer who had spoken to her before, as he clamped a hand on her arm.

Lily yanked her arm away, but she couldn't shake his grip. He released her, but only after ensuring she realised it was his decision. Lily turned.

"Giles, please return to the palace separately and ensure the Royal Guard are prepared to meet me and resume responsibility for my security. I wouldn't want to impose on the HSP longer than necessary. I will speak with you on my return." Lily looked at him meaningfully, but Giles was way ahead of her.

"Of course, Your Majesty." He bowed and strode quickly away.

"Right then," said Lily, projecting a confidence she no longer felt. "Let's all head back to the palace. I have work to do."

3

Lily glared at the HSP officers as they shut the door to her rooms, leaving her alone with Naomi. A high-pitched yip came from the direction of her bedroom.

"Kevin!"

Lily crossed the floor and met her tiny pelotromo, who came bounding towards her, his little triangle of a tail wagging excitedly.

"Miss me, buddy?" Lily picked him up and nuzzled him against her face, screwing up her eyes, his tiny tongue tickling as he licked her. "Yeah, I missed you too."

Naomi kept a wary distance from the reunion, reminding Lily that, while they looked like tiny puppies, pelotromos could suddenly grow to the size of a woolly mammoth if they felt threatened.

Ignoring Naomi, Lily patted and tickled Kevin until he indicated he wanted to be returned to the floor. As his little paws hit the floorboards, Kevin bounded off, back towards the bedroom. He turned to look at Lily from the doorway, and after giving a final yip of excitement, scurried out of sight.

Lily wandered over to the doorway, wondering if it had

been a yip of "come and follow me" or more a yip of "catch you later". She scanned her empty bedroom and saw no movement.

Guess it was the latter.

Vaguely wondering where Kevin had gone, Lily wandered back into the main area and joined Naomi, who had taken a seat on a couch. Lily sank into the couch opposite, suddenly feeling overwhelmed and utterly exhausted.

She had thought it would be better back here. Having spoken briefly to Giles and Jenkins while in her home dimension, Lily knew things weren't good in Highacre—Minister Bellingham and Addison had been arrested and the HSP were oppressing everyone—but despite that, she had felt like she could at least do something about it, unlike what she had found on her return home.

Her family had disintegrated in the six months following her disappearance to Highacre. They had lost the farm, and then her father lost his life. Her mum had a breakdown, her brother turned to drinking, and her older sister was trying to take care of her younger sister, who seemed to hold Lily responsible for everything. Not that Lily could blame her.

Lily closed her eyes, rubbing them. She had felt so powerless to help her family. The idea of coming back to Highacre, where she had some authority and could fix things, had given her something to work towards. But now she had returned, and it seemed she was every bit as powerless as she had been back home.

A title only gives you power if everyone agrees.

Lily felt a stab of yearning for her advisors. They always knew what to do. Minister Bellingham typically took charge, and the others fought to get their ideas in the mix. How was she supposed to do this without them?

Tears slid down Lily's cheeks and before she could stop

herself, she was hunched over, sobbing. Embarrassment filled her as Naomi moved beside her, rubbing her back and murmuring words of comfort. Lily tried to pull herself together. Naomi had been through goodness knows what while Lily was gone, and she wasn't crying on the couch. And Lily was meant to be queen.

"Sorry," Lily sniffed, trying to wipe her face.

"Don't apologise, Your Majesty. You've been through a lot."

Lily nodded. "I just don't know what to do," she said, desperately trying to keep her voice from cracking. "I wish the others were here."

"I do too, Your Majesty," Naomi said softly. "But you're here. That's what matters. So long as you're here, we can fight."

Lily sniffed, wiping her face again. It was nice of Naomi to say that, but it wasn't true. She couldn't do this alone. No one recognised her authority. The prime minister had friends, politicians, and his own personal police force. What was she meant to do against all that? She needed the others.

"What matters is getting the others back. They'll know what to do."

Naomi sat back, lips pursed. "You're the queen, ma'am. I'm all for getting everyone back if we can, but we would do that so they can help you. Not so they can fix things. You're in charge here."

Lily closed her eyes, breathing deeply. It was a nice sentiment, but she couldn't bring herself to believe it. Didn't Naomi see how Lily had been treated by the HSP?

"We can prioritise retrieving your advisors in accordance with how they fit in with your plan—"

"I don't have a plan!" Lily shouted, springing to her feet. "This is hopeless. I don't know what I'm doing. How am I meant to fix all of this?" The last question came out as almost a whisper, with Lily's anger leaving as quickly as it had come and her fear taking over.

Naomi stood and put a hand on Lily's arm. "I know you can do this," she said with feeling. "And you're not alone, Your Majesty."

Lily smiled at Naomi, wiping her tears. Naomi's confidence in her did make her feel better, but it was the unwavering solidarity that brought her back. Naomi was all in. So Lily would be too.

The moment was interrupted by the door opening. Quick as a flash, Naomi positioned herself in front of Lily.

"Knock, knock." A head poked in, looking around to see if it was okay to enter. "Ah, Your Majesty. Welcome back. I trust I'm not interrupting?" Richard gave a quick but respectful bow before raising an eyebrow at the tension.

"Not at all, come on in," said Lily, gesturing for him to take a seat.

Lily glanced at Naomi and saw realisation dawning on her face. Lily had told Giles to have the Royal Guard replace the HSP so she could get the prime minister's cronies out of her hair. But both she and Naomi had forgotten that with Richard replacing Jason as the head of the Royal Guard, he would, of course, come by for some face time with the queen.

Lily had not had a lot to do with Richard, though the man did once protect her from a drunken gunman. Everything she'd heard about him from others painted a picture of a rich boy looking to make his own way, albeit while using the connections his privileged upbringing afforded. Lily thought about how Jason must have felt, being replaced by the subordinate he fired. She decided to not like him in solidarity with Jason.

Lily darted a look at Naomi. *Jason!* Lily felt terrible not asking how he was. Then she remembered it was only a few hours ago that Naomi had told her about the failed raid. It felt like weeks ago. Lily thought about his damaged eye and mangled leg. How was he going to play with his kids?

He'll get better. He has to.

"I'm sure Naomi has told you, ma'am, but I have replaced Jason as the head of your guard," Richard began amiably, with a respectful nod to Naomi. "The prime minister has also appointed me head of palace security."

"Isn't that the same thing?" Lily asked.

"Excuse me, ma'am?" Richard asked, confused.

"Jason covered palace security as head of the Royal Guard. So isn't your second appointment redundant?"

Naomi leaned forward on the couch next to her to catch a glimpse of Richard's reaction, eager for his response.

"Yes, of course, Your Majesty. Jason did take care of that, but things have changed while you were away. The prime minister thought it important to have a contingent of HSP officers based here for your security. The HSP have their own command structure, ultimately overseen by Minister Toot. But having multiple command and control structures can be confusing, and so as head of palace security, all HSP personnel based here report to me."

"Of course, the Royal Guard are also now overseen by Minister Toot," Naomi added.

"What?" Lily looked from Naomi to Richard. That made no sense. Jeremy Toot was the laziest person Lily had come across. It had surprised her that he was the defence minister, given the recency of the last war with Meridia. But to hear he was now also in charge of the HSP and Royal Guard was just ridiculous.

"The prime minister feels that defence of the nation and defence of the sovereign are one and the same," Richard explained with an answer that sounded rehearsed. "And so it makes sense that all aspects of national and palace security fall under one portfolio."

Lily stared at Richard. If Toot was in charge of the HSP, then he was clearly Reginald Toth's man. He had crossed to the other side. And if Toot was Richard's boss, then Richard couldn't be trusted either.

"I've had the pleasure of speaking with both men," Richard puffed up, obviously enjoying bragging about his connections. "And I can assure you, Your Majesty, that they are highly intelligent and capable, and one hundred percent focussed on ensuring your safety and security."

"Get out."

"Your Majesty?"

"I said get out."

Richard recovered himself quickly. "I'm sorry, ma'am, but I can't in good conscience leave. The threat to your safety is too great. I wouldn't feel right—"

"Get out before I have you thrown out." Lily leaned back on the couch, letting Richard know he wasn't worth her personal intervention. She looked directly into Richard's eyes to ensure he knew she was serious. "And I think Naomi can take you."

Richard looked from Lily to Naomi, his cheeks flushing with the embarrassment of being undermined in front of a subordinate. Weighing his options, Richard seemed to decide he could retain the most dignity by pretending that they were all on the same page.

"You must be tired, Your Majesty," he said, standing. "I'll leave you in Naomi's capable hands, but I'll be right outside if you need anything."

"Why don't you head back to Toot's office," Naomi muttered.

"Sorry, what?" Richard asked in a tone that told Lily he had heard what Naomi said.

"You heard me, *sir*. Most of the guys here thought you were alright. But a few thought you were a spoiled, power hungry knob. We all reveal our true colours in the end." She looked him up and down. "I guess the few were right."

"Naomi," Lily hissed. If Naomi got fired, she didn't know what she'd do.

"What do you mean?" Richard, to his credit, seemed more confused than offended by Naomi's sudden, aggressive insubordination.

"Why don't you take a closer look at what your bosses are doing? They don't care about her safety. They want to get rid of her so they have more power. They're the enemy."

Richard stared at Naomi, clearly confused and unsure what to say. He buttoned his jacket. "It's been an emotional morning, what with your return and the declaration of war. Why don't you both rest here? I'll make sure some food is brought up. Naomi, we can talk later."

As the door shut behind him, Naomi relaxed, but Lily looked at her in alarm.

"What was that about? He's probably going to fire you," said Lily.

"He won't," said Naomi, not sounding completely convinced. "I don't think he's a bad guy. If he opens his eyes, he might just come over to our side. I just need to avoid that meeting until he's looked a little closer at Jeremy Toot."

Lily wasn't sure that was the right approach to recruiting, but she was more focussed on getting her team back than adding to it.

"Okay, so I know some of what's been going on, but perhaps you can fill me in? I know Jason's in the hospital and Minister Bellingham and Addison are in prison, but do we know how they are? And where are Claire and Austin?"

Naomi exhaled loudly, moving back to the couch opposite Lily and considering where to start.

"I'm not sure how Minister Bellingham and Addison are, but I know they're in prison, because when the warden refused to let me see them, he did confirm they were there. Which is more than he did for Claire. She was arrested about a week ago, but I haven't been able to find out where she's been taken."

Lily paled. Three of her advisors arrested, one in hospital, and one gone to the prime minister's side. It didn't look good. And Claire was someone Lily had come to rely on. If she couldn't get Claire back, it was going to hurt their side immensely.

"Hudson disappeared at about the same time as Claire. He's an old army buddy of Jason's who was helping us with tech support," Naomi explained, seeing Lily's blank expression. "I haven't been able to get any information on him either. It's possible that he was taken, but I'm hoping with his affinity for technology he had early warning and got away and is staying off the grid."

Lily nodded. "What about Austin? He could help us."

"Ma'am, Austin was the insider working against you."

"What?"

"And a war criminal, as it turns out."

"What?" Lily said again, her mind struggling to comprehend this new revelation.

"Claire and I looked into him closely. He's got a history of anti-Meridian behaviour and nationalistic activities. Claire found the evidence we needed right before she was arrested. Of course, with her arrest, nothing was done to Austin. Instead, he left the palace and joined the prime minister." A look of anger clouded Naomi's face. "He's now the head of the HSP, working under Toot."

It was all Lily could do to stop from asking "what"

again. Austin had always been so nice to her. She was struggling to reconcile the man she knew with a war criminal who was involved in the death of her family and who had been trying to bring about her downfall.

"Well, if he's gone over to their side, at least he's out in the open. We know who the enemy is."

"Yes," agreed Naomi, "but it looks like Austin was lower down the food chain. He seemed to be working for someone calling themselves the Patriot. We think that's who is behind everything."

"Don't suppose you know who that is?"

"Claire figured it out, but then she was arrested and disappeared. We think she sent us an email with the information, but her entire online existence seems to have been wiped."

"That doesn't bode well," said Lily. She couldn't imagine anyone who had gone to that length intended to give Claire back. She might already be dead.

No, we will get her back. It's just going to be more difficult.

Pushing the negative thoughts from her mind, Lily asked Naomi for her ideas on the Patriot's identity.

"I think the leading suspect is Ezra," Naomi said. "Jason thought it was him because Claire didn't seem like she'd uncovered a bombshell, and she was so sure Ezra was up to something. I was thinking it could be one of our politicians, maybe even Minister Bellingham—"

"But she's in prison."

"As far as we know," said Naomi. "If it was her, that would be excellent cover. But now I think Jason was probably right. The failed raid was at a warehouse owned by one of Ezra's companies. If he did steal the felixium, it seems likely that he's the one behind everything."

"And he was in the room with the interdimensional travel machine."

"Yeah, we know. But we tried to minimise his contact with it—"

"No," Lily interrupted. "He was in the room before I entered. The machine was already on, and he knew what it was."

Naomi frowned as she processed this new information. "If he's the one who powered up the machine, then he'd have to be at least involved in the theft of the felixium. He steals that and then pushes you through—"

"He didn't push me," Lily corrected Naomi. "A hooded figure entered after Ava and Alexei and pushed the three of us through."

"Maybe Austin? If Ezra is the Patriot, he could have set up the machine and then had Austin come and push you through."

"Maybe. But why? I still don't get why he had me sent home."

"I know. Why not just kill you?" Naomi nodded, thinking.

Lily shifted, uncomfortable. Even though she agreed it was odd that no one actually seemed to be trying to kill her, especially given the assassination of the rest of the royal family, she didn't appreciate everyone else loudly mentioning how much easier that would be. After a slightly awkward pause, Naomi continued.

"Okay, so we might have Ezra masterminding some or all of the incidents and using Austin as a lackey. Ezra then gets in the prime minister's pocket..."

"Or puts the prime minister in his."

"True. That seems more likely. Together they set up the HSP and increase Toth's powers, get rid of you, and then declare war on Meridia. Why?"

Lily searched her brain for an answer. Why would Ezra want war between Highacre and Meridia?

"He must stand to gain something," Lily mused out loud. "Which means he thinks Meridia will win."

"Or he knows they will because he can interfere at this end. If he's controlling the prime minister..." Naomi responded.

"It doesn't feel right," said Lily, standing and moving to the window. She gazed out at the amazing view, thinking. "We're missing something. But I suppose the 'why' can wait. What matters is that we know he's probably running the show and we'll need to stop him."

"Alright, Your Majesty. Where would you like to start?"

Lily considered her options. She wanted to visit Jason to see how he was. She had relied on him so much; she needed him to be okay. A selfish part of her also hoped to see evidence of a speedy recovery so that he could re-join the team. She also wanted Claire back, but that sounded next to impossible. The easiest start point would be busting Minister Bellingham and Addison out of prison, but who knew how difficult that was actually going to be.

I wish Ava was here.

She missed being able to bounce ideas off her friend, and Ava's practical take on everything. Naomi was great, but Lily just felt like Ava gave a different perspective. Not to mention she wanted to find out why Ava hadn't told her about Ezra.

I can't believe he's her dad.

Lily was still reeling from the revelation. How much had Ava known about what Ezra was up to? She thought about Ava's urgent need to get back to this world. To get back to the father she'd just reconnected with. What had she said? Something about stopping him from making a mistake? Maybe he had revealed his plans.

"I might pop over to the diplomatic wing and see how Ava is," said Lily. "I'd like to run some of this past her, and see if I can't have her released. Alexei too."

A charged silence met Lily's words, and Lily had the distinct feeling that Naomi was tempering her reply.

"It's understandable that you want to check in on your friends, ma'am. I'm sure you went through a lot together and grew close while you were away. And them being detained like that must have been alarming. But I think we need to be cautious with Ava. At least until we understand more about what involvement she's had with Ezra. We've just figured that he's the most likely candidate for being behind all of this. And we've only just found out that he's her father."

"She's only just found that out too," said Lily defensively.

"And yet, she didn't tell us."

Naomi's words scraped over the recent wound and Lily shifted uncomfortably. Why hadn't Ava told her? There was no reason, particularly while they were so far removed from all of this in the other dimension, for Ava not to have mentioned her father was Ezra. She wanted to think she was embarrassed somehow, or there was some other reasonable explanation for the omission, but nothing immediately sprang to mind. And that fanned the flames of suspicion.

"Ma'am, I do think we need to entertain the possibility that it wasn't an accident that Ava went through the portal with you. That her being with you was part of whatever Ezra's plan is."

"But to what end?" Lily was struggling to understand the motivation behind any of this. Ezra seemed to zig whenever a reasonable person would zag.

"Probably the same end that's seen her befriending you for the past few months."

Lily's face burned. That was her biggest fear. Her biggest insecurity. She had been so sure about what she felt for Ava. Had it all been a lie? Lily realised Naomi was still talking.

"... growing close to you for influence, perhaps. Or to report back on what we're doing. Or even whether you're in charge or largely being led by your advisors. Information is key in Ezra's world."

Lily nodded mutely. What Naomi was saying made sense. But the idea that everything she'd forged with Ava was a lie was too much. She'd needed the strength of her friends during her time at home. Having them ripped away from her now was overwhelming. How was she supposed to decide who to trust?

"Ma'am?" said Naomi softly, looking at Lily in concern.

Lily could see the question in her eyes. Close as Naomi knew her and Ava to be, Lily could tell she sensed something more in Lily's reaction.

"We... we grew close while we were away," Lily said.

"Of course." Naomi nodded, not understanding.

Lily cleared her throat. "Really close. We... we're together."

Naomi was still nodding, but as realisation hit her, she stopped. "Oh. Oh! Well—I was about to say that's great, but under the circumstances..." Naomi's eyes darted around the room, her mind processing the latest complication and assessing the increased risk.

Lily could feel what was coming. And she understood—her intimacy with Ava compromised her objectivity when it came to determining the ambassador to court's loyalties. But she needed to know.

"I think it's best I confront her. We're not going to know what we're dealing with until we ask her and get her reaction and explanation." Lily hated herself a little bit for still wanting the comfort of Ava's presence. Even as she imagined the painful confrontation, asking if it was all a lie, she felt her heart relax at the idea of being near Ava again.

"I think we need to leave it for now, ma'am," said Naomi firmly. "It's best you take some time so that when you do see her reaction, you have perspective."

"I think—" Lily began to argue.

"Not to mention," Naomi said loudly, cutting her off, "your loyal advisors have been fighting for you back here. Countering the prime minister's narrative and ensuring you could be crowned, finding a way to get you home, and trying to uncover and defeat the threat. Maybe you might like to start with those who are in prison or hospital?"

Lily's cheeks heated with shame. She bit back her defensive reply. She did want to see Jason. Make sure he was alright. Well, as alright as he could be with his injuries. And to get Minister Bellingham and Addison out of prison. But she longed for her friends. She hadn't considered that they wouldn't be helping her fix things when they arrived back in Highacre.

"You're right, I'm sorry," she said softly. "I'd like to see if we can visit Jason, and if not, perhaps we head to the prison and try to get Minister Bellingham and Addison out."

"Sounds like a plan, ma'am," said Naomi approvingly. She checked her watch. "Visiting hours don't start for a couple of hours, so perhaps prison, then hospital."

"Oh, what's wrong with Alexei's father?" Lily asked, suddenly remembering what Sergei had said.

Naomi looked concerned. "There have been rumours he's really sick. The Valmeadians are downplaying it, but the impression is that he's dying."

"Oh no, poor Alexei," said Lily, empathising with her friend. She would have to see to it that he could go home.

"Poor us," countered Naomi. "The guy standing in for

him, Klaud Gutzmer, is unpredictable and hates Highacre. If the Great Leader dies and that guy replaces him, it's likely Valmead will enter the war on Meridia's side."

"But Alexei will replace his father," said Lily. "I know it's not officially hereditary…"

"Alexei can't replace his father if he's stuck here."

"All the more reason to have him sent home."

"It might not be that easy," said Naomi gently. "With the public sentiment being whipped up by the prime minister, showing preferential treatment to your foreign friend—and especially allowing a potential new leader to return to Valmead to lead them into war against us—won't be popular. It's all we've been able to do to have the people accept that you are the rightful queen, and you passed the confirmation requirements. If you let Alexei go, you may play into the prime minister's hands and lose the support you greatly need."

"Alexei would never go to war with us," said Lily angrily.

"That's not what the people think," Naomi said, raising her hands to show she wasn't trying to argue with Lily. "The prime minister has had control of the media for months. It's only that the judges got straight in front of the cameras after the Trials that our narrative about your legitimacy managed to get out. He's eased off his argument that you failed, though he drops it in every so often for good measure. But he's been emphasising that your closest friends are foreigners while delivering a steady propaganda campaign designed to make the people wary and even fearful of foreigners."

Lily exhaled, running her hand through her hair in frustration. Sending Alexei home was clearly going to be harder than she thought. But she would send him home. She hadn't had the opportunity to say goodbye to her own father, and there was no way Lily was going to prevent her friend from having that chance.

"Right, prison then hospital it is." Lily tried to refocus. "So, how do we get out of here?"

"I was thinking we'd drive," said Naomi.

"But they've confined us to the rooms."

"The prime minister wanted you returned to the palace for your security. I, as your bodyguard, assess the threat level of our plan as permissible. And I have been learning more about my fellow guards. I have enough that I know are loyal to you that would be happy to re-educate any HSP officers who think they can curtail your movements."

Lily smiled at Naomi gratefully. "Alright. Let's get out of here."

They reached the garage with minimal interference from the HSP roaming the palace. Only one officer had been silly enough to try to stop them, but he was so alarmed by Naomi yelling for him to back away from the sovereign that his attempt was short-lived.

Naomi snapped her seatbelt on, adjusted her mirrors, and opened the garage door. "We'll be followed, naturally," she said, moving the car slowly towards the exit.

"Oh." Lily's heart sank slightly.

"Of course, they've never tried to follow me."

An evil smile flickered on Naomi's lips as she hit the accelerator, and they shot out of the garage into the sunlight.

$$4$$

"I WANT to see my advisors right now."

Lily was getting frustrated. She and Naomi had talked their way through the entrance gate and the front entrance of the prison. Having been escorted into the reception area, she had spent the last five minutes arguing with the warden. He was a short, older man who seemed to enjoy having power over the sovereign.

"I'm terribly sorry, Your Majesty," he said in a voice that did not sound the least bit sorry. "But I just can't find you on the visitor's list for either inmate."

"I don't care if I'm on the list or not," Lily reiterated through clenched teeth. "You will bring my advisors to me now."

"I would love to do just that, Your Majesty," said the warden jovially with a little laugh. "But if you're not on the list, there's really nothing I can do."

Lily leant towards the little man. "Put me on the list."

The group of guards who had been watching the exchange, enjoying the warden jerking the queen around, all flinched at the dark look on Lily's face and her dangerous tone. But the warden simply brightened.

"Well, I suppose we can make an exception for the queen! Just this once." The warden turned to his screen, typing furiously for a couple of minutes before turning back to Lily. "Name?"

Lily blinked. He was really going to do this. "Lily."

"Address?"

"The palace."

"Occupation?"

"Queen of Highacre."

"Relationship to inmate?"

"Uh, employer. Look, do we really have to do this?"

"Got to have the paperwork in order." The warden smiled at Lily. "Purpose for visit?"

"Just put me on the list," she snarled.

The warden flinched, but recovered quickly, glancing furtively at the watching guards, clearly not wanting to be seen to be scared of a young woman.

"Right you are, Your Majesty," said the warden.

He focussed on his computer, happily hitting buttons on his keyboard. The room was silent but for the typing and clicking of the warden's mouse, but the energy was charged. As time stretched on, some of the guards shifted uncomfortably.

As Lily opened her mouth to demand that the warden hurry up, he hit a key with a flourish and beamed back at her.

"There now. All of that should be in order. You can expect a response in ten to twelve business days. Our decision will be mailed to you, as you have elected not to provide an email address..."

Anger burned behind Lily's eyes as she glanced over at Naomi. Naomi nodded subtly. The Royal Guards who had met them at the prison stood taller, ready to move.

Lily looked back at the warden. While a small vindictive part of her would enjoy this, she hesitated. She did not want to be like the prime minister. But Naomi had warned her on the drive over that in the current climate, Lily would have to be tough. That she may have to take a hard line to show she was serious. That she was in control.

Lily shifted her weight and closed her eyes. Taking a deep breath, resolve settled within her. Her eyes opened.

"Arrest him."

The Royal Guards moved swiftly. Confusion pierced the warden's eyes. Then terror.

"Wait, no..."

Lily's guards grabbed him, securing his arms behind his back before they escorted him away.

Lily looked at the remaining prison guards. None were smiling now. All looked scared, though some were shifting their weight, hands moving towards batons.

"Who is in charge now?"

The guards all looked at each other, none wanting to attract attention. Eventually, their eyes all found a large man in the back corner who was failing spectacularly at trying to look inconspicuous.

"Ah, I guess that would be me," he said hesitantly, wiping his hands on his stained white shirt and shuffling towards Lily. A crooked name badge on his chest identified him as the deputy warden.

"I trust you will be more helpful than your predecessor."

"Yes ma'am, er, Your Majesty." He fumbled with the computer, trying to see what the warden had done. "Let me just... here we go... ah, okay. Looks like Juliana Bellingham is in with the general population, cell block B, and Addison Grange is in—oh, solitary. Ouch."

Lily's mind raced at the idea of Addison in solitary confinement. It hurt her heart to imagine the bubbly, motherly woman locked in a tiny dark room, all by herself, with no one to talk to. And Minister Bellingham was sharing a cell and the facilities with a mix of prisoners? The haughty, confident woman could unintentionally put people off. What if that had resulted in violence? An image of Minister Bellingham getting jumped popped into Lily's head.

Please let them be alright.

"Pardon," Naomi said quietly behind Lily.

"Yes?" replied Lily, assuming Naomi's formality was because of their audience.

"Pardon, ma'am."

"Yes, Naomi, what is it?" Lily said, getting frustrated.

Naomi rolled her eyes. Moving close to Lily, she whispered, "Just pardon them and have them released."

"Oh!" Lily felt her cheeks redden and willed the blush away, clearing her throat before addressing the deputy warden. "I officially pardon Addison Grange, Juliana Bellingham, Claire Jones, and Hudson... er..." She looked at Naomi, who shrugged. "Um, please search your records for anyone named Hudson, and we'll deal with him if he's here. But the others are pardoned and I order their immediate release."

Lily had no idea if that was something she could do—unilaterally pardon and release prisoners—but she focussed on projecting confidence and hoped no one would question her authority.

The deputy warden paled, his shoulders dropping as if he wished he could fold in on himself and disappear. He glanced about frantically, but none of his guards would look at him. Loosening his tie, he looked at the computer as if it might give him answers before looking at Lily as if he might cry.

"I'm not sure if I can without..." He faltered, remembering what happened when the warden insisted on procedure being followed, before whispering, "I don't know what to do."

"Do what your sovereign has ordered you to do."

Lily jumped, not having heard anyone else enter the room, but the deputy warden visibly relaxed.

"Yes sir. Right away." Responsibility taken from his shoulders, he began furiously typing on his computer. Lily saw the other guards spring into action, eager to carry out the command now that approval had been given by the newcomer.

Lily, annoyed that this hadn't been the response to her own direction, turned towards the door, noting Naomi and her guards had already repositioned themselves to protect her.

"Hello Ezra."

"Your Majesty." He swept into a respectful bow. "How are you? And welcome home. I apologise for not welcoming you appropriately earlier. I was so taken with having my daughter back."

Lily flinched internally at the reminder of Ava's deception. She remembered Naomi suggesting that it was Ezra's fault they had all been pushed through the interdimensional travel machine in the first place. Not to mention everything else he was likely behind.

"Of course, I expect you were quite overcome with relief. What brings you down here?"

"I was informed that you were here, Your Majesty. And of course, I came right away to ensure you were being taken care of. I know how pesky bureaucracy can be. And…" Ezra made a show of looking embarrassed before leaning in towards Lily. "With the prime minister not accepting your ascension of the throne, it makes it more difficult for the lower-level decision-makers to know what to do." He smiled politely, but the subtleties in his tone told

Lily this was designed to show who was in charge in Highacre.

"How thoughtful." She smiled. "Perhaps we can avoid all of this paperwork in the future by you not arresting my advisors."

Ezra chuckled as if Lily had made a mildly humorous joke. "Quite right, Your Majesty. Of course, I'm not in charge of arresting anyone. Perhaps you should mention it to the prime minister. Or your advisor, Minister Toot. He *is* in charge of the HSP, after all."

Lily considered Ezra. What was his game? His rhetoric was consistently insistent that he had little power, even though it was clear that he was very powerful, if not pulling all the strings.

And why had he come here personally? Let alone help her secure the release of her advisors? Surely it would benefit his side for Lily to be tied up and focussed on releasing her friends, rather than getting in his way, trying to defeat him and the prime minister? And given how poorly things had been going before he turned up, she would have been stuck here a while. As much as it irked Lily that the prison staff had snapped to action for Ezra, she knew he was the only reason they were releasing her friends so quickly.

It didn't make sense for him to help her.

Is he helping me?

Try as she might, Lily could not figure out what Ezra's angle might be.

Ezra grinned genially at Lily, but something in his smile turned her stomach. Suddenly, Lily wanted to be as far away from the man as possible.

"What is taking so long?" she called to the deputy warden, who was still hen pecking at his keyboard.

"Out-processing can take a while, Your Majesty,"

answered Ezra before the deputy warden could open his mouth. "They have to ensure the inmate is medically fit and that all of their belongings are returned to them. Why don't you head back to the palace? I'll ensure everything moves swiftly here, and we will provide your advisors transport to meet you there within the hour."

She looked at Ezra, dumbfounded. Did he *really* think she would entrust him with the responsibility of safely returning her advisors? Her friends?

He smiled placidly back at her, his eyes betraying his curiosity at what she would do. He had to know she was at least very suspicious of him, having found him alone with the interdimensional travel machine, and him with far too much knowledge about its existence and operation.

But what was his game here? She reached out, feeling for his mind. A brief wave of relief flooded her at being back in Highacre, with her familiar magic at full power. It felt easy, like the first few meters of a jog when you've had a couple of days rest.

The relief was short-lived, as her power stretched for the rings of his mind and was rebuffed, as if she had gone to reach through a window and hit glass. Trying not to let the confusion show on her face, she focussed on his mind. She could see the rings, just like with everyone else. But when she tried again to access them, she couldn't get close.

Lily had never encountered anything like this. When she'd come up against barriers in the past, they'd felt like a void, or a limitation on accessing all of a person's thoughts. She'd never been prevented from even touching the rings of someone's mind before.

Ezra continued to look at her, waiting politely for her response. If he'd noticed her failed attempt to read his mind, he wasn't showing it at all.

"I can spare an hour for my friends who have been

locked up because of their affiliation with me," said Lily pointedly. She sat in one of the uncomfortable plastic chairs that lined the wall. Naomi sat next to her.

"As you wish," said Ezra, as if her decision either way was of no difference to him. He sat across from Lily, crossing his legs and watching the muted screen mounted on the wall. Lily glanced up and saw it was news coverage of the prime minister's declaration of war. Her heart sank as she watched footage showing the first shots had already been fired.

Lily's eyes drifted back to Ezra. It was bothering her like an itch she couldn't scratch. What was he doing here? Why had he stepped in? He should have been happy to let her flounder, trying to liberate her allies instead of regaining her power from the prime minister. And if he'd hoped to spirit her friends away, perhaps to a black site—and given his background in intelligence, he'd surely know the locations of a few—her decision to remain didn't seem to bother him.

Panic gripped her. What if he was keeping her here in the reception area, while having her advisors taken away? He could be kidnapping them right now and she was just sitting around, letting it happen. What if he took them to Meridia? She'd never get them back, especially not now they were at war.

Lily took a breath and concentrated on the deputy warden. His mind was simple, three large rings, easy to penetrate and access what she wanted. She relaxed a little at finding he was unaware of any subterfuge. If Ezra was stealing her friends, he was doing it without the deputy warden's knowledge.

Lily did a quick scan of the assembled guards. It was equal parts enjoying the use of her magic, wanting to confirm she shouldn't be unduly worried, and boredom. None of them were aware of anything out of the ordinary, and in fact one was getting updates from the corrections officers in the prison that indicated everything was progressing as it should.

Her relief curdled. Then *why* was Ezra here? She ran through literally anything she could think of that he might get out of this current interaction, but the only thing that made the slightest bit of sense was that Ezra had an insatiable need for information.

She had no doubt that he could have monitored the release of her advisors from the comfort of wherever he spent his days, but in coming here, he was able to gather information on her.

He was testing her. What would she do if the warden refused to help? Would she assert her power? Would she let Ezra take over the release? Did she trust him?

She felt like a lab rat. And then, unsettlingly, she wondered how he would satisfy his need for information when he wasn't able to simply show up. He was no longer welcome at the palace. Would he try and draw her out? Or find a way to weasel back in?

"Ma'am," Naomi broke into Lily's thoughts. Lily blinked. She hadn't even noticed Naomi get up, but her bodyguard sat back down, putting her phone away. "Jason's been released from hospital. He's on his way to the palace now."

Lily stood automatically, elated to hear he was well enough to be discharged. But then she faltered. She desperately wanted to be at the palace to welcome him back. She owed him that much, with all he had lost for her. But she couldn't leave before the others were free.

"I'm happy to wait," Ezra offered again. "It shouldn't be too much longer, and I'll ensure the ladies are back with you as soon as the processing is complete."

Like hell.

Lily shot a furtive look at Naomi. She was the logical choice to leave here to ensure that her advisors were freed. But could she risk losing Naomi too? If Ezra was capable of spiriting three of her allies away, why not four?

She could leave the small group of Royal Guards there, but would they be a match for Ezra if he tried anything? Lily wasn't even sure *she* was a match for the man.

Feeling like she was letting Jason down, Lily sat back in her chair.

If he was here, he'd tell me to wait for them.

She knew Jason would understand her decision to wait for their friends. He might even be upset to learn she'd abandoned them for him if she left. But it felt wrong, and Lily was almost certain that Gwen, Jason's wife, wouldn't forgive her for not being there to welcome Jason back.

"Naomi, call Giles. Tell him to meet Jason and Gwen when they arrive and make sure they have everything they need. And ask him to tell Jason I'll be there as soon as I can."

Naomi gave a short nod and walked away, dialing as she went. Ezra watched the exchange with a look of disinterest, though his eyes shone. Seeming to sense Lily observing him, Ezra began fiddling on his own phone, tapping away, though not as if with anything important.

Barely a minute after he put his phone away, Ezra called to the deputy warden.

"Is there any way to hurry this up, Brent? I'd hate for Her Majesty's time to be wasted any longer."

"We just have to—oh. It looks like they're bringing them over now."

"Ah, perfect," Ezra smiled over at Lily. She did not return it.

Five minutes later, a side door buzzed open, making Lily jump. She almost didn't recognize her friends as they entered the reception area. The two women had lost weight and had the pale look of those who had not seen the sun in a while.

Lily's heart, overjoyed to see Addison and Minister Bellingham, faltered as the door closed behind them.

Where is Claire?

Lily looked at Naomi and saw her unspoken question echoed there. Lily indicated to the deputy warden, and with a nod Naomi went to question him.

Addison's eyes were darting around as if frightened. She reminded Lily of a rabbit, sure it was being hunted, but not sure by whom. Minister Bellingham also scanned the room, but there was something wild in her eyes. As if she knew she was being hunted and was looking for a fight.

Both women seemed to see Lily at the same time, and their faces brightened as they started towards her. They'd barely taken two steps before they saw Ezra smiling at them and their steps faltered.

Minister Bellingham glared at him. It was the prime minister who'd had her arrested, and Ezra was now his special advisor. Ezra opened his mouth to greet her, but she strode angrily past him, embraced Lily in a slightly aggressive, though brief hug, and then walked out the door.

Addison scurried in Minister Bellingham's wake. She embraced Lily tentatively at first, then more warmly once Lily pulled her in. Lily's happiness at having her friend back was tinged with sadness as she felt Addison's bony body shake slightly as she held her.

"They don't have her. According to their records, they never did," whispered Naomi, reappearing at Lily's side.

Lily glared at Ezra. He knew where Claire was. She was sure of it.

"Where is she?" Lily demanded.

"My apologies, Your Majesty. Who are you referring to?"

"Claire Jones. She was arrested too, but apparently she was never brought here. Where is she?"

"Oh dear. That is very concerning," simpered Ezra. His face was a perfect mask of concern, but his twinkling eyes betrayed the lie. "I do hope she's alright."

Lily took a step towards Ezra. "If you've done anything to hurt her..."

Ezra affected shock. "Your Majesty, I assure you, I would never harm anyone. And certainly not one of your advisors. I will make inquiries at once. There are a couple of other facilities she might have been taken to. Once I find her, I will let you know."

Lily made to argue with him. To threaten him. She wanted to make him tell her where Claire was. But she knew he wouldn't, and there was nothing she could do here to make the man talk. Plus, if he was the one holding Claire captive, the last thing Lily wanted to do was make it worse.

"Come on, let's get you home," Lily said, putting her hand on Addison's shoulder and gently turning her towards the door.

Lily opened the door for Addison, and Ezra called, "We'll do tea soon, Addy."

Lily saw Addison freeze. Ezra remained where he was, smiling as ever. Lily took a few steps protectively towards Addison, but the older woman's hesitation lasted only a second and she continued towards the door without acknowledging Ezra at all.

Lily followed her, frowning. Had there been a hint of an order in his voice, or had she imagined it? Surely Ezra didn't think he and Addison would still be friends? Not after all that had happened, and certainly not with them now so clearly on opposite sides.

5

SSAT in the back of the vehicle as Naomi drove them back to the palace, Lily, Addison, and Minister Bellingham swapped brief stories of what had happened since they were last together. Most of what Addison and Minister Bellingham had to say, Lily already knew, and she didn't want to go into much detail herself, well aware that she would need to go over it again soon when all the advisors were gathered.

But she did fill them in on everything the team knew and suspected about Ezra, thinking it best to warn them that he might be their main enemy, lest something happen before the meeting. Minister Bellingham got angrier as more pieces fell into place, and Addison became more agitated.

"I can't believe I thought he was my friend," Addison said, clearly upset with herself.

"If it makes you feel better," Lily said, "I got closer to Ava than you ever did to Ezra."

A brief look of surprise crossed Addison's face, before understanding hit her, and then she looked at Lily sympa-thetically.

"What do you mean?" asked Minister Bellingham.

"Ava is my girlfriend," said Lily. "Was. Is." She shook her head. "I don't know."

"Oh," said Minister Bellingham darkly, her expression one of distaste.

"Is that an issue?" challenged Lily. For some reason she had been more cognisant of the potential for negative reactions to her relationship back in her home world. She didn't feel anyone in Highacre knew her well enough to have an opinion one way or another about her sexuality, and she'd not noticed anyone here caring about such things.

"No. Well, I mean..." Minister Bellingham shrugged, gesturing as one does to indicate it's none of their business when they clearly have strong opinions on the matter. "Meridians aren't for everyone. But each to their own. No judgement here. Though her being Ezra's daughter and all..."

Minister Bellingham's tone indicated Lily should be embarrassed for her poor choice, and she began to feel that way before remembering Minister Bellingham had as little idea about Ava's parentage as she did when she entered the relationship.

"I only found out a few hours ago."

"Even still."

"*You* only know because I just told you!"

"Yes, well, at least now we do know. We can take appropriate precautions."

"I didn't know you didn't like Meridians," said Addison, frowning at Minister Bellingham.

"Oh, I don't have a problem with them." Minister Bellingham waved her off. "I just mean they can be an acquired taste. I dated a Meridian once. When I was at college."

Both Lily and Addison stared at Minister Bellingham in

surprise. Lily couldn't put her finger on it, but for some reason she just couldn't imagine Minister Bellingham dating. To be fair, she couldn't imagine her at college either. Minister Bellingham was one of those people who you assumed had just always been the age she was at now.

"Terrible idea," Minister Bellingham continued, unaware of her companion's surprise. "He always wanted to *test* things. Experiment. Find out how they worked. Drove me crazy. I kept telling him, 'stop playing around and start *doing*'."

They parted ways upon arriving at the palace. Addison and Minister Bellingham were reunited with Giles, who led them away to freshen up, while Lily and Naomi hurried up to her office to find Jason.

"We checked all the other facilities," Naomi said when Lily asked about Claire. "No luck. But I will check them again."

They entered the anteroom, where people who came to meet with the sovereign waited. An attendant informed them that Jason and his wife had decided to wait on one of the balconies to enjoy the fresh air. She left to get them, and Lily paced the room anxiously.

The room was small, but the high ceiling gave the impression of space. Chairs and couches were spaced out, lining the walls that were adorned with oil paintings and knickknacks, which were apparently gifts from foreign dignitaries. She vaguely remembered Giles telling her it was one person's entire job to ensure the appropriate gifts were displayed depending on who was visiting.

Lily crossed to the windows, gazing out. The weather was stormy, but the landscape still looked beautiful. The lake was grey, mirroring the clouds, and the mountains looked magnificent but ominous. As if hiding secrets.

What secrets is Ezra hiding?

Her mind returned to Minister Bellingham's comment about her old boyfriend. She felt like that was exactly what Ezra was doing. Observing them. Testing them. As if they were all ants in a glass case, and he was watching to see what they did in response to whatever he threw in there.

He had to have a motive beyond pure interest. Something to gain from everything he was doing. But none of it made sense to Lily.

The door to the anteroom opened, and Jason and his wife Gwen entered.

The last time Lily met Gwen, she had found her warm and welcoming, bringing Lily into her home and chatting about family. This Gwen regarded Lily warily, with a frosty gaze.

Lily's eyes darted quickly to Jason, and she suddenly felt immense relief. She hadn't realised until seeing him how much she missed him and his reassuring presence. Just as quickly, her heart sank. A bandage was still wrapped his head, securing the gauze in place over the hole where his left eye used to be. He leant heavily on both the cane in his right hand and his wife, and Lily noted that the arm around Gwen's shoulders was bandaged. Lily's initial relief at seeing two shoes was replaced with worry—what if he had lost the leg but already had a prosthesis?

She felt ill. The only reason Jason had gone to the Disputed Region was to secure the felixium to bring Lily home. And in the end, she had been able to get herself home, which meant his failed operation had been pointless. And now he was permanently maimed. Because of her.

The look on Gwen's face told Lily that she also parked the blame for her husband's condition at Lily's feet, and the way she was angrily whispering to Jason let Lily know she didn't agree with Jason being here.

"Jason!" Lily hurried over and gave her bodyguard a

hug. She could tell he'd lost weight and felt tears burning her eyes. "It's so good to see you."

"You too, Your Majesty. Welcome home." The genuine affection in his voice melted her heart, and Lily hurriedly wiped the tears before turning to Gwen. Lily moved to hug her, but pulled back at the icy stare.

"It's good to see you too, Gwen," Lily said with feeling. "How is he? Really?"

"He shouldn't be out of bed, for a start," Gwen said, shooting Jason a look.

"They said I needed to start moving around."

"Moving around the house, not out to the palace and back to work."

A thump made them all jump as Naomi unceremoniously placed a chair next to Jason before looking pointedly at him, and then at it.

With a look of resignation, Jason allowed the three women to help settle him into the chair, fussing about and making sure he was comfortable.

"I'm just going to have to get up again to go into the office," Jason complained.

"And we'll help you with that too," said Naomi before returning to her position near the door.

"I'm fine, really," Jason insisted to Lily. Lily raised an eyebrow and looked at Gwen.

"They did say he's recovering really quickly," admitted Gwen grudgingly. "But that's only because you were following doctor's orders," she added before Jason could comment. "It's only been three weeks, and while the healers are powerful, there's only so much they can do."

"I'm fine," Jason insisted again. "And I do think it's good for me to get out and about. Get things back to normal."

"Doctor Zarka said you shouldn't push it. She said to ease your new leg in."

Lily's stomach dropped. *So he did lose it...*

"It's fine," Jason insisted, tapping the metal with his cane. "Meridian technology. Not sure how I feel about that..."

"It's let you get up and about faster than anything we produce would have. You wouldn't even be ready for a prosthesis if we didn't have their medical products," Gwen said.

"And all that matters is you're okay," Lily insisted, catching Gwen's glare out of the corner of her eye. Jason was not okay.

"I heard the prime minister's announcement," said Jason, seemingly oblivious to the tension in the room. "This war might be even worse than the last. We're both more technologically developed and we know each other's tactics from last time. So we really need to get started with—"

"Woah, woah, woah. Hold on there, Jason. There's time enough for shop talk later," said Lily.

Jason looked rebuffed, and Gwen looked pleased.

"Look, I know you have ideas about what we should do, and how we should prepare. Your experience is invaluable."

"Exactly, and that's why I need to come back and prepare the troops."

"It's why I need you to get better, and then come and be my war advisor."

Silence met Lily's pronouncement.

"I'm honoured, Your Majesty," said Jason, sounding disappointed. "But, I mean..." He rubbed his neck, looking uncomfortable. "Not to toot my own horn or anything..."

"Toot away," said Lily, smiling.

"I'm more of a commander in the field. You know, leading the battle. I know it's too big a step up from my previous role to be the general, but I thought I might at least be one of the main battle commanders."

"It's exactly that experience that I need with me, Jason.

We have plenty of commanders we can deploy to the field, but I need someone by my side advising me on the overall strategy so we can shape the battle plan."

"That sounds right up your alley, sweetheart," Gwen added, beaming at Lily now that she knew Jason would not be sent back into danger.

"I'm grateful for your faith in me, ma'am, but I'm just not suited to the strategic or political level. I'm a grunt at heart. I plan operations and win battles."

"Jason." Lily looked him directly in the eye. "You know my advisors. I have plenty of people who can tell me about the political ramifications of this or the strategic implications of that. What I want—what I need—is someone who knows how they all talk, which you do, and can tell me what the impact will be for our soldiers on the ground. I need you to help me make sure that when I make decisions, I really understand the possible consequences. I know I will have to make decisions that will result in people being injured. I know that some of my decisions will cost people their lives. I do not want those decisions to be uninformed or made in ignorance of the likely outcome."

Jason considered Lily's words. She could see that his heart still wanted to be in the fight with his soldiers. But she could also see he understood her point. That he could make a difference; that he could help his men and women by advising her. She knew Jason would still feel the guilt of being safe at home while others risked their lives, but he would just have to deal with that. She couldn't risk losing him.

He nodded slowly. "Thank you, Your Majesty. It would be my privilege to serve in this way."

"Of course, your new role will come with a pay raise."

"Well, why didn't you open with that?"

6

THE GENERAL CHATTER died down as Lily sat up straighter and cleared her throat. She looked around the room. So much had changed since she was first led to this office by Giles. That felt like a lifetime ago.

And scanning the faces of her advisors, they also looked like they had lived a lifetime since then. Jason was pale, and though he had assured Gwen he was fine as he gently extracted himself from her care, leaving her in the ante-room, he looked tired. Naomi, though not a royal advisor, had been permitted to stay for security purposes given Jason's condition, and she had positioned herself so she could protect Lily while still monitoring her old boss in case Jason needed anything.

Minister Bellingham and Addison had returned not long ago, having refreshed themselves and changed clothes. Addison had lent Minister Bellingham an outfit, and the minister looked quite out of place in the homely floral blouse and slacks. However, where the old Minister Bellingham would have been irritated at wearing something so far from her usual style, the woman before Lily now hadn't even mentioned it, aside from thanking Addison for her generosity.

Addison remained quiet. She seemed more relaxed now that she was home, but there was still a sense of unease about her. Lily couldn't quite put her finger on what seemed to be bothering Addison and put it down to the length of time she had spent in solitary confinement. Surely the sudden influx of people would be difficult for anyone.

Minister Bellingham, on the other hand, was like a woman reborn. Far from being at odds with her cellmates in the general population section of the prison, it seemed she had managed to fit right in, to the point of making friends and bonding with the other women there. "I think I'm even in a gang now!" she exclaimed happily to Lily. "Did you know that most of those women are in there simply because they don't have enough money to support their children or themselves?"

"Er, no, I didn't..." replied Lily, embarrassed to realise she hadn't given it much thought.

"Yes." Minister Bellingham nodded enthusiastically, her face serious. "They start out poor, and because of that they can't get a good education, and because of that they can't compete for higher paying jobs, and the cycle continues!"

"Oh, that's—"

"It's a problem we need to fix, that's what it is," said Minister Bellingham with a fervour that made Lily think the older woman might do just that. "They're all smart women. And they have such amazing skills. Trace made a shiv out of a toilet roll holder! I'd never even think of using a toilet roll holder!"

Waiting for the meeting to begin, most of the advisors chatted happily, catching up with each other. However, when Minister Jeremy Toot entered, the conversation lulled, stony eyes watching as he strode to his chair, seemingly oblivious to the collective detestation.

Lily's eyes fell on the two empty chairs. Conspicuous by their absences were Austin, who hadn't been invited, and Claire, who had failed to return. Lily frowned, wondering again where Claire was, and if she was okay. Naomi had told her that her inquiries had found nothing. None of the facilities that Claire might reasonably have been taken to following her arrest had any record of her. Though Naomi had left clear instructions that if any of them happened to find themselves with a Claire Jones in custody, she was to be released immediately.

The best case scenario was that Claire had already been released from whatever secret facility she had been held in, and had gone to ground. But Lily couldn't see her not reaching out to let them know she was okay. Unless she had decided not to return. Lily couldn't blame her if that was the case. She had been through a lot; perhaps she had decided the fight wasn't worth it.

Lily pushed the thought, and the pain it brought, aside. More likely, Claire was somewhere off the books. A black site, or somewhere else she couldn't be found. The idea that they couldn't help Claire made Lily feel sick.

She liked Claire. Respected her. The idea of trying to defeat Ezra and Reginald Toth all while stopping a war without her help seemed impossible.

Lily noticed the eyes on her and brought herself back to the present. She would open the meeting, and then no doubt Minister Bellingham would take over and Lily would help the team come up with a plan. She swallowed, preparing to speak.

Before Lily could start, Minister Toot placed his glass of whiskey on the table loudly and cleared his throat. "Your Majesty, I think I speak for all my colleagues here when I say welcome back. You were sorely missed." He smiled at her, sickeningly sweet, though his eyes remained cold, regarding Lily with the same disdain he had always held for her.

Lily noted the reactions of her assembled advisors. Some merely averted their gazes, their faces showing they had no time for Minister Toot's simpering ingratiation. Naomi rolled her eyes, earning her a look from Jason. Minister Bellingham cracked her knuckles as if wanting to test out some of her new prison skills on him.

"Thank you, Minister Toot," said Lily, returning his fake smile. "You're fired."

The rest of the advisors perked up, looking at Lily as if she had just told them it was Christmas. All except Minister Toot, who looked flabbergasted. He opened and shut his mouth, eyes goggling. Lily could see the cogs of his mind creaking, trying to decide how to respond. He downed his whiskey in one gulp, collecting himself before addressing Lily.

"Your Majesty, whatever do you mean?"

Playing it dumb, then. Typical.

"I mean just that, Minister Toot. Your services are no longer required. I thank you for your dedication to Highacre in your capacity as royal advisor over the years, however, all good things must come to an end, mustn't they?" Her smiled broadened as he continued to stare at her.

"But, Your Majesty—"

"Your role in aiding the prime minister is in direct conflict with your role as my advisor. Therefore, your place here is no longer tenable." Lily leant forwards, meeting Minister Toot's now hostile glare, her eyes steely and cold. "I again thank you for your service, and wish you well in your future endeavours."

Minister Toot did not get up.

"Now, if you'll please leave us. I don't think we need to mar your service by having you escorted from the palace, do we?"

Minister Toot opened his mouth, but Minister Bellingham beat him to it. "Jeremy, don't make a tit of yourself. Be a good chap and bugger off. There's a good boy."

A dangerous shade of red began climbing Minister Toot's neck. Again, he looked like he wanted to respond, but Naomi took a step forward as if ready to escort him from the room. The realisation dawned on Minister Toot's face that his situation was unsalvageable. Muttering a curt, "Good day," the minister snatched his hat and coat and left, banging his shoulder on the door in his effort to sweep majestically from the room.

The remaining advisors smiled around at each other, the mood in the room livelier.

"Good riddance, I say. Well done Your Majesty," said Minister Bellingham. The weight loss had left the angles of her face more severe, but her eyes seemed more alert somehow. Lily also noticed she startled more easily, and sometimes seemed to be looking at something that wasn't there.

Perhaps prison wasn't as easy as she's making out.

She was still pompous and had definitely retained her upper-class accent, but something about her, despite her new edge, was now more down to earth, more accessible.

"Thank you, Minister Bellingham. I don't know if this is appropriate, but I must say it almost seems like prison agreed with you."

To Lily's relief and surprise, Minister Bellingham laughed. "You know what? I think it did. And please, Your Majesty, call me Juliana. I think I ceased being a minister when I got arrested."

"Right," said Lily after a slightly awkward beat where everyone was waiting for someone else to start. "Looks like we have another vacancy. With Jason becoming my war advisor, I'll need someone to fill the security position. Naomi, are you interested?"

"Ma'am?" said Naomi, shocked.

"That was rude of me, springing it on you like that," said Lily, seeing her shock and worrying that Naomi wasn't interested. "You can, of course, think about it—"

"No need, ma'am, I accept," said Naomi quickly before sitting in the chair next to Jason. She kept her face impassive, but her eyes were shining.

Lily looked around the room, again waiting for someone else to step in and take charge. In her first few meetings with her advisors, she'd barely managed to get a word in. But now… she was hit by just how much of a toll the last few months had taken on her advisors. They seemed shadows of the people she'd met. Tired, worn down, and the hope they had projected that everything would be fine seemed to have evaporated. They were not the people she'd met all those months ago.

But then, neither was she. Gone was the lost, scared, timid girl who had been pulled from her home dimension and thrust into the political crisis gripping Highacre. She had been tested. She had suffered loss. And she was stronger now, more confident. Lily had found herself to be much more capable than she had ever given herself credit for.

And she was queen.

These were her people.

Her family.

She could do this.

"Right, well, now that he's gone, welcome back. Particularly to Juliana and Addison, who have endured being in custody for too long. And to Jason, who I know we're all glad is recovering."

Lily faltered. She hadn't planned an agenda for the meeting, as she'd assumed that her advisors would take over. She should have come up with a plan. Lily remembered Ava telling her she was capable of anything, so long as she didn't get in her own way. Lily was hit with a pang of longing. It was at odds with the souring of her stomach, thinking of Ava's betrayal, but despite that, she knew Ava had meant those words. And Lily didn't have to do everything herself. That's why she had advisors. She just had to lead them.

"I'm going to need all of your help to figure out the best way forwards. We don't need to do all the planning today, but the way I see it, we need to make Highacre safe again. That means getting rid of the prime minister and anyone working with him and making peace with Meridia. At the same time, we should plan for the worst, so we'll need a war strategy. I don't know how we're going to do any of those things, or if they need to be done sequentially or concurrently, but that's what we're going to figure out together."

Lily looked expectantly at her advisors, hoping that they weren't all as defeated as Addison looked.

"I think a key piece of information that none of us in this room possess is the demeanour of the Meridian and Valmeadian heads of state," said Juliana. "None of us were involved in whatever conversations the prime minister has had, and so we don't know our opponents' appetites."

"You think they might want war?" asked Naomi.

"It is possible," replied Juliana. "We won't know until someone talks to them. We can't rule out that they might be open to peace. But don't forget that a Meridian terrorist group claimed responsibility for the attack on the arena. We don't know if it was state-sponsored. If the Meridian government wasn't behind it, it's possible that President Taylor will forgive our declaration and the ensuing hostilities if we forgive the terrorist attack. But the attack could have been back by the Meridian government with the intention of driving us towards declaring war, in which case we have no hope."

"What we need to know is whether Ezra is working for Meridia, or if everything he's doing is for his own gain," said Jason. "If he's acting as their agent, then we should plan on war until we can take care of him. If he's not, then we might have a better shot at negotiating peace with the president."

"Ezra's the real deal," Addison said randomly.

The room turned to stare at her, and she turned a deep red.

"I mean, that's what I thought. But he tricked me. I mean, he can be tricky." She sighed, as if frustrated that she couldn't articulate what she wanted to say. "I just think it'll be difficult to figure out what side he's on. Sometimes things are not what they seem."

The advisors nodded sympathetically, murmuring words of comfort to Addison. She of all of them had been taken in by Ezra. Clearly she was beating herself up about it.

"Okay, so it sounds like the first step might be that I call my counterparts and sound them out," said Lily.

"It would be usual protocol for you to have a video call with them anyway, Your Majesty, having assumed the throne. It's a little more unusual following the declaration of war. But noting they made it in your absence, it would not be out of line for us to reach out and set up a discussion," said Giles.

"And whether they agree to the meeting or not will give us a good idea of their receptiveness," added Addison.

"Excellent point," said Lily, too enthusiastically. She silently cursed herself. She wanted to encourage Addison to participate, especially after her stumbling earlier, but if she was too obvious, she'd just send the woman back into her shell.

"So, if they don't want to talk, or won't agree to peace... then what?" Naomi looked around the room.

"We need contingency plans," said Jason. "If you're happy with it, Your Majesty, while you're making your calls, I can lead the development of a war plan. And perhaps Minister Bellingham might take the lead on planning how to deal with the prime minister."

"Juliana," Minister Bellingham corrected Jason with a warm smile. Jason looked distinctly uncomfortable; Lily wouldn't be surprised if he never used her first name. "And I agree with Jason. He and I will lead the respective planning efforts, seeking support of you all as required. I will prepare you for your call, Your Majesty, and then get cracking. After Her Majesty has made contact with the heads of state, or been rebuffed, we can reconvene in here. Jason and I will present our plans, and together we can refine and amend them as required."

The meeting drew to its natural conclusion, with everyone seeming slightly more positive than when the meeting had started. Having a way forwards gave them all energy, and even Addison seemed eager to help Juliana with her planning.

Even Lily felt like they were moving, taking steps toward victory. But Jason was right—if Ezra was working with Meridia, then nothing would stop the war other than defeating Ezra himself.

She paused, suddenly hit by the complexity of the situation. It was so easy to want to simplify things. To make Ezra the villain, so they could focus their efforts on one target. But even if he was working with Meridia, others in the country would have their own goals. Meridia had lost land in the Disputed Region at the end of the last war. It wasn't beyond comprehension that they might embrace the chance to get back what was once theirs.

But violence wasn't the only response. Lily had to believe that she could find a way forward with Meridia. To come to an agreement so that people didn't have to die in a needless war. The price of peace would likely be high. Meridia had Highacre over a barrel. Despite this, Lily had confidence that she could make a deal that would work for Meridia and be palatable to the Highacren Parliament.

Because while Meridia would drive a hard deal, no one actually *wanted* war.

Right?

7

LILY SAT IN THE CHAIR, trying her best to relax and look calm and confident. The room featured nondescript, plain solid colours like every government building she had ever been in. Juliana and Addison fussed around, making sure she had water nearby. They dabbed at her face with tissues, blotting the perspiration spotting on her forehead and nose due to her nerves. Lily sat back and concentrated on her breathing.

In five minutes, the room as Lily saw it would transform, and she would be in a virtual meeting room with the President of Meridia and the representative of the Great Leader of Valmead, Klaud Gutzmer. She had been told that it was almost impossible to tell that it was not real, similar to an immersion device.

Lily grabbed her water bottle and took a swig. Her hands shook slightly, and she glared at them, willing them to steady.

"You'll be fine, Your Majesty," said Addison. The warmth in her voice was reminiscent of the old Addison, but her smile was still worn and tired. Lily smiled at her gratefully.

"Thanks Addison. I just have to keep telling myself not to be intimidated about meeting the president and acting dictator. That I'm also a leader of a nation."

"That you are, Your Majesty." Her smile reached her eyes this time. "And you have nothing to be intimidated about. The president is a jerk and this Klaud, from all accounts, is just like a highly motivated Jeremy Toot. And you already took care of him."

"Right." Juliana marched up to them. "You should have everything you need. Once we shut the door behind us and the scan confirms you are the only one here, the door will not be able to be opened again until you authorise it yourself. Do you have all the information you need on both men?"

Lily quickly ran through what she knew. The Meridian president, Dan Taylor, was an old university friend of Ezra's. He had been a career politician, though low-level, and no one thought he would achieve much. Then the old Meridian president screwed Ezra over, blaming a military disaster on a catastrophic failure of intelligence and sacking him from his position as the Director of the Meridian Intelligence Agency. Ezra had turned to business and done extraordinarily well. He then funded the election campaign of his old friend Dan Taylor, who was elected president.

Juliana had told Lily that old HIA files suggested that the president took Ezra's advice in most things, but notably any important matters of state. They had considered Ezra essentially a de facto president. Even his appointment as the ambassador to Highacre had been at Ezra's request.

Information on Klaud Gutzmer was more difficult to find since the HIA had been disbanded. Lily should have been able to simply ask Alexei about him, but her advisors had all been strongly opposed to this idea. Their issue was that Alexei would insist on his release in exchange for the information. This seemed like a win-win to Lily, who had been intending on having Alexei released as soon as was practical. However, Juliana insisted that releasing either ambassador at this point would be reputational suicide. With the people of Highacre suffering and the prime minister running such an effective campaign about Lily's over-familiarity with foreigners, doing anything to give an air of truth to his words would turn the public against her.

Knowing that she couldn't yet send him home to be with his sick father dampened Lily's enthusiasm to see Alexei. How was she meant to look him in the eye, knowing that he had been there for her when she learned of her own father's death, and tell him he couldn't go be with his? Cursing herself for being a coward, Lily tried to believe her advisors when they told her that under the circumstances Alexei probably wouldn't give her the information anyway. She knew him better, though. Alexei was more honourable than any of them, herself included. Nonetheless, Lily had dropped it and directed her advisors to find what they could on the Acting Leader of Valmead.

All they had been able to dredge up was what was in the public domain. Gutzmer was widely seen as a man who traded on the power of others. He enjoyed his close position to the Great Leader, often using the dictator's name to achieve his own goals. The relationship worked because Alexei's father was able to keep him in check. Now that Gutzmer was holding the reins, already the wheels were falling off. He was restricting freedoms and access to essential goods and services for regular Valmeadians in favour of ramping up military recruitment and production. It seemed inevitable that with Gutzmer in charge, Valmead would enter the war. It just wasn't yet clear whether they would pick a side, or take on both Meridia and Highacre.

An arrogant, narcissistic puppet, and a delusional wannabe tyrant. Great.

"Yes, Juliana, I think I'm good to go."

Juliana eyed Lily suspiciously. "Are you sure, Your Majesty? You seem a little... nervous."

Lily cursed her trembling hands. The nerves were getting to her, sure, but her mind kept jumping back to the briefing that she had received that morning. The war had begun with bloody force. There had been a string of battles within and around the Disputed Region and over two hundred people were confirmed dead so far. Some were soldiers on both sides, but there were civilians among the casualties. Men, women, and children who had just been living their lives, but had the misfortune of living in an area that became a war zone.

Lily had been expecting casualties. That's what happened in war, and she was used to hearing news reports back home. But they had been about distant countries that she'd never been to. Sad yes, but she hadn't felt a connection. But this was her country. Her citizens. And her soldiers who had been sent to war by her order.

Well, by the prime minister's order.

But she had been unable to stop him or negate his decree. With the help of her advisors, they had lodged an urgent injunction with the courts. However, their legal advisor had warned that with the prime minister challenging Lily's right to rule, the case might take a long time, even if given priority.

Lily took a deep breath. While she was nervous about meeting the heads of state, she hoped this would be a relatively easy meeting. So long as Ezra wasn't acting on behalf of the Meridian president, then there was a chance for peace. After all, Meridia was taking casualties too, so surely the president's aim would be to cease hostilities as soon as possible. And without Meridia and Highacre at war, it would be suicide for Valmead to attack either of them.

If she could just get Meridia to set their terms for peace, she could bring that to the Parliament and convince them to revoke the declaration. And if Juliana could come up with a plan to defeat the prime minister, getting the treaty through Parliament would be relatively easy. In fact, if the prime minister was out of the way completely, she might not even need the Parliament—she could agree to the peace herself.

If all sides were focussed on achieving the same outcome, all that would be up for discussion were the terms of the peace treaty. Lily was worried about the negotiation process; she had never been good at that sort of thing. But closing her eyes and seeing the images of the casualties, knowing that more would follow if she was unsuccessful, the pressure was overwhelming.

"I'm good. I'm fine. Everything's fine," Lily said unconvincingly.

Juliana and Addison exchanged a look, after which Juliana gestured towards Lily meaningfully. Addison hesitated, then sat down next to Lily.

"Your Majesty, would you like some help? Perhaps I could just take the edge off your nerves? Or get rid of them for you?"

Addison's magic allowed her to alter other people's emotions. Lily recalled being very upset when she had realised that Addison had been keeping her calm when she was first brought to Highacre. Now it seemed like a fantastic idea.

"Would you? That would be great."

Addison beamed and gently grasped Lily's arm. Lily instantly felt better. She still had the gravity of the situation in mind, but she felt calmer, more confident. She thanked Addison and the two women left Lily alone in the room.

Nothing happened for about a minute, but just as Lily was beginning to relax in the peace and quiet, the room suddenly shifted, becoming a large space not dissimilar to her own office. It was bright and airy, with one wall displaying a beautiful view.

Across from Lily sat two middle-aged men, each in a chair similar to hers. A coffee table had appeared in the middle of the room, complete with coasters and books. Given that this was all some kind of holographic construct, Lily wondered briefly at the point of such detail.

Behind each man was a large image, signifying their country. Lily glanced briefly behind her seat and saw a large Highacren flag waving majestically despite the lack of a breeze. The Meridian president was framed by the Meridian crest. It was dominated by a symbol that comprised two beakers, their stems crossed, with three inter-locking ellipses in the background. Lily had been told that the image was intended to depict scientific research, and that the words beneath it, which were in a language that Lily did not recognise, said "knowledge is power".

The Valmeadian imagery was far simpler. It was an enormous oil portrait of Nicholai Rosovski, the Great Leader. Alexei's father was a strong, imposing man. Unfortunately, with his image in the background, the flaws of the man in the chair were thrown into stark relief. Where the image of the Great Leader gave the impression of a man who made decisions and took action, Klaud Gutzmer looked to be the type of man who was always scheming and calculating, determining which course of action would be better for himself. He wore a smirk designed to make others think he was bored. That he already had all the information or had made a decision, but was generously meeting with lesser people in an effort to help them gain even a fraction of what knowledge he already had. Lily had dealt with people like Klaud before. Usually they were the least knowledgeable person in the room.

Sensing that the Meridian president was about to speak, Lily quickly opened the meeting. She had called it; she would control it.

"Gentlemen, thank you for meeting with me. I know we are all very busy."

"Yes, well, busier now that you have declared war on us," said the president. His tone had some bite, but he did not seem angry, more curious about Lily and what she would do next. He flashed her a smile that was a less smarmy version of Klaud's smirk. Lily was struck by the similarities between the men. Klaud fed off the Great Leader's power, and Taylor wouldn't have any without Ezra. Though the president had the air of someone used to receiving deferential treatment, he also seemed like the type of man who received it because of his position, rather than his actions.

"And that is precisely what I have asked you here to discuss. As you may know, the declaration of war was made by the Highacren prime minister in my absence. With my return, things have changed. I prefer diplomacy to violence, and too many have already lost their lives when we can resolve matters here, together."

There was a slight hesitation before the president replied. Lily saw Klaud shoot Taylor a glance, though the president kept his eyes on Lily.

"Forgive me, Your Majesty, but what exactly has changed? You were not here, true, but presumably there were legitimate reasons for your prime minister declaring war on Meridia. And presumably those reasons remain? Unless, of course, he was under the mistaken impression that Meridia was responsible for your absence, and that was the cause for all of this bloodshed."

Klaud Gutzmer nodded. "We also noted the lack of reasoning behind Highacre's declaration. Quite unsettling, I must say. Makes Valmead distinctly nervous. Not to mention your refusal to return our ambassadors. This is quite distressing, especially when we are not currently at war. I must reiterate our demand that you return our countrymen."

Lily watched the two men bounce off each other, almost as if rehearsed, and was hit by the realisation that they had already spoken.

Of course they have.

Lily inwardly cursed herself for not considering that the Meridian and Valmeadian leaders might side against her for the negotiations. By working together, they could drive up the cost of peace.

Lily settled herself. The grounds on which Highacre had declared war was the main lever Meridia had against Highacre. Under international law, a country could not simply declare war on another country without cause. The prime minister had largely hung his decision on the terrorist attack at the arena. However, following the claim of responsibility by the Meridian terrorist group, the Meridian government had publicly condemned their actions. They claimed to be doing everything possible to locate those responsible and bring them to justice.

Time enough hadn't passed for Highacre to justifiably make a claim that Meridia was not trying to locate those responsible, or worse, was shielding them. But then, the prime minister hadn't gone into specifics when he sent them all to war, merely stating that the attack was the basis. However, a country that declared war without appropriate grounds was liable to pay compensation or suffer sanctions. That seemed to be where the other leaders were steering this discussion.

Lily needed to somehow maintain that the prime minister's grounds were legitimate, but that the situation had escalated more quickly than she would have liked. She would then need to offer an incentive for peace. Her advisors had suggested ceding some land in the Disputed Region to Meridia.

"Travel is currently restricted due to the conflict," Lily said, trying to remove the monotone from her rehearsed statement. "Your ambassadors will be returned once we can ensure their safe passage. As for the prime minister's declaration, the reasons were clear," said Lily, trying not to choke while declaring her support for Reginald Toth's actions. "Hundreds of Highacren citizens lost their lives as a result of the terror attack at the arena. The attack for which a Meridian group has claimed responsibility. And I do hope you are not going to deny or downplay Meridia's provocative actions in the Disputed Region."

President Taylor shifted uncomfortably, but said nothing. Gutzmer continued to smirk.

"I support the prime minister's declaration insofar as I agree with its legitimacy. However, having returned, I would like to see if we can't resolve these issues without the loss of more lives."

The president chuckled. "How very interesting. Highacre slaps us across the face with one hand and then asks us to shake the other. Forgive me, Your Majesty, but is Highacre having a crisis of personality? Who is in charge there?"

"I am," Lily said sharply, leaning forwards. "There is no issue here, no confusion. The circumstances are simple. In my absence, the prime minister was in charge. He responded to the attack and your illegal seizure of the Highacren mines in the Disputed Region. But now I have returned, and wish to examine whether we may find a less extreme solution."

"Highacre does not want war," Klaud Gutzmer stated. "Scared, perhaps?"

"Highacre is prepared for war." Lily looked Gutzmer dead in the eye. "But we do desire peace."

President Taylor and Acting Leader Gutzmer looked at each other. Gutzmer gave a barely perceptible nod, and both men returned their gaze to Lily.

"Your Majesty," said President Taylor, his voice dripping with condescension. "Meridia also desires peace. We tend to indicate this by not declaring war on our neighbours."

Gutzmer snorted.

"However, Highacre's somewhat... erratic behaviour concerns us. We also remain concerned about Highacre's seemingly inconsistent leadership structure. How can I be sure that, if I accept your offer of peace, you won't disappear again? And then the prime minister—who may continue his military preparations during this proposed peace—might launch another attack on Meridia." He shook his head. "No, no. It is too uncertain. I can't ask my people to live in those conditions."

A little warning bell began to sound in Lily's head. She was waiting for the president to signal his price for peace, but so far there was no hint about what he wanted.

"Well, would you consider a ceasefire? That way, our people don't have to die and you have legitimate grounds for keeping your forces on whatever level of readiness you desire."

President Taylor smiled his patronising smile. Acting Leader Gutzmer simply looked down at his hands, as if embarrassed.

"Yes, well, I suppose that is one option," said President Taylor. "However, I do have to consider my people."

"Yes," agreed Lily. "That would be the ceasefire bit, where none of them die needlessly."

"Quite. Of course, many of my people are still angry after the last war. They feel—rightly or wrongly—that Highacre came out on top through deceptive means. They lost their land. Some lost their livelihood. And tragically, many lost their lives."

"The last war was a tragedy that still touches us all," said Lily firmly. "I assure you that many Highacrens—rightly or wrongly—feel the same about Meridia. But we don't address these issues between our countries by repeating the same mistakes."

President Taylor nodded, rubbing his mouth as if made uncomfortable by what he was about to say. "I can imagine you feel that way, Your Majesty. Of course, Meridia's wounds are harder to heal when so many still feel that Highacre covered up, rather than investigated, such widespread allegations of war crimes against our people. I, of course, desire peace, but how could I refuse the families of those massacred by rogue Highacren soldiers the opportunity for justice?"

Shit. The alarm in her head was now almost drowning out her ability to think.

"Justice? Please be clear, President Taylor, exactly what you mean by justice?"

The men looked at Lily pityingly. She didn't understand the political game. The nuances. The unspoken code. They were meeting with a twenty-year-old woman, not a queen. And as angry as their attitude made her, she was infuriated to realise that she had walked into this meeting extraordinarily unprepared.

They did not want peace. She saw it now. She used to think that any leader would do anything to protect their people, but that assumption had been fundamentally flawed. She was disappointed, and any hope she'd had that so long as there was no connection to Ezra, there was a chance to discuss peace, fizzled and died.

Both her rivals saw Highacre as weak. They saw the leadership squabbles. Saw the prime minister oppressing the people with the HSP. They would be seeing the result on an international scale through productivity and trade.

Lily saw now that war had been inevitable. The only reason Meridia or Valmead hadn't moved already was that they were waiting for Highacre to tear itself apart internally. The more degraded Highacre was, the easier it would be for them to come in at the end and crush them.

Lily looked at the president. She dearly wished she could wipe the shit-eating grin from his face.

She saw his play now. He wanted land. The entire Disputed Region. Maybe more. He would demand Lily give it up in exchange for peace. And if she offered it all, he'd increase his price. There would be no real negotiation—he was too confident that he would win the war.

"Surely your people would be even angrier if you send your soldiers to their deaths when you had an opportunity to stop the war?"

Both men smiled patronisingly at her naivety.

"Your Majesty," said Klaud Gutzmer, "you are new to this. A military is a tool of the state. Brave men and women volunteer to fight. They accept the dangers and they, and their families, in the event of their death, are appropriately compensated. You cannot rule a country worrying about the individual lives of soldiers."

"Don't you have conscription?" Lily asked.

The Acting Leader waved his hand dismissively. "All Valmeadians would gladly give their lives for their country. But you miss the point. You must lead with your head. The heart is fickle. It breaks too easily. Lead with your heart, and the country dies."

Lily stared at him before returning her gaze to President Taylor, who was smiling at her as if she were a simple girl who should stick to playing with her dolls. Lily realised there was no room to negotiate with these men. She couldn't give up the entire Disputed Region. They needed the felixium, if nothing else. And if the leaders weren't willing to treat fairly, that meant only one outcome.

War.

She felt sick.

"Well. It looks like there is little more for us to discuss. I remain willing to speak with you if either of you realise that violence is not the answer. But otherwise..." She looked each man in the eye, holding their gazes in turn. "I'll see you on the battlefield."

8

Lily strode confidently down the corridor, the echoes of her advisors in her head. A sense of defeat had settled in the room after she told them of her meeting with the heads of state. Lily could tell that they, like her, had all been hoping no one wanted war. That once Lily had negotiated a peace treaty, they could focus on the slightly more manageable task of defeating the prime minister and restoring order to their country.

However, when Lily informed them of her intention to speak with Alexei, they had all become animated, united in their opinion that this was a bad idea. Only Giles, who had remained quiet during the discussion, now accompanied her to Alexei's room, with Naomi present but remaining far enough behind Lily to let her know she didn't approve.

Overwhelmingly, her advisors felt nothing could be achieved with anyone from Valmead, Alexei included, without releasing the ambassadors and allowing them to return home. They were also in agreement that doing this before garnering enough public support would hand Highacre to the prime minister on a platter.

Lily stopped outside Alexei's door, hesitating. What if they were right? She knew it was going to be extraordinarily difficult to speak with Alexei, knowing that his father was ill and she was the one with the power to send him home. And there wasn't much Alexei could do to help her from here. But the war was already bloody; the latest casualty reports were still turning her stomach, and if Valmead entered the fray, it would be catastrophic. Lily had to do anything and everything in her power to try to prevent that from happening. And even if Alexei couldn't *do* anything to help, he had always helped her think more clearly about a problem. She was sure that together they could figure out what to do.

Closing her eyes, Lily knocked on the door.

And besides, what kind of friend has you detained and doesn't even visit?

Guilt had been gnawing at her over the past few days about the treatment of her friends. Not for the first time, she wondered if she was doing the right thing in following her advisors on this matter. Was it really so important for Ava and Alexei to be locked up? Maybe the public would understand?

The door swung open, Royal Guards permitting Lily entrance. Alexei and Brigadier Sergei Romanovich were sitting on a couch by the window. At Lily's appearance, Sergei's face darkened, and he excused himself under the pretence of allowing Lily and Alexei privacy.

His rejection stung, but Lily couldn't blame him. Lily looked to the guards, who moved to the corridor, though Naomi and Giles remained in the room, neither open to leaving Lily alone with Alexei.

Lily bristled at the implication that unsupervised, she might be persuaded to let Alexei leave, but then decided that it wasn't out of the realm of possibility.

And maybe I should, regardless of who's watching.

Lily moved towards Alexei. He sat up straighter, but wouldn't look at her. He also remained sitting. The Alexei she knew would have stood, if not to embrace her, at least out of respect. Lily took a seat in an armchair across from the couch, pulling it slightly closer.

"How are you?" she asked.

The look Alexei gave her conveyed exactly how stupid he thought her question to be. Then his eyes softened, revealing the desperation deep within. "I'm worried about my father," he said, looking imploringly at Lily. "And with him sick, my siblings are in danger. My stepmother will be pushing for my brother to be declared Acting Leader, and Gutzmer is ambitious..."

Lily resisted the urge to lean forwards and hold Alexei's hands. He looked so lost, so worried about his family.

"You understand," he said, looking directly at Lily. Her stomach dropped. She absolutely could understand. She had spent the last month or so doing everything she could to help her family. And Alexei had been right there with her, at times more focussed on helping them than even she had been. "Please, let me go home."

"She can't," Giles responded before Lily could. "It's just not—"

"I'm not talking to you!" Alexei roared, exploding to his feet and startling Lily. Naomi moved swiftly to her, the protective movement breaking Alexei's focus on Giles and calming him slightly. Giles had paled and stood rooted to the ground as if unsure of what to do.

Alexei took a breath, clenching and unclenching his fists. "You should have told me. When we spoke through the communicator. You should have told me that my father was sick."

Lily stared at Giles. She hadn't even thought about that. When they had spoken, Alexei even asked about things in his home country and Giles had simply said that little news was getting through. But they had known about his father. And said nothing.

Giles opened and closed his mouth, unable to find the words to explain his actions.

"I deserved to know," said Alexei, quieter now. "I would have made very different decisions."

"We felt, under the circumstances, that upsetting you while you couldn't do anything about it—"

"But I could have done something about it!" Alexei shouted, anger engulfing him again. "I pushed to stay. To help Lily's family. We could have come home earlier. Gotten here before the declaration. You wouldn't have locked me up. I would have been home."

"We couldn't have known—"

"My father is dying!" Alexei's voice broke, pleading overtaking the anger. Lily blinked furiously, her heart breaking for her friend. Alexei turned, looking at Lily now.

"Leave us," she ordered her advisors. Giles turned for the door, clearly eager to escape. Naomi didn't budge. "You too."

"No, Your Majesty," said Naomi simply, her eyes on Alexei.

"He won't hurt me."

"No, he won't."

Lily took a breath, refocussing on her friend. At her indication, Alexei sat heavily on the couch, his face in his hands.

"I'm sorry, I shouldn't have yelled," he said. "I'm worried about my father, and about my siblings. And I'm frustrated at being trapped here, unable to help them. But it is good to see you." *Finally.* The word hung between them, an unspoken accusation at how long it had taken for Lily to visit.

"I'm so sorry I haven't come before now," said Lily. She bit back an explanation. An excuse. Alexei deserved an unreserved apology. She *should* have come before now.

Her apology softened Alexei. "I know you've been busy," he allowed. "Are we at war?"

Lily shook her head. "Just Highacre and Meridia at this point. But I spoke with President Taylor and Acting Leader Gutzmer, and I think Gutzmer is planning on joining in."

She explained the meeting to Alexei, who nodded, unsurprised by what he was hearing. "Gutzmer is a weak man seeking power. He likely sees Meridia as the powerful side for the moment, but will wait to see who starts winning. Then he'll enter on their side and see how much he can gain while the main battles are being fought by others."

Lily relaxed, relieved that Alexei saw the man as she did. "I need your help, Alexei. We need to make sure Valmead doesn't enter the war. I'm having a hard enough time stopping the conflict while it's just the two countries. There'll be no chance if all of us are involved. Not to mention the unnecessary casualties."

Alexei sat up, beaming at Lily. "Of course. Of course I'll help. Once I'm home, I'll be able to counter Gutzmer's influence."

Lily's heart sank. Alexei saw her expression, and his own faltered.

"Alexei, I can't let you go. Not yet. Right now, the prime minister has everyone suspecting I'm a traitor. If I let you go home before I can counter that narrative, I'm as good as handing Highacre to him. Even if we win the war, Highacre will be lost."

Alexei's face fell. He stared at the floor, nodding, and swallowed thickly.

"But I will do everything I can to change things so I can send you home as soon as possible," Lily said.

Alexei nodded again, still not looking at her.

"I mean, maybe... maybe you could provide assurances you won't declare war on Highacre? They might make you Acting Leader instead of Gutzmer, right? And so maybe, if you said that, or put it in writing, then I could ask if we could send you home. We could tell everyone it was to prevent war," Lily finished weakly, knowing that it was a stretch.

Alexei finally looked up at Lily. "How could I possibly do that?"

"Sorry?" asked Lily, confused.

"How could I promise we won't go to war?"

Lily stared at Alexei, stunned. "What are you saying?" she asked slowly.

"I thought I knew you, Lily. But my friend would never have locked me up and kept me here, unable to see my dying father. You *know* what it's like to lose your father. And you're doing it anyway. I don't know you at all."

Lily sat back in her chair, feeling as if the wind had been knocked out of her.

"And under these circumstances," Alexei continued, "I can't be sure that you wouldn't come for Valmead if you thought it in Highacre's best interests. So no, I can't provide assurances that Valmead won't prepare and protect itself."

Lily felt sick. She had enormous respect for Alexei. During their time in her home dimension, he had been the voice of reason. Of morality. And he was right. Why should he trust her? Why would he still want to be her friend when she was standing between him and his father?

An image of her own father popped into her mind. She

could see the disappointment on his face that she was denying anyone, let alone a friend, the chance to say good-bye. The chance she herself had not had.

Lily closed her eyes, breathing deeply, willing the tears away. She was queen. She did not have the luxury of being Lily, Alexei's friend. She had to be Lily, Queen of Highacre. Her people were dying. More each day. While she wanted more than anything to let Alexei return to his family, she needed to protect her people, even those she didn't know. She couldn't let them die because she wanted to help a friend.

Steadying herself and trying to ignore the hurt in her heart, Lily looked again at Alexei. "You have my word. I'm the same person you knew, Alexei. But I'm queen now, and I need to think of more than just what I want. What we both want. I'm doing my best in shitty circumstances, and I know I'm getting it wrong, but I am doing my best."

Alexei slid to his knees, kneeling in front of Lily, grasping her hands and staring pleadingly into her eyes. "Then send me home. Your people will understand given the circumstances, and I will work with you—we'll be a team again. Send me home, Lily. Show me you're the Lily I grew to love like a sister."

Lily looked at Alexei, hit by the desperation and pleading in his eyes. There was nothing she wanted more than to let him go home and be with his family. His father. Alexei saw her resolve slip.

"I promise you, Lily. Once I'm there, I'll do everything I can to stop Gutzmer from entering the war. I'll make sure Highacre has nothing to fear from Valmead. Maybe I can even convince them to enter the war *with* Highacre. With both of us together, Meridia would have to seriously consider peace."

He was telling Lily what she wanted to hear. She could

sell that, surely? Surely her people would be in favour of sending a son home to be with his dying father. A son who would then be their advocate in his own country. It made sense, and Lily was certain she could spin it. She would have a press conference, tell the people all Alexei had already done for her—for their queen. He had returned her to them. They were friends who would work together as leaders. Her people would have to understand, even support, the decision to send him home.

Lily turned to tell Naomi her decision and have her rally the advisors to make the arrangements. But Naomi stepped forwards, her eyes on Alexei. "Can you really do all that?"

"What?" asked Alexei.

"Stop Gutzmer from entering the war. Forge what amounts to an alliance with Highacre. Can you actually do that? It's just that Gutzmer *is* Acting Leader. Not you. At least until your father passes. At which time, I assume, you become his strongest competition for the role of Great Leader. Why would Gutzmer do anything you asked for?"

Lily's insides froze. Naomi was right. She didn't for a second doubt Alexei's honesty. She was sure he would do his best for Highacre, especially because in this instance, Highacre's interests aligned with Valmead's. But how effective could he really be? Gutzmer was not going to want to work with him, let alone allow even an implication that Alexei was influencing him and his decisions. Alexei advocating for Highacre might actually work against them.

Alexei looked from Naomi to Lily, panic behind his eyes as he saw the tide turn.

"Lily... please."

Lily stood. She had known Alexei would help her gain clarity. And he had. Unfortunately, the decision clarified had not been in his favour.

"I'm so sorry, Alexei," Lily said, her heart breaking further. "I promise I will send you home as soon as I can. I'll have my advisors start to set the conditions immediately."

As she turned and walked to the door, Lily saw Alexei sit on his couch, his face in his hands. His shoulders shook as he cried. As her own tears fell, Lily exited his rooms, closing the door behind her.

9

Lily knew she needed to find Juliana and work with her to finalise the plan to oust the prime minister. With Meridia uninterested in peace, and Valmead likely to join them against Highacre, the sooner they got rid of Reginald Toth and unified Highacre, the better their chances at survival.

But after her discussion with Alexei, Lily needed a moment to collect herself and told Naomi to escort her to her rooms instead. The walk was a blur, and Lily suddenly found herself in front of the door to the Lodge. She pushed it open, hoping Kevin was there. She could use his snuggles.

Lily heard a cry and turned to see Austin behind her, blasting Naomi out of the room before the door closed. She heard banging, coupled with frantic voices demanding to be let in, but whatever power Austin was using to seal the door shut was working.

Backing away from Austin, Lily wracked her brain to remember what his magical abilities were, but she couldn't remember being told. Right now, that seemed like a significant oversight.

"Your Majesty." Austin gave a respectful but abbreviated bow and approached Lily, his face excited. "Welcome home."

Lily backed up another couple of steps, confused. "Thank you?"

Austin was the palace insider. He had been working against them for months; he was the cloaked figure who had pushed Lily, Ava, and Alexei through the portal, stranding them in her home dimension while the prime minister took over, turning Highacre into a police state.

Not to mention a war criminal.

According to what Claire, Jason, and Naomi had found out, Austin was directly responsible for the death of her grandfather, and at least indirectly responsible for the deaths of her immediate family.

So why is he standing in my rooms acting like I should be pleased to see him?

"I know you must have questions for me," Austin gushed, "but he said they'd explain everything to you on the other side of the portal."

"He?" asked Lily, still trying to get her head around what was happening.

"The Patriot. He's trying to combat the Meridian influence within Highacre. They're who have been trying to bring us down from the inside. They're the ones who killed your family."

Lily stared at Austin, dumbstruck. *He really believes he's one of the good guys.*

Quick as a flash, Lily reached out, penetrating Austin's mind, confirming her suspicion.

"Your Majesty," Austin tried again, taking a step towards Lily. She instinctively took a step back. Austin hesitated, confusion coating his face. "I'm not going to hurt you," he told her slowly, as if that should be obvious.

"You pushed me through the portal," Lily said.

"Yes. To get you away from the other advisors so that the Patriot, or his men, could explain the situation to you." A sliver of doubt crossed his expression. If all had gone to plan, Lily should know all this. "We're not sure how many of the advisors have been compromised. But Your Majesty, didn't they explain all this to you?"

"Austin, there is no 'they'. There was no one waiting on the other side of the portal." Lily felt anger bubbling up, but tried to keep a cap on it. She was trapped alone with Austin. Upsetting him probably wasn't the smartest move. Her mind flickered to what she had been told her genial, soft-spoken war advisor had done to innocent civilians. It was difficult to reconcile the advisor she knew with the murderer he was.

"Something must have happened," said Austin, looking worried. "They had to extract early, or maybe someone messed with the machine. Sent you to the wrong place."

"Austin," said Lily as gently as she could manage, "nothing went wrong. They didn't want me sent somewhere for an explanation. They wanted me out of the way so the prime minister could send us to war."

He shook his head, pacing now. "War was inevitable. We need it to beat back the Meridians. They think they're strong. That they can interfere with our sovereignty. Attack us without consequence. But they were meant to explain all this to you."

Lily watched as Austin became increasingly agitated. He believed what he was telling her, which meant he had been lied to. But it was his patriotism that was being used against him, and he seemed loyal to her. Maybe she could bring him around?

"Austin, we're in alignment about the Meridian influence. I know they're trying to interfere in our government. Destabilise us. Bring us down from the inside."

Austin's attention snapped back to Lily, relaxing slightly.

"But you've been lied to. The Meridians, they've been using you. Playing on your patriotism. Your loyalty. We think Ezra Brown is the Patriot. That he's behind all of this."

Austin backed away from Lily, shaking his head. "No, no. See? This is what I was afraid of. They've interfered with our plan to show you the truth and fed you lies to turn you against us."

"Austin—"

"No!" he shouted. "He said they would bring you on to our side."

"Ezra—"

"Is not the Patriot," Austin insisted, clearly angry and upset by the allegation.

"Have you met him? This Patriot?" Lily could see by his reaction that Austin had not. "Then how do you know, Austin? It's not your fault. There's still time to—"

"It's not him!" he shouted again, pointing at Lily aggressively. "I would know. I'd never work with them. I hate the Meridians."

Spittle began flying from his lips as Austin deteriorated before her eyes. He was now casting glances at the door, realising he was not safe like he had assumed and looking for an exit. She saw him repeatedly touch his radio, as if checking it was still there. Remembering he was now head of the HSP, panic gripped Lily. If he called them in, it would result in a fight between them and her Royal Guard.

Trying to bring him on side wasn't working. She needed to get him out of her room before he decided to take matters into his own hands and fight. Austin was still ranting.

"If you'd just listen—"

"Listen? You have no evidence, Austin. All I have is

your word, and you haven't even met the Patriot! I've seen the evidence that the others found. It all points to Ezra being key in all this. And now he's the prime minister's right-hand man? The former head of the Meridian Intelligence Agency? Why isn't your Patriot going after him?"

Austin paused his pacing, frowning. "He said we would. That we will take him down. When the time is right—"

"And when's that, Austin? Your organisation is allegedly focussed on battling the Meridian influence in our political system. And there is a glaring example of it. Right out in the open. And you're going to, what? Get to it later?"

"The Patriot has a plan—"

"His plan is to destroy Highacre! Austin, can't you see you're helping him? You're helping the wrong side! You helped kill the royal family! My family!"

Austin shook his head furiously, running his hands through his hair. "No, no, no!" He looked up, glaring at Lily now. "You're one of them. You're on their side! You and your Meridian girlfriend."

Austin advanced on Lily, who saw him preparing to attack. She felt panic rise in her chest.

Well, this is an inopportune time to realise no one's trained me to defend against unknown magical attacks.

Lily backed away, trying to buy space. She realised she would only have time for one option—either fight Austin or exploit his focus on her while she got the door open.

She could fight him, focus on using her powers to bring him down. But she had no idea how to block or counter his magic, whatever that even was. All he'd need was a lucky shot, and she'd be helpless, separated from her guards. And what if he was impervious to whatever she tried to fight him with? Her mind returned to the arena and her battle with the fire-eaters.

As Austin raised his arms to strike, Lily made her choice. Focussing all the power she could muster, Lily reached with her telekinesis and flung open the door. The door opened, spilling Royal Guards into the Lodge. Austin slashed his arms down in Lily's direction. She felt something pass over her. Energy of some kind. But nothing hurt, and glancing down, she saw no injuries. Lily cast a look over her shoulder in time to see the furniture behind her crumble as the banners hanging from the rafters were slashed to ribbons.

Lily glanced at Austin, seeing her confusion mirrored in his face. She readied to defend herself against a second attack, but Austin saw the guards running at him. He fled towards the balcony, crashed through the glass, and vaulted over the railing.

Naomi ran towards Lily, her eyes scanning for threats or injuries. Seeing none, she hurried to the balcony, peering over the railing, searching for Austin.

"He's fleeing the grounds," she called back. "Try to stop him at the gate."

"No," Lily countered, causing the guards who had turned to follow Naomi's orders to jerk to a halt. "Let him go."

"Ma'am?" Naomi reentered the room, looking at Lily with concern.

"He's head of the HSP. The last thing we need is them storming in here to rescue their leader. We know he's a threat now and we can plan for it. But I don't think he'll come after me again."

Naomi didn't look as confident about that, but nodded at her guards to stand down.

"Oh dear," Giles said as he and Addison bustled into the room. Giles went to the broken window and Addison fussed over Lily, checking for injuries.

"I'm fine, thank you," Lily said, warmly but firmly.

"I'm just taking care of you, Your Majesty. Just like—" Addison cut off suddenly, looking confused and alarmed. She gave Lily a weak smile. "But you seem fine." She nodded and went to help Giles repair the glass. Once that was done, the two excused themselves, leaving with the bulk of the guards.

When it was just Lily and Naomi left, the bodyguard checked Lily over herself.

"I'm fine, really," Lily insisted.

"But how? Austin can cut through objects with energy. You should be sliced open, bleeding everywhere," Naomi continued to examine Lily, lifting her arms and poking her chest.

"Maybe it doesn't work on me?" Lily suggested, pushing Naomi off her.

"Maybe. Perhaps a new power? Some kind of defensive magic?"

"I shielded her."

Both Naomi and Lily jumped, whirling to see a small girl sitting primly on a couch in the back of the room.

10

"Who the hell are you?" Lily asked in alarm.

"I am Prudence. Lady Octavia's replacement." The girl, who looked all of five years old, bowed her head respectfully when mentioning her mentor.

Lily ogled the small girl for a minute before it all became too much.

"I know it's not easy," she began softly, turning to Naomi, "but I really feel that we need to step up security. At least a touch."

"Yes ma'am. Of course, ma'am," said Naomi apologetically, sensing that Lily's anger was just getting started.

"I mean, how in the hell," Lily began shouting, "can everyone just waltz into my rooms whenever they want? I'm meant to be the queen! I'm meant to be a target! I know I'm not the only hope for Highacre, but I feel like it would be really inconvenient for me to die right now!"

Naomi nodded, head down in shame. She had no words; she clearly knew she had failed. Lily took a breath. Yelling at Naomi would achieve nothing. She knew Naomi would beat herself up worse than Lily ever could. And that everything *had* been done to keep her safe. Austin got in because he was the head of the HSP. And who knew what powers this girl had.

Lily took another deep breath, calming herself as best she could.

"Sorry, it's just…"

"Don't apologise, Your Majesty. You're right. I've failed you."

"No, I know you've done everything you could. But I think you should go now."

"Yes ma'am," said Naomi, hurrying for the door. Lily knew she would remain right outside. "I will increase security immediately."

"Seems redundant," commented the girl. "Her Majesty is powerful enough that she *should* be able to take care of herself."

Lily's frustration turned inwards. "And yet I can't. If only I'd had more time with Lady Octavia."

A sad silence drifted between them. Lily had been so worried about Lady Octavia after finding evidence of a fight in the courtyard where they were to meet for Lily's final lesson. But then so much had happened, and it was only after her return that Naomi had confirmed Lady Octavia's death. And everything was so hectic that Lily hadn't really had time to digest her mentor's passing. She had liked and respected Lady Octavia. The woman had a presence.

Lily looked at Prudence with more sympathy. Lady Octavia must have been even more of a mentor to this young girl. It suddenly struck Lily that the child spoke more like Lady Octavia than a five-year-old. Perhaps this girl was not what she seemed.

"I had heard they found her. I'm sorry." Lily crossed the room and sat in a chair to Prudence's right.

Prudence nodded, acknowledging Lily's condolence. "Her death was not completely unforeseen, but still. I feel her absence."

"So, are you the detector now, then? Does that happen automatically, or do you need a ceremony or something?" Lily asked, thinking of her own journey to become queen.

"The role passes automatically," said the girl simply. "A new detector is usually discovered a few years prior to the passing of the current one. They are trained up and then step in once... the need arises."

Lily nodded. Lady Octavia had been instrumental in helping Lily connect with the magic within, but it now struck Lily that she had no idea what Lady Octavia did day-to-day when there was a normal monarch who had grown up with their abilities.

"I'm embarrassed to admit I don't know much about your new role, Prudence. And is there a reason you're in my room? Can I help you with something?"

"I'm here to help you, Your Majesty." Prudence smiled up at Lily, her short legs swinging, unable to reach the floor. "Ultimately, the role of the detector is to help the monarch. How that assistance manifests will change depending on the circumstances. Obviously, Lady Octavia's main role was to help you with your magic, and that is certainly something that I can continue to assist with. However, my main role is to help you with what is to come."

The ominous tone with which Prudence made her final statement made Lily shiver, and she swore the light had dimmed theatrically. "And what is to come?"

"That is not for me to say."

"Okay. Then how are you going to help me with what is to come?"

"For now, it is to provide you with information."

Lily waited for Prudence to continue, but when she did not, she tried to prompt the small girl. "Great, what is it?"

"It is information of utmost import, not just for the current issues plaguing our land, but for calamities foretold that will befall our descendants."

"You don't talk like a child," Lily said, slightly accusingly.

"Quite," replied Prudence, reminding Lily strongly of Lady Octavia. The little girl continued, determined not to be distracted. "We normally do not reveal much of our roles to the monarch. Some of what I am to tell you has been shrouded in secrecy for hundreds of years. I am to reveal it to you now, so that you understand. This understanding will help you with what is to come."

"Which you can't tell me about."

"I cannot."

"Okay, shoot."

"It is well known that each generation has a detector. However, the detector is one of three powerful roles, all of whom work harmoniously. This knowledge has been forgotten by most. Forgotten... quite deliberately."

"You're not really as young as you appear, are you?" Lily couldn't help interrupting.

Prudence sighed, and Lily thought she heard her muttering something about a lack of appreciation for tradition. Lily could swear that as Prudence had been speaking, the lights, now back to normal, had taken on a candlelight feeling, and now that the mood was broken, Lily had the distinct feeling that soft music had been playing, though she had no idea where it had been coming from.

"I am, in fact, five years old, Your Majesty. However, along with being the detector, I possess an extremely rare ability. I can visit people's memories and experience their lives from beginning to the present time. I can be in and out of your head in the blink of an eye. However, when I visit, I experience a person's memories as if in real time. I have lived several lifetimes alongside both important and everyday people from all over the world. And with the help of my mentor, I discovered that if I am in proximity to someone's remains, I can also view the lives of the dead. You might say I am quite experienced despite my years."

Lily blinked in amazement. That was quite a power. Lily couldn't imagine already having lived all those lifetimes as Prudence had done. Perhaps that was why she lacked the sense of urgency that Lily was feeling. Or maybe Prudence had witnessed the rise and fall of nations to the point where the current crisis felt mundane. A thought occurred to Lily.

"Have you... er... popped into my memories?" Lily asked, feeling very uncomfortable about the idea.

"No, Your Majesty."

Despite her discomfort, Lily felt immediately offended that Prudence hadn't, and became defensive. "Why not?"

"Your Majesty?"

"Why don't you want to visit my memories? Are they not good enough for you?"

Prudence looked patronisingly placating. "Of course they are, Your Majesty. It's just, you have so much more life to live. I would prefer to experience the whole story. You're most certainly on my 'to live' list."

Lily wasn't sure that made her feel any better, but she indicated for Prudence to continue with what she had come here to tell.

"As I was saying." The lights dimmed and Lily could definitely hear some kind of soft, eerie, orchestral music. "Along with the detector, each generation has a reassigner and an oracle."

Lily sat up at the mention of the oracle. Lady Octavia

had disappeared once, saying she had to consult the oracle. Was she finally going to discover what Lady Octavia had found out?

"The reassigner is mostly immortal and centuries old. He is the first recorded reassigner that Highacre has had."

Mostly *immortal?*

"His gift is to take powers from one person and reassign them to another. If he were here, he could give me your control of fire, or give you my ability to live memories. Monarchs of old abused Cyril's power for their own gain, and as a result, he lives a reclusive life, where he employs his talent for the good of the world, not for the power of men. The oracle, as the title suggests, can see the future. However, the oracle is unaware of their gift."

Prudence shifted in her seat, drawing herself up and looking at Lily with a look of great importance on her face. "At present, the oracle is..." Prudence paused for dramatic effect, "Addison Grange."

"Addison!" Lily sat back in surprise. "Addison is the oracle? And she really has no idea?"

"None at all. Knowing the future is a great burden, and one we detectors bear for the oracle. The oracle is possessed of prophetic dreams. Detectors are able to visit their dreams, and over time, we have learned their meanings. We record these prophecies and act accordingly."

"Wait, so they don't see the exact future? Just dreams that you then interpret?"

"Yes, but we are quite skilled and very accurate."

"No doubt, but you can't so much *see* the future, as make predictions about it, right? Like horoscopes."

"I'm not sure what horoscopes are, Your Majesty, but I assure you, our work with the oracle is as much of an exact science as... well, science," the young girl finished weakly.

"Uh huh," said Lily. "So you and this reassigner fellow

work with Addison, who's the oracle, but she doesn't know she's the oracle, nor that you're working with her. And she just has dreams which you then ascribe meaning to. Is that it?"

"In a sense," said the girl, not looking overly comfortable with Lily's description. "But I tell you that as background for you, so that you might understand what I came here to reveal."

Lily leant back and looked at Prudence expectantly. She wanted to hear what the little girl had to say, but she was getting antsy about reconnecting with Juliana and Jason. Prudence shuffled, perhaps expecting more awe from Lily. "Yes, well, I came here to reveal why Lady Octavia never told you what your powers were. Why she couldn't tell you about the prophecies. And why the fate of the world is in your hands."

"Great. Are you able to cover it in the next ten minutes? Because I really need to go and find Juliana to see about ousting the prime minister."

Prudence seemed put out by Lily's reaction, as if she had pictured the revelation of her closely guarded secrets being met with more enthusiasm. More interest. The small girl sighed and muttered something about "royalty these days", before composing herself and looking Lily dead in the eye.

"Lady Octavia was of the opinion that one hundred and eighty-three prophecies recorded over the last several hundred years were about you. This is highly unusual—it is rare to find two prophecies that refer to the same individual. But all of these refer to cataclysmic events, and you being the one to prevent them. The one to save the world."

Lily appreciated Prudence dropping the dramatics, however, the blunt revelation that she was responsible for saving the world felt like a blow to the head.

"What are these events?"

"I cannot say."

Lily glared at Prudence. "As in, you don't know, or you won't tell me?"

Prudence shrugged apologetically. "A little of column A, a little of column B. Unfortunately prophecies aren't an exact science—"

"But you literally just said—"

"And sometimes too much interference from those of us who know of the future can alter it. As such, we strive to nudge people in the right direction so as to achieve the desirable outcome without losing sight of what is to come."

"And the desirable outcome here is?"

"The world not ending."

"Ah. I see." Lily suddenly felt a lot of pressure. How was she meant to save the world when she couldn't know what she was saving it from?

"Lady Octavia did not tell you of the full extent of your powers because, in the prophecies, you will become the strongest magical being the world has ever seen. She worried that if you were told that, rather than having to strive to discover your powers, you would not reach your full potential. And if you did not, then you could not save the world."

"So when you say you're here to help me, what you mean is you're here to subtly nudge me in what you think is the right direction to ensure the future remains as Addison the Oracle dreamed it, but with me ensuring the more positive outcome."

Prudence considered Lily's description. "Yes," she nodded slowly. "I'd say that is accurate."

Lily stood. This was all too much. Facing the prime minister and Ezra was enough, even without throwing in a war and separating her from her friends. Her heart ached at the reminder of her friends. Were they even her friends anymore? Alexei must hate her, and Ava... Lily was struggling to decide whether any of that had been real. She knew she could figure it out if she just talked to her, but understood why Naomi thought that unwise at the moment. Besides, she had other urgent matters to deal with. Which apparently now included saving the world.

"Okay, well, thanks for stopping by. I guess I'll continue trying to stop the war that's going on, and you'll swing by to nudge me as required?" Her tone came out frustrated, but she couldn't hide the tiny crack that betrayed how close she was to tears.

Prudence leant forwards, sliding off the couch and landing on her small feet. She smoothed the skirt of her dress before looking up at Lily. Her tiny hand slid into Lily's, giving it a soft squeeze. For some reason, this small comfort was almost too much, and Lily drove the nail of a finger on her free hand into the padding of her thumb to keep from crying.

"I understand that this is frustrating, Your Majesty. But I am here to help, and it is vitally important that we work together."

"Yes, I get it. If we don't, then everyone will die."

Prudence suddenly looked sad, and Lily worried that her flippant attitude had upset the little girl. "Sorry, I didn't mean... I wasn't trying to offend you. I get it. You'd tell me if you could. And I trust you, Prudence, as I trusted Lady Octavia."

The little girl beamed at the comparison.

"What might be useful, if you have time, would be if you could help me with my magic. Lady Octavia got me going, but I need to be better. I mean, if I'm the one to save the world, I at least need to learn to save myself."

"It would be my honour, Your Majesty," said Prudence,

dropping into a tiny curtsey. "I will do everything in my power to help you realise the true potential of your own. We are in very troubled times, and even with the best possible outcome, people *will* die. I just hope, in working together, we can minimise the damage."

11

THE EARLY MORNING sunlight permeated the canopy, lightly brushing the branches and trunks of the trees as it reached for the ground. It was peaceful in the forest. Quiet, but for the occasional rustling and chirping of the birds and other creatures foraging for their breakfast.

Lily had not ventured this far into the forest before. Naomi had been reluctant to let Lily enter the forest alone, but had, in the end, agreed to wait at the entrance to the extended grounds. If Lily wasn't back at the appointed time, Naomi, and no doubt most of the Royal Guard, would come looking for her.

Lily had headed to the extended grounds with the dual purpose of clearing her head and finding Kevin. He had not turned up in her rooms last night, and while this was not unusual for Kevin, Lily had missed his comfort. With all that was going on, she found herself morbidly worried that something had happened to her little pup.

She had barely slept, running through everything from the last few days and replaying the conversations she'd had over and over in her mind. And without Kevin to pat, Lily had spent most of the night waiting for morning.

Though the forest was soothing, Lily was still on edge. She felt sick about how she was treating Alexei. Her friend had been nothing but kind to her during their time stranded in her home dimension. And he had genuinely cared for her family, to the point of wanting to ensure they were secure before coming home. He had snapped at Giles that he would have wanted to come home immediately if he had been informed of his father's illness, but Lily suspected that even then, he would have sought a balance of helping Lily's family and returning to his own.

Lily ran a hand through her hair in frustration. *No one said being queen would be easy.* She knew the country had to come first. She couldn't put the lives of thousands in jeopardy for her friend. But she needed to find a way to help him. To do what she knew he would for her.

Hearing a rustle to her right, Lily paused, straining to see through the brush, hoping for a tan streak to come bounding out. Instead, two small birds exploded out of the leaves at her, swerving to miss her at the last minute, but not before she squealed and jumped, ducking her head and protecting her eyes with her hands.

The shock had her heart beating a mile a minute, and her hands shook even once the birds had gone and she knew there was no threat. Feeling silly, Lily glanced about, ensuring she was alone and no one had seen her.

For a beat, Edmund passed through her mind. He could control small birds, and while he obviously wasn't hidden somewhere sending his minions to dive-bomb her, the birds reminded Lily of him. She wondered where he was now. Probably not somewhere jumping at shadows like she was.

"Get it together," she whispered to herself, fisting her hands to stop their shaking. If she was going to save the world, she'd need to have stronger nerves. Her lessons with Prudence couldn't come fast enough.

Lily swallowed, blinking hard, trying to banish the tears that suddenly threatened to fall. How was she meant to save the world? She didn't even know what she was supposed to save it from.

Lily had already felt an intense pressure at being queen and knowing that her decisions would affect the lives of so many, for better or for worse. But hearing that she was prophesied to be the one hope to save the world from... what was it? Cataclysmic events? That was a whole new level of pressure. It was all too much.

She longed for the simple life of her family farm. All of them together and safe, and the biggest worry being the fields or the livestock. But that was gone now, too. She would never again ride on the tractor with her dad, help her brother with his chores, or play with her sisters in the garden, their mum yelling at them to mind the vegetables.

Suddenly, the tears that had threatened wouldn't come. Lily stood, staring into the trees, feeling numb. It was all too much. She longed for someone to talk to. Someone to share the burden. But she had locked up her friend, and her girl-friend was the daughter of the person who was likely behind everything that was going wrong.

Loneliness gripping her chest, Lily sniffed before wiping her nose on the back of her sleeve and continuing on her way. She would find Kevin. His presence was comforting, and somehow patting him always made her feel better.

Lily had barely gone another few steps before she heard a loud rustling to her right and saw branches moving at eye level.

"Kevin?" she said quietly, knowing he wasn't that big. *Unless...* Lily had been told that pelotromos could "explode", suddenly growing to the size of a woolly mammoth. She had never seen it happen, but what if something had spooked Kevin and he was now barrelling towards her like a frenzied truck?

Lily backed up, still unsure what was in the bushes, but certain now it was headed right for her. It was too big to be her little Kevin, but seemed too small for an exploded version. Too late, she realised she should have moved farther down the path so as not to be directly in line with whatever was speeding towards her.

Lily tried to leap out of the way, but kept her eyes on the path of the creature and so failed to see the root poking out of the ground. Just as a man burst onto the path in front of her, Lily tripped, landing heavily on her backside.

"Ah, found it," said Jenkins, happily nodding at the path. "Not lost, just temporarily geographically displaced. Always travel south. Never fails."

Suddenly, he saw Lily sitting on the ground. Jenkins seemed more puzzled by her position than to have run into Lily all the way out in the forest. "Odd place to sit. Tired, perhaps?" he muttered to himself in a clearly audible tone. Raising his voice unnecessarily, he addressed Lily, "Do you require assistance?"

"No, thank you, Jenkins." Lily stood and brushed the dirt and debris off her pants. She liked Jenkins. He was a genius and unapologetically himself. Though to be fair, his brain was so caught up in inventions and scientific theory that he likely didn't think about other people and how they might view him enough to consider apologising or other-wise. If it were possible, that idea made her like him more.

He looked very out of place in the forest. He was still wearing his lab coat, but she had never seen him away from his equipment and inventions. Now that she thought about it, she had never seen Jenkins outside the palace. Let alone outside of his rooms.

"What are you doing out here?" she asked curiously.

Jenkins blushed and started fidgeting, casting his eyes about him.

"I mean, it is a nice day for a walk—"

"Yes! Walking. That's it. Jenkins is walking. For, er, exercise. Yes, exercise. Very important." He nodded so enthusiastically Lily worried his glasses may fly off.

"Uh huh. Jenkins, you're not doing anything out here that you shouldn't, are you?"

"No! No, no, no, no, no. Nope. Huh uh." Jenkins pressed his mouth closed and, still shaking his head, began rocking from his toes to his heels.

Lily raised an eyebrow at him. Genius he may be, subtle he was not.

"Okay, well, I might just head off this way." She moved around him, pointing into the forest where he had emerged. "Continue my walk in the direction you came from."

"No!" Jenkins leapt around so that he stood in Lily's way. "Terrible idea. No comfortable seating that way. Better to go back to the palace."

"I'm not going back to the palace. I'm looking for Kevin, my pelotromo."

"Still, best not to go that way. Opposite direction is much better—" Jenkins's eyes snapped to Lily's face. "Pelotromo is missing?"

Lily nodded. Jenkins looked worried. He started pacing, muttering to himself and glancing back in the direction he had come from.

"Jenkins." Lily grabbed his arms, stopping his pacing. "Are you alright? What's going on?"

"Nothing. Ha, ha. Everything is fine." He spoke like a robot, his eyes darting about nervously.

"Okay, well, I'm going to head off this way, then." Lily started pushing through the bushes before Jenkins could respond.

After a panicked beat, Jenkins crashed after her. They continued on, backtracking along the path Jenkins had made through the undergrowth. Jenkins chattered the whole way, still trying to persuade Lily to turn back. The more agitated he became, the more convinced she was that she needed to see what he was up to.

When she first met Jenkins, he had revealed himself to be the creator of the machine that enabled interdimensional travel. During that conversation, he had casually mentioned that he might develop a way to travel through time as a summer project. Maybe that was what he was hiding—a time travel machine? Or who knew what other device. Lily started to feel excited. Maybe whatever Jenkins had invented this time would give them the edge they needed.

Without warning, the dense forest gave way to a small clearing that served as an entrance to a large, ominous cave. What had Jenkins been doing in there?

"Ah, a cave. Most interesting. From the outside. No need to enter," Jenkins babbled rapidly at Lily as he positioned himself once again in front of her. Lily sidestepped him easily, ignoring his words, and walked purposefully towards the cave's entrance.

As they entered the gloomy cavity, Jenkins fell silent, falling into step behind Lily. She could tell he was still worried, but had accepted there was no stopping her now.

Just as the light from the entrance dimmed, a soft glow appeared up ahead. It was so faint that if she had simply wandered into the cave herself, she would have missed it and turned back for fear of becoming lost in the darkness.

The light grew stronger as Lily approached, though the cave narrowed. She had to duck as the tunnel she was following contracted. As they continued, Lily hoped whatever was being lit was in an open space. She was now almost doubled over, and worried about needing to crawl the last few metres.

Lily spied the end of the tunnel, and was relieved to see it did open up into another large cavern lit by a fire in the middle. Suddenly, a huge shadow appeared on the cavern wall, backlit against the light. Lily recoiled in fear. It was a massive beast. Rearing back on powerful hind legs, its wings spread wide, the creature let loose a bloodcurdling shriek that echoed around the cavern, followed by a terrifying roar.

12

Lily froze, having second thoughts about entering the enclosed space. But Jenkins was directly behind her, preventing her from backing up. And besides, this was clearly what Jenkins was hiding. Lily needed to see this through. A memory knocked at her mind, trying to remind her of something, but she brushed it away, readying her magical abilities and preparing to defend herself, wishing she had already started training with Prudence.

Lily dropped into the cavern, followed by Jenkins, who seemed to sense Lily's defensive posture and moved swiftly between her and the beast. Casting his arms out protectively, he looked at Lily, pleading in his eyes.

Lily hesitated. The creature couldn't be that dangerous if Jenkins was comfortable turning his back to it. Maybe it was like the fire-eater—dangerous if misunderstood. Steeling herself, Lily took a step to the side to get a look at what they were dealing with. She felt a slight twinge of embarrassment that moved quickly to disbelief.

"Jenkins, you didn't."

The terrifying creature was positioned directly behind the small fire lighting the cavern, which magnified its shadow significantly. Jenkins smiled at Lily, relieved to see she wasn't going to hurt the beast. He walked to the fire, plopping down on the ground beside it. The creature immediately hopped onto his lap, nuzzling into him as he gently scratched its tiny head.

The baby dragon wasn't much bigger than a small dog, though it was about three times the size of Kevin. Lily noticed a discarded, cracked eggshell off in a corner. It couldn't be that old.

Lily approached with caution. The dragon eyed her suspiciously, but Jenkins enthusiastically waved her over.

"Yes, yes, come closer. She won't bite. Well, untrue. She nips. But playing. Only bites if provoked."

"How old is she?" Lily cautiously extended her hand for the dragon to sniff. It did so, mirroring her caution.

"Three weeks," said Jenkins proudly. "She is a fire-breathing red belly."

Lily nodded appreciatively, as if she knew what that meant. The dragon nipped playfully at her fingers, then licked the tip of one with her hot little tongue.

"She likes you," Jenkins said.

"What's her name?"

"Geraldine."

"And where did she come from?"

"I brought her back from another dimension." Jenkins was completely focussed on the dragon, besotted. "They are curious creatures. Solitary. Leave the nest very young. Equipped for violence, though appeared to be living in peace. Very intelligent. Human level. Studied them as much as possible during the expedition, but there wasn't enough time. Considered risks of bringing one back. Considered benefits. Decided worthwhile. Worried though, others may disagree. Decided not to tell them."

"People need to know she's here, Jenkins," Lily said

gently. "What if someone stumbles upon her? She's so small, they might hurt her. And when she grows, she might hurt them."

Jenkins nodded. "Seems appropriate. Just... Jenkins worries about her. Doesn't want her hurt. Doesn't want her locked up."

"How big do you think she'll get?"

His eyes lit up. "In home world, they get very big. Growth is much faster than ours. Will be too big for this cavern soon."

"And what were you going to do when she is too big to live here?"

Jenkins looked confused. "That is a later problem. At least three weeks. No need to waste time considering now. She may not grow that big. Different world, different food, different environment. Will wait to see how big she grows and find a new home then."

Lily sat back and sighed. She had to admit, Geraldine was cute. And watching Jenkins with her was like watching a child with their first pet.

"Can she fly?"

"Only a little. Too small. Wings not developed. But when she grows, yes."

"Jenkins, how are we going to make sure she doesn't fly off and hurt somebody?"

"We'll tell her not to." Jenkins looked at Lily, seeming surprised at her apparently stupid question.

"You can talk to her?"

"Fire-breathing red bellies have telepathic abilities," Jenkins said, as if everyone knew that about this particular type of dragon.

Lily eyed the dragon warily.

Hello, a soft, high-pitched voice said.

Lily jumped at hearing the little voice in her head. The

dragon seemed pleased at her surprise. Lily sighed again and tried to think. *If* the dragon would do what they told her to, then it should be relatively low risk. And if it came to war, having a massive fire-breathing dragon might be somewhat useful. But they would need to handle this carefully. Geraldine would need to be integrated appropriately. And trained. Or raised? If she had human-level intelligence, they would need to ensure she was treated accordingly. And her wants would need to be taken into consideration.

"Jenkins," Lily said gently. "What if she wants to go home?"

"This is her home," said Jenkins simply.

"What if she wants to see her home world? Meet other dragons. She may want a family someday."

Jenkins looked at Lily, but his gaze was distant, his giant brain at work. "Will need to make a larger machine. Won't fit though at full size. Or maybe smaller. Portable portal? More convenient all round. Need felixium first, of course."

Lily blinked. She had thought they would need to have a long discussion about letting her go if she wanted to leave. But it seemed Jenkins had no concept of wanting to keep Geraldine if she didn't want to stay. His mind went straight to how to make it happen.

Lily watched Jenkins tickle Geraldine. The dragon squealed with joy and accidentally let out a small puff of flame that singed Jenkins's coat. He gave a small chuckle as he patted the embers away.

Lily felt an intense longing for Kevin, seeing the two of them together. The dragon peered over at her, sensing her mood dip. With a little hop, helped by a frantic flapping of wings, Geraldine landed on Lily's lap and nuzzled her hand. Lily smiled wearily, patting the little creature. She was so cute; it was hard to imagine the terror she could wreak when she was fully grown. Despite Jenkins's assurances, if Geraldine could be dangerous, it would be best to address it now, while she was small. The idea turned Lily's stomach. She was sick of having to make difficult decisions. Having to put the needs of the people she loved behind the needs of people she had never met. Alexei strode back into her mind, and she tried to push him out, focussing on the baby dragon instead.

"How can you be sure she won't hurt people?" Lily asked, tickling the thinner scaled area under Geraldine's wing. "She's little now, but when she grows, she could take out an entire town."

"Risk management," Jenkins said simply. "I assess the risk as low. Will teach and monitor to ensure it remains low."

"But I mean, what we're really doing is prioritising Geraldine's needs, who we know and can see and is very cute, above the safety of countless people we don't know and can't see. We're gambling the risk of death to them to make sure Geraldine is safe and comfortable. How do we justify doing that?"

Jenkins cocked his head to the side, considering Lily's question. "Understand the quandary. Concern about preferential treatment for friends." Geraldine hopped up, flapping her wings and jerkily gliding her way to Jenkins, landing on his shoulder and knocking his glasses off. Jenkins beamed proudly at her, his glasses forgotten in the dust.

Lily picked them up, polished the lenses, and handed them back to Jenkins. He looked at them in surprise and replaced them on his face before looking at Lily and remembering her question. "It's an equation. Weighing up the benefit of a dragon against the potential damage to others. Likelihood of harm, et cetera. All equations have answers. Some are favourable. Others... less so."

"Okay, but what would you do to appease the people?

What if they found out you have a dragon and they didn't like dragons—"

"Seems unlikely. Who doesn't like dragons?" Jenkins muttered.

"—and because you wanted to take care of your dragon, who you know and have spent time with and you know is on your side, they all decide that they don't like you and instead are going to be friends with another scientist. An evil scientist."

"Well, I'd—evil scientist? Who is the evil scientist?"

"No one, it's hypothetical."

"Why are they evil?"

"It's just someone who doesn't want what's best for the people."

"Evil is subjective."

"Yes, okay, they're not evil per se, they're just selfish and if the people support that scientist instead of you, bad things will happen."

"What is their field of study?"

"Jenkins!"

"What?"

"How would you appease the people?"

"What? Oh, right. Easy. Talk to them."

"You'd talk to them? That's it?"

Jenkins nodded, patting Geraldine gently with a dopey grin on his face as happy puffs of smoke came out of her nose. "Explain she's not a threat. People fear the unknown. Make it known, then they don't fear."

Lily looked at Jenkins. The man had a brain the side of a planet and was the preeminent scientist in all of Highacre, probably the world. Yet, here he was happily patting his pet dragon as if he didn't have a care in the world.

"How do you do it?"

"I add the processor to the fluxuator before the fuel. Must be good fuel. Sometimes extra egg shells."

"Huh?"

"That is how I do it."

"Wait, what 'it' are you referring to?"

Jenkins looked slightly alarmed. "What 'it' were you asking about?"

"I was wondering how you deal with the pressure. You're called on to invent technologies, make them work, improve them. With all of Highacre depending on you. Doesn't the pressure get to you?"

"Oh." Jenkins frowned, looking up at the ceiling of the cave. He seemed perplexed by the question, but considered it nonetheless. "It's my job," he said simply. "I have to do it. So I do it. There is no angst. It just is. People might have expectations. They are theirs, not mine. All Jenkins can control is what Jenkins can do. So Jenkins does his best. If this is not good enough for them, that is their disappointment to deal with."

Lily thought about his answer as she watched Geraldine struggle to fly up, the little dragon trying to see things from Jenkins's point of view. Lily sighed. It was a nice sentiment.

"It's not that simple when people will be dead rather than disappointed if you fail," she said quietly.

"Constant risk management," said Jenkins, frowning slightly. "Invention needs continuous assessment of likelihood of success. If Jenkins might fail, tell others. Ask for help. Worst case, now they know—less disappointed. Most often, they help." Jenkins reached out quickly, catching Geraldine, who seemed to have forgotten to beat her wings and was plummeting to the floor. The little dragon let out a surprised and happy gurgle to find herself in Jenkins's arms. "Pressure comes with responsibility. But multiply the team, and the odds of success increase too."

Lily looked at Jenkins and his dragon and couldn't help but smile. He was awkward with people, but maybe he understood them better than she did. He was right. She needed to be mindful of her responsibilities, but she didn't have to shoulder the burden alone. And she needed to do what she knew was right. To communicate with her people, and trust that they would understand. She knew what needed to be done.

A small yip sounded from outside, eerily echoing through the cavern. *Kevin!*

Thanking Jenkins, Lily got to her feet, dusting off her pants.

"Okay, here's what we're going to do. You can move into the guest villa in the palace grounds. Geraldine can live with you there while she's little. Addison told me about the old palace dungeons; there's three stories of cells. We don't need those, so they can be gutted and turned into a more permanent home for her for when she's grown."

Jenkins looked like it was Christmas morning. "And procure a flock of sheep. Maybe goats."

Lily paled a little, but moved on. "But we'll need to figure out the best way and the best time to tell everyone. Until then, you need to keep her hidden. No flying around the town, scaring the citizens. Last thing we need is the prime minister using her against us."

At the mention of the prime minister, Geraldine snorted and small flames exited her nostrils. Jenkins paled suddenly. "Giles..."

Lily smiled. She remembered how angry Giles had been when she announced she was keeping Kevin in the palace. She couldn't imagine what his reaction might be to discovering that they would be housing a dragon.

"Leave Giles to me," Lily said to Jenkins's immense and

obvious relief. "You just make sure no one finds out about her yet."

13

Lily hesitated at the entrance to the diplomatic wing of the palace. Though it was called a wing, it was actually a separate compound on the palace grounds. It was here that the Meridian and Valmeadian ambassadors, and the ambassadors to court, resided. Each had their own apartment with its own entrance for privacy.

Lily stood looking at two doors, side by side. The one on the left led to Ava's apartment, the one on the right to Alexei's. A distant rumble sounded from the north. Lily turned to look, seeing the angry grey clouds light up again, and she waited for another growl of thunder to roll in. Strange to see the storm in the distance when the weather was fine here, but it wouldn't be long until the rain reached the palace. Lily picked a door and entered.

If Alexei was surprised to see Lily again so soon, he didn't show it. He had answered the door himself, hesitating slightly before gesturing for Lily to enter. Naomi waited outside with the other guards, hopefully making the calls Lily had instructed her to make.

Alexei stared at Lily, waiting for her to explain why she was here. He looked tired.

"I'll cut to it." Lily smiled gently. "We're sending you home. Naomi's making arrangements as we speak. As soon as you're ready, you and Sergei will be taken back to Valmead."

Alexei nodded, dropping his gaze to the floor. "Thank you."

Lily frowned. She hadn't expected him to throw himself on her in gratitude, but she had expected a more enthusiastic reaction.

Sniffing, Alexei returned his gaze to Lily. "My father passed last night. I appreciate the opportunity to return home to bury him."

"Oh, Alexei." Lily reached for her friend, but he stepped back. "I'm so sorry."

"Thank you," he said mechanically.

They stood awkwardly, Alexei's shoulders slumped. He didn't seem to want her to leave, and so Lily tried again, moving to Alexei and holding him. This time he didn't move away, and after a minute he wrapped his own arms around Lily, returning her embrace.

After Alexei went briefly to tell Sergei they were leaving, he and Lily moved to the couches. Alexei told Lily that Sergei had heard his father died through diplomatic channels. He hadn't yet spoken with his family and didn't know how they were.

"When I get home, I want to see my siblings, but I don't know if my stepmother will let me. She'll see me as my brother's main competition for my father's role. If she won't talk to me, it'll make funeral preparations much harder."

Lily listened and made sympathetic noises. She hadn't been there for her own father's death. Hadn't had to help with the funeral. Hadn't had to deal with tense family relations. It sounded like Alexei was heading back into a storm of emotions.

"Sergei has told me the factions are already posturing. Gutzmer is publicly giving the impression that his ascension into the role is a matter of time. Just waiting for the burial out of respect. My stepmother has already visited several influential families. And apparently my backers will be waiting to meet me when I return."

"Surely it'll be you, though," Lily said. "Isn't that how it works in Valmead?"

"There is an election, but yes. Usually the eldest son of the Great Leader succeeds him. This is a little different because I was away. Gutzmer being Acting Leader gives him a stronger claim than other opposition usually has. And no doubt my stepmother has used my absence to campaign for her son."

"I don't suppose it means much in the current climate, but you, of course, have Highacre's backing. You'll do so much good for your country, Alexei."

Alexei smiled at Lily, nodding as he sipped his water.

"And obviously you as Great Leader would be great for Highacre right now."

Alexei's face darkened, and Lily hastened to clarify. "I mean, we know each other. I know I can trust you. I don't have to worry about you joining Meridia. And obviously you can trust me not to do anything that would harm Valmead."

Alexei stared at his glass, swishing the water. "So long as it is in Highacre's interests not to."

"Sorry?"

"You wouldn't do anything that would harm Valmead so long as that suited Highacre. I don't think you'd actively seek to harm Valmead, but if it were in Highacre's interests not to act in a situation where Valmead might suffer harm, I'm not so certain. I know you wanted to send me home right away, but you hesitated because keeping me here was in Highacre's best interest. It's okay, I understand. You're a leader now."

Lily felt like she had been slapped, though she couldn't fault him for feeling that way given how she'd treated him recently. "It was a mistake to keep you here. And I'm sorry. I will forever regret not realising my mistake before your father died. And it's still not going to be easy to explain letting you go, but I know it's the right thing to do."

Alexei's head snapped up. He looked at Lily with a curious expression. "Did you really not learn of my father's death before I told you?"

Lily blinked, confused. "Of course not."

"Are you sure? You're not just letting me go now because it suits Highacre for me to be Great Leader?"

Lily inwardly cringed. Of course it looked that way. She had steadfastly refused to let him go home. Then his father died, it would benefit Highacre for Alexei to take his father's place, and suddenly she has a change of heart.

Why did I have to say that I wanted him to be Great Leader? Why did I have to mention politics at all?

"I promise you, Alexei—even though I know that doesn't carry much weight—I didn't know. I decided to let you go without knowing your father had died. I didn't..." Lily's voice cracked. "I didn't realise he was that ill."

Alexei frowned at the floor, trying to decide if he believed her. Lily wanted to hug him again. To let him know she was his friend. To comfort him. But she knew doing so now would be interpreted as manipulative. Trying to bring him back on side. She blinked back tears, wanting to cry for her friend, for the damage to their relationship, but worried that too would be misunderstood.

Alexei stood, and Lily rushed to stand with him.

"Thank you for releasing me," he said, formality in his tone. "I should prepare to leave."

"Of course," said Lily sadly. "Let me know if you need anything. Even to chat. I'm always here for you, Alexei."

The words felt empty, given what she'd done, and she saw in Alexei's eyes that he felt the same. Lily forced herself to leave the room rather than throw herself at his feet, begging his forgiveness. She emerged into the charged atmosphere outside as another rumble of thunder, much closer now, rolled overhead.

As she looked up into the bulging grey clouds, the first drops of rain began to fall.

"Thanks Naomi, I've got it from here."

Naomi respectfully inclined her head to Lily, glared at Ava, and shut the door behind her, leaving Lily and Ava alone in Ava's rooms. An awkward silence descended. Lily looked around. Ava's apartment was a mirror of Alexei's. The main living area, where they currently stood, was comfortable but also formal enough to be used to receive visitors. A couple of doors led off to more private living areas, and there was a small balcony where it looked like Ava had been sitting before Lily entered.

"How are you, Your Majesty? How's it all going?" Lily noted Ava's tentative tone and reversion to her title, even though they were alone. She didn't correct her.

"Fine. I trust you are comfortable enough here?"

"Beats an internment camp," Ava said. Her tone was light, but Lily also noted the reference. The prime minister had recently ordered his HSP to round up all Meridian citizens and hold them in hastily constructed internment camps. It was unclear whether he intended to have them returned to Meridia, or held there until the conclusion of hostilities. Clearly, Ava was still receiving information from somewhere. Probably her father.

"So, we're still at war, then?" Ava tried again to engage Lily.

Lily considered how much to tell her. Given Ezra's intelligence capabilities, there probably wasn't much she didn't already know, or wouldn't find out anyway. Lily hated having to vet their discussion. She desperately missed her talks with Ava. Her advice. Her friendship. But the sting of betrayal was too raw. It was an odd feeling. Relief had washed over her, just being with Ava, but she was also immediately irritated, remembering her treachery.

"Yes. I spoke with your president and the Acting Leader of Valmead. Both see Highacre as weak. They think they can gain more for themselves through violence than diplomacy." Lily sighed. She was still processing the fact that the continuation of the war was inevitable. She was going to have to project power to succeed. And currently, the only power Meridia seemed to acknowledge was violence. As more reports of casualties came in, Lily had begun to realise that to bring Meridia back to the table, she would need to turn the tide. Her generals were currently under orders to simply hold Meridia back, but Jason and his team were creating a plan to go on the offensive.

"How is Alexei?" Ava asked with genuine concern.

"I'm sending him home," Lily said simply. She knew Ava deserved more. Ava and Alexei were such good friends. But Lily was still drained from meeting with him. She needed to process it before she could talk about it.

Ava smiled sadly. "It'll be good that he can attend the funeral."

"You're well informed," Lily snapped. "Is your dad keeping you up to date?"

"I'm sorry," Ava said simply. She sounded genuine. "I'm

sorry that the leaders won't strike an accord. Sorry for the suffering that will result. I'm sorry you were put in that position with Alexei. And Lily—Your Majesty—I'm sorry for not telling you that Ezra is my father."

"Yes. That might have been good to know before."

Before we became friends.

Before I confided in you.

Before I fell for you...

"I know, I'm sorry. It doesn't excuse it, but I only found out that he's my father right before I took up the post here. I don't think I've ever introduced him as my father, or him me as his daughter. I'm not used to telling people about him."

Lily tried not to have sympathy for Ava's position. Ava was abandoned by her parents when she was very young and had been raised by an aunt until her aunt had, in turn, abandoned her and she had gone into foster care. In all her internal ranting about Ava's betrayal, Lily hadn't considered that Ava wouldn't have known her parents until she was an adult. She may still not know who her mother was.

As if reading her mind, Ava said, "Ezra told me my mother is dead. She was another agent in the agency, apparently. They had a brief fling during training and she dropped out when she found out she was pregnant. She didn't tell him, or at least, that's his story. He says he didn't find out about me until a few years ago. Then he tracked me down and observed me. Thought I'd be a good fit for the agency. He claims he didn't tell me who he was then because he didn't want me to think I'd gotten any special treatment to get into the academy or during training. He only told me after I got selected for this role. He said since we'd be working together, he wanted to be open and honest with me."

"Did he get you this position?"

"No. Well," Ava hesitated, frowning. "He told me I was

selected through the normal channels and he didn't influence it. I don't know. He seemed genuine, but I guess it is a hell of a coincidence."

Lily watched Ava. She did seem to be genuinely re-evaluating whether she believed Ezra had pulled strings or not. Lily had no doubt that Ezra had ensured her selection.

"It's hard, Lily," Ava said, pain in her voice. "He seems so genuine, and I want to believe him. But honestly, I don't know him that well. I want my father to turn out to be a wonderful man. But I can't rule out that he didn't ensure I was chosen to accompany him here. And if he's lying about that..." She shrugged. "What else is he lying about?"

Lily was hit again with unwanted empathy for Ava. She could imagine, with Ava's background, that all she would want was a family. And then she found her father, someone to love who loved her back and wanted what was best for her. Lily tried to put herself in Ava's shoes. She would believe anything the man said. Would look for whatever clues she could find to show he was a good man. Would ignore the neon flashing signs to the contrary.

"I just... why didn't you tell me? We had so many deep discussions. Or I thought we did..."

"We did." Ava went to move closer to Lily, but Lily stepped back. Ava stayed where she was. "I should have told you at the beginning. But you had already been introduced to him when we met. It seemed weird to mention he was my father. And then we started getting closer. I don't know, I just didn't know how to randomly drop it into conversation. We were talking about our lives, and to be honest, he's not been a part of mine."

"I would think that discovering and meeting your biological father would have been a big life event. Or perhaps even relevant when we were talking about my father..." Lily's voice cracked and she frowned, trying to regain her composure.

"You're right." Ava seemed to be fighting against her instinct to comfort Lily. "You're absolutely right. I should have found a way to tell you. There must have been dozens of openings in our discussions for me to tell you, and I missed them, or I felt too awkward, or whatever. But I should have told you, and I'm sorry."

Lily looked at her. Ava seemed genuine, but the trust had been broken. Was this a lie, too? Could she trust someone who was trained to be a spy? Maybe it had all been an act to get close to her.

Lily went to reach for Ava's mind and hesitated. When she and Ava had first got together, Lily had resolved not to read her girlfriend's mind. Mind reading was something she had discussed at length with Lady Octavia during their training sessions. It was a powerful gift, but it was not without its drawbacks.

Lady Octavia had likened it to having faith.

"You can't have faith in something if you keep demanding evidence," Lady Octavia had said. "That's not faith, that's knowledge. When you can read minds, you're at risk of losing your ability to trust."

Lily had nodded appropriately, but she hadn't really agreed with her mentor at the time. Of course reading minds could help her trust. If she could check that people were telling her the truth, then she would know if she could trust them.

But when she started her relationship with Ava, she suddenly understood what Lady Octavia had been trying to tell her. If she read Ava's mind, she wouldn't be trusting her, she'd be relying on her own assessment. She didn't want to spend her life needing to verify for herself if those she loved were honest with her. Not to mention that mind reading was such an intrusive action. Surely in doing so she would be the one breaching Ava's trust?

However, now that she was home, and Ava had shown her deception, no matter how understandable it might be, she felt conflicted. On one hand, it was stupid under the circumstances to have this power and not use it. But on the other, reading Ava's mind felt like closing the door on the possibility of their relationship. And locking it.

Lily knew she wasn't ready for that. Perhaps it was selfish, but look what had happened with Alexei when she'd put everyone else first. Lily felt she really knew Ava. They had grown so close, and despite the betrayal, Lily couldn't shake how she felt about her. Looking into Ava's eyes again, it was like coming home. All she wanted was to fall into Ava's arms.

She knew her advisors would be disappointed, but Lily rationalized. Ava was detained. Despite the decision to release Alexei, there was no current plan to free Ava. There was time enough for Lily to confirm trusting Ava was the right decision.

"Look, I can understand that. I really wish you had told me, but we all make mistakes," she said, thinking of Alexei. "If I can't forgive you, how could I expect anyone to forgive me?" *And it's not your fault your dad's a megalomaniac.*

Ava's eyes brightened immediately, and suddenly Lily was in her arms, and they were kissing. Lily lost herself in Ava, all her worries, guilt, and anxiety forgotten. After what felt like a lifetime, they breathlessly pulled apart, each still holding the other tightly, foreheads lightly touching.

"Do you really think you can forgive me?" Ava looked at Lily, eyes huge and beseeching. Did she really have to ask after that? Ignoring her initial instinct to joke, Lily considered Ava's question. If they were going to do this, be together, Lily would have to genuinely forgive Ava. Trust her again. She didn't want to be in a relationship where past hurts were pulled back out in future conflicts. And especially with her position, if she couldn't trust Ava, she shouldn't be with her. Lily turned and wandered towards the fireplace.

"No more secrets?" she asked in a serious tone.

"No more secrets. I promise."

Lily's heart decided instantly, but she made a show of considering it. "Maybe. In time. Perhaps you can make it up to me."

Ava caught the playful tone that had permeated Lily's voice. "I'm sure you'll think of an appropriate punishment, Your Majesty."

Lily's stomach flipped excitedly at the implication. She avoided looking back at Ava, knowing as soon as she looked at her, she'd be back in her arms. Lily's eye caught an ornate box on Ava's mantelpiece. It looked familiar somehow. She hadn't seen it before, she was sure of that, but something about it pulled at a thread of memory. It was a simple wooden box made of redwood. The iron lock contrasted beautifully with the wood and curled around it in ornate swirls.

Suddenly, it clicked. *The key*. Lily turned and walked to the door, surprising Ava, who asked where she was going. Lily ignored her. When she first arrived in Highacre, she had received mysterious notes from someone who signed them "A Friend". One of those notes had been accompanied by an old, ornate key. A key that Lily now thought looked like it might fit the lock of the box on Ava's mantelpiece.

"Naomi," Lily called, opening the door. Her bodyguard appeared immediately. "Do you remember that key that came with the note that appeared in my room?"

"This one?" Naomi produced the key.

Lily started. "Um, you've been carrying it around with you?"

"I move around the palace a lot. I figured it was better to keep it on me in case I found its lock. It's not like it's big or bulky," she added defensively.

Lily took the key from her and strode back over to the box. Naomi stepped into the room, keeping a suspicious eye on Ava, who looked utterly bewildered about what was going on.

Ava's eyes grew wide as Lily took the box from the mantelpiece.

"That's not mine," Ava said quickly. She was scared, and the words came out guiltily.

Naomi rolled her eyes and watched as Lily put the box on a table. Lily hesitated before trying the key. *Please don't fit.*

The key slid home into the lock and turned easily. Heart heavy, Lily opened the lid and saw a small metallic cube sitting in crushed velvet.

"What is this?" she asked Ava.

"What is what?" Ava asked. Unable to see into the box from where she stood, she approached Lily, leaning to see inside.

Naomi moved closer to Lily as Ava approached.

"Quit playing, Ava, and tell me what this is."

"I'm telling you, that's not my box. I don't know what's in it. Let me see..." Ava stopped abruptly when she saw the device.

"You recognise it then," said Naomi. She was now positioned between Ava and Lily.

Lily reached out to pick up the device. Naomi grabbed at her arm, trying to stop her. "No, ma'am, we need to take this to—"

As Lily's fingers brushed its surface, a blinding light

emitted from the device before all went black. Lily blinked furiously, trying to clear her vision, then began to panic when nothing changed.

"This is a top-secret level governmental briefing," said a comforting female voice. "All unauthorised personnel should now be removed from the immersion experience."

An immersion device. Lily exhaled the breath she hadn't realised she was holding. It looked different from the ones she had used before. Maybe because it was classified? Or perhaps Meridian immersion devices just looked different.

Suddenly, a room appeared and Lily saw Naomi and Ava looking around, as confused as she was. They were in a laboratory with scientific equipment decorating the tables and lining the walls. Through a panel of windows, she could see people in white coats and safety goggles moving around busily, carrying beakers and test tubes and running experiments.

Naomi looked around nervously, eyeing the scientists. Lily studied Ava's expression for any hint of recognition, but either she was an amazing actress or she hadn't seen this projection before.

"Hello, and welcome to BioTech Mechanica Lab One, ModTech's most secure facility where we work to satisfy all of your technological needs."

All three women jumped and stared at the man who had just materialised in front of the windows. He looked and sounded like a telemarketer from one of those ads on television at one o'clock in the morning.

The projection droned on for a bit about all the wonderful things the company was doing, and Lily began to wish for a fast-forward button. What she did pick up on was that the Meridian government had given ModTech a grant to design next-level implants. With a start, she remembered

Ezra was the director of ModTech. She saw Naomi was already looking at Ava, studying her as Lily was for any reaction. Ava's face remained impassive.

"Today, this briefing has been arranged to introduce you to our biggest breakthrough yet."

The room changed, and now they were inside the laboratory with the scientists. They were all tinkering on something small, using magnified screens to manipulate tiny parts and configurations.

"BioTech has created a prototype implant that far exceeds the operating capabilities of the current government-grade SecurityMod implant. The FreeMod One has five times the capabilities of the top-of-the-line implants available today. With the FreeMod One, the implantee can access up to ten of the fifty-three available abilities. That's double the capacity of the currently leading implants! FreeMod One also enables the user to operate up to three of those abilities concurrently."

Lily recalled Addison telling her that if an implant user tried to access too many capabilities, they would overload, which sounded a lot like having a stroke. She had read reports that suggested most implants allowed the user to access only three abilities. The top-of-the-line models, usually reserved for high-level government workers, could allow five to be used safely. Highacre was not aware of an implant that allowed for the concurrent use of abilities, though. That must be new.

"The FreeMod One can be loaded with classified abilities up to the secret level for government agents," the advertisement continued. "Your agents will now be able to scan for threats while accessing up-to-date maps and building plan data to easily plot an exit if required, all while remaining invisible.

"BioTech is also proud to unveil new capabilities only

accessible with a FreeMod One implant. While still undergoing testing for regulatory approval, the FreeMod One can provide security-cleared users with mind reading abilities. Further, BioTech scientists are currently working on illusory capabilities and mind control elements.

"And if all of that wasn't enough, each FreeMod One implant can link to other FreeMod One implants, allowing users to communicate and share information telepathically. For our top-level restricted users, FreeMod One implants can remotely access inferior implants and interact seamlessly with their operating systems."

Lily's mind reeled. Meridia had managed to make implants that allowed users to become invisible and read minds? And from the sounds of things, these higher-level users could control other Meridians by accessing and overriding their simpler implants. She looked again at Ava, but her face mirrored Lily's shock.

"How do we know it works?" the recording continued, oblivious to the reactions in the room. "FreeMod One has already been field tested. Having successfully completed trials at home, the FreeMod One is in use by our current ambassadors in Valmead, and our ambassador and ambassador to court in Highacre. FreeMod One has proven to not be adversely affected by enchantments or magic, and its new capabilities have yet to be detected by current countermeasures employed by either country.

"But I'm sure that's more than enough of me talking, and no doubt you have questions. Your BioTech representative is waiting to answer all of them for you."

The scene faded, and suddenly they were all back in Ava's room. A stunned silence engulfed the women.

"Look," Ava began.

"No more secrets, huh?" Lily looked at her, hurt etched on her face.

"Lily—"

"You literally just promised."

"I can explain—"

Lily didn't want explanations.

She wanted to be alone.

Heart breaking all over again, Lily turned and left, ignoring Ava's pleas.

14

Lily had been to the Tower several times and not once could she say it had been a pleasant experience. The building that housed the Parliament of Highacre was an odd yet imposing structure. The ground floor was a huge rectangular space with ridiculously high ceilings that encompassed the public areas, including a reception hall filled with artefacts about Highacre's history and the large auditorium where the politicians sat and bickered.

High above the public areas of the Tower was the spire that gave the building its name. Lily had not been inside the spire before now, and given its proportion comparative to the ground floor, she had thought the rooms within would be small. However, the politicians' offices were as vast and sprawling as if each were housed in their own small office building. Each floor held at least four politicians and their staff, though Juliana had told her that the top floor was reserved for the prime minister alone.

Lily had followed Juliana closely as the older woman moved through the ground floor halls to the private elevator needed to access the spire. Now they were enclosed in the small box shooting upwards and Lily watched Juliana's face in the reflection of the steel doors. There was something on her mind—something Juliana clearly wanted to say. Normally Lily would have jumped in and provided an opening, but today she waited. Still reeling from the pain of Ava's lies, she didn't think she could take much more negativity. If it was bothering her that badly, Juliana could bring it up herself.

"The public relations campaign is in full effect," Juliana began.

Ah, that's what it is. Alexei.

"Admittedly, more time to prepare would have been better. Much better. But we're doing what we can, and early reports seem positive."

Lily watched Juliana's reflection. Juliana did not look at Lily.

"You don't approve."

The ex-foreign minister pursed her lips. "I do not."

The old Lily would have been hurt by the disapproval. She would have clamoured to make it up, to seek forgiveness, to regain favour. But now, Lily found that she simply understood why Juliana wouldn't approve, and that was okay. It was okay that she would have done things differently. That didn't make Lily's decision wrong.

"I do, however, respect you making an informed and well thought out decision." Juliana looked at Lily for the first time. "You didn't just do the easy thing, the thing you desperately wanted to do, and release him straight away. Which would have been a disaster," she added as an aside. "No, you put your country first. Placed responsibility to your people over your own personal preferences. You are a far cry from the lost girl who arrived so many months ago. You have truly become a queen."

Lily stared at Juliana in shock before turning away and fighting the tears that were suddenly welling. She cleared her throat. "Thank you, Juliana. It means a lot coming from you." Lily looked curiously at the older woman. "You know, from what you've described, it doesn't seem like many people come out of prison changed for the better. But you may just be the exception to the rule."

Juliana let out a loud laugh. "I usually am, Your Majesty. If I had a dollar for every time I heard that from my mother's lips. But how anyone expects a person to come out of that place motivated and eager to become a productive member of society is beyond me. It's a lunatic's dream. That said, I did receive some constructive feedback while I was doing my stint in there. I'm so used to only stepping in when there's a problem. I would let my staff run things until something went wrong, and then I'd step in and fix it. But that also means that they only really heard from me when they failed. Or felt they'd failed. And so all they'd get was criticism." Juliana shook her head at the idea of the woman she used to be.

"But, if you don't tell people they're doing a good job, or at least ensure they know things aren't their fault when they're not—if they don't know you appreciate them, then they lose motivation. They lose the desire to help, to be part of the team. The feeling that there even is a team. And then when Big Karly comes for your commissary, there's no one to even tell you about it, let alone help you stop her."

The elevator pinged and opened its doors, letting the women out into a spacious and clean reception area. Lily's eyes were drawn to the floor-to-ceiling windows on her left that offered an amazing view of the city and beyond. Juliana made to walk up to the reception desk where a young lady was on the phone, but Lily grabbed her arm, looping it through her own, and guided Juliana over to the window.

"So, what is the plan?" whispered Lily.

"We're going to wing it," Juliana whispered back brightly.

"Okay, but what purpose are we winging it towards?"

"My planners have been hard at work, but the problem is that we don't know what weaknesses to exploit. They've run modelling on campaigns against the prime minister based on abuse of power with the HSP, but everyone already knows he's doing that. And the campaign won't inspire the people to rise up against him, because they're too scared of the HSP. We need something else. Some chink in his armour. Some indisputable evidence that will either make the people rise up en masse, or cause his rich and influential supporters to drop him like a rock. Preferably both. So the plan, such as it is, is to burst into his office and rile either him or Ezra enough that they trip up and expose a weakness. You're here with me to both irritate the prime minister and to listen carefully to whatever they say so we can go over it later. And if you can use that mind reading of yours, that'd be a help too."

Lily fought an automatic blush, still feeling as if her attempt to read Ezra's mind at the prison had been her own failure. Of course, now having seen the classified briefing regarding his implant, it made much more sense.

This made her think of Ava, and Lily quickly brought her mind back to the task at hand, and Juliana's plan.

"That sounds... um..."

"I know it's not much, but it's better than doing nothing."

Lily wasn't altogether convinced that was true.

"At any rate, Your Majesty, don't forget your mental barrier. We don't know that you'll be able to stop that implant of Mr Brown's, but it can't hurt."

"Can I help you?" the timid voice of the receptionist called across the room.

Juliana strode over to the desk while Lily moved to look at a glass cabinet built into the wall. There were several artefacts with plaques telling the viewer that they were from the early inhabitants of Highacre. Pots, weapons, and paintings from different eras told the story of the evolution of the country Lily was in charge of. The country she didn't even know. Though Addison had prepared her well for her confirmation hearing, Lily felt her knowledge of her country was woefully inadequate. She made a mental note to try to rectify that. Perhaps after she put a stop to the war with Highacre's neighbours.

Lily felt a pang in her chest comparing the bright, bubbly Addison who had taught her to the quiet and withdrawn woman who had emerged from prison. Lily had tried checking in on her, but Addison waved her off each time, becoming increasingly agitated about taking Lily's time, which should be better used addressing the threats to Highacre, and if Prudence was to be believed, the world.

The last time Lily checked in, Addison had burst into tears, apologising profusely for her friendship with Ezra, clearly wracked with guilt about what she may have wittingly or unwittingly told him. Lily had tried to reassure her, but Addison politely dismissed Lily, telling her she was tired and needed a cup of tea.

Juliana's raised voice drew Lily's attention, and she moved towards the desk.

"Don't you know who I am?" Juliana boomed. "I have never experienced a greater level of disrespect in my life!"

The young girl burst into tears. "I'm sorry, I'm just an intern," she sobbed. "It's my second day. The receptionist is at lunch and I don't know anything."

Juliana took a small step back, looking slightly alarmed at the level of distress the girl was in, and seeming unsure of what to do about it. She looked imploringly at Lily, who shrugged, unsure of how to help, and of the opinion that Juliana should fix her own mess.

Hesitantly, Juliana took a step towards the girl and awkwardly patted her on the shoulder, muttering, "There, there."

"What is going on out here? Emily, what's wrong?"

Ezra Brown strode into the reception area, his face concerned at the distress of the intern before hardening slightly at seeing Juliana and Lily. Then, in a flash, his face became the usual mask of polite friendship that he wore so well.

Before he could greet them, Juliana rounded on him. "We're here to see Reginald, but you'll do, Mr Brown. After all, you're involved in all this. You're probably running the whole damn thing. Why don't you just come clean and tell us why you're doing it? And what have you done with Claire? Where is she? Is she even alive?"

"What is all the commotion?"

Juliana and Lily's jaws dropped in tandem as Claire herself emerged from the inner offices to see what the fuss was in the reception area. Claire's eyes fell on Juliana and Lily, and her face fell. "Oh, hello," she said in a tone that clearly communicated she was not pleased to see them.

Juliana, restricted by the reception desk, walked its length to stand closer to Claire. "Claire! Are you alright? What are you doing here? Is this terrorist holding you against your will?"

Claire looked at Juliana in shocked confusion. "What? No. I'm not being held by anyone. I'm at work."

Lily and Juliana reeled back, stunned by her reply. Ezra gave a small chuckle. "I can assure you ladies that we are not in the business of kidnapping. Claire, like our other staff, is free to leave at any time."

At this, Emily let out a strangled sob and ran towards

the stairs, clutching her purse. Ezra watched her go, tutting and looking sympathetic. He turned to Claire. "Have someone check in on her, would you? Make sure the ex-minister didn't upset her too much."

Claire nodded, making a note.

Lily walked along the reception desk, her eyes on Claire. She felt Claire monitoring her approach, though Claire gave no outward indication that she noticed. Lily moved past Juliana and stopped directly in front of Claire. Claire finished making her note and looked up, meeting Lily's eyes for the first time.

"Claire, what are you doing here?" Lily worked to keep any judgement from her voice, her tone only revealing her concern. At the same time, Lily worked to penetrate Claire's mental barriers, seeking access to her mind. Expecting to be met with the void that Claire had manifested once before, Lily worked to keep the surprise from her face as she easily entered Claire's thoughts.

"I had time to think," Claire replied. "While I was... detained. And I realised what we were all doing was not what was best for Highacre. We had the best of intentions and were all trying to do what was right, but..." Claire trailed off.

"What in the world do you mean?" snapped Juliana.

"The royal family was tragically killed. As a result, the prime minister had to step up in order to keep the country running, and that is exactly what he did. When the Meridians, the likely party responsible for the assassinations, infiltrated the government to continue their sabotage, the prime minister put measures in place to tighten security and avoid further violence. He wasn't trying to consolidate power for himself, he was trying to keep it from being used to further interfere with our way of life. When Meridia moved to steal our essential resources in the Disputed Region, he was willing to fight to get them back." Claire looked from Juliana to Lily and back, smiling reassuringly at them.

"He was being hit with violence and he met it with strength. The HSP isn't oppressing our citizens, they're protecting them from the nefarious foreign influence that has been allowed to permeate our borders. I mean, look at it this way. If a dangerous virus broke out and he ordered people to stay in their homes, you'd say he was keeping them safe, not unlawfully detaining them, right?"

Juliana scoffed. "You sound like the spokesperson for his re-election campaign. But oh, that's right. He doesn't need a re-election campaign because he 'postponed' the election due to the 'current security situation'." Her air quotes were violently scratched into the space between them.

Lily was alarmed to find that Claire believed everything she was saying. She scoured Claire's mind for any indication that she was lying. That she had been tortured or brainwashed into believing what she was saying. But there was nothing. Her memories supported her story that this had all occurred to her while she had time to think.

"Claire, he's arresting people just because they oppose him. He arrested me for that very reason. He imprisoned you!" Juliana cried.

Claire smiled politely. "Yes, but I deserved it. He was doing everything he could to battle the nefarious foreign interference that was focussed on destroying Highacre's way of life. And there we were doing everything we could to get in his way! All that served to do was open the door for Meridia."

Claire turned to look at Lily. "I have no problem with you personally, Your Majesty, nor do I in any way dispute your claim to the throne. But was the appropriate first step following the assassinations really to locate and retrieve a teenage girl who had no idea about Highacre, let alone ruling a country, and try to install her as the leader? How was that meant to protect the people of Highacre? To project power to our enemies as they took action against us?"

Lily shifted uncomfortably, and she noticed Juliana, who had opened her mouth to argue, close it again, a puzzled expression on her face.

"The prime minister was taking care of Highacre. He took control and ensured the country kept running. He closed ranks to keep out the infiltration. He took immediate action to protect our people. Putting you on the throne took over six months. What were any of us doing during that time for the people of Highacre?"

Lily and Juliana gaped at Claire. Lily was dumbfounded. She knew she should argue, rebut Claire's assertions. She knew Claire was wrong about the prime minister's motives. At least, she thought Claire was. But Lily found it awkwardly difficult to argue against Claire's points. Maybe they did do the wrong thing. Maybe she was on the wrong side. Should she have at least tried to work with the prime minister?

Ezra moved closer to the women, startling Lily, who had forgotten he was even there.

"No one is accusing anyone of having unscrupulous motives," he said kindly. "Of course, you all had the best of intentions. But often, those following their good intentions blindly can do more harm than good."

Lily felt her anger reignite at Ezra's faux sympathy. She remembered he was the prime minister's right-hand man. And he had his fingers in all the pies that were tied up in this conspiracy. The prime minister was either bad or a puppet. *I did the right thing.*

"But I can see, Your Majesty, that you are starting to

think and act for yourself, rather than at the behest of your advisors," he nodded, smiling at Juliana. Lily half expected the woman to shiv him right there. "I heard you released Alexei Rosovski so that he might attend his father's funeral. I hope my daughter might also be safely returned to me soon."

Lily saw red at the insinuation that Ava was being detained in any way that might cause her harm. Ezra's daughter was currently in luxury accommodations at the palace, unlike the scores of Meridian citizens who had been rounded up and forced into makeshift internment camps by the prime minister. And how dare he use Ava like that. The daughter he hadn't claimed for years. Who he had brought with him to help with his plan to destroy Highacre. How dare he pretend to worry about her now.

"You are behind all of this; I know it," Lily hissed at Ezra. "You are manipulating the prime minister and putting not only the Highacren people at risk, but your own citizens. How can you live with yourself, sending our countries to war for your own gain?"

Ezra took a step back, looking startled. "I don't know what you're talking about, Your Majesty."

Lily marvelled at his control. She almost believed him. "You were behind me—and your daughter—being exiled to another dimension. You are behind the nationalist movement, the HSP, and probably behind the assassinations of my family that started this whole thing."

"This is exactly what I'm talking about, Your Majesty," said Claire sadly, shaking her head. "You're so focussed on this personal vendetta against Ezra that you've lost sight of what's best for Highacre. What's best for the people."

Lily looked at Claire and saw a deep disappointment in her eyes. It cut Lily to the core. She had always respected Claire. Cared what she thought of her.

"I think it might be best if you both just leave," Claire said sadly.

Lily made to argue, to plead with Claire to drop the act and come back to their side. They would protect her. But Juliana put a hand on her shoulder and, glaring at Ezra, guided Lily back to the elevator.

Lily stared at the descending numbers, blinking, determined not to cry and trying to convince herself that Claire was not lost to them forever.

15

"We can't rule out that Claire is being held against her will and forced to say those things," Juliana said hopefully as she finished briefing the royal advisors, who had gathered to hear the results of their trip to the prime minister's office the day before.

Lily shook her head sadly. She and Juliana had discussed this already, but she understood the older woman's desire to think Claire hadn't simply ditched them for what she thought was the winning team.

"I read her mind," Lily said gently to the other advisors, needing to tell them the facts but also wanting to avoid the appearance of undermining Juliana. "She believed everything she was saying. I just don't understand why she joined them. I don't buy her whole 'I had time to reflect' line. But I couldn't find anything in the time we had that would explain it."

"Maybe they brainwashed her?" suggested Addison.

"Possible," said Juliana eagerly. "Or tortured her. I know Meridia has some clinical methods of interrogation that can have severe impacts on the mind."

Lily shook her head again. "I found her memories, and

there was nothing about torture or brainwashing or anything that would explain her switching sides, other than what she told us."

"Then they've hidden them somehow," said Juliana forcefully, trying to keep the hurt from her voice.

"But if she hasn't been tortured or brainwashed, why would Miss Jones abandon us like this?" asked Giles. He looked imploringly at the faces of the other advisors, clearly wanting someone to explain away the sting of rejection.

"Claire was quite ambitious," said Jason tentatively. He had a more permanent eyepatch now, the bandage on his head no longer necessary, and he was stronger, his body adjusting to his injuries. An icy silence met his comment.

Naomi cleared her throat. "I read her file. Without fail all of her instructors and supervisors noted she would do whatever it took to succeed and come out on top. I know it's hard, but I think we have to wonder if any of us really knew her at all. When she arrived, she was an undercover operative for the HIA, not the etiquette advisor you all thought her to be. Maybe everything was a lie."

The icy silence melted and turned morose as the advisors considered Naomi's point. Lily frowned at the table in front of her. Was it that simple? The Claire they knew was a lie and the real woman was just looking to get ahead? Lily didn't believe it. But was it untrue, or did she simply not want to see what was in front of her?

"You spent the most time with her once we knew her background; what do you think?" Juliana asked Naomi.

Naomi considered the question, before blowing out a breath in frustration. "Casting my mind back to the time we spent together... I'm as stunned as you are," she conceded eventually. "This behaviour does not match the person I knew her to be. And while that could all have been an act, she did save my backside a number of times."

Lily looked around at the tired faces. They looked about ready to give up. Claire had jumped ship, the other heads of state were refusing to come to the table and discuss peace, and the war was going poorly. As if on cue, Jason announced he was going to provide an update on the war effort. "The good news is, for all of that, morale is reasonably high and recruiting is slightly above peacetime levels," he concluded after clinically detailing casualty estimates and rattling off a long list of battles they had lost.

"What's the bad news?" Lily asked.

"The bad news is that we've lost ground. And we've lost a lot of people ensuring that we didn't lose more. Our current strategy is to try to push Meridia back, even out of the Disputed Region, in the hope that it will cause Meridia to negotiate peace. But we can't even hold the line against them at this point, and from the sounds of your discussion with President Taylor, success might not achieve that effect even if we did push them back. I'll convene the war council," he said wearily, rubbing his hands over his face. "Get everyone strategizing."

"I'll keep half my people looking into the prime minister," added Juliana. "They'll have to find something we can use, eventually. And maybe with him out of the way, Taylor would be more likely to respect your position, Your Majesty."

"What are the other half doing?" Lily asked, only mildly curious, her mind still reeling from the cost of war.

"The other half are planning strategies to bring him down. Once we have the fuel, the pyre should already be built and we can put them together."

Polite nods around the table with weak smiles told Lily that, like her, all of this sounded like a lot of work occurring with little being achieved. They felt hopeless. Lily felt it too. She remembered feeling hopeless when she was trying to learn how to use her powers. She'd tried everything, but nothing worked. But now, this hopelessness was different. Frustrating as learning magic had been, she'd known it was within her power to achieve. This felt out of control. Like nothing she could do would have any impact. She felt the echo of powerlessness in her advisors.

Lily took a deep breath. She needed to lift the mood. To get them back on track. They were her team, and they needed her to lead. She could be depressed on her own time.

"None of this is going to be as quick or easy as we'd all like," she said, looking around and making eye contact with each of them in turn. "I know I was hoping that I could solve a huge conspiracy that's crippled our country and sent us to war in one phone call, but that was wishful thinking. But just because it's going to be a hard process, just because it's going to take longer than we want, doesn't mean it's not going to work."

Slow nods. They heard her, but she could see their exhaustion at the idea of what they were going to need to do.

"We need to regroup and start again." Lily tried to infuse her voice with motivation and positivity. She needed to get them all back up and going. "Juliana, re-prioritise your team's efforts so they are all looking for the chink in the prime minister's armour. We can figure out the plan to take him down once we've found the target, but that's wasted effort until we know what we're hitting him with."

Juliana nodded, making notes. Lily saw her shoulders roll back.

"Jason, have the war council come up with options to achieve one big victory. I'm not talking about pushing them back into the DR. We need something big that will shock Meridia and have them second-guess their chances of overall success. We need to remind them who they're dealing with."

Everyone sat a bit straighter, nodding more enthusiastically. Jason also made himself a note, his forehead creased.

"I'm happy to hear suggestions that are outside the box," Lily clarified. "A display of power, a demonstration of a new weapon, whatever you all think might work, and we can go from there."

"Yes ma'am," Jason said, nodding and adding to his notes. "The most likely thing to get a response from Meridia at this point would be a large, decisive battle. We're going to need more people..."

"Then have someone get on recruiting. I don't want to conscript if we can help it, but I'm not ruling it out. I think voluntary recruitment is also probably a good metric for the public mood. Maybe have them plan a drive to get the numbers we need. From the sounds of things, we need a big recruitment push, anyway."

Jason hesitated. "You know Minister Toot will get in the way. He *is* still the defence minister."

"I'll handle Toot in the short-term," said Lily with more confidence than she felt. "Juliana and her crew will give us the way to clear the decks for good."

Lily looked over at Juliana, her eyes emphasising the need for Juliana to expedite her efforts. The lives of many Highacrens depended on her. Juliana nodded gravely; she understood the importance of her role.

"Right," said Lily, looking around and happy to see the mood lifted. "If you don't have another task, please support Jason and Juliana as much as you can, and we'll meet back here in a few days."

"How's it going?" Lily asked as she approached Giles.

They were standing in front of the old dungeons. Lily had expected to see various large pieces of construction machinery surrounding the three-storey building. And while a couple of massive skips were scattered about filling quickly with debris, all she could see were workers rushing around to prepare Geraldine's new home. The noise was incredible, even at the distance she and Giles stood.

At the command of a supervisor, three people lifted their arms, and walls that were no longer needed crumbled. As soon as it was safe, ten more people surged forward, each taking control of the destroyed concrete and bricks, hovering them across the ground toward the various skips. Lily smiled as she saw a few of them making a competition of it.

On the right-hand side of the building, where the walls had already been cleared away, Lily watched as they began building the enclosure: conjuring materials, lifting and placing beams and supports, and enlarging a window to a size the dragon should be able to use as an exit.

Giles glanced at Lily, his annoyance plain on his face. "The *construction* is going perfectly well, Your Majesty. We're on schedule."

Lily fought to suppress a smile. Giles had not been enamoured with the task to begin with, muttering about a "royal menagerie" and standards slipping. But despite his distaste, he maintained pride in his work, and his tone had conveyed a hint of offence at the mere idea that he would not complete it as specified. It gave Lily reassurance that the old Giles was still here.

"Thank you, Giles. I really appreciate it."

Giles grunted, trying to hold back from saying something. Lily allowed the silence to stretch, confident the old man would not be able to keep it in for long.

"I mean, *really* Your Majesty," he began, and Lily couldn't keep the smile from her face this time. "A dragon? A *dragon*? In the palace? What was Jenkins thinking? What were *you* thinking? Though of course you are the queen and of course you may do whatever you like, but still. A *dragon*?"

Lily felt like hugging him. With all the changes and stress and pressure, the familiarity of the butler she had met when she first arrived was like a salve to her bruised heart.

"Honestly," Giles went on, oblivious to Lily's reaction. "First a pelotromo, and now a dragon. At least the dragon will be out here. But the palace is no place for a..."

Giles broke off, staring at the huge enclosure he was constructing. Lily saw the light of the idea glisten in his eyes.

"No, absolutely not."

"But Your Majesty—"

"Kevin is not moving down here, Giles."

"But it makes so much sense—"

"It's not happening, and I don't think you could make him move out even if I did allow it. Which I won't."

"Well," Giles faltered, unwilling to let go of the dream so soon. "Couldn't you talk to him about it? You know, in his mind?"

Lily shook her head. "I've tried connecting with him like that, but it doesn't work. I don't know if it's just different, or if he's blocking me. But with all you've told me about pelotromos, I thought it best not to push it."

"No, no. Quite," said Giles quickly.

Lily felt lighter than she had in ages. She could almost forget everything that was weighing her down. She was simply a queen arguing with her butler about the palace pets.

As if cued by her happiness, Giles's face fell.

"Your Majesty," he began seriously.

"Giles, if you're going to apologise again, you can save it. You've explained what happened. You thought you were protecting Addison. Toot *made* you think that. And you still made sure not to compromise Jason, Naomi, or Claire. No one blames you."

"I blame myself."

Lily looked at Giles, her heart breaking at the pain in his voice. She reached out, gently touching his arm. "I know. But at some point you're going to have to forgive yourself. Just like the rest of us have."

The moment was ruined as a large roar from behind made both of them jump.

"Oooh, construction!" said Jenkins, clapping his hands. "How exciting."

Geraldine stood behind Jenkins and Lily started before staring up at her. It had barely been two weeks, but the dragon was now almost twice as tall as Jenkins, and quite a bit wider. She roared again, stretching her wings.

A crash at the construction site drew Lily's attention.

"Giles, you *did* tell them what they were building, and why, right?"

"Ah, no, Your Majesty."

"That would explain it."

The workers were staring with understandably shocked expressions at the enormous dragon sitting only a few hundred metres from where they were working.

"Jenkins," Lily called as he started toward the workers, "maybe tell her not—"

Geraldine bellowed again, this time emitting a strong bolt of fire into the sky.

"—to breath fire," Lily finished redundantly.

"Where is that man going?" said Giles, watching as

Jenkins ran after the terrified workers, calling to them that everything was fine. "Jenkins!"

Lily watched, amused, as Giles followed Jenkins, trying to catch the man while retaining his composure, which meant he was walking like a speed walker, his hips swinging in a distinctly un-Giles-like fashion.

Lily turned to the dragon, remembering that she could ask Geraldine to avoid scaring the workers herself, but as if wanting to get a better view of the chaos, Geraldine launched into the air, eliciting more screams from the poor construction workers below.

"Oooh, a dragon," came a small voice from beside Lily.

"Hello Prudence."

"A fire-breathing red belly, if I'm not mistaken."

Lily stared down at her.

"And so big. Must be at least two weeks old."

Lily continued staring until Prudence had to look up at her. Lily raised an eyebrow.

"I spoke to Jenkins earlier," the little girl admitted. "I like him."

"Everyone does." Lily smiled, turning back to watch the chaotic scene before her.

"Are you ready?" Prudence asked.

"Yes," said Lily, turning reluctantly away; she wanted to know how the situation ended up. "Teach me to defend myself."

16

A FEW DAYS LATER, Lily was sitting on her balcony, sipping coffee. The latest casualty reports were beside her. When they first started coming in, Lily had poured over them, making herself read every word as if to not do so would dishonour those who had given their lives.

Now she scanned them, tracking the losses but aware that she served her people better if she kept her head clear rather than drowning herself in the losses of those she did not know, and now never would.

Lily was distracted. Her training with Prudence had gone better than expected. She had a good grasp on her magic, and Prudence was a surprisingly adept teacher. Lily had mastered a basic shield quickly. It would not help for anything other than not dying during a surprise attack, but that alone put her in a significantly better position than she had been before the lesson.

No, her magical progress was not what was bothering her. It was what Prudence had said as they were leaving the courtyard.

"Have you noticed anything different about the oracle?"

Prudence had asked the question as if merely asking after

an old friend. However her use of the title "oracle" rather than Addison's name, and something in the brief hesitation before she asked, told Lily something was on the little girl's mind.

"Not really," said Lily as they'd walked into the palace grounds. "I mean, she's quieter since she came back. And she's beating herself up about her friendship with Ezra."

"Hmmm." Prudence had furrowed her brow at Lily's comment but said nothing further.

"Have you noticed anything?" prompted Lily.

"Her dreams are... different."

"Different how?"

"Less prophetic, more..." Prudence had clicked her fingers, searching for the word. "Running and hiding. Like she's anxious. Worried about something. She's conflicted."

Lily could tell by Prudence's expression that her words had been unable to capture the feeling that Addison's dreams conveyed, but Lily thought she understood.

"You think she's hiding something?" Lily had asked, frowning. She still couldn't imagine what it could be. Unless she told Ezra something important and hadn't confessed it yet. But there wasn't anything left that was important. Even if she was the one to tell him about the interdimensional travel machine, that ship had sailed. It didn't really matter anymore how Ezra had found out. Unless that avenue of information was still open to him, and clearly, if Addison had been the one to tell him, it was not.

"I do get that impression," Prudence had said, selecting her words carefully. "But it's not as straightforward. Something is murky."

They'd walked in silence the rest of the way, each lost in their thoughts.

"Be careful, Your Majesty," said Prudence as she turned to leave Lily. "And trust sparingly."

Lily put her coffee down. She loved the view from her balcony and took every opportunity to spend some time here. Though with Prudence's words echoing in her head, she wasn't enjoying it as she usually did.

"Ma'am." Naomi came out onto the balcony, breaking into Lily's thoughts. "I have a peace offering from the Meridian ambassador to court."

Lily blinked in surprise. She had tried not to think about Ava with everything else going on, but her mind kept wandering back to her unbidden. She missed her terribly. Missed the person she had known. Missed the relationship they had forged.

"What is it?" Lily asked, grabbing her papers and flicking through them as if looking for something and not eagerly awaiting Naomi's response.

"It's another immersion device. Ava passed it to the guards on her door and said it was for you and you alone. I've had it screened as best I can, but it seems to be locked for your eyes only. I can't tell what's on it, but Jenkins assured me that using it wouldn't cause harm."

Lily turned the small metal box over in her hand, only half listening to Naomi. She knew it wouldn't hurt her. Ava wouldn't do that. She may have withheld some information—some rather pertinent information—but Lily knew deep down that Ava would not cause her harm.

But then, why is she here? Why did Ezra bring her to Highacre in the first place?

That man had plans within plans, and he did nothing without it somehow serving his ultimate goal. But Lily didn't know what that ultimate goal was, and so she had no hope of figuring out how Ava fit into it.

Lily looked up and realised Naomi was awaiting her instructions.

"Thanks for looking into it so thoroughly. I'll activate it now and see what Ava wants to tell us."

Naomi hesitated, clearly uncomfortable with the idea of Lily using the device alone.

"You're welcome to join me, if that would make you more comfortable."

"Thank you, ma'am," Naomi said, obvious relief washing over her. "It would be better if I were with you. And don't worry, if it's a recording of Ava declaring her undying love for you, I will exit the immersion immediately and leave you to it."

It'd need to be something more than that at this point. Lily felt her heart pulling towards Ava, but the sting of her subterfuge was still too recent. She desperately wanted to believe her, but Lily just didn't think she could.

"Let's do this," Lily said and hit the button.

The space around them changed immediately, transporting them from a lovely day on the palace balcony to the view from a window in a tall building. Lily felt like she was in an office, but didn't know why she felt that. This immersion experience was different from the others she had encountered. Rather than being able to see all around them, the image was limited, as if only showing the view from one person's perspective. She could hear someone droning on in the background, but it was muffled, as if being tuned out.

"Oh I hate these," Naomi commented. "Seeing out of someone's eyes. I much prefer the third person perspective."

Lily had to agree with her, and found it slightly nauseating as the view moved, the subject turning to face the person who had been talking.

Naomi swore softly as the prime minister came into view, his belly jiggling as he laughed gratuitously at something he himself had said.

"I mean, I knew the plan would go well, but there *were*

doubters. No one cares about them now though, do they? I have complete control. Don't even need them anymore."

"No, I don't suppose you do," said a familiar voice that Lily struggled to place without a visual aid. Lily assumed it was the person whose memory they seemed to be observing.

"I must say, when I first agreed to killing the entire—"

There was a sudden burst of audio and visual static and Lily and Naomi were forcibly ejected from the immersion device, finding themselves back on the balcony, rubbing their ears and squinting at the sun.

Recovering, the two women looked at each other, stunned.

"You know what he was about to say," Naomi said.

"That he was involved in assassinating my family," said Lily.

"Sounded like more than just 'involved'," said Naomi.

"But it's not enough," Lily said, eyes narrowing. "He almost said it, but he didn't. We'd need him to actually say it to bring him down for good. The key part is missing. I'm going to have to go speak to Ava."

Naomi pursed her lips, clearly thinking what Lily herself was wondering. That it was possible Ava had held back the key part of the recording to make sure Lily did just that. Visit her.

As they crossed the palace grounds to the diplomatic wing, Lily stopped and turned to Naomi. "I'll go in alone."

"No—"

"Yes," said Lily firmly. "I trust Ava. At least not to harm me. She's had plenty of opportunities. Whatever her game is, she's not a physical threat."

Naomi nodded slowly, and they set off walking again. "I'll be right outside, though."

"No, take this to Juliana and her team." Lily passed her the immersion device. "Tell them I'm working on getting the complete recording, but to switch their effort to plan on bringing the prime minister down based on this footage."

"I'll put her in touch with Hudson," said Naomi. "Once we have the footage, they'll need a way to put it out there."

Lily's cheeks burned with shame. She'd forgotten about Hudson with everything else going on. Not having met him, he wasn't as prominent in her thoughts as Claire, but he had been an integral part of the team while she was missing, and she was angry at herself for not asking after him.

"He's okay then?"

"Yes ma'am," Naomi assured her, sensing her embarrassment. "Hudson was never captured, after all. He saw the HSP closing in on him and went off the grid for a bit to evade them. He's managed to reinforce his online security protocols and is currently flitting in and out of the system in order to thwart their attempts to find him. But I spoke with him a few days ago and he's keen to be tasked with something."

They reached Ava's door and Naomi informed the guards that they were responsible for Lily's safety. Both men snapped to attention, hyper alert. Naomi nodded, satisfied that Lily would be safe, and walked as fast as she could back towards the palace.

Lily took a deep breath, knocked once, then opened the door and stepped inside.

Ava stood by the window, staring out, her expression melancholic. Lily's breath caught as she stared. Ava's hair, swept over one shoulder, caught the light perfectly. She looked like a tragic princess trapped in a tower, stoically refusing to let it break her. She looked beautiful.

As Lily took another step forwards, she could tell Ava knew she was there, but Ava didn't turn or acknowledge Lily's arrival. Lily frowned. What had changed?

"I got your message," said Lily, moving closer to Ava.

Ava turned, finally looking at Lily, who almost flinched seeing the pain in her eyes.

"Why don't we sit out here," said Ava, moving out to the balcony without waiting to hear if Lily objected.

Lily followed, concern creasing her brow. She fought the urge to touch Ava, to ask what was wrong. Instead, she sat beside her friend and waited.

Ava continued to stare at the view, the wind gently blowing her hair. Lily kept silent, trying to give Ava the space she needed, ignoring the growing impatience to prompt her to get the information she required and spring into action against the prime minister.

"All I ever wanted was a family," Ava said. "Somewhere to belong. Someone to take care of me. To want me. To love me."

Ava looked over at Lily, her eyes dark but full of longing. "I thought that was him." Ava pulled her gaze from Lily and turned back to the view, but not before Lily saw the pain again. Lily kept silent, letting Ava talk in her own time.

"I was so focussed on biology—on finding my real father. He even looks like me. It blinded me, and I missed the signs. I missed that he only engaged with me when it suited him. Only cared for me when there was a benefit to him. Only loved me when he wanted something."

Ava scowled, staring down at her hands. "Even when I met Alexei and you. When I had a perfect example of what family was. What it was like to be loved and cared for unconditionally. I still craved his attention. His love. Because he was my father. And I hurt you to protect him. I'm sorry."

Lily's heart softened as Ava's voice broke on her apology. She could sense the pain and sadness and self-loathing in her voice.

"I understand," Lily said. "I was hurt. Because I care

about you. So much. But I understand that need you had for his attention. His approval. And I forgive you."

Ava's eyes snapped to Lily's, searching for validation of the truthfulness of her words. Her eyes brightened, seeing Lily meant it, before the sadness returned.

"Thank you, Lily. But I'm not sure I can forgive myself." She returned her gaze to the view again before adding, "I'm not sure you should forgive me either."

Lily frowned, trying to think of what to say, how to reassure Ava. Everything that came to mind sounded trite.

"I didn't know about the implants," said Ava quietly. "I mean, of course I knew I got a new one, but I didn't know about everything it could do. He didn't tell me."

Lily felt her hatred for Ezra bubbling up. Games within games. Why bring her here with a high-tech implant without telling her about it? He was treating everyone like his toys. His puppets to play with. Even his own daughter.

Ava sighed. "I knew the box was his. I'm sorry—when you found it, I panicked. Honestly, I'd forgotten about it, but then you saw it and all I could think was you'd think I was working with him. It was locked when I took it, and I had no idea you had the key..." Ava trailed off, knowing she wasn't making it any better. "I panicked and lied. And I'm sorry. It won't happen again."

Lily nodded. She could understand Ava's reaction, but on top of everything else...

"You can read my mind," Ava said imploringly. "Please? Lily, I want to make it up to you. I want you to know you can trust me."

"Why don't you tell me what happened, and then I'll have a look and see?"

Ava nodded, brightening at the chance to win back Lily's trust. Lily felt duplicitous. She knew it seemed to Ava as if Lily was wanting to give her the chance to explain herself, but in reality, it would focus Ava's thoughts. If she was lying, telling her story would also bring the true memories to the foreground as she concentrated on hiding the truth. That would make it much easier for Lily to find them.

"I saw him hide it in your office. I thought that was odd, and I was curious, so I tried to open it while you were both talking. But it didn't open, and then you said something to me and I couldn't put it back without being caught, so I took it. I dropped it back in here, thinking I'd return it when I got the chance, but to be honest, I completely forgot about it."

Lily checked Ava's mind and found this was true. "He expected me to see this months ago then," mused Lily. "Why?"

"He wanted to make you distrust Meridia," said Ava. "Looking at what's happened, I think he would have wanted you to see that recording and expel us both. I can't imagine anyone would be willing to let us stay with this technology. But sending us home would have increased the division between Highacre and Meridia, inching the countries closer to war. In his mind, you wouldn't be strongly opposed to war when things deteriorated, given our duplicity. Especially mine. He would have then used your actions in expelling us and cutting ties with me to draw me in closer to his side, citing the typical anti-Meridian behaviour to be expected from Highacre."

Lily considered this. It did sound like something Ezra would do. "I get it, but it feels a bit weak. I don't think I would go from being annoyed at you both lying about your implants to war."

Ava smiled weakly. "No, you wouldn't. And I think it's safe to say he consistently underestimates you. But I think part of his plan was for us to develop our relationship so that the betrayal would sting all the more. That's what he does. He gathers information and then adapts his plan to incorporate what he learns. He could see we were getting close. That I liked you..."

Lily smiled sadly at the memory. All those hours with Ava in the woods when she was trying to learn magic.

"He started really encouraging me to get to know you better. I told him to butt out, but he kept going. He was saying that befriending the Highacren monarch would be good for my career, and having a friend my age would be good for me, especially here, where most people are older. Before we were pushed through the device, we had a bit of an argument about it. He was so insistent, it was getting weird."

"I remember you telling me you fought," said Lily. "That was why you wanted to get back so quickly." But as she said it out loud, it didn't make sense. If the argument was about spending time with Lily, then Ava should have wanted to stay where Lily was.

"No, it wasn't that argument," said Ava. Lily flicked out with her power, confirming Ava was still telling her the truth. "He had been talking with Toth. Mentioned he was thinking about leaving his role as ambassador and going to work with him. He was excited about it, because he said I could have his role and be full ambassador."

Ava paused, blinking again furiously. Lily, still connected to her mind, could feel the raw pain Ezra's deception had caused his daughter.

"I told him I didn't want that," she whispered. "That I liked working with him. He said we'd still work together, but I didn't know how. Not with Toth being so opposed to you. I tried focussing on that. Told him Toth was bad news, that his plans weren't something we wanted to be a part of. But he wouldn't listen. He just kept telling me not to worry. That's what I wanted to get back to deal with. I was terrified

I'd get back and he'd already be working with the prime minister."

Lily realised with a jolt that this was exactly the scenario that Ava had walked back into. Just far worse than she had imagined. Lily bit back the choice words she had for Ezra. Though Ava was clearly as upset and angry as Lily—perhaps even more so—Ezra was her father. The rejection was still raw and Lily verbally bashing the man wouldn't help Ava. Instead, she considered Ava's theory. It did seem to fit. But again, Lily wondered what Ezra's endgame was. What did he gain by bringing Ava and Lily together and then driving them apart, other than perhaps some perverse sense of control? A distraction? It seemed like a lot of effort to merely pull Lily's mind from the disasters befalling Highacre. It wasn't like she would be up for war with Meridia because her girlfriend lied.

Ava continued, breaking into Lily's thoughts, "After we saw the briefing, I tested the implant out. It was hard at first, but the functions were all there. I managed to figure out the link to Ezra's implant, and through that and the mind reading capability, I got into his memories." Ava looked embarrassed. "At first I was looking for why he'd treated me like this. I wasted time trying to answer my own questions. I'm sorry."

Lily shook her head. "I would have done the same."

"Eventually I got over myself and looked for what he was up to. I figured he must have some reason to be doing all this. And then I saw the memory I sent to you. Where he's talking to your prime minister, who says he agreed to the assassinations of your family. I was shocked, but I tried to move quickly, engaging the recording function. Unfortunately, he noticed me and blocked me out. And then he switched off my implant."

Lily looked at Ava in horror. She tried to reconcile the

worried father embracing his daughter when they arrived back from Lily's home dimension with a man who would so coldly reject her like that. Now she understood Ava's demeanour. Not only had her father rejected her, but she had lost access to her implant.

Lily could understand some of what Ava must be feeling. She had begun to rely on her own powers, and she would certainly feel the emptiness now if they were taken away. But Ava had grown up with an implant. Used it daily. It would be like losing a limb. The shock of that loss must be awful, but coupled with the rejection from her father?

"Ava, I'm so—"

Ava interrupted, waving off Lily's sympathy. Lily watched as Ava fought to maintain her composure. "In a memory I saw before I was locked out, the prime minister mentioned a visual archive. Ezra was questioning him about it, clearly thinking it was a liability, but I could tell he also wanted the information to potentially use for his own gain as required." Ava paused. Lily saw pain cross her face, probably thinking about how Ezra had so coldly used her too.

"Do you know what this archive is?" asked Lily. She'd not heard of such a thing before.

To her surprise, Ava snorted. "Toth has been backing up his memories. You can do that with immersion devices, but it's very expensive. It's rare for someone to back up one memory. Toth has been backing up everything for over a year. The man thinks he's such a pivotal figure in history that generations to come will want to know everything about him."

Lily found herself unsurprised in the sense that she knew Toth was a narcissist, but she was still galled at the depths of his delusion. Of course, in this case it was to her benefit, and so rather than try and grasp the kind of person who would expend the time and resources to document themselves so thoroughly, she was grateful for the gift of evidence.

"If we can access that archive, we'd have access to the full footage I sent you. And more. If we get that and release it, the prime minister would be finished."

We. Lily's heart gave a brief flutter. She knew Ava was signalling that she was on their team against Ezra and Reginald Toth, but Lily couldn't help but think Ava might be feeling out a return to their relationship. Cursing herself, Lily turned her mind back to the matter at hand. Her love life could wait.

"That's amazing Ava, thank you."

"I'll tell you where it is." Ava turned to Lily, her eyes blazing with an intensity that almost made Lily look away. "No matter what, I will. But I want to help more. I want to bring him down. I'm yours, if you'll have me."

Lily hesitated. Her advisors would be against bringing Ava in. Not only was she Meridian, but they did not know whether Ezra could use her implant to spy on them even if it was dormant. *Shit, he could even be listening now.*

Ava caught Lily's hesitation and turned away, hurt. "Of course, you'll have to discuss it with your advisors." Her tone was all business now. "And no doubt you would need to limit my access to information."

"Ava, I'm sorry—"

"The archive is in the old HIA building. I think the HSP is operating out of there now. You'll need to hurry. I've no doubt Ezra will review what I accessed, if he hasn't already. If he figures out I know about the archive, it might be moved, or its security increased. Or they may even destroy it."

Lily reached out and grabbed Ava's hand, trying to convey through touch what she couldn't find the words for.

That she still trusted her. That she cared about her. That she loved her.

But Ava didn't respond, instead staring pointedly at Lily, who knew she needed to get moving. Ava was right. They didn't have much time, if it wasn't already too late.

Lily stood and left the balcony, striding for the door to the apartment. Her heart was screaming at her, tearing at her chest. She reached out, placed a hand on the door's handle, and froze. Time was of the essence, but she did love Ava. That was clear to her now. She couldn't leave it like this.

Turning, Lily hurried back across the apartment as Ava re-entered from the balcony, looking up in surprise to see Lily still there. Lily walked right up to Ava and embraced her firmly, holding her tight. She felt Ava freeze, then relax, returning the embrace. Lily nuzzled her face against Ava's and their lips found each other, kissing tenderly but intensely.

Lily felt time stop. There was nothing and no one else in the world but Ava. She felt whole. Eventually, Ava broke the kiss and rested her forehead lightly against Lily's, her eyes shut.

"Go," Ava whispered.

Lily gave Ava a soft kiss goodbye and left. As she walked down the corridor, she brought her head back into the present.

Time to talk to Juliana.

Time to bring down the prime minister.

Lily watched a snufflepidgeon fly in a lazy loop past the window, allowing her mind the brief distraction. She thought again of Edmund, wondering where he was now, but the thought exited her mind almost as soon as it entered, distracted as she was by the bickering in the room.

Why couldn't anything be easy? She thought they would seize the momentum they had created, seamlessly flowing from the discovery of the prime minister's archive to the mission to retrieve the memory that would be his downfall. But here they were, Lily and her advisors, gathered in her office, pulling apart Juliana's plan.

It made sense for them to go over it, offer suggestions, and review it to find the holes. But those who hadn't been involved in the planning wanted more detail than the brief overview Juliana had given contained, and Juliana was a little too attached to her plan, which meant she was less than willing to receive feedback.

Lily tried to return her attention to the discussion at hand. At least Juliana wasn't being defensive due to ego. She had built her team with women she had served time with who had since been released, and she was keen to show them in a positive light. To let everyone know they were capable. However, her vigorous defence of their plan was more in keeping with someone asserting her team were infallible.

"Okay, but once you have the device—" Naomi began before being interrupted by Jason.

"Is it a device? What if the memories are on a whole server system?"

"Or in the cloud," suggested Giles.

"No, they wouldn't be in the cloud," said Jason dismissively.

Lily watched as Giles sat back as if rebuked. She had been trying to include Giles and Addison as much as possible. She knew both felt guilty about their actions while Lily had been away and she was keen to make them feel like valued members of the team again. However, the current issues were not really in their ballparks. She knew Jason hadn't intended to dismiss Giles. He was just focussed on the plan. But the effect was still the same, and Lily frowned.

"It's a small device," Juliana said, exasperation lacing her tone. "Maybe the size of a paperback novel. Really, this level of detail is only important to those of us carrying out the plan. I thought we were just meant to be examining the higher-level detail."

"Yes, which brings me back to my question," said Naomi quickly. "Once you have the device, are you planning on exiting the way you entered? I don't see an alternative route marked here on the map."

The occupants of the room looked as one at the 3D holographic model projected above the coffee table.

"We have identified a couple of alternative exit routes, though we could also use the entrance path. At this stage, without time to conduct appropriate surveillance of the building, we thought it best to leave the extraction as flexible as possible."

"Good point," said Lily, cutting off whatever Naomi was going to say in response. "Giles, Addison—do either of you have anything to add?"

Both advisors looked alarmed to be put on the spot, and while Giles seemed to start wracking his brain for anything he might say, Addison simply shook her head.

"Come on," Lily said in what she hoped was an encouraging tone. "You've got a background in intelligence, Addison. Surely you have some questions?"

Addison shrugged. "With Ezra taking care of Highacre —er..." Addison shook her head. "I mean helping the prime minister, I'd say my intelligence background is severely outmatched. Plus, it wasn't long after you aband—after you left." Addison closed her eyes and took a deep breath, her frustration at fumbling her words palpable. "After you were pushed through the machine, that I was arrested. So the others have a much better picture than I do."

Lily frowned at Addison. She wasn't normally so nervous when speaking among the advisors. Not to mention Juliana was arrested quite a while before Addison had been. And she was the one running the plan. Prudence's words echoed in Lily's mind.

Trust sparingly.

"So anyway," said Juliana quickly, taking advantage of the pause, "once we have extracted the device from the premises, we will rendezvous back here where I will hand it over to you two"—she nodded at Jason and Naomi—"and you can give it to your chap to upload."

It took Lily a beat to realise that Jason and Naomi's "chap" was Hudson. Lily noticed Naomi's eyes lock on Juliana and sensed she was waiting for a chance to challenge the implication that Juliana and her team were doing all the heavy lifting and all Naomi and Jason were good for was handing something to someone else. Lily could understand her being sensitive about that, particularly with how much Jason and Naomi had done while Juliana was in prison.

"Thanks for the briefing, Juliana," Lily said before Naomi could get in and signalling that the discussion was over. "Can you tell us about the team you're taking?"

Juliana's chest puffed up at the chance to discuss her crew.

"Of course, Your Majesty. Most have done time and so have excellent sneaking and fighting skills—either from their time inside, or from their previous lines of work that led them to being locked up."

"If they got caught, them perhaps they're not so good at evading capture..." muttered Naomi, earning a glare from Lily.

"I have one girl who can disrupt monitoring devices, including magical ones, and another girl who is a lock breaker."

"Which type of locks?" Giles asked.

"Any of them," said Juliana proudly.

"And offensive capabilities?" asked Jason.

Juliana shifted her weight, uncomfortable. "Yes, well, that's not our strongest area I'll admit, but the plan relies on us flying under the radar, so offensive capabilities aren't as important."

"Sure, but you'll need something more than what you have in case something goes wrong. No plan survives—"

"Yes, yes, I know," huffed Juliana. "Like I said, we can all fight. Even I got into a brawl or two during my time inside."

"I don't mean any disrespect, but this is a highly

defended facility. If something goes wrong, you'll need more than prison brawlers."

Silence followed Jason's words and Lily tried to think what the answer might be. According to Juliana, they needed to keep the team small to evade detection, but Jason was right. From the sounds of things, if they were detected, they'd be captured instantly. Or worse.

Juliana cracked her knuckles, drawing the focus back to her. "Well, maybe it's my time to shine. I come from a long line of dissuaders. I can make people suddenly want to go somewhere else. A rather handy ability, I'm sure I don't have to tell you."

Everyone stared at her. That was not what they were thinking in terms of the firepower needed.

"Oh. That's great, Juliana," said Lily, a smile plastered on her face. "How powerful is your ability?"

"I can do two at a time," Juliana replied. Sensing the room deflate, she added, "But if I'm really concentrating, I can do two more straight after without a break."

Juliana looked around the room, seeing no one was overly impressed with her ability. "I'm also a pretty good lie detector," she said defensively.

"For a group of insurgents, you do seem a little light on firepower," Naomi said.

"I'll go with you," said Lily before Juliana could respond to Naomi.

As one, the room shot down Lily's suggestion.

"The mission would be for nothing if something happened to you, ma'am," said Jason. "We need you ready to take charge once the prime minister is out of the way."

"But he's not going to be out of the way if we don't get the device," Lily argued. It was vital to get the device, but she also didn't like the idea of sitting around safe in the palace while others risked their lives. "Besides, people keep saying that I'm the most magically powerful person around. What's the point of that if I never use any magic?"

"I don't doubt we'll need your powers before the end, Your Majesty," said Jason, a note of sadness in his voice. "But you're too important to put in danger when it's not absolutely necessary."

Lily knew it was true, but she still didn't like it. She had a pang of longing for Claire. She would be perfect for the mission, and she worked well with Juliana.

"I can go," Jason started.

Naomi put a hand on his arm. "I'll go," she said firmly.

Jason looked like he wanted to argue, but saw the resolve in her eyes and sat back, nodding.

"I really don't think it's necessary," said Juliana, looking put out.

"What's the issue?" asked Lily. "You need more fire-power. Naomi has magic and muscle."

Juliana looked embarrassed. "It's just... this is my mission. With my girls." Her face flushed and Lily could tell Juliana could hear how silly it sounded out loud.

Lily understood where Juliana was coming from, but this was too important for pride. "It's still your mission with your girls," she said kindly but firmly. "But Naomi will join you. She's a powerful revealer and can paralyse up to three people for five minutes. She will help your mission succeed, and she will be under your command."

Lily glanced at Naomi to make sure she understood. Naomi nodded, looking over at Juliana to ensure the older woman saw that she knew Juliana was in charge.

"Fine," said Juliana, nodding back at Naomi.

"It's still not much firepower," said Jason.

Before anyone could respond, there was a knock at the door, causing them all to jump, with Naomi and Giles leaping to their feet. However, where Naomi moved towards Lily, Giles backed up, away from the door.

The door opened a fraction and Richard's head poked in.

"Sorry to interrupt," he said tentatively, stepping into the room as Lily and the advisors continued to stare at him. "I, er, wanted to see if I could help."

Lily saw her stunned expression mirrored in her advisors' faces. Juliana seemed to recover first. "Should we lock him up?"

Richard paled and backed up a step, raising his hands as if warding her off. "What? No, why would you lock me up?"

"Clearly you're a spy," Juliana spat.

"If I was a spy," said Richard, recovering quickly, "I'd hardly walk right in and ask what you're up to."

"Oh, so you know we're up to something," exclaimed Juliana, as if she'd cracked the case.

"Of course you're up to something! It'd be a pretty terrible insurrection if you weren't."

"Oh, so you know we're insurrectionists."

"We're not insurrectionists," Lily said, interrupting the bickering.

"I am," huffed Juliana.

Lily glared at her. "We're not insurrectionists because I am the queen, which means I have authority. If anyone's an insurrectionist, it's the prime minister."

"Look, I can understand your scepticism," said Richard, bringing them back to the matter at hand. "But I took Naomi's advice and looked more closely at who I was working for. And I didn't like what I found. I didn't ask questions when they offered me the job. I was just full of myself for getting it, and probably a bit focussed on beating Jason." Richard had the grace to look embarrassed.

Lily glanced at Jason, noticing most of her advisors doing the same. Jason was studiously examining his hands, brow furrowed.

"I'm sorry, Jason," said Richard earnestly. "You taught me better than that."

Jason took a deep breath before finally looking up and meeting Richard's eyes. After a beat, he nodded, and the tension in the room dropped considerably. Lily saw Richard relax as if the main hurdle had been crossed. He looked around at the advisors before resting his focus on Lily and Juliana.

"I want to be on the right side here. I want to help. Please. Let me help."

Lily studied Richard's face. He seemed genuine, and a quick scan of his mind showed her he believed what he was saying. But that didn't necessarily make it true.

"Juliana?" Lily prompted.

"String him up."

"I wasn't asking for your opinion. Didn't you just say you were a lie detector?"

"Oh," Juliana blushed. "Well, I must admit that Claire and Ava are more talented in that area than I am. Though I suppose with her implant offline, I might have the edge on Ava for the moment."

"Well, they're not here," Lily snapped. She took a deep breath. She could understand Juliana propping herself up earlier and panicking now that they needed to rely on her power. But she missed Claire intensely, and hated that she couldn't bring Ava into these discussions. She felt like she was running low on close friends and just wanted Juliana to channel the overconfident woman she usually was. Lily would prefer to have her opinion and balance it against her own knowledge than for Juliana to hold back her thoughts for fear of judgement.

"What changed your mind?" Jason asked Richard, and Lily was grateful to him for providing Juliana with another opportunity to assess Richard. "I mean, sure, you looked into things and didn't like what you found. But what was the exact thing that made you want to switch sides?"

Juliana concentrated, squinting at Richard as he paused to think.

"It was Toot, really. I didn't agree with some of his decisions. He seemed more interested in creating a façade, and I wanted to do the job properly. I questioned him about it, and he told me to shut up and follow orders."

The room was suddenly full of scoffing and Lily's advisors expressing their opinions of their old colleague. Only Lily and Juliana remained focussed; Juliana checking for lies and Lily continuing to monitor Richard's mind to see if he believed what he was saying.

"After that, I moved the people I trusted into a few key positions and went home. I'd been living in the barracks at my old job and then moved straight here to the palace. Hadn't been home in months. No need to, really." He shrugged. "But I needed a break after the run-in with Toot, so I went and walked through my old neighbourhood. The first thing I noticed was that no one else was out. Usually people were out walking their dogs or playing with their kids, but it was like a ghost town. I saw one of my neighbours; I used to work on cars with her husband. She spotted me and practically ran back inside her house. She was terrified.

"Finally, I ran into Joan. She's an older lady—we used to call her 'neighbourhood watch' because she knew everything that was going on. She didn't run, just stared at me defiantly. I asked her what had been going on, and she told me. She told me what the HSP has been doing. That people were terrified. Missing. Dead."

Richard's voice broke, and he coughed, trying to cover it before quickly composing himself. "This is not my High-acre. We're better than this." He looked over, holding Lily's gaze. "I can fight. I can manipulate water, including the water in people's bodies. I can stop them, kill them if I have to. I can also heal. Please, let me help. I want to serve my country."

Silence met Richard's heartfelt plea.

"He's got my vote," said Jason simply. Richard nodded gratefully at his old boss.

Jason's opinion meant a lot to Lily, but she couldn't risk this mission on heartfelt speeches. She hadn't found anything in Richard's mind to indicate he was deceptive, but she looked over at Juliana, who was still glaring at Richard. Juliana's expression was less hostile, and she frowned, as if considering her options. She noticed Lily watching her expectantly.

"He's genuine. He's in."

18

Lily was sitting in Addison's living room, the air thick with awkward tension. Lily was eager to *do* something. While she understood why she shouldn't be part of the mission to retrieve the prime minister's archive, she was frustrated about having to remain safely at home while others risked their lives for her.

For our country.

But she couldn't help feeling she wasn't carrying her load. And so she had resolved to get to the bottom of what was going on with Addison. There was definitely something off about her friend. And while Lily knew Addison had been through a lot in prison, especially if she'd spent so long in solitary confinement, it didn't feel as if her behavioural changes could be solely explained by her incarceration.

Even now, it felt like Addison didn't want her here. She was fidgeting and kept looking at her watch. Her answers so far had been short and she seemed overly cautious in considering her words.

"I'm worried about you Addison," Lily said, deciding to be direct. "You're not yourself."

"Well I was locked up for a long time," Addison

snapped before closing her eyes as if silently berating herself.

"Even so," said Lily. She looked at Addison, who looked anywhere but at Lily. Lily decided to change tactics.

"You haven't even asked about my mum."

Addison's eyes flew to Lily's, embarrassment mixing with something Lily couldn't identify. "I didn't... I wasn't sure... I didn't know if she told you."

"She did tell me," said Lily. "About you being the one to ask her to take me in. But the old Addison would have asked about how it was seeing my family even if she didn't think I knew. The old Addison would have wanted to know about her oldest friend."

Addison opened and closed her mouth, clearly unsure of how to ask now that she had been called out for failing to do so.

"Mum told me you were in the HIA together."

"Oh yes," said Addison, her old smile breaking out across her face. "Belinda was my best friend. She was so good at everything. And I was terrible." Addison laughed, her eyes unfocussed as she lost herself in the memory.

Lily cautiously reached out with her magic. She noted how reliant she'd become on mind reading. It seemed she was having difficulty trusting almost everyone close to her.

Trust sparingly.

"This one time, we were supposed to locate and follow a target. We had to work in pairs, and Belinda would always pick me even though she would do better with one of the other candidates. So Belinda found the guy and followed him to a park, where I was supposed to take over. I was never good at concealment, so I thought I'd be smart and hide in plain sight. I took a seat on a bench and waited to see the target enter the park."

Lily kept the smile on her face, but internally she was

frowning. She could see Addison's memory as she told her story. It felt like the Addison she knew. But if Lily tried to go further into Addison's mind, it felt murky. Fractured. She didn't dare probe further in case Addison noticed her. Something told Lily that if Addison realised Lily was reading her mind without her knowledge, she'd be lost forever.

"This guy sits next to me," Addison continued happily, oblivious to Lily's inner turmoil. "And he sees me looking around and asks if I'm waiting for someone, like he's worried he's taken their seat. We get to talking and after a while I tell him I'm on a course and we're playing a game and I have to find someone before they find me. And then he says he loves games and they used to do things like that all the time when he was at the academy."

"Oh no," said Lily, pulled back into the story.

"Oh yes. Of course, I'm so naïve, I thought it was the most amazing coincidence. We sat talking for another thirty minutes before he broke it to me that he was the target and let me know I failed." Addison's smile faded. "You'd think I'd have learned about talking to people I don't know."

"Addison, you can't—"

"How is your mum?" Addison cut Lily off. "Is she well? I miss her a lot."

"She's not the best, actually. But she's better now than she was." Some instinct told Lily to push, and so she told Addison everything that had happened to her family in her absence. She forced herself to expand where she wanted to gloss over the details, and she kept going, even when the tears came as she told Addison about her dad.

"Oh Lily," said Addison, crying herself. "You poor thing. Your poor mum."

Addison suddenly collapsed into wracking sobs and

Lily moved closer, holding Addison and stroking her hair, murmuring words of comfort.

Eventually, Addison regained control of herself and took some deep breaths.

"Addison, what is going on?" Lily asked softly.

"I think they did something to me," Addison whispered. "When I was locked up."

"What do you think they did?"

Addison tried to speak, but unable to find the words, gave up and tapped her head. Lily nodded and re-entered Addison's mind. It felt less fractured than before, but the experience was still jarring. Lily had an overwhelming feeling of uncertainty as to what was real.

She looked for Addison's time in prison and found an unpleasant but uncontroversial memory of being in solitary confinement. She quickly searched, finding nothing unusual about her time incarcerated. But then there was a schism, like a record scratching, and Lily heard a voice echoing in Addison's mind.

The Prime Minister and Ezra are taking care of Highacre.

Alarmed, Lily kept searching, eventually triggering another message.

The princess is weak and ran away at the first sign of trouble. She has abandoned you.

Lily hesitated at pressing further, the memory of the police officer lying broken on the street running through her own mind. But she wasn't going to change Addison's memories. It should be safe. Gently, she pushed, prodding the memories, looking for evidence of anything fake.

The Prime Minister and Ezra are the real deal. They're the good guys.

Suddenly the image of Addison sitting in her cell morphed into Addison strapped to a chair. The propaganda messages were playing, and someone was seated behind Addison, doing something that was causing her pain.

"Oh!" Addison exclaimed in shock. Lily withdrew quickly from her mind, worried about hurting her. Addison blinked in confusion. "I don't remember that."

"Addison, I think you were brainwashed."

Addison paled, her attention caught by the exposure of the hidden memories.

Lily sat up, horror filling her. "When we left the prison, Ezra suggested you catch up for tea. Did you go to see him?"

"No, I wouldn't," said Addison quickly, before something struck her. "But... I think I did. I—oh Lily, it's all a blur. I don't know what's real."

"That's okay," said Lily, trying to be gentle despite her urgency. "Why don't you tell me anyway and we'll figure it out together."

Addison nodded, trying to compose herself. "I think I met with him once, shortly after we all met the first time."

"And what did you talk about?" Lily felt sick. What had Addison told Ezra?

"We talked about the advisors," said Addison, closing her eyes and straining to remember. "That Toot was fired and Austin was gone. And that we didn't know where Claire was."

Lily felt like a hand was squeezing her heart. *Claire!* She must have been brainwashed too. Lily hadn't noticed anything, but nothing had been apparent with Addison either. Not until she had pushed. They needed to help her. But how?

"And he wanted to know if you trusted him," Addison finished.

"What did you tell him?" Lily asked, refocussing on Addison.

"I said you didn't. And then he asked why, and I said

because he was working with the prime minister. He seemed happy with that."

Lily leaned forwards, squeezing Addison's hands reassuringly. "Addison, this is important. Have you met with him since?"

"I..." Addison closed her eyes, screwing up her face in concentration. "I don't think so."

Lily relaxed a little.

"But I can't be sure," Addison said, her eyes opening and fixing Lily with a look of alarm. "I don't know what's real," she whispered.

"It's okay," Lily soothed.

"No, it's not," said Addison, her alarm growing. "I can't trust my memories. I don't know what's real. And," she dropped her voice to a whisper, "I think I'm hallucinating."

Lily looked at Addison in alarm. She wouldn't have thought brainwashing would cause hallucinations, but then she wasn't exactly an expert in the matter. Maybe whatever they did to Addison was too much for her.

"What is it you see?" Lily asked.

"There's this little girl I see in my dreams sometimes. It's weird, she doesn't even seem to be a part of the dream, and she turns up no matter what the dream is about. Just watching. I guess it sounds creepy when I say it out loud, but I don't get the feeling she's malicious or anything. But"—Addison nodded to the corner behind Lily, dropping her voice again—"I can see her in that chair over there now, and I'm not asleep. At least I don't think I am. Unless this is a dream..."

Lily's eyes snapped to the chair Addison pointed to and jumped at seeing Prudence sitting there, her legs swinging, unable to touch the ground. Prudence smiled at Lily and gave her a little wave.

"Prudence, stop being so creepy. You're making Addison think she's having a breakdown."

Addison looked at Lily in shock and whispered, "You can see her too?"

"I can, Addison. She's real. Prudence? Tell Addison you're real."

Prudence turned to Addison and said, "I'm real."

Perhaps catching Lily's glare, she added, "I'm sorry I gave you a fright, Addison. I'm Prudence. Lady Octavia's replacement."

"Oh!" Addison's face broke into a delighted smile at the mention of her hero, and then her face fell, remembering she was dead.

"Do you remember seeing Lady Octavia in your dreams too?" Prudence asked.

"No," said Addison thoughtfully, "I mean, sometimes she was a part of my dreams, but never just watching like you do."

"Interesting," said Prudence.

"But why would I see either of you?" asked Addison.

"I believe you've been seeing me because I am the one meant to reveal to you your true role."

"My what now?"

"You are the oracle, Addison. You are one of the three pivotal roles that underpin our world. You are vitally important, and you always have been."

"Oh, gosh!" said Addison, covering her mouth, eyes wide. "I always wanted to be important. I'd hoped to be a detector, but obviously that wasn't to be," she said, gesturing to Prudence.

"The oracle is every bit as important as the detector," Prudence said simply.

Lily marvelled at the little girl's emotional intelligence

and ability to sense what was important to Addison. What she needed to hear.

Addison laughed nervously. "I used to dream of having an important role. But my mother laughed at me. Told me not to be so stupid."

"Your mother never should have said that," said Lily, feeling a wave of anger towards Addison's mother. "You've always been important, oracle or not. I never would have gotten through the confirmation hearing without you. Or through the Trials. And I would have freaked out and never even accepted what was happening if you hadn't been there that first day."

Addison beamed at Lily, her smile genuine for the first time in weeks. Lily had the sense that Addison was over-whelmed and frightened by the revelation of what had been done to her in prison. It was easier to ignore that in favour of something positive. It didn't strike Lily as the best approach, ignoring all of that, but she let it go for now. There would be time enough to deal with what had been done to Addison, and what she may have unwittingly revealed.

Addison turned to Prudence and asked curiously, "Tell me more about the oracle?"

"The oracle has prophetic dreams. But in line with the nature of dreams, the dreamer rarely remembers, or at least, not in great detail. Luckily, the detector can visit the dreams of the oracle, and as such can record the prophecies you see."

"Wait," interrupted Addison, suddenly looking worried, her cheeks flushing. "You don't visit *all* my dreams, right?"

Lily noticed Prudence was suddenly uncomfortable. "No, only the prophetic dreams."

Lily watched the blush burn the little girl's cheeks and wondered if that might not be true. Prudence hurried on, clearly eager to leave the topic.

"Addison, forgive me for eavesdropping, but it seems that someone has hurt you."

Addison's face fell, the joy at learning her new role gone and replaced with the fear of before.

"I had noticed some changes in your dreams, and it makes sense now. But we need to heal you. As I said, you are one of three important figures. Along with me, there is also Cyril, the reassigner. He is visiting with me in my home at present, and I thought it might be nice for you to come and stay with me too. We could all spend some time together, and while you're with us, I can use my other power to get a better idea of what has happened to you."

Lily looked up at Prudence gratefully. Prudence could experience Addison's life and see what had happened. Lily wasn't sure what Prudence would see about Addison's time in prison—whether her power would let her see the truth, or what Addison's damaged mind remembered. But at least she would be able to see what Addison had done since returning. And what she might have told Ezra.

"That would be great," said Addison, smiling again. "Oh, but only if that's okay with you, Your Majesty."

"Of course it is," said Lily. "You don't have to ask."

Prudence slid from her chair, landing lightly on her tiny feet. "Excellent. Her Majesty and I will leave you to pack." She stared meaningfully at Lily before moving to a door that led from Addison's rooms to the garden.

Closing the door behind her, Lily looked gratefully at Prudence. "Thank you."

The little girl waved her away. "It's nothing, but it's probably best she's out of the palace until we can resolve the matter. I'll check the damage and then see what she needs. There's a healer I know who works well with the mind."

"Thank you," said Lily again, and Prudence blushed, trying not to enjoy the gratitude. "Well I'd better—"

"I did need to speak with you on a separate matter, Your Majesty," said Prudence, stopping Lily from making her exit. "It's about the prophecies."

Lily felt a spike of irritation. She had been mulling over the frustration of not being allowed to know the contents of these prophecies for a while now. Prudence's explanation for why she couldn't know made sense, but still, Lily felt like it'd be easier if the little girl would just speak plainly.

"Are you here to deliver more veiled comments that aren't actually useful?"

Prudence flinched back, surprised at the switch from gratitude to snark. "We're snippy today, aren't we, Your Majesty? Hormones?"

Lily knew she was joking, but the enormity of what she was facing suddenly felt crushing. "The prime minister is oppressing the country. We're at war. People may or may not want me dead. Ezra is brainwashing my closest allies, and apparently the fate of the world rests on my shoulders. I don't need hormones to be snippy when apparently I'm responsible for saving everyone, but I'm not allowed to know what I'm saving them from or how."

Lily hadn't meant to take out her frustrations on Prudence, but the little girl abruptly turned from Lily, walking over to the pond. After a beat, Lily heard a sniff and felt guilt bubbling in her stomach. She had just made a small child cry. She needed to control herself better, no matter what was going on.

Lily moved slowly over to the pond, careful not to startle Prudence or crowd her space. "Look, I'm sorry. I shouldn't have yelled like that."

Prudence waved Lily off, producing a large handkerchief and blowing her nose loudly. "It's just allergies."

"Regardless," said Lily, crouching beside Prudence so that they were at eye level, "I shouldn't have taken my frustrations out on you. I am sorry. None of this is your fault. And if you can't tell me things, or speak plainly, then you can't. I know you're not doing it to mess with me. You're doing it because you need to. I trusted Lady Octavia, and I trust you."

Prudence wiped her tears and gazed up into Lily's eyes, her own big and full of happiness at Lily's words. "Thank you, Your Majesty. I accept your apology."

"Now," said Lily, relaxing and trying to sound upbeat, "what did you need to speak with me about?"

"Oh yes," said Prudence brightly. "It's about you saving the world."

"What about it?"

"In order for the world to live, you must die."

Lily stared blankly at Prudence. She had been starting to like the little girl, but sometimes she thought she might hate her.

19

THE ROOM WAS SWELTERING with no air circulating and so many bodies packed in together. Naomi thought she could hear everyone's heartbeats, and she definitely felt someone breathing hard on her neck.

"Keep it down," Juliana hissed, as if her crew could instantly calm their breathing. Or perhaps stop it altogether. Naomi tried to shift, craning her neck and watching as Juliana pressed her ear to the door, not content to rely solely on the girl who could sense if any living thing was nearby. What was her name? Ricky? Renee? Rose, that was it.

"Hush," Juliana whispered again, straining.

"It'd be easier if we could split up. Just saying," said Naomi, not for the first time.

"Well, Bella can only disrupt the surveillance assets in a six-foot radius," Juliana shot back defensively.

"And muffle the noise of the locks breaking," complained Naomi. "I'm surprised we've made it this far."

"I said Jo was a lock breaker," said Juliana, annoyed now. "What part of that had you misunderstanding that she would be breaking the locks?"

"I didn't think it would be literal."

"Well, you shouldn't assume."

Naomi sighed, frustrated that she hadn't been part of the planning, or able to interrogate the plan the way she would have liked before the mission began, and exasperated that Juliana refused to accept that the plan might not be going as intended. Naomi had assumed they would break into smaller groups and take different routes, and was severely dismayed to find the group of eight moving as a pack so that Bella could ensure no one was seen by cameras or magical abilities.

All of those issues coupled with the loud snaps and clunks of Jo literally breaking any locks they encountered into bits had Naomi convinced they would be discovered much sooner than she had estimated.

She took a deep breath. There was nothing she could do about it now, and arguing with Juliana would only make things worse.

"I'm not trying to criticise," she said softly, willing all the apology she could muster into her tone, but unable to help but add, "I was just saying all of this would have been good to know earlier."

She sensed Juliana warring within herself with the desire to have the last say, and, similarly to Naomi, realising that they needed to shut up and work together.

"With the restrictions and noise, it *is* likely we'll be discovered sooner," Richard piped up, voicing Naomi's concern. "But it just means we'll have to move a bit faster." His tone was upbeat and positive, and a good circuit breaker for the tension.

"It's refreshing to hear some positivity," commented Juliana pointedly.

Naomi closed her eyes and exhaled. *Be the bigger person.* "I agree. I'm sorry for being negative, Juliana."

She felt the stunned silence, but something else too. Disappointment, maybe?

"Oh. Yes, okay," said Juliana, less pleased that Naomi had expected. "I am too, of course. It's just... I quite enjoy our verbal sparring. Got quite a kick out of it in Parliament, you know, and now, well... I've missed it."

Naomi raised an eyebrow, surprised that the ex-foreign minister would see her as a worthy opponent. "I'm flattered that you chose me."

"Well, you know what they say, any port in a—"

"Why don't we save the banter for after the mission?" Naomi interrupted to keep Juliana from ruining the moment. "Our current strategy is... well, anyway, we need to get a move on."

"Quite right," said Juliana. She made a demonstration of listening at the door again, ignoring Rose, who stated in a bored voice that there was no one outside.

The group moved off, once again traversing the corridors in small bursts. Juliana took the lead, Rose telling her when she sensed people coming and Juliana using her power to make them suddenly feel that they should be elsewhere. Naomi followed Juliana closely, ready to step in with her own power should Juliana miss anyone, or if they encountered a group too large for her to influence.

Not far from their objective, they were looking for cover when Rose hissed that a large group was coming straight for them.

"You got it?" Naomi whispered to Juliana.

Juliana shook her head. "Negative. Too many, and I'm tapped out anyway."

Naomi could hear them now, moving towards the group. In seconds, they would be found and it would all be over. The device would be moved or destroyed and their group killed or captured. Naomi had a vision of her and Juliana in adjoining cells, no one coming for them.

"Over there," Richard hissed, pointing to what looked like a reception desk.

Without hesitation, the group hurried to the barrier, sliding in behind it as the footsteps rounded the corner and stomped right past them. They stayed frozen in place, listening intently and barely breathing as the footsteps and voices faded.

"We're clear," said Rose, earning her hisses from everyone to be quiet. She shrugged, clearly confident that no one was around to hear them, and stood up.

Juliana tentatively stood too, furtively looking around before moving over to Naomi. "Did you see her?"

Naomi nodded.

"It's a relief Claire didn't see us."

"Agreed," said Naomi. "Though I could have sworn she looked right at me as I slid behind the counter."

Spooked, the group hurried away, determined to cover the remainder of the distance to their objective in a single bound. Naomi kept glancing behind them, the hairs on her neck raised, feeling like someone was following them.

"There," said Juliana, excited.

Naomi saw the huge secured door looming at the end of the corridor. The group spontaneously broke into a jog, anxious now and desperate for the mission to be over. Without another word, Jo moved to the door and began working on the lock.

With effort, Naomi bit back the urge to provide helpful tips like "hurry up" or "keep the noise down". The nerves were getting to her. She never did well when she didn't feel in control. Naomi paced to the intersection of corridors, glancing down the one that crossed theirs. She didn't know what she'd thought the old Highacren Intelligence Agency offices would look like, but she hadn't expected this. Far from a normal office building, it seemed to be a labyrinth of corridors, all leading off goodness knew where. And so far, they'd only found storage and briefing rooms in the doors they had hidden behind. Where did everyone work?

A loud clunk sounded behind Naomi, causing her to flinch. Way too loud. But at least the coast was clear. For now. Swearing from Jo told Naomi the lock was still intact.

A minute later, Rose spoke just as Naomi heard them.

"People coming. Loads of them."

Naomi poked her head into the intersection, listening. She could hear boots coming from each direction, along with excited voices. She could catch sporadic words of "wall", "hole", and "breach".

"They've found the main breach. They know we're here," Naomi called back to the group.

"That was quick," said Juliana, eyes wide in alarm.

"Not really; your girl blew a giant hole in the wall."

"Not the time, ladies," said Richard, cutting off Juliana's response.

Juliana and Richard moved beside Naomi and they faced the opening together, ready to try to stop anyone coming down the corridors. The rest of the crew, other than Jo, who remained focussed on the lock, unsheathed small knives and weapons and stood ready behind the three in case their magic was insufficient. Naomi looked at Juliana and watched the realisation that their firepower really was inadequate dawn on her face.

"We got this," Naomi said quietly, but with feeling. Juliana looked back at her with resolve, nodding, a grim smile spreading across her face.

"Ready girls?" she said to her crew.

They all nodded, with Richard calling back, "Ready," in a slightly higher pitch than his usual voice.

The guards were close now. In a few seconds, they would turn their respective corners and see the intruders.

"Charlie team, return to the front and secure the breach," a voice commanded. Naomi heard the group approaching on the left halt and start moving back the way they came.

"Bravo, head to the centre. Secure the boss. Be prepared to escort him from the premises."

After a loud grunt of affirmation, the group on the right also withdrew.

"Alpha, reinforce Delta on the perimeter. I want roving patrols. This facility needs to remain secure."

"Yes ma'am," came the reply from the group that had been heading straight for the intruders. They had almost reached the corner that was the only thing preventing them from seeing Naomi and the team. A few more paces would have brought the groups face to face. But with a relieved exhale, Naomi listened to their boots clomping away, back in the direction they had come from.

"That was fortunate," commented Juliana, stunned. "What's this?" Juliana began grasping at something in the intersection.

Naomi turned to see Claire standing in front of them. Claire was chameleoning and therefore all the rest of the group could see was a slight shimmer. As a revealer, Naomi could see Claire easily.

"Don't shoot," Claire said as she materialised. Juliana, her girls, and Richard jumping as Claire suddenly appeared.

Naomi gave the corridors a quick scan, unnerved that Claire had gotten so close without spotting her.

"I've bought you some time, but not much. Once you have the device, leave through the south corridor—it is the least protected. Third door on the right leads to a maintenance room with a waste disposal tunnel. It's not glamorous, but it's a more secure, and certainly a more subtle, egress route than your way in."

"I don't see anything wrong with—"

"Thank you, Claire," Naomi cut Juliana off quickly.

"No time for that. Just get it done."

Naomi heard Claire moving away quickly to run further interference and felt a wave of conflicting emotions. Was she on their side? In that brief interaction, Naomi had sensed nothing other than the woman she had worked so closely with. She was the old Claire, no nonsense and down to business. And it had seemed like she was genuinely helping them. But Lily hadn't sensed anything to indicate Claire wasn't working with Ezra when she and Juliana ran into her in the Tower. What if Claire was setting them up? Though if that was the case, Naomi couldn't think of a reason for her not to have arrested them all right then. Even if she wanted them to get the device first, she could have just waited, hidden, and nabbed them as they exited the room.

Naomi desperately wanted to believe that Claire was on their side. That no matter what had been going on when Lily saw her, Claire was with them now. Naomi had grown close to Claire and she missed her friend.

But if that was true, then Claire was working as a double agent. That was so dangerous. Naomi knew what Claire was risking, and what would happen if she was discovered. She felt more afraid for Claire than she was for herself. Maybe they could somehow bring her with them when they escaped, but Naomi didn't know how she'd be able to find Claire again to rescue her.

A loud thump from behind accompanied by a satisfied whoop from Jo jolted Naomi from her thoughts and told her they were through. Juliana ducked into the vault, emerging triumphant moments later with the device held tightly.

They immediately moved to the southern corridor, Naomi and Richard in the lead now. No time for discussion. They were being hunted, and any guards they encountered would need to be dealt with.

"On your left," called Richard, flinging an arm to stop Naomi while pointing his other at two guards heading towards them from a side corridor. They froze mid-stride before falling to the floor, not moving.

Naomi looked gratefully at Richard, who simply smiled back before returning his gaze to the front. Naomi took a step towards the guards, squinting at their uniforms. *HSP? What were they doing here?* Juliana's brief had said normal guards were protecting this facility. Either they were here protecting someone, or Ezra had realised what Ava saw in his memories and security had been increased. *Hadn't Claire mentioned a boss?*

With no time to mull it over, Naomi let Richard know about the HSP and the group hurried down the corridor. Naomi and Richard quickly dispatched everyone they encountered.

"Locked," Richard called when they finally reached the third door.

"'Course it is," one of the girls muttered as Jo hurried over and got to work on it.

Naomi and Richard faced back the way they had been travelling, ready to protect the group from any threats that came. Rose was just behind Naomi, having been scanning their route for guards.

"Rose, can you—" Naomi started to ask her to cover their flank, but it was too late.

"Shit!"

The cry came from one of the half a dozen scrappy ex-prisoners who were now tussling with two HSP officers. The girls were all over the two officers, hanging off them, punching, kicking, and stabbing at the flailing forms.

"Richard?" Naomi asked.

"No good," he said, frustration lacing his voice. "I need to be precise, otherwise I'll dehydrate one of the girls."

Naomi swore. She didn't need the same level of precision, but the mound of wriggling bodies was making it difficult to get a bead on her targets. She squinted, concentrating on getting a good line of sight to one of the HSP officers.

A gap appeared and Naomi seized the opportunity, letting out a whoop of satisfaction as he fell before concentrating on the remaining threat. The lock snapped loudly behind her and she called to the girls to withdraw before she quickly pushed Jo through the door with her. Richard followed, assessing the room to ensure it was clear. The rest of the team started spilling through, a couple of the girls dragging Juliana.

"We need to get her body," Juliana argued, clearly upset.

Naomi peered outside and saw the two HSP officers on the ground, along with one of the girls. The pool of blood around her head and the angle of her neck told Naomi she was beyond help.

"There's no time," she said firmly to Juliana, moving past her to help look for the tunnel.

"It's okay, Jules," another girl said thickly to Juliana. "Debbie would have wanted it this way."

The other girls, wiping tears and snot, all nodded and offered grunts of concurrence.

Naomi's forehead creased, confused by the comment and wondering why Debbie would have wanted her body left in a top-secret governmental facility. But there was no time to consider what she'd meant, and Naomi concentrated on getting the team going, shifting the objects lining the walls to find the exit.

"Here," called Richard. He had moved some boxes, exposing a metal grate as tall as he was, secured by a simple padlock. Through the bars, Naomi could see a large, dank tunnel. There was no indication as to where it went, however it was clear by the smell that travelling through it was going to be unpleasant.

Jo ripped the small padlock off, and without complaint about the smell or the strange goo on the floor, they all rushed into the tunnel.

Halfway through was the first time Naomi really considered that Claire might be lying. It was pitch-black and stuffy, and with no way to know how far they'd gone, or how far there was left, Naomi started wondering if this wasn't an elaborate trap her old friend had laid out. She shook the thought away, reminding herself that if Claire was against them, she would have captured them outside the vault. It would have been much simpler to grab them there. No potential witnesses. The entire group could be disappeared and no one would know what happened to them.

Unless they don't want to get their hands dirty. If we die in here, no one will ever find us.

The girls started complaining. It was hard to breathe, and the smell was becoming overwhelming. The tunnel was large, but not so big that they didn't have to stoop, and everyone's back was hurting. The complaints increased as the tunnel suddenly grew smaller, requiring everyone to crawl through the thick muck coating the floor. She heard someone vomit behind her and was instantly grateful not to have to crawl through vomit on top of whatever she was already covered in.

Richard called something back, and a cheer went up. Naomi craned her neck, straining to see past those in front of her, and her heart lifted upon seeing light ahead. They were almost there.

A moment later, she tumbled onto the gravel under the tunnel, rolling to ensure whoever was behind her didn't fall out on top of her. Gasping for breath, Naomi resisted the urge to wipe her face with her dirty waste-tunnel hands.

"Okay Helen, you're up," called Juliana.

Naomi sat up, eyeing the huge chain-link fence standing between them and freedom. All that way through the tunnel and they were *still* inside the compound. Naomi glanced around. The tunnel had terminated three feet off the ground. Sludge from inside it seeped down into a small ditch that ran the length of the perimeter fencing.

Looking left and right, Naomi couldn't make much out. The fence line wasn't well lit, and to her left was a slight embankment, rising up and blocking her view. The buildings of the compound sat farther up the hill, away from the stinky tunnel. She frowned. It would be hard to see anyone sneaking up on them, though the lack of nearby buildings would hopefully mean they would hear any guards approaching.

Naomi moved to the fence, peering through. Large bleak buildings loomed out of the darkness, and Naomi visualised the map of the area she had looked at earlier. Warehouses and storage units. Perfect.

"No can do, boss," called Helen, the girl who had blasted their way into the compound. "I can only do solid objects. It won't work on this."

Naomi opened her mouth to comment that this information too would have been good to know before the mission, but sensing her, Juliana called, "Not the time, Naomi."

Instead, Naomi turned to Jo. "Don't suppose you can do anything with this?"

Jo shook her head. "Needs a lock."

Naomi nodded, expecting that answer, and turned to the group. "No one thought to bring wire cutters?"

The group of ex-cons shifted, embarrassed.

"I don't see you whipping a pair out, Naomi," shot back Juliana.

Naomi shrugged, nodding to herself at the fair comment. The relative silence was broken when loud voices came from their right. Naomi turned, straining in the dark to find the source. She heard more loud voices to their left, and Naomi shared a look with Juliana. The guards were closing in. It wouldn't be long now.

A loud sigh came from behind the group and Naomi turned, peering in the shadows by the tunnel and spotting a figure.

"Someone's behind us," Rose commented redundantly as a pair of wire cutters flew through the air, landing at Naomi's feet. A brief flash as the figure hurried away revealed their saviour. Juliana raised an eyebrow and Naomi nodded.

"Thank you, Claire," the group said together in soft, sing-song voices, all abashed to need her help again.

Naomi snatched up the wire cutters and got to work on the fence, carving out a small hole and bending the remaining wire back. "Come on," she urged as the sounds of the patrolling guards got louder.

Naomi gestured to Juliana, allowing her to go first, but Juliana shook her head. "I was the first in, and I'll be the last out," she said, urging her crew through the hole.

Richard followed the last of Juliana's women through the hole. Then he turned, grabbing the folded-back fence from Naomi so that she could squeeze through.

As Naomi ducked down, lights appeared over the slight rise to their left, the indistinct voices louder now, as if having spotted something. Naomi squeezed through and stood on the other side of the fence. A shout rang out, followed by shots.

"Come on," she urged Juliana unnecessarily. Juliana was already squeezing through the gap, with Richard letting the wire ping back into place as she stood.

"This way," Juliana said, leading the group away from the old HIA facility and into an alleyway. Naomi hoped the size of the hole might hold up their pursuers, but too soon she heard footsteps racing after them, and vehicles in the distance.

"We need to hide," she called to Juliana.

"Great idea," Juliana called back, sarcasm dripping.

"Well, let's do it quickly, okay? They're right behind us."

Naomi heard Juliana grunt, annoyed, but the pace increased and they continued snaking their way through alleys and between buildings until Juliana finally led them into an abandoned warehouse.

Naomi glanced around, looking for where they could hide. The building was enormous, but largely empty. A staircase led up to what looked like an office overseeing the expansive warehouse floor, but they would be found there in a heartbeat. Some boxes were stacked haphazardly in a corner, and Naomi moved automatically towards them. They didn't offer enough cover for the group, and they were coated in dust. The minute they moved anything, it would give them away. They were stuck.

Naomi turned to look at Juliana, who was at the door, listening to find out how close their pursuers were.

"We have time; they're in the next alley over," said

Rose. Juliana nodded at her, but continued listening for a beat all the same.

"Right," said Juliana, taking charge before Naomi could voice her concerns. "Shelly, can you hold them?" Juliana nodded at the boxes.

A younger woman, who Naomi assumed was Shelly, nodded and moved to the boxes, the group following. She raised her arms and the boxes rose into the air, remaining grouped as they were on the ground, dust and all.

Under the boxes was a trapdoor, which was opened by Juliana. Once everyone was safely down in the basement, Shelly, who had been guided down the steps, her arms still raised, concentrating on the boxes, carefully lowered her arms, putting the boxes and dust back over the trapdoor. Naomi had to give it to Juliana—it would look as if they had never been there.

Someone switched a light on and Naomi, relaxing slightly, looked around the group. "Is everyone okay?" The escape had been so frantic this was the first time she could check that no one had been injured.

"I've been hit," came Juliana's stoic voice.

Naomi rushed to the older woman's side. She was sitting on a box, clutching her thigh. There was blood all over her pants.

"Richard," Naomi called over her shoulder as she peeled Juliana's hands off the wound.

"Oh." Naomi slumped in relief. "It's just a graze."

"It's a bullet wound," argued Juliana, affronted to have her injury made light of.

"It's a minor flesh wound. You don't even need stitches."

Juliana huffed as Naomi turned to Helen, who was sitting next to Juliana. She had caught herself on the fence and had several gashes that looked at least as bad as Juliana's injury.

"Does it hurt?" Naomi asked Helen.

"Oh, I don't mind the pain," answered Juliana. "It's an honour to put my body on the line to save the country."

Helen smiled back at Naomi, shaking her head. Naomi rolled her eyes and looked over her shoulder to see if anyone else was injured. Some girls were huddled in a group, but the rest were recovering and drinking water.

"Richard?" she called again, surprised he hadn't already come to help.

"He's here," called one of the women in the group. "He just collapsed."

Naomi rushed over as another woman commented, "He doesn't look too crash hot, does he?"

Naomi slid onto the floor beside Richard, who looked pale and clammy. She joined the other two women in inspecting his body, looking for the source of his condition.

"I think he's been shot," said Jo, uncovering a small hole in his side.

Blanching, Naomi pulled Richard's shirt back on the other side of his body, where the bullet would have exited. His skin there was torn apart, with blood rushing out of the wound impossibly fast.

"Pressure," said Juliana, appearing at Naomi's side and putting folded shirts against both the entry and exit points.

"I think it's gone through his lung," Naomi told her, taking Jo's place and looking for something plastic to put over the hole.

The two women worked together, doing their best to stop the bleeding and bring Richard back, but nothing seemed to help. Their efforts became more frantic as the blood continued to leave his body and his face became increasingly slack.

Minutes passed, then an hour. Gradually, the girls from

Juliana's team faded away, sensing what Juliana and Naomi refused to accept.

"I think he's gone," Juliana eventually whispered.

Naomi nodded, sitting back, staring at Richard's damaged body. She hadn't known him that well, but it had taken strength to be handed everything he had ever wanted and then give it up to do what was right.

Someone brought over a sheet and covered Richard's body. Silently, they all retreated to their own spaces in the basement and waited for the guards to give up their search.

20

Tʜᴇ ᴍᴏᴏᴅ ᴡᴀs sombre for a celebration. Lily had asked for the Lodge to not be decorated, as a mark of respect for Richard, but she still thought it was important for her team to gather to celebrate their victory and blow off some steam.

Small tables had been assembled in the centre of the room, spaced to allow people to mingle, and they were covered in glasses full of various drinks and trays packed with finger food. Hastily mounted flat screens ringed the walls, each displaying different news feeds, but all currently broadcasting the prime minister's very public fall from grace.

Her advisors were chatting with each other, enjoying their success, but they all seemed mindful of the cost.

"To Richard," Jason eventually called, lifting his glass and turning to the group. "A true patriot and a loyal guardsman."

"To Richard," the room replied, lifting their glasses before drinking, all remembering the young man who had given his life.

"And to Debbie," toasted Juliana. "Though she

defrauded the government for most of her short life, she showed herself a true Highacren in the end."

"To Debbie," they all replied, before returning to the general chatter and watching of the screens, though a strained vibe still permeated the space.

"Maybe I should go," suggested Ava.

"Don't be silly," said Lily. "We wouldn't have been able to do any of this without you."

Ava raised an eyebrow, but simply sipped her drink. It was not the first time she had offered not to come, or to leave, having arrived to an icy reception from Lily's advisors. Lily was frustrated that they were not being more welcoming to Ava. It was true—they wouldn't have known about the archive without Ava, and she very much doubted they would have removed the prime minister quite so completely without it.

The drive Juliana's team had recovered contained the footage Ava saw through her connection to Ezra, and much more. There was no way for the prime minister to excuse away all of it. And so Lily felt Ava had every right to celebrate with them. She was definitely part of their group, no matter her nationality, and no matter who her father was.

Lily tried to tell herself that was the reason for her insisting that Ava stay. But she couldn't deny that she missed Ava. Missed being around her; missed being able to run things by her. She knew her advisors were uncomfortable about the connection between Ava and Ezra's implants, but Ezra had shut Ava's down. Thinking of the cost Ava had suffered doubled Lily's resolve for Ava to be included.

"Jolly good result," said Juliana, moving up beside Lily. "If I do say so myself. It will be good to get together to talk about next steps, Your Majesty. Sooner the better."

"We can do that now," said Lily. "We're all here."

"Yes," said Juliana reluctantly. She glanced pointedly at Ava. "Perhaps in the morning."

"If you feel that would be best," said Lily, trying to stem her anger, "but Ava will still be with us."

She felt Ava shift uncomfortably.

"Is that wise, Your Majesty?" said Juliana, glancing again at Ava and offering a quick, "No offence," which Ava waved away.

"We wouldn't be here without her," Lily said again.

"Of course, I completely agree. I don't mean to doubt Ms Harrington's motives. I'm merely nervous about the connection between her implant and her father's. How do we know he's not listening in now?" Juliana whispered the last part loudly.

"He turned her implant off. He can't hear anything," Lily said, frustrated.

"Did he?" Juliana asked, looking curiously at Ava. "Or did he turn off her ability to control it, leaving open his own access?"

Lily's eyes grew wide. She hadn't considered that. She looked at Ava quickly, seeing her expression mirrored. Ava hadn't thought of that either.

"Can he do that?" asked Lily.

"I don't know," said Ava. "I don't think so. I think I'd feel it if the implant was still on, even if I couldn't access the functions, but I can't say for sure."

Lily tried to put herself in Ezra's mindset. Spying through Ava's implant was absolutely something he would do. But surely if he was able to do that, he would have thwarted their mission to retrieve the prime minister's archive?

"Unless all of this plays into his larger plan," said Juliana softly when Lily posed the question out loud.

But what was Ezra's plan? Lily felt frustration flood her. None of it made sense, and nothing in the archive thus far had shed any light on what the man was trying to achieve. Why had he pushed her through the machine rather than kill her like he had her family? Why hadn't he had her killed during any of the dozens of opportunities he'd had? Why had he released her advisors? None of it made any sense to any of them, and so Lily had decided to stop focussing on trying to divine his plan. Rather than trying to stop his, she would simply focus on implementing her own.

"To Claire," said Naomi loudly, breaking the tense silence. "Without her help, we would have failed the mission and been captured or killed. She's a loyal ally and has been through who knows what kind of hell to see our side succeed."

"To Claire." The room toasted Claire before falling back into a charged silence, still waiting for Lily's decision about including Ava.

But Lily was distracted by the toast. Where was Claire now? No one had heard from her since the retrieval of the archive. Lily oscillated between thinking this was a good sign—if her cover was intact, she couldn't very well be calling them to let them know she was okay—and worrying that her silence meant she had been discovered.

Lily had been thrilled to discover Claire was on their side after all, but she worried about the dangerous situation her friend had placed herself in. *Did she place herself?* Lily's mind drifted to Addison, still absent as Prudence worked to ensure the damage to her mind was reversed. Had Claire been brainwashed too? Though if she had somehow shaken Ezra's control, as it certainly seemed she had, then she must have also decided to stay. Lily envied her bravery.

"To Reginald Toth," Juliana declared loudly, her champagne held aloft. "Without his narcissistic personality, there wouldn't be a handy archive of every single one of his evil deeds to display to the people and turn in for the judiciary's consideration. May his stay in prison be much, much worse than my own."

The group chuckled, joining in Juliana's toast. Though smiling, Juliana returned her heavy gaze to Lily, still wanting to resolve what to do with Ava.

"I might head off," Ava said quietly into Lily's ear.

"No," Lily turned, putting a hand on Ava's arm. "I mean, please go if you feel uncomfortable, but let's sort this out first. Juliana? What do you propose we do?"

"Well, there are a couple of options," said Juliana eagerly, clearly prepared for this discussion. "We have excellent surgeons available, some of whom studied in Meridia. We could try to remove the implant—"

"No!" Ava said, horrified.

"—or see if they could destroy it in place."

"Absolutely not." Ava glared at the idea, crossing her arms defensively.

"We'd make sure to get the best people," Lily assured Ava, curious about her heightened response. Sure, the idea of brain surgery wasn't pleasant, but didn't she want any chance of Ezra getting in her head removed? It wasn't like her implant was working anyway. "And our healers are top notch. Look at how well Jason's doing so soon after his injuries."

As Lily followed Ava's gaze, she realized her example probably wasn't as useful as she'd intended. His recovery was remarkable, but as Ava looked at him Lily saw her register the lost eye and metal leg. Her expression indicated she wondered what damage she might suffer.

"It's not that," Ava said, tearing her eyes away from Jason. "It's just... an implant is a part of you. We get them so young. It's like another limb."

"Yes, but yours doesn't work, does it?" said Juliana, slightly insensitively.

"No, but it could." Ava's eyes brightened, and Lily could see the strain of being without her implant. "I could learn to control it properly. Keep Ezra out. Maybe even figure out how to get into his. I could spy on him for our side."

Juliana looked away, as if embarrassed by Ava's naivety.

"I'm sure you could, Ava," said Lily gently, squeezing her girlfriend's hands. "But even if you could turn it back on and control it, that doesn't solve the issue of what to do until then."

"I'm not—"

"I don't think we need to jump straight to brain surgery," Lily interrupted Ava's protest, giving a pointed look to Juliana, who looked ready to argue. "How about we see if Jenkins can do something for us? Maybe he could—"

"Great idea, Your Majesty," said Juliana quickly. "But perhaps it's best not to hypothesise about what he might do. You know, given." Juliana nodded meaningfully at Ava's head.

"How does that sound?" Lily asked Ava.

"I think that's the best option," said Ava. "And when he makes sure my implant is safe, I can help bring Ezra down."

"You'd really turn in your own father?" Juliana asked.

Ava turned, squaring up to Juliana. "The person behind all of this is responsible not only for the hardships that have befallen Highacre, but for sending Meridia to war. That person is an enemy of both countries, and I am all for bringing them down. Even if it is my father."

Juliana nodded, accepting that Ava would do what was right, no matter the personal cost. But Lily noticed Ava's wording. There was still hope there that maybe her father wasn't the mastermind behind the terrible conspiracy.

Lily couldn't blame her, and though she felt sad that Ava wouldn't be able to work with her in the short term, she felt comfortable in her decision. She was sure Jenkins would be able to find a way to shut Ezra out. And until he could, there was a good reason for Ava to be kept away from the planning efforts.

"I might go," said Ava, smiling to let Lily know she wasn't upset. "See if I can find Jenkins now and get started."

"Okay," said Lily, giving her a quick kiss. "I'll see you later."

Lily turned her attention to a news report showing footage of the prime minister lazing in his office, a glass of whiskey in his hand.

"Sheep, that's what they are," he said happily to the room. Oddly, the footage showed the prime minister alone, despite the fact that Lily knew he had been talking to Ezra. So far, it appeared that Ezra had somehow erased himself from all the footage they had recovered.

Maybe he is spying through Ava's implant, and he erased himself from the footage rather than stopping us from stealing the archive?

"I mean, look at them. Compliant, fearful, stupid." The prime minister snorted into his glass. "They outnumber us significantly, but they're not even thinking about rising up against us."

Lily glared at the screen. The prime minister talking so disrespectfully about the citizens of Highacre was great for their purposes, but it still made her mad.

"I couldn't have asked for a better group of people to oppress," the prime minister continued to dig his own grave.

"And the HSP is such an easy to run organisation, even an imbecile like Toot can be in charge! Stupid fool."

Lily turned away from the footage of Reginald Toth burning every bridge he had and moved over to Jason.

"So, this is going out all over Highacre?" she confirmed, not for the first time.

"Yes ma'am," said Jason patiently. "Hudson sent it to every news outlet, and has it looping on all the main public access devices. He's actually enjoying playing with the HSP's attempts to stop it. Every time they try to take down one of his feeds, he takes over three more public access screens and adds the footage there. He says it's driving them crazy thinking it's something they're doing themselves."

"Won't be long until the HSP are out of his way," said Naomi. "They're too big to just shut down, but they're being dismantled as we speak."

"It's a shame none of the footage shows who he's talking to," said Giles, joining them and nodding up at one of the screens showing the prime minister guffawing at something. "I mean, we know it's Ezra, but the public doesn't."

"Surely they'd assume," said Naomi. "I mean, Ezra's his special advisor. Who else would he be talking to?"

"They can assume, but without him in the footage... you're right, Giles. It would have been great to bring them both down at once," said Jason.

Lily felt a momentary twinge of failure before she pushed it away. It was important to recognize what they'd achieved for the success it was. They still had Ezra to deal with, but the prime minister was gone, and with him a major bar to brokering peace with Meridia.

A smile brushed Lily's face as one of the screens broke away from footage of the prime minister to show political prisoners being released. She wiped a stray tear as she watched families sobbing as they were reunited.

Yes, this was a victory to be celebrated.

A young guard appeared at Jason's shoulder, whispering urgently in his ear. Jason nodded at the girl, who turned and left the room as quickly as she could. Jason put down his glass and put a hand gently on Lily's shoulder, guiding her away from the group.

"A large contingent of our troops were being transported through Highacren-held Disputed Region territory when they were ambushed by Meridian forces. The losses are... significant."

Lily's stomach dropped. Her sadness at the loss of life was compounded by her guilt as she looked around the Lodge. Her people were dying while she held a party to celebrate with her friends. What had she been thinking? What kind of leader was she?

"I want to go to the front line to visit our troops," she said firmly.

"Your Majesty—"

"The last time I asked, you said I shouldn't go at this stage of the campaign. But now is when they need me. When we're at our lowest. Not when things are looking up and it's safer. I want to see our troops."

Jason sighed, looking torn. "And they want to see you, ma'am. Nothing boosts morale like a visit from the queen to show she cares. Well, except maybe food. Or a letter from home." He shook his head. "What I mean is, they'd really appreciate it, but if you were killed... it'd be catastrophic. Especially now that the prime minister is gone. It's great that he is, but until he's replaced, it's just you. If you were to die now, there'd be no clear leader for Highacre, and the country would collapse. We can't win this war if we keep having to fight political battles for leadership at the same time."

Lily understood his point and waved Juliana over.

"How long until we have a new prime minister?"

Juliana cocked her head, thinking. "An election needs to be run, and that will take time. But in the absence of a prime minister, and in our case a deputy prime minister, given Minister Hastings was also caught up in the archive scandal, the party the prime minister belonged to may nominate an interim prime minister. I believe the party is meeting in the next few days to hold a vote."

Lily nodded, satisfied that it was all in motion. "And, er, are you still a member of the party? Given that you're now out of jail?"

"I am." Juliana nodded happily. "And they've even reinstated me as a member of Parliament after they saw some of the footage."

Lily couldn't imagine there were many contenders for the interim role. And likely not too many volunteers. The state of the nation at present meant a lot of hard work, with more opportunities to look bad than good. Not to mention actually running the country would eat into the campaign time for the eventual election.

Lily turned back to Jason. "In a few days, either Juliana will be acting prime minister or will be in a position to influence whoever is. I hear you about the risk, but I do think it would be feasible to visit the front line now. However—" she cut him off as he went to argue, "I acknowledge the cost benefit analysis you outlined before. Giles," she called the older man over. "Please coordinate with our generals. I want supplies sent to the front lines. Chocolate, ice cream, whatever the generals think the troops might want, and can be transported quickly."

Giles nodded and hurried off, obviously pleased to have an important task. Lily turned back to Jason.

"Where can I visit that is safer than the front line but might still be appreciated?"

Jason thought for a second and said, "Forward HQ is probably doable. It's close enough to feel the effects of the action, but protected enough that you should be fine, and the security overhead won't be crippling. Plus, the field hospital is there. You can visit the wounded."

Lily nodded. "Excellent. We leave in an hour."

21

THEY WALKED QUICKLY from the armoured vehicle to the headquarters building. Lily glanced around. For some reason, she had been expecting rows of tents with men, faces painted in camouflage, yelling into radios. But the headquarters building was in the middle of a compound with proper brick buildings, all of it surrounded by huge, thick concrete walls. She saw some large tents off to her right that Jason explained were transit lines for military personnel moving through the area, and to her right was a large open gym with men and women working out despite the heat of the day.

"This might be difficult, ma'am," Jason said again.

"I hear you, Jason," said Lily, reminding herself that Jason was worried about her and trying to keep the exasperation out of her voice. "I did consider how difficult a visit to a war zone might be when I was asking to go to the front lines."

"Yes, but hearing about the war and actually seeing it are two different things."

Lily paused as Jason opened the door to the building for

her. "I get that too," she said gently. "I'm as prepared as I can be, and I'll deal with whatever happens."

Jason nodded, seeming to accept that he couldn't protect her from everything, and stood back as Lily entered the HQ.

A crack sounded as the assembled soldiers and officers snapped to attention, saluting Lily as she entered. Panic gripped her. Was she supposed to salute back?

"Tell them to rest," Jason whispered from behind her.

"Thank you, please rest," she called out, relieved as they all relaxed.

A strong, efficient-looking woman with hair pulled into a severe bun approached, bracing up in front of Lily.

"Your Majesty, welcome to the DRHQ. We are grateful for your visit."

Lily shook her hand. Her grip was firm, but not crushing. "Thank you, Brigadier James. I appreciate you hosting me. I trust you will all be able to carry out your duties and I won't be too much of an impediment."

The commander of the Disputed Region Headquarters hesitated slightly, but Lily caught it.

"Perhaps I should put it this way. I know my visit will interrupt your business as usual. And I expect that if you, or anyone else escorting me, is required elsewhere, you will leave immediately and attend to whatever needs your attention. I am quite happy to entertain myself, or wait patiently in a designated location. And if I need to leave earlier than expected, I can do that too. This visit isn't supposed to be about me."

The commander relaxed, nodding appreciatively. "Thank you, ma'am. We are excited to have you here, and the team wants to show you what we do, but I will let you know if we need to focus back on the task at hand."

Rules set, the brigadier took Lily on a tour of the building, introducing her to men and women, some young enough to remind her of her younger sister April. They were doing everything from analysing intelligence on Meridian forces through to assessing targets for strikes. Lily had never really considered everything that needed to go into a war. Sure, Jason and her generals had tried to explain it to her, but Jason had been right; hearing about the process of war and seeing it in action were two very different things.

An aide walked swiftly over and spoke to the commander, who apologised and handed Lily over to her second-in-command before hurrying away down the corridor.

"Sorry, Your Majesty, they need the boss's decision on something time-sensitive," said the young man with a smile. "I'm Jake."

Lily looked at Jake curiously. He couldn't have been much older than she was, and yet apparently he was the one who would run things if for some reason the brigadier couldn't. Lily felt equal parts impressed by him and ashamed that she hadn't achieved more with her life.

"I imagine they need her decision on a lot of things all the time," Lily said, shaking his hand, amazed at everything under the brigadier's control on the base, let alone out in the field.

"It's not too bad," Jake said, leading Lily out of the building. "Brigadier James is a great delegator. She's clear with us about her direction and expectations and then leaves us to achieve her goals without micromanaging the details."

"She sounds amazing," said Lily, looking around the sprawling base.

"She is," said Jake, his respect for his boss clear. "So, if it's okay with you, ma'am, I figured while the boss is tied up, I'd show you the base and take you to the hospital. Then I'll bring you back here and she can brief you on the war effort."

"Great." Lily smiled.

The base was bigger than Lily had thought, even after the walk to the headquarters building. There were hard-standing accommodations alongside the transit tents she had seen, a smaller indoor gym with equipment that couldn't be stored out in the elements, and a large shop where people could buy snacks or toiletries and even books and games.

"What would you do if you needed to leave in a hurry?" Lily asked, gawking at the dining hall.

"We'd leave it all," said Jake, shrugging. "But realistically, the Meridians would have to fight through most of our troops to get here, so we should know they're coming in advance. And if they attacked us by surprise, then we'd stand and fight."

Lily glanced at the young man with admiration. He spoke so easily about needing to fight. Lily imagined gunfire opening up and bombs exploding all around and thought she'd be terrified. But it was just a fact of life for this young man. For all the troops. The base felt so secure; she imagined it must feel removed from the battles, and she asked Jake about the difference between being here and being back at his home base in peacetime.

"Oh yeah, this is like Bolivar Barracks, where I'm posted, just rougher. But we do go out. We conduct regular patrols and sometimes we need to push forward to relieve a unit when someone's hurt or killed, or they need a special-ist. And we do get the odd attack here—"

Jason coughed loudly, and Jake flushed red. "Oh, but not in ages. It's really safe here." He nodded enthusiasti-cally, and Jason rolled his eyes.

"What kind of attacks do you get here?" Lily asked Jake

while glaring at Jason. "I know you'll all take care of me, so I won't be scared."

"Mainly rockets. They send explosives over the walls. But the latest is self-driving trucks. They load them up and send them as close as they can get to the perimeter walls and then blow them up."

"But surely that doesn't do much with those walls?" Lily asked, staring at the massive blocks of concrete that were as wide as a car.

"With a big enough explosion they can do damage," said Jake seriously. "So far, they seem to be haphazard, and we have countermeasures to interfere with the self-driving capability as the trucks get closer to the base. But our intelligence analysts assess that the Meridians monitor the vehicles closely. They must have other explosives or forces stationed nearby in case one of their trucks manages to breach the wall, but we've not found them. Each time we locate a self-driving truck, we scan the area with different technologies. It's a good opportunity to try and defeat their cloaking abilities."

Jake paused, pointing out scorch marks, and Lily could also see a reinforced part of the wall, where another massive block had been erected behind a damaged one.

"How do they get so close?" Jason asked.

"They mask the radar signatures usually. Though, with the last one, they cloned one of our own truck's signals. Tell you what, if we had self-driving trucks, they'd probably be able to drive one of our own right in here and blow us to pieces. But as it is, anything without troops inside is identified quickly and dealt with."

Lily marvelled at the professional soldiers calmly discussing how the enemy might kill them all. She had a newfound respect for anyone who served in the military. They were either at the pointy end, fighting for their lives and those of their fellow citizens safe at home, or in a place like this, where it felt safe, but at any moment you might be blown up.

Jake opened a door into a huge building and Lily was dismayed to find it was the hospital. Part of her was hoping the hospital might be a smaller building, but she knew that was wishful thinking, given the casualty reports she read daily.

She was introduced to the doctors and nurses, and gave them the same direction—that their real job had priority. They were polite, but met this declaration with slight confusion, clearly comfortable with the idea that they would leave Lily in a heartbeat for something more important. Lily felt silly for even mentioning it.

Her personal embarrassment quickly faded as she was introduced to men and women, young and old, missing limbs or with head injuries, some now blind or deaf. She noticed Jason moving among the injured too, showing them his false leg and explaining to a young woman with an eyepatch similar to his how he got it to stop itching his nose.

She listened to the man in the bed in front of her bemoan that the war was with Meridia and therefore he wouldn't be able to get a bionic arm, as Meridia were the only ones with the technology. An older man in the bed next to him spat he couldn't be paid enough to take anything from Meridia, and the man without an arm should feel the same. She saw the conflict on the armless man's face and loudly said that the war was separate from medical treatment, and once an arm was available, there was no shame in getting one.

The amputee smiled at Lily, relieved to hear her say it was okay, but the older man scowled at her, turning over in his bed. *Guess I don't have his vote.* Then she smiled, remembering she wasn't elected. She still wasn't entirely comfortable with the notion of hereditary rulership, but she did enjoy not needing to worry so much about not offending anyone.

Eventually Jake reappeared, telling Lily that the commander was available to brief her now, and she reluctantly said goodbye, telling Jason on the way out that they needed to visit the hospitals more regularly. Expecting an argument, she was pleased when he nodded, telling her he'd already made a note.

Lily saw the brigadier waiting outside the conference room as she walked down the hallway. She peered into each room as they passed, coming to an abrupt stop at seeing several people in a large, empty room, all standing around, staring at nothing discernible.

Jason managed to not run into her, and Jake took a couple of steps back to see what Lily was looking at.

"They're in a battle immersion," said the commander, having walked down the hallway to join them. "They're currently reviewing the recent ambush, seeing what we need to improve and what we missed. Also looking for intelligence on Meridia."

"May I see it?" asked Lily. She was curious to see what an immersion device was like for a battle. How would they be able to review such a large event all at once? It had to be much more expansive than the normal ones. Also, knowing Jason was likely never going to let her near the front lines, this seemed like a safe way for Lily to learn a little bit about what combat was like for her people. Those she sent into danger.

She saw Jason and the commander exchange a glance, clearly not liking the idea.

"How about I put it this way," Lily said, remembering who she was and her position. "I would like to view the footage. Now."

The commander entered the room first, pausing the device and pulling her men out to brief them on the fact that the sovereign was about to join them. Jason followed Lily into the room, ushering her to the side and doing his best to describe to her what she was about to see. Lily listened, trying to steel herself for something she was sure nothing could prepare her for.

"Your Majesty, are you ready?" the commander called. Lily nodded, and the device was restarted.

22

Lily was standing next to a large convoy travelling along a dusty road, the landscape barren. Cliffs lined one side of the road, and the other opened into a plain that stretched out of sight. She could see the cliffs flattening out ahead of the convoy, and about four hundred metres down the road, they were gone.

The first difference about this immersion device that Lily noticed was that no one was moving. Every other time she had experienced a memory, it had started as soon as she used the device. When the sergeant started moving towards her on her left, he drew her focus.

"When they review battles like this, it's a lot of stop and start," Jason said beside her. "They can control the flow. Usually one person is designated controller. I suspect it's him."

"Ma'am, sir." The soldier nodded to them. "I am the controller for the review of this battle footage. As you will be joining us, we will simply run through it this time, but if you wish for me to stop or replay anything, please let me know. Also, if you wish to leave, you can do so as you would with any immersion experience."

The sergeant then explained to Lily that they could position themselves anywhere in the memory with this particular type of immersion device.

"I recommend viewing the battle from a high point." The sergeant pressed something on a small handheld device, and suddenly everyone who was viewing the memory appeared to be standing in mid-air, several feet above the convoy.

"It can take some getting used to, but the vantage is much better."

Lily nodded, feeling apprehensive about standing in mid-air, but reminding herself that her feet were firmly planted on the floor of a room in the headquarters. She looked around nervously before taking a couple of steps. Satisfied that she wasn't about to plummet to the ground, she started to enjoy it, feeling strangely liberated.

"Are you ready to start, ma'am?"

"Yes, thank you."

The sergeant used his device again, and the convoy sprang to life under their feet. Lily moved with Jason and the sergeant to the left, then walked alongside the vehicles, leaving enough distance to ensure a good field of view.

There were five large trucks in the middle of the convoy. Canvas covered the backs, where Jason said the troops being transported were. He pointed out the armoured vehicles, and the sergeant piped up, explaining that they were both escorting the convoy and contained strike teams that would operate out of the new forward operating base they were supposed to set up.

They fell into silence as the convoy kept moving, the three of them walking alongside it. They had started out at the front of the convoy, and as the vehicles emerged past the cliffs into the open, they were just beyond the middle of the procession.

"It'll start now," said the sergeant softly.

Lily still jumped as the rocket hit the lead armoured vehicle. She watched as the rest of the convoy tried to pull around it and escape, but then the first truck was hit. Not as protected as the lead vehicle, it exploded, spilling vehicle and body parts across the road. Lily could hear the screams of the injured now, but stopped the sergeant when he suggested to Jason he turn the sound off. She needed to hear them. She needed to experience what had happened.

She could sense the conflict in whoever was in charge of the convoy, of wanting to get the vehicles away, but knowing that doing so risked them being picked off along the straight road. They decided to fight the ambush, and Lily watched the vehicles arrange themselves to provide protection and firepower before the small figures of the soldiers spilled out, taking up cover and returning fire.

More rockets exploded, but she saw the Meridian forces now. Hundreds of them were firing from hastily dug trenches, with cover from snipers and rockets up on the cliffs behind the convoy. Despite knowing the outcome, Lily's stomach sank, seeing how outnumbered the Highacrens were. There seemed no way any of them could survive.

The immersion recording overlaid colours on the rounds used by the Meridians; blue for rockets, green for grenades, and red for bullets. Lily watched, morbidly fascinated, as the rounds swerved slightly, their firers having limited control via their implants.

"They're better over distance," the sergeant commented, seeing her focus. "More time to manipulate the trajectory."

Lily's attention was shifted by a barrage of bullets on her far left suddenly dropping to the ground and she watched as her countrymen and women fought with weapons and powers alike. A group of soldiers to her right protected a smaller man. Periodically, he pointed his hand at an enemy, who would drop to the ground, dead. It was a very useful power, but in an ambush of this ferocity, it was like a drop in a bucket.

Three soldiers in the middle of the convoy moved their arms in a complicated fashion and a tremendous gust of wind buffeted the middle of the enemy position. Some were knocked to the ground, others lost their grip on their weapons. It was short-lived, but provided a much-needed respite for the Highacren side, and Lily watched as several teams repositioned before the Meridians could recover.

As the battle raged on, Lily could hear Jason and the sergeant discussing it in the background, debating strategies and tactics. But her eyes were fixed on the people below. People falling, injured or dead. The frantic and chaotic nature of the fight. The amazing ability of the commanders to bring order to the chaos. Wrenching her eyes from her own people, she saw people falling on the Meridian side too. It seemed fewer were, though if that was only because they had superior numbers, she didn't know.

It all seemed so futile. All those people below her, maimed and killed, and for what? Land? Resources? Ego? Guilt swelled inside that she hadn't done more to stop the war. She should have run onto the parliamentary floor when the prime minister made the declaration and reversed it. She should have tried harder with President Taylor. She shouldn't have focussed on removing the prime minister so completely at the expense of those fighting.

She knew her decisions had consequences, but never before had they been laid out so plainly in front of her. She wiped the tear that spilled down her cheek, steeling herself. Those below didn't have the luxury of tears.

Lily noticed Jason and the sergeant moving closer to the

rear truck and followed them, seeing some of the soldiers huddled around, receiving orders.

"You can see the Meridians positioning to envelop the convoy now," said the sergeant, and Lily looked up, noticing for the first time that the Meridians were pushing their forces to the left and right. "The commander of the rear truck saw them moving and decided to push his team out to prevent their manoeuvre."

"But there's so few of them," Lily said, aghast, staring at the Highacren team of about fifteen people and then at the advancing horde of Meridians.

Both men remained silent, and Lily realised the commander was just doing his best to fight a losing battle. Something familiar caught her eye. One soldier, how he moved. Lily walked closer, staring at the soldier who was now huddled against the rear of the truck before he darted across an opening and pressed himself against the front of an armoured vehicle.

Lily wheeled on Jason. "What is Edmund doing there?"

Jason's focus whipped to the man Lily had been watching, his eyes going wide before his face fell. "It, er, was a misunderstanding," he said, sadness in his voice. "I wasn't paying attention, and he somehow decided that I'd suggested he join the army."

"What?" Lily was furious and terrified at the same time.

"I hoped he wouldn't, but I guess he did," Jason said, gesturing weakly at the image of Edmund.

Lily squeezed her eyes shut. It would be okay. There were survivors. And when she was attacked during training, Edmund had hidden in a haystack. He would be fine.

"I'm sorry," muttered Jason, clearly devastated to see Edmund there.

"No, it's not your fault, Jason," Lily said, her anger dissipating instantly. "He told me he always wanted to join the army. I've no doubt he was ready to read into anything you said to support what he wanted to do. Goodness knows he was happy to read into whatever I said."

"I should have stopped him," Jason continued, shaking his head.

"You couldn't have known. And besides, maybe he'll be fine."

At that, both returned their focus to their friend, who was pinned down as the Meridians grew ever closer. Suddenly, the intensity of the attack increased. Meridia, sensing victory, charged, trying to bring the battle to a close. From her vantage point, Lily could see that the minute the Meridian forces got around the vehicles, the Highacrens would be slaughtered.

"How did they get so many here?" Lily wondered out loud.

"That is something we are looking into, ma'am," replied the sergeant. "This is Highacren territory. The convoy is less protected than normal because of that. We have no idea how they managed to get a force this size into our territory without our knowledge. And then out again," he muttered.

"They escaped?" Lily asked, aghast.

"Those who survived," the sergeant said, a glint now in his eye as he looked back at the battle. Lily and Jason followed his line of sight, watching as the Meridians on the left made their final charge.

Edmund dashed out of cover, running around the front of the vehicle. He cried out, a pained, frustrated cry of anger. His arms stretched skyward. Lily's heart dropped. She couldn't imagine a way for Edmund to survive.

A sudden shadow fell over the battle, then an intimidating rustling sound, like a blanket being flapped right next to your ear, coupled with a weirdly terrifying cacophony of chirping.

Thousands upon thousands of tiny birds were shooting through the sky, called to the battle by Edmund. The fighting all but stopped, the soldiers stunned by the bizarre sight. Edmund cried again, this time in pure anger, and pointed his arms at the advancing forces.

As one, the birds aimed themselves at the Meridians, like a wave of self-guided arrows. Lily heard the cries of the Meridians as the birds flew into them at top speed, piercing and stabbing and pecking. She saw birds dive-bombing the attackers, clawing at their eyes. Others lay dead, embedded in the bodies of their kills.

The Highacrens pressed the advantage, firing into the Meridians left standing, and it wasn't long before the invaders retreated, still harassed by the flock of tiny weapons. A cry went up on the Highacren side, the victory made sweeter by the prior certainty of defeat.

Lily grinned at Jason, who returned it. Edmund was a hero! And to think, he'd been teased mercilessly about his power, and here he was, saving a doomed convoy of troops with it.

Lily turned back to watch him celebrate.

But he wasn't celebrating.

He was lying on the ground.

Motionless.

Lily choked back a moan as her hand flew to her mouth. It wasn't real. It couldn't be real. Something wet dripped onto her shirt, and she realised she was crying.

Edmund had left the safety of cover to direct the horde.

He had sacrificed himself for his fellow soldiers.

Lily forced her eyes to remain with Edmund's body, trying to convince her mind that it was true.

Edmund was dead.

I never got to say goodbye.

23

THE FIRE CRACKLED COMFORTINGLY in the main fireplace of the Lodge. Lily watched the shadows dance across the walls. She was completely exhausted. Wanting to project strength for the soldiers, she had pulled herself together earlier, furiously wiping her tears away. But now, back in the privacy of her rooms, all she felt was devastation.

"He wouldn't have joined if not for me."

"That's not entirely true. He always wanted to join the army," Ava countered gently.

"Sure, but if I'd stayed engaged to him, he wouldn't have been able to."

"Technically, you were still engaged to him," said Ava. "The intervening factor here is that we got pushed through that machine and stuck in your home dimension. If you're looking for someone to blame, this is another thing that can be laid at the feet of the person behind all of this—my father."

Lily sat up from the couch where she'd been lying in Ava's arms, turning to look at her. "I'm sorry, I didn't mean—"

Ava waved Lily's apology away. "I wasn't intending to take the focus from you. It's important that you let it out when you can. Especially if you want to maintain a stoic appearance for your followers and advisors. You need somewhere safe to feel your feelings."

Lily lay back, pulling Ava's arms around her. Sadness and grief rolled through her body, filling her completely and threatening to drown her. "First Richard, and now Edmund."

"I didn't really know Richard," Ava said, slowly tracing circles on Lily's arms. "But he did help save us that time in the training yard."

"Yeah, along with Austin. At least Richard saw he was on the wrong side. I don't think Austin will ever be able to acknowledge that about himself."

"Not surprising," said Ava, her tone harder. "Given he's a war criminal. I don't usually associate high moral development with people like him."

Lily nodded, though she felt more conflicted. She had known Austin better than Ava had, and it was hard for her to reconcile the genial man who wanted to help, who wanted to serve his country, with what she now knew he'd done. She always thought war criminals were pretty straightforward. Devils. Monsters. And she supposed that was what Austin was. But he'd never acted like that with her. He just didn't seem evil. Lily was hit with an image of herself being interviewed on the news. She'd be the neighbour who said he seemed so nice and quiet. How could she still be so naïve?

Shaking her thoughts away, Lily returned her focus to the present—on lying on the couch with Ava. On the lazy patterns Ava was tracing on Lily's skin with her fingers. On the feel of Ava's skin under her own.

If only this could be the main focus of her life. Shouldn't that be what your twenties were like? Where the biggest issues were navigating relationships and dealing with heartbreak. Not leading a country at war and being responsible for millions of lives.

Her mind flicked to Jason. He had remained in the Disputed Region to discuss options with the brigadier, but messaged her a little while ago, letting her know he was back and meeting with the war council. The brigadier had identified a heavily guarded signal tower that intelligence now suggested was key in relaying signals essential to the Meridians' implants. If they could take the tower out, Meridia's combat power would be significantly reduced, and they would have to at least engage in peace talks.

But where Jason seemed buoyed by this plan, Lily felt like she was drowning in dread. Heavily guarded meant high casualties. And if this one tower really was so key to Meridia's success, they would no doubt throw any and all reinforcements at it if they even thought Highacre was considering launching an attack. Lily couldn't imagine the operation not coming with a huge cost, and that was without a guarantee of success.

Still, if there was a chance at peace, they had to take it, right? Even with the losses Highacre might suffer in this operation, the cost of ongoing war would be catastrophic in comparison. She squeezed Ava's arm tighter.

Her mind returned to Edmund unbidden. She suddenly felt guilty that he was dead, and she was lying here with her girlfriend. Then Richard's face entered her mind, and the guilt intensified that she was more upset about Edmund because she knew him better when Richard had sacrificed his life just the same.

Her stomach dropped as she thought about the hundreds of soldiers she watched die in the immersion replay of the battle. The thousands who had died on both sides during the conflict so far. Did their lives matter less than her friends? She was so focussed on her personal grief she had barely thought about her people. Sure, she read the reports and felt sickened by the numbers, but what of their families? How many of her people were crying in their houses having lost a parent, sibling, or child?

"I don't think this is the last of it," Lily whispered. "I'm so scared we'll lose more before the end."

Ava's hand stilled briefly as she hesitated. Eventually, she said, "I don't want to insult you with pleasant lies."

"Sometimes pleasant lies are nice," said Lily.

"Oh, well, in that case, Meridia will wake up tomorrow and decide they've had enough of this war business. And Ezra will decide that it was wrong to be an evil mastermind, and he misses home and wants to move back there and find a remote shack where he'll enjoy the quiet life and never bother anyone again."

Lily smiled, but it faltered quickly. *Ezra.* Was he listening in right now? Jenkins's preliminary assessment, delivered direct to Lily when she arrived home, was that he couldn't tell if there was a way for Ezra to use the implant to spy, but he was sure he could create something to block it if he was. What Lily gathered, from the excited explanation that had followed, was that Jenkins would build something that would interfere with certain frequencies.

"It will be vulnerable to attacks on the same frequency, but it's a Meridian frequency, so unlikely they will attack it—"

"Jenkins," Lily had interrupted. "Can you do it?"

"Yes, of course."

"Great. Please make this device as a matter of priority."

Jenkins had nodded and gone to leave.

"Jenkins," Lily stopped him. "It's late; you can start in the morning."

He'd given her a weird look, as if wondering why he wouldn't *want* to start right away, and left, muttering excitedly to himself.

Lily brought herself back to the present. She wished Ava's lie were true. That everything would magically resolve itself and they were just two women, in love, spending time together.

"Perfect," Lily said. "Can we sleep in then?"

She felt Ava hesitate again. "Am I sleeping over then?"

"If you'd like," said Lily, trying to sound casual while the butterflies in her stomach ramped up.

A high-pitched yip grabbed their attention, and they turned to see Kevin sitting next to the couch, his tiny tail wagging like a dragonfly's wings. When Lily didn't immediately reach down to pick him up, Kevin yipped again before launching himself at the couch, getting his front paws over the seat, his rear legs scrambling to push his body up.

Eventually, he pulled himself over and promptly bounced up onto Lily's stomach, slamming his front paws down and giving another yip.

Lily obliged, patting him and moving her fingers over the spots he guided her to while murmuring at him. She felt Ava tense beneath her and remembered Ava was uncomfortable being underneath Kevin, lest he blow up into an enormous version of himself, crushing her beneath him.

Lily sat up, still cuddling her fluffy little buddy.

"What are you so excited about? Huh? You're so cute, yes you are." She could practically feel Ava roll her eyes, but she ignored her, fussing over Kevin, who was playfully trying to catch her fingers with his mouth. "We're having a sleepover, aren't we? A sleep over!"

"Yip!"

Ava chuckled. "I mean, if Kevin's sticking around, maybe I'll go back to my apartment."

Kevin gave a playful little growl.

"You will not," said Lily.

She stood, deposited Kevin on the floor, grabbed Ava's shirt with her other hand, and pulled her into the bedroom, kicking the door shut with her foot.

24

CLAIRE KNOCKED TWICE and opened the door, peering cautiously around.

"You asked for me?"

"Yes, yes. Come on in. Shut the door."

Claire moved cautiously into Ezra's office, closing the door carefully. She took one last glance at the corridor before the door shut. Her mind, sensing that something was off, was screaming for her to run. Having shut her only real escape route, Claire plastered a pleasant smile on her face and turned towards Ezra, who was sitting comfortably behind his desk.

She concentrated on her breathing, trying to slow her heart rate. She was worried, but trying to convince herself she was just being paranoid. They hadn't really spoken since the device was stolen, as the focus lately had been on moving from the now ex-prime minister's offices and into their new base—the old HIA building. The building the device had been stolen from.

But surely if Ezra knew, or even suspected, that Claire had any involvement in the raid, he would have mentioned it before now. Right? She looked at his face, checking his eyes for any hint that she'd been made. Nothing. The man was just so damn hard to read.

"All the critical infrastructure is up and running," she began when Ezra gave no indication that he would start the conversation. Best to keep it light. "And most of the staff are settled in. They are a little curious about what their role will be now that the prime minister has been arrested, and so presumably your position is defunct."

Shit, shouldn't have drawn attention to the raid.

"Yes, that was most unfortunate, wasn't it? I mean, I must say I didn't really care for the man personally. Even so, he had his uses. And his untimely demise was... inconvenient."

Claire froze.

He knows.

She forced herself to respond appropriately, looking concerned. Maybe he didn't know. Maybe he was just venting about the unfortunate events. She noted he didn't engage at all about his staff and what they might do now. And his voice had an edge, though that could just be his frustration at things not going his way. When was the last time that had happened?

Still. Claire had reviewed the camera footage and was sure that she had either been close enough to be covered by Juliana's disruptor or her magic had ensured she had blended into her surroundings. But the screen was small, and she hadn't been able to spend much time reviewing the footage. Had she missed something?

Stop it. Spinning out of control wasn't going to help. *Assume he doesn't know until he proves you wrong.*

Ezra was still staring at Claire, his eyes hard.

He can't know, can he?

The mood was broken by Ezra's phone ringing. He snatched it up, answering immediately.

"Oh, you are? Brilliant. Thank you."

Hanging up, Ezra grabbed a remote control and pressed a button, turning on the large screen mounted on his wall.

Claire's mind flashed back to the day she had pressed that button. The day she got her mind back. It was just after she'd seen Lily at the Tower. She had entered Ezra's office to drop off some documents. The office was empty, with Ezra off who knew where doing who knew what. Claire had gone to place the papers on his desk when something caught her eye.

A folder, lying where she was about to deposit her own. She'd never have touched it, but something about it caught her eye. A sheet, peeking out from under its cardboard cover.

Memory manipulation results.

A deep curiosity that had not been quelled by whatever had been done to her caused Claire to reach out, flicking open the folder. She'd scanned the page, quickly becoming alarmed at what she was reading.

We're brainwashing people?

They'd had lessons about the subject in the academy, and it was the only part of her training that had given her the heebie jeebies. The idea of someone manipulating her mind. Changing her thoughts, opinions, memories. The essence of who she was. Without her even knowing.

Unsettled, she'd reached out to pick up the folder to read more of the contents. Her finger hit a button under the folder, and the screen mounted on the wall lit up. The image was split into twelve tiny boxes, all showing different camera feeds from different cells.

Claire had known they had some prisoners in the building, but not that many. And she had not seen those cells before. Half of the prisoners had someone sitting behind them, doing something that was clearly causing them extreme pain. The other half were positioned so that they couldn't avoid watching screens on the walls of their cells. Something bright and colourful was blaring at them.

The images were alarming, but there was something else digging at Claire's mind. Something was familiar about the images. As if someone had similarly sat behind her back. As if she had been bombarded with propaganda.

The memory crashed through and Claire had dropped to her knees. Her eyes swivelled, alarmed as she tried to make sense of the conflicting memories. As she'd regained control, she worried at how long she'd been in Ezra's office, and hurriedly turned the screen off and left.

***

Now the screen lit up again, grabbing Claire's attention, and showed just one camera feed. The room was dark. One of the underground cells. And sitting in the chair in the middle was an old man being tortured.

Her mentor.

She had spoken to him just that morning. Claire's brain went into overdrive trying to determine what the old man could tell them, and what it meant that Ezra was showing her. Nothing good, that was certain. Ezra was watching her closely, looking for any reaction. She fashioned her expression into one of surprise and shock, with just a hint of confusion as to why he was showing her this. Escape was seeming less and less likely. Maybe she could talk her way out of this?

Please don't tell them anything. She willed her mentor to stay strong.

Ezra pressed another button, and the sound of her mentor's screams filled the room. Whatever they were doing to him was causing an enormous amount of pain. It seemed to go on forever. Screams, questions, more screams. After what felt like an age, the old man had enough.

"Okay, please stop! I'll tell you everything!" her mentor cried.

She made sure her worry remained internal. *Don't react.* He wouldn't sell her out. He'd make something up. Say it was just him.

"I remembered," he sobbed. "I remembered everything. It came back about a week ago. I've been trying to sabotage you ever since."

His head hung low as his body was wracked by huge, heaving sobs. The torturers worked on him some more, interrogating him about what he had done and who he was working with. Eventually they gave up, and one moved to a phone mounted on the wall. Seconds later, Ezra's line rang. It drove Claire crazy that she couldn't hear what was being said.

Ezra's expression remained neutral. Eventually he simply said, "Approved," and hung up. Claire watched as the torturer also hung up and nodded at his colleague, who moved back towards her mentor.

He didn't give me up.

Ezra switched the screen off before Claire could see what they did next. She allowed shock and dismay to cross her features.

"He turned against us. I'd never have believed it without hearing it from him," she nodded at the screen as if grateful Ezra had shown her that. "They broke him quickly."

Ezra nodded. "They did indeed. We've developed a new technique to... encourage people to be truthful. Much faster than traditional methods, and far less messy. It seems to be working well." Ezra looked directly into Claire's eyes. "Have you been truthful, Claire?"

Her stomach sank. Her heart began racing.

He knows.

Claire managed a look of polite confusion. "Of course."

"The break-in was regrettable," Ezra said, apparently switching topics, his voice genial again, his gaze softer. He stood, crossing casually to the window and looking out over the grounds. "Highly regrettable."

Claire mentally ran through options for escape. Could she simply run out the door? He'd radio his guard, and she'd be caught in an instant. That's assuming he hadn't put guards on the door after she entered. The window then? She could push him out of the way and dive out. But she was fairly certain the glass was impenetrable, and either way, the fall would kill her.

Might be a better way to go.

Subdue him? That might be the only option. Either knock him out and make a break for it, or take him as a hostage until she was out of the compound.

"Security was terrible, I agree," she said, matching his tone and appearing frustrated. "But it's been rectified, and there's no chance of a similar failing. I am personally overseeing the remediation and have selected certain personnel for retaining and upskilling."

Ezra turned, smiling at her. "Thank you, Claire," he said warmly. Pointing the remote, he turned the screen back on. It was footage of the break-in.

Her body screamed at her to run. To do whatever she had to do to escape. But her mind kept her glued to the spot. She'd reviewed this footage. She was clear. Wasn't she?

The footage showed Claire directing the HSP away from the intruders, though she saw nothing to indicate she was doing anything other than commanding the response. Having cleared the area, she saw herself walk out of the camera range, and then nothing. Ostensibly she had moved somewhere else in the compound. In reality, she had cloaked herself using her chameleoning talent and moved into the radius of whatever had kept Juliana and Naomi from being seen on the cameras.

Why was he showing her this? Juliana's team was undetectable. Claire looked at the footage closer. Had there been a brief shimmer? She didn't think so. *But then why show me?*

The footage shifted, now showing the fenced area where the group escaped. She watched as wire cutters appeared from nowhere and flew across the screen before disappearing again. As the footage repeated, slower this time, she did see a brief, distinctive shimmer where she had been standing.

Chameleoning wasn't the same as invisibility. You were still visible, just taking on the appearance of your surroundings. The shimmer was a dead giveaway, but then, she wasn't the only one with the power.

Claire's brain worked overtime trying to identify a way out, quickly discarding weak argument after weak argument.

Ezra pushed another button, displaying an infrared overlay. *Since when did we have infrared surveillance?* Claire stared at the red spot that had lit up, noting that Juliana's group remained undetected. She was used to seeing indistinct blobs when infrared cameras were used. But this one showed her silhouette clearly. She could even see the tight bun on the back of her head.

Before she could say anything, Ezra pressed the remote again, and now the screen showed his office. Claire flinched, turning around and trying to spot the camera she hadn't known was there. She watched as she went to drop off her documents and accidentally turned the screen on.

Her mind continued scrambling for an excuse, an explanation, a way out. But it found nothing.

"Well, shit."

"Indeed," Ezra replied. He walked casually back to his desk before taking a seat and leaning back, his fingers steepled in front of his face as he considered Claire.

"Claire, Claire, Claire." He shook his head. "What *are* we going to do with you?"

25

THE TWO WOMEN sat on the floor of the office, surrounded by papers. Some, they themselves had emptied from drawers and cabinets, but most had already been there, discarded during the exodus of the prime minister's staff.

Having received the all-clear from Prudence, Addison had re-joined the fold. Lily had asked her to search Ezra's parliamentary office for anything that might help incriminate the man. Though she didn't say it, Lily felt Addison had the best chance at finding something. After all, she had known him better than most.

Lily had missed Addison, and with nothing else to distract her from her worries, she had decided to join her friend. They'd completed a quick check of the office to see if there was anything of obvious value, then resigned themselves to scanning the abandoned documents for any evidence. Anything to incriminate Ezra.

"So, overall it's been great," beamed Addison, who had been regaling Lily about her time with Prudence and Cyril. Lily was just happy to have her friend back. Discovering she was the oracle, coupled with whatever the healers had done, and spending time with Prudence and Cyril seemed

248

to have restored the old Addison, which made Lily's heart happy.

"Prudence takes some getting used to," said Addison thoughtfully, dropping another document into the discard pile next to her. "She's so serious for a five-year-old. But she's really lovely. A bit like Lady Octavia. You can tell they were close. And Cyril seems nice. Very quiet. Doesn't say much. But he doesn't seem to mind if I natter away at him."

"What is Cyril doing at Prudence's house?" asked Lily, frowning, trying to figure out what the document in front of her was about.

"You know, I'm not sure," said Addison, lowering her document as she considered the question. "He doesn't seem like he really wants to be there. You know, he just keeps to himself. But I guess he's visiting. Probably a good thing. Can't live all by yourself for hundreds of years and not go a little batty."

They fell into silence, each focussing on the various pages and documents. The task was boring but Lily was enjoying having the old Addison back. It felt relaxed and easy, just like it had before Lily had been pushed through the machine. Addison sighed, dropping a thick bundle of paper into the ever-growing pile to her right.

"These documents are all so confusing and wordy. Why can't they have a simple description of what they are right up the top? No wonder politicians take so long to get anything done. They're spending all their time trying to figure out what these documents are."

"I know," agreed Lily. "I mean, what even is 'a treatise on the symbiotic relationship between the electromagnetic ion cyclotron wave and solar particle events'?"

"I got lost halfway through that!" laughed Addison as Lily dropped the paper on her discard pile, giving it a disgusted look. "I mean," Addison said, picking up another document and considering it, "it's pretty unlikely Ezra left anything incriminating here. At least nothing that incriminates him."

"I agree," sighed Lily. "This is probably pointless. I don't expect we'll find a document titled 'How I Took Down Highacre and Why'."

Addison laughed again. "That's a good title for a fiction book, because he hasn't taken down Highacre, and he never will. Not with you here to stop him." She beamed at Lily.

"Not with *us* here to stop him," corrected Lily. "We're all a team."

"I know we needed to get rid of Reginald, but it feels like we spent so much time focussed on him, and almost none on Ezra. And Ezra is the real threat!"

"I know. Toth needed to go so we'd have a better chance at stopping the war, but you're right. It feels like we got caught up in the distraction and now the real bad guy has gotten away."

"He won't get away. We'll stop him."

Lily heard the feeling in Addison's tone. This was personal for her. Ezra had used her and then thrown her away.

"What do you think his endgame is?" Lily asked. "I mean, you knew him best of all of us. What's your insight into the man?"

Addison flushed and stared at the papers in her hand. "I don't think I really knew him at all."

They lapsed into silence, and Lily wondered if she shouldn't have said anything.

Eventually, Addison sighed. "This is why I was no good as an intelligence agent. I really have no idea about Ezra. Honestly, the man I knew is not the man who is behind all this. It's like he was a mirage. He doesn't exist. I thought I knew Ezra. I thought we were friends."

"We *were* friends."

Both women jumped, turning to see Ezra striding into his old office, with Austin at his side. Lily stared at Austin, who was looking everywhere but at Lily. Panic gripped Lily's chest. The last time she saw Austin, he'd tried to kill her. Was this it? Had Ezra decided she had outlived whatever usefulness she had? Although, Austin *was* the head of the HSP. Perhaps Ezra would simply have her arrested. Lily wondered which would be worse.

How about we don't find out?

Lily steeled herself, shaking off her initial panic. Though she hadn't had as many lessons with Prudence as she would have liked, the little girl was an effective teacher, and Lily was able to shield herself against most of what her advisors could throw at her. Would her shield defeat a blast of energy of the kind Austin could wield? She supposed she would soon see.

The two men looked out of place, standing together. Ezra, the refined businessman, and Austin, the battlefield soldier turned war criminal. It was jarring, unlike when Lily had seen Ezra with Claire.

Claire!

Lily's mind again turned to her friend. Why hadn't Ezra brought her with him? Had he discovered she was a double agent? Or had he simply brought Austin to drive home how many of Lily's advisors were now seemingly on his team? Maybe he'd bring Jeremy Toot next time. Lily hoped not. Toot annoyed her.

She glanced towards the door. Naomi had accompanied her and Addison to the Tower, but having cleared the offices to ensure the place was empty, she had then positioned herself in the reception area near the elevator and fire exit—the only way to access this floor. But then, how did Ezra and Austin get in without her seeing them? Lily blinked, realising for the first time that Ezra and Austin had come from within the offices, not from the direction of the reception desk.

A secret entrance?

"What are you doing here, Ezra?" Lily asked, projecting all the confidence she could muster into her voice. "Forget something?"

Ezra laughed easily. "No, Your Majesty. No, this place has been thoroughly cleaned out." He picked up a document at random, looking at it with passing interest before letting it drop back to the floor. "But old habits die hard, and I'm used to reviewing the efforts of my subordinates. It seems they have left you somewhat of a mess."

Lily turned her gaze to Austin, who still wouldn't meet her eyes. "And how are you, Austin? Has your HSP destroyed many families today?"

Ezra laughed as if Lily had made a witty remark, answering before Austin had a chance. "No, of course not. The HSP are keeping the people safe." His eyes twinkled, enjoying the irony of the propaganda of the organisation he had created to enable his enemies to destroy themselves.

Lily focussed again on Austin, jerking her head at Ezra. "Gonna let your Meridian buddy do all the talking for you?" Austin flinched, but didn't respond. He continued staring fixedly away from Lily. It bothered her that he wouldn't look at her, given all the time they had once spent together. She worried that he was distancing himself. Maybe Ezra really did want her dead this time. "Why won't you look at me, Austin? Ashamed of something?"

"No," Austin muttered, but he still wouldn't meet Lily's eyes.

Lily glanced at Ezra, who had picked up some ornament and was turning it over in his hands, looking at it with benign interest.

What was he doing here? If he wanted Lily dead, he'd have killed her before she even noticed he was there. He'd had the jump on her, the element of surprise. Even if he wanted her to know he'd won, he should have killed her by now. But then, what did he want?

Think!

But Lily had never been able to figure out what the man wanted. His plan seemed so alien to Lily, she couldn't even begin to try and put herself in his head. He seemed to have layers upon layers of schemes and multiple feeds of intelligence.

Wait... that's it!

Now that she looked closer, Ezra's eyes kept flicking to Addison. He didn't know that she had recovered. Perhaps she had missed a meeting? Lily stood a little straighter. And if Jenkins's block had worked for Ava's implant... he'd lost his lines of information on Lily's activities. And the blind spot had forced him to come out himself.

"Let's cut to the chase," said Lily, staring at Ezra, a sly smile on her lips. "Did you come here to see me, or Addison?"

Ezra's eyes flashed to Lily, the twinkle gone, his smile slipping briefly.

"Because Addison's recovered from her stint in prison," Lily continued meaningfully. "She's back to her old self."

"Well," said Ezra, fixing his smile but unable to make it reach his eyes. "Isn't that just wonderful."

"It really is." Lily beamed. "And Ava's feeling more herself too. Have you spoken to your daughter lately? I thought you missed her?"

Ezra's eyes grew harder, boring into Lily with an intensity that had her instincts screaming to look away. But she forced herself to hold his gaze.

"Oh, no, that's right. You don't care about your daughter. You used her, and then when she served her purpose, you switched her implant off. How could you do that to her? Your own daughter?"

Ezra's hand twitched toward his pocket, but otherwise he didn't respond.

"No snappy comeback?" Lily wondered if it was wise to taunt him, but Ezra always seemed impossibly unflappable, and having found a chink in his armour, she couldn't help but poke. "You've lost your live feed. Your brainwashing doesn't work. And your best ally is a war criminal."

Lily braced herself, sure she had gone too far, but Austin flinched at the description and spoke before Ezra could.

"I might have made some mistakes," Austin began. He closed his eyes briefly, giving an almost imperceptible shake of his head and finally looking directly at her. "I *have* made some mistakes," he corrected. "But I always thought I was doing what was best for Highacre. I love Highacre. I'm loyal to Highacre."

"Like hell," said Addison, glaring at Austin.

"I am," Austin said, looking imploringly at Addison before returning his focus to Lily. "I'm loyal to Highacre. And I'm loyal to you."

Before Lily could blink, Austin drew his pistol and turned, aiming at Ezra. A small pop made Lily jump, and she and Addison both let out short screams. It was quieter than she'd expected a gunshot to be, but still loud in the small room.

She looked at Ezra, expecting to see him fall, but he was standing with his own pistol pointed at Austin.

Austin fell to the floor.

In her peripheral vision, Lily saw Addison clamp her hands over her mouth. But her eyes were fixed on Austin's body and the pool of blood forming under his head.

Murdering his subordinate seemed to have calmed Ezra and restored his confidence. He casually crossed to Austin's body. Fiddling with his pistol's silencer, he peered down, a look of disgust on his face while he nudged Austin's body with his toe.

"Good help is so hard to find. And it's been a rough week. That's two people I've had to let go."

Addison stood, recovering enough to glare at Ezra.

"You monster! You're a psychopath, killing anyone who gets in your way. You are not the man I thought you were. I didn't know you at all."

Ezra looked blandly back at Addison, head cocked.

"What's going—oh!" Naomi entered the room, drawn by the screams, and pulled her pistol as she fully took in the tableau before her.

Ezra raised his pistol and almost lazily pointed it at Lily.

"Over there next to Ms Grange, please, Naomi."

Naomi moved quickly, her pistol still aimed at Ezra, who seemed supremely untroubled about it.

"Now, if you'll just come over towards me, Your Majesty."

"She will not," said Naomi forcefully.

Ezra ignored her, looking directly at Lily and then pointedly moving his aim to Addison's head. Lily made to move.

"No!" Naomi commanded. "You cannot go with him, Your Majesty."

"She's right," said Addison. She smiled bravely at Lily, though it was clear she was terrified with the gun pointed at her. Lily could see her shaking.

"But... Addison," Lily started.

"I'm waiting," Ezra said loudly in a sing-song voice.

"It's fine," Addison said, nodding, tears pricking her

eyes. "Naomi's right. You can't go with him. And he won't shoot me."

A small crack sounded followed by a small red hole appearing in Addison's forehead. Her eyes lost focus, and she dropped to the ground before Lily could process what had happened.

Naomi was moving, jumping over Addison and standing in front of Lily. She could hear her talking to Ezra, but she couldn't make out the words.

Then Lily was on the ground, staring at Addison's body. Whether Lily fell or dropped on purpose, she didn't know. She stared at Addison's vacant eyes. How could someone's spirit leave so quickly?

Lily reached out hesitantly, stroking Addison's face. It was slack, but still warm. For some reason, she had expected it to be cold. Addison felt different, though. Something had irrevocably changed. Addison was gone.

Her mind couldn't process it.

She wanted to go back in time.

To take it back.

To make Addison not dead.

All Lily could hear was her own heartbeat, which made a cruel mockery of Addison's broken and silent body.

It's not her. She's not here anymore.

Lily looked over her dead friend at Ezra, blind hatred in her eyes.

He was staring at Addison with a benign curiosity. "I guess she was right. She didn't know me."

"How could you?" said Lily, grief mixing with rage.

Ezra shrugged. "She served her purpose."

"You are a monster," Lily spat.

"I'm not a monster. I'm a businessman."

Rage took Lily, and she flung a huge fireball straight at Ezra, hitting him dead-on. But the fire deflected around him, exploding into the wall and setting some papers on the desk to smouldering. She fired three more, then, in frustration, reached out with her telekinesis and grabbed everything her skill would allow, hurling it all at Ezra. Ezra simply stood there, looking unfazed and unharmed.

Lily felt an arm on her shoulder and was surprised to see Naomi. She'd forgotten she was there. Naomi was trying to pull Lily's arms down, and Lily realised she had been reaching for lightning. The air around them crackled as if charged. Fuelled by her anger, a single bolt would likely destroy the Tower and everyone in it.

Except Ezra, it seemed, who was apparently impervious to harm. Lily strained to see the barrier protecting him, reaching out with her magic. She could feel it. Something was engulfing him and protecting him from magic. She tried to access his mind, but the barrier stopped that, too. Just like it had in the prison.

All magic then. What is it?

Naomi moved in front of Lily, firing a shot at Ezra as she did. But her foot caught some of the debris from Lily's futile attack. Her ankle turned and the bullet hit whatever was protecting Ezra and ricocheted into the wall.

Ezra turned his attention back to Naomi, a nasty glint in his eye. Lily saw what he intended, and yelling, "No!" stepped in the line of fire before Naomi could stop her.

Ezra's expression returned to one of amusement. "So ready to die for your bodyguard, Your Majesty?"

"You're not going to kill me," Lily bit back, trying to keep her voice from shaking. It was a gamble, and one with the highest price. But if he meant to kill her, Lily was sure she'd already be dead. Whatever Ezra's sick plan was, he seemed to need her alive. Although, if she was wrong...

Ezra looked at Lily with an odd expression that she couldn't quite place.

"Ha! So confident." Ezra trained the pistol on Lily, aiming right between her eyes. Lily held her breath, forcing her eyes to remain open and ignoring the voice in her head telling her to move. She felt Naomi shift behind her. Lily knew as well as Naomi that Ezra could shoot Lily long before the guard could take her place.

With a wry smile and eyes burning with hatred, Ezra relaxed his aim.

"Unfortunately, Your Majesty, you are still necessary." Lily exhaled in relief before he added, "You *are* coming with me though."

The hell I am.

Lily took a breath, centring herself as she had learned in her lessons with Prudence. It was all about control. She controlled her magic, her magic did not control her.

Concentrating on the floor just in front of Ezra, Lily called a precision bolt of lightning. It crashed through the high windows, making them all jump, and blasted a hole in the floor directly in front of Ezra.

As the three began to recover from the shock, the floor in front of Ezra started to crumble. He started to move back, but the hole expanded, taking him with it. Lily and Naomi rushed forward, peering through the hole in the floor, seeing Ezra on his back. The women smiled at each other just before the surface they were standing on bowed and broke, sending them tumbling to the floor below as well.

Lily peered through the dust, pushing herself off the floor and looking for Ezra. He'd been forced back to the ground by the debris that accompanied Naomi and Lily, but was stirring, just as Naomi was next to her.

They all regained their feet and as Naomi, having lost her pistol, went to lunge at Ezra, he pointed his pistol at her.

"Now," he said, slightly out of breath. "Where were we?"

Ezra's free hand was patting his chest pocket, and a look of alarm spread across his face. He scanned the floor, Lily's eyes mirroring his as she tried to see what he was looking for. She spotted the small glass cube at the same time Ezra did, but she didn't realise it may have been the source of his shield in time.

She reached for Ezra's mind as he reached for the cube, but as his hand clenched around it, she was expelled. Not, however, before she caught a glimpse of his thoughts.

They were of Ava. He loved her. Well, as much as a megalomaniacal psychopath could love anyone. It shocked Lily though. She hadn't expected him to truly care for Ava. Not after what he had done. But the man did love his daughter, and he wanted to avoid causing her pain.

Sirens sounded in the distance, and Ezra seemed to make up his mind.

"I'm afraid you'll have to excuse me, ladies," he said, giving a small, mocking bow. "But I expect we'll see each other again. Very soon."

26

Prudence and Cyril sat by the fire, neither talking, both listening to the soothing crackle of the flames, their expressions those of sadness.

The door burst open, slamming into the wall behind it. Neither jumped. Instead, they both simply took another sip from their mugs.

Lily glared, their lack of reaction enraging her further. She strode up to Prudence, stopping in front of the little girl's chair.

"How could you let her die?" Lily demanded. "She's the oracle. She's important. Vital even. How could you just let her die?"

Prudence shrugged, eyes still on the fire. "There is another. We are all of us replaceable."

Cyril stood and shuffled to the door with his mug of tea, leaving the women to their confrontation.

Lily continued staring at Prudence, barely registering the sound of the door closing behind Cyril. Her rage was fading, turning quickly into grief. She tried to hold on to the anger, needing it to mask the pain, but then it was gone. She slumped into Cyril's now vacant chair.

"How could you let her die?" she asked again, softly now.

"I know it's hard, Your Majesty," said Prudence, fingering her necklace. "Loss always is. But sometimes, it's just the way of things."

Lily's eye caught on the pendant. Recognition hit her suddenly. She had seen Lady Octavia wearing it.

"But why not me then?" Lily asked, frustrated.

Prudence shot a look at Lily, her eyebrow raised.

"I mean, I don't *want* to die. But it feels like I'm the one meant to have been in danger all this time, and there Ezra is, protected by some barrier that I can't penetrate, holding a gun. And he just says I'm still necessary. Still not sure how he even got in there in the first place," Lily muttered.

A huge manhunt had been organised amid the clean-up effort. Naomi had recovered her pistol and protected Lily until help arrived, but neither the workers sent to fix the damage to the Tower, nor the dozens of Royal Guards who scoured the building, could find how Ezra had entered or exited without so much as a trace. The man was a ghost. Untraceable. Unkillable.

Prudence took a sip of her hot chocolate. "You have great power, Your Majesty."

"Yeah, yeah." Lily waved her away, frustrated. "Most powerful person in generations or whatever. Doesn't explain it. Doesn't help. And it didn't let me save Addison."

Prudence paused, frowning in annoyance at the interruption. "You have great power. A unique power," she continued quickly before Lily could interrupt again. Lily glanced over, curious now. "It's never been seen before. Though to be fair, it likely couldn't have been identified in earlier times and wouldn't have been much use. Lady Octavia recognised it the first time you practiced together. It is the key to Highacre's survival. You are the one who will save us all."

Prudence returned her gaze to the fire. Lily watched the young girl expectantly as she took a slurping sip of her drink.

"Well? What is it? What's my amazing power?" Lily eventually asked.

"You can emit a pulse of energy that negates technology."

Lily stared at Prudence, floored.

"Obviously, this will be vitally important in the coming battles," Prudence said, taking another sip from her mug.

Lily's anger returned in a flash. A memory played in the back of her mind of when she had connected to her power that first time. It had seemed like nothing happened, though there was a noise, and a man stumbling outside the court-yard before calling to Jason that he was fine. That voice. *Ezra.* Her power must have hit his implant.

Lily's anger turned to rage. All this time, it had been there. She could have used it. Addison. The mission to get the drive. Maybe all of this could have been avoided. How many times had they trained together? And not once had this been mentioned by Prudence. Lily thought they had grown close. That at least Prudence had a level of respect for Lily and her situation.

"Why the hell haven't you told me before now? I could have stopped him. I could have done something. Addison would still be alive." Lily's voice cracked, and she balled her fists, refusing to cry.

Prudence shrugged, sipping. "You were not meant to know before now. And she was not meant to live."

Lily's vision flashed white, pure rage enveloping her body, her thoughts reduced to a high-pitched whine that could be screams. She marvelled at the control she had developed over herself and her powers. There she sat in her chair, glaring at the little girl, wishing all manner of horrible, painful things to befall her, and not once did her magic attempt to make it so.

The pain of betrayal stabbed at Lily's chest. She'd told Prudence about her grief. Of losing her father. Losing Richard and Edmund. That she couldn't bear to lose anyone else.

With an effort, Lily made herself stand. She needed to leave.

Prudence went to take another sip, pausing to examine the remains of her drink. "You have not yet learned the lesson."

Lily closed her eyes, telling herself to leave. To just walk out. She didn't want to know what the lesson was. It would just make her angrier. But for some reason, she needed to know.

"What lesson?" she asked between gritted teeth.

"You alone cannot succeed."

Lily wheeled, leaning over Prudence menacingly. "And what the *fuck* is that supposed to mean?"

Prudence glared back up at Lily, defiant and appearing supremely unfazed. "If you don't get your shit together, we are all going to die."

Lily stood up straight, still looking down at the little girl. "And what's that? Another prophecy? Another vague reference to something I'm not supposed to know, but somehow need to figure out or else the world will explode? I'm sick of it. I'm sick of you! And you know what? I'm done. I'm done with you and your veiled comments. They don't help. They're not even vaguely useful. You put too much stock in fortune telling. Reading the tea leaves of some random person's dreams. And for what? So you can not tell me about it? So you can not tell me how to fix things? How to save the people I love? Well, you know what? I make my own fate." Lily turned and stormed out of the room.

Prudence returned her gaze to the fire, her body tense, uncomfortable with confrontation, and muttered, "I knew you were going to say that."

27

Lily threw open the door to her office and strode inside as the door banged against the wall, making her gathered advisors jump.

"We need to implement the mission to take out the signal tower," she said, looking at Jason. "Right now."

Jason sat forwards in his seat, nodding. "We're ready. Everything is in place. But we can't move before nightfall. We need the cover of darkness. If we go too early, they'll see us and repel our forces before we get close enough."

Lily hesitated, impatient, but she nodded. Moving now might make her feel better, but blowing their one chance because she was angry and hurting from the loss of Addison was stupid.

"The good news is our scouts report the tower is not nearly as well protected as it was even just a few days ago." Jason smiled around the room. "We seem to have picked our timing perfectly."

"Maybe things are finally going our way," said Juliana, smiling too.

Giles sniffed beside Juliana, and he tried to pass off wiping away a tear as brushing something from his face.

Lily felt her heart breaking again and willed it to become stone. There would be time enough for grief once the threat to the country was gone.

"Giles, can you work with Juliana to set up a meeting with President Taylor?"

Giles nodded, happy to fix his mind on a task. "When do you want it scheduled for?"

Lily looked around at her advisors, struck suddenly at how small the group was now, even with Ava joining them, though she looked like she wanted to fade into the wall. Lily wondered who would be left in the end.

"Thoughts?" she asked, banishing the morbidity from her mind. "Should we call President Taylor before blowing up his tower and offer him a chance to avoid the damage, or after it's a done deal?"

"After," said Jason and Naomi together.

"Well now," Juliana said, thinking. "Before might help our countries heal quicker and return to normal relations."

"You're assuming peace, though," said Jason. "We won't get to the table if we give them a chance to protect the tower."

The debate heated up, all of Lily's advisors jumping in to discuss the options. As she had hoped they would. Everyone was hurting, but she needed them at the top of their games, and figured debating the issue was not only a way to focus them on the task at hand, but to distract them from the pain of loss.

In her mind's eye she saw Ezra, expressionless, shooting Addison in the head. Lily shook herself, trying to dispel the memory that had been intruding on her thoughts at inopportune moments.

Vaguely listening to her advisors debate, Lily stood and crossed to the window, staring out into the darkness. The stars twinkled down at her, and the lights of Burlaron, muted by the forest of the palace's extended grounds, sparkled up from the city.

Lily tried to make out the mountains in the distance and blinked as a huge shadow flashed across the sky. She tried to follow it, but it was gone before she could focus. Jenkins's dragon, perhaps? What was her name again? Geraldine? Lily made a note to ask why he'd picked that name, wondering briefly why she hadn't asked before and feeling guilty for not checking in on both of them. Reminding herself she'd been somewhat busy, Lily still felt bad and decided to head down in the morning, after the assault tonight.

In order for the world to live, you must die.

Lily tried to flush Prudence's prophecies from her mind, but snippets of their conversations continued to invade. *Cataclysmic events.* Lily's anger grew, along with a visceral hatred for the prophecies. *And I'm the one meant to prevent them.* She felt stuck, like she was being funnelled in one direction, a helpless slave to fate.

But what if they're true?

Lily was happy to buy into the idea that she could save the world. Sure, it was a massive burden, but so was being queen. She had managed to adjust to that. She could suck it up and do her best to save the world. But having to sacrifice herself to do so? That felt like too much to ask. Especially when she hadn't asked for any of this.

Staring out into the darkness, she thought of Edmund again. Had he been afraid to die in his final minutes? As he stepped out from the safety of the armoured vehicle, had he worried about dying at all, or was he just focussed on saving his friends? Had he realised that he would be killed, and accepted it? Lily wished she could speak with him. Ask him about it. She wished she had his courage.

Feeling tears prick her eyes, Lily listened to the voices

behind her, and satisfied that her advisors were well ensconced in discussion, she opened the door to the balcony and stepped out into the cold.

The lights of Burlaron, stronger from out here, twinkled softly through the trees as they blew in the wind. A sudden urge to test out her new power gripped Lily. To see if she could switch them off. *I suppose the power isn't new*. Lily kicked lightly at the balcony in frustration. So many secrets. If only Lady Octavia had told her back then what Lily had done. What she was capable of doing.

You were not meant to know before now.

An idea was stirring. But hopefully it would not be needed. Once they took the tower, they could return to peace. Lily had already decided she would call President Taylor after the signal tower was destroyed. She didn't trust the Meridians not to take advantage of Highacre's generosity if they offered a warning. And a small part of her wanted Meridia to hurt as Highacre was hurting. Lily didn't want to acknowledge that small part of her, but it was there all the same.

In order for the world to live, you must die.

What if she sacrificed herself and it didn't work? She would happily sacrifice herself if she could only know for certain that it would fix everything. That everyone would be safe. She would be terrified, but she'd do it. Well, she hoped she would. It was easy to make promises while in the safety of her balcony in the palace. The memory of Edmund crossed her mind again. He had strode out with no hesitation.

Lily's mind turned to the others she had sent to war. The hundreds of others like Edmund that she didn't even know about who had given their lives, if not directly for their comrades, then for their families, friends, and country. They had died in the hope that people they had never even met might be safe. They had died without knowing if it would make a difference. A strong sense of pride in her countrymen swelled in Lily's chest.

She could sacrifice for her people, too.

She thought of her friends. If the destruction of the signal tower didn't work as planned, they might need to put themselves in harm's way. She needed to find a way where they could be free to choose whether or not to do that. Sacrifice required a choice. The options available to choose from might not always be great, but the freedom to choose was still important. She would need to give them that freedom and accept the risk that she might lose more people she cared about. She wouldn't be able to protect them. And they would need to similarly accept that they couldn't protect her. Her fate was already sealed.

"Your Majesty?"

Jason appeared in the doorway. Lily glanced behind him, seeing that the rest of the group were still in animated discussions.

"Are you alright?"

"I'm fine, thank you Jason," Lily said, turning her eyes back to the view and letting the cool breeze caress her face.

Jason moved to the railing, standing beside Lily and looking out into the darkness too. "It's hard. Losing people."

Lily nodded, not sure she could answer and keep it together.

"Richard. Edmund. Addison. Even Austin."

"I don't want to mourn him," Lily said, her face hardening at Austin's betrayal. Of her, but more of his country.

"That's fair," Jason said simply. "At least now we know you can negate technology. That will make things easier."

"Would have been good to know that before," said Lily bitterly.

"If we had known before, the attempts on your life

would have been more serious," said Jason reasonably. "Ezra certainly wouldn't have let you live back in the office."

He wouldn't have had a choice. Lily imagined herself blasting him with her electromagnetic pulse power and killing him before he could shoot Addison. A fantasy that she'd indulged in many times since he'd murdered her friend. But Lily's mind was stuck on Jason's first comment. He was right. She never would have even made it to the office. With a power that dangerous to anyone with an implant, Ezra would never have let her live once he found out about it. And with a sinking heart, Lily realised it probably would have been Addison that would have told him.

A sharp rap at the door drew Lily and Jason's attention, and they both moved back into the office as the Chief of the Highacren Military marched in. He scanned the room, saluting as he saw Lily.

Lily returned the compliment as Jason had taught her, her eyes taking in the general's neatly pressed dress uniform, the lights catching the four stars on each of his shoulders. She wondered how he was always so immaculate as she pulled at her own top, creased and crinkled from the day's activities.

"Your Majesty. DRHQ has been overrun."

"What?" Jason asked, taking a step forwards as if wanting to spring into action.

"A huge force just appeared. We had no warning. They didn't show up on any of our surveillance equipment and no one sensed anything."

"The people?" Lily said, her mind on the brigadier and her staff, and all the people in the hospital.

The general shook his head. "We don't know yet, ma'am, but I'm afraid I can't say I hold high hopes."

"Can we muster enough troops for a counterattack?" Jason asked.

The general shook his head, his eyes returning to Lily. "The Meridian forces didn't stop at DRHQ. They are advancing south through Highacre."

Gasps and cries came from her advisors. Lily stared into the general's eyes and asked the question she already knew the answer to.

"Where are they headed?"

"Here, ma'am. They're advancing towards Burlaron."

Lily saw movement and heard muffled reactions around her, but everything felt blurry, a now familiar high-pitched ringing in her ears.

Lily forced herself to take a couple of deep breaths and focus. She heard Jason's voice. "We need to pull troops back. Form a blockade."

"We can't. Meridian ships made landfall in the north near Monkronia. We already sent troops up there before the attack on the headquarters."

The general looked at Lily, and she realised he was waiting for orders. No, a decision. Her brain finally caught up. She could leave things as they were and save Monkronia, but the capital would be destroyed. Or she could sacrifice Monkronia and its people and recall the troops to save her city.

The magnitude of the decision was paralysing, and Lily wished she had Brigadier James's decisiveness. She wondered if the woman was still alive.

"And..." The general's tone drew the attention of the room once again. "Scouts report ships to the east."

"How in the world did the Meridians get that many ships?" Jason asked. "I thought we were monitoring production."

"It's not the Meridians." The general's tone was flat. "It's Valmead."

Everyone froze. The enormity of the situation filled the room like a heavy gas.

Lily closed her eyes briefly, willing the fear away.

"What forces do we have on this side of the Meridian advance?" she asked.

"There are always some troops stationed here to defend the city," the general answered. "And we have a few garrisons nearby. But some were redirected towards the bay once we had word of the Valmeadian ships landing."

"The Royal Guard is ready," Jason said, Naomi appearing at his side and nodding. "We can fight."

"I don't want to fight in the city," Lily told them. "I won't put my people at risk."

She turned to her military chief. "General, find me a battlefield. Somewhere between here and the Meridian advance. I want somewhere we will reach first. Then gather all the troops you can, who are not already committed, and send them there to prepare it."

"Do you mean to leave the city unguarded?" the general asked.

"Yes," Lily said. "Send your troops to secure the battlefield. We may need help with transport, so commandeer civilian and commercial vehicles as needed."

The general snapped to attention and gave a sharp nod.

"Naomi, get the Royal Guard and prepare to evacuate the city. Do we have plans for this? Somewhere for the people to go?"

"The extant plan is to move into the mountains," Naomi said. "There are some caches of supplies up there, but the plan was made with natural disasters in mind. We've never thought the Meridians would make it this far south."

Lily nodded. "Gather everyone who can fight and send them to the battlefield. Leave a small contingent to protect those who can't fight and send them into the mountains."

"Is Alexei with the ships?" Ava asked, speaking for the first time.

"Jason?" Lily called. Jason was at her desk, talking on the phone.

"Yes, he's leading them," Jason called, covering the mouthpiece with a hand and mouthing "Hudson" at Lily, confirming who was pulling the information for them. "Alexei was made Great Leader last week after striking a deal with his stepmother."

"His stepmother?" Juliana said, confused.

"She was making a play for her eldest son to take the role," Lily said.

Juliana raised an eyebrow. "I knew she was ambitious, but for her to hold more power than Gutzmer…"

"What was the deal?" Lily called to Jason.

"Alexei wanted to lead a force and go to the Disputed Region," relayed Jason in a tone that indicated he was kicking himself for not asking Hudson to monitor Valmead before now. "His little brother is in charge in his absence. They've apparently made some arrangement whereby if Alexei doesn't make it back, the brother steps up."

"He wanted to go to the DR but they landed to the east?" Lily asked.

"Correct," said the general as Jason hung up the phone and returned to the group. "Perhaps they saw the Meridian advance?"

"Or were told about it," said Jason gravely. "Hudson's going to see what he can find out."

"Thanks Jason," Lily said. "I want you to go with the general. You'll ensure integration between the military, the Royal Guard, and everyone else we can gather."

Jason nodded, the gravity of his role settling on his shoulders.

"Naomi, as well as the evacuation, consider if there are

any HSP that we can use. I know some have been saying they didn't know what was going on, or they were coerced, families threatened and so on. Use them if you think you can. Leave them detained if you can't trust them. We're going to need any citizens who can fight and are willing. But I want volunteers only. We need numbers, sure, but I'm willing to sacrifice volume for quality."

Naomi nodded at Lily, already scratching notes in her notebook.

"Juliana," Lily said, seeing the older woman already looking at her intently, awaiting her orders. "Get your ladies ready and have them reach out to anyone else they know who can fight. I'm looking for scrappers and insurgents. People who can cause chaos and get behind enemy lines."

"On it," Juliana said with passion.

"Ava." Lily turned to see Ava react with surprise at getting a role. "Reach out to Alexei and see if you can make contact. He's probably more willing to speak with you than me at the moment. Also, try to reach out to any contacts you have in the Meridian military. I'm thinking more soldiers than officers here. Tell them we don't want to fight. We'd prefer to end this without any more bloodshed, if possible. But if they force our hand, we will wipe out every last one of them."

Ava stared at Lily, eyebrows raised.

"I mean, put it nicer than that, but you know what I mean. I want them to hesitate. If we can make this happen without further loss of life, that would be great."

"Okay," said Ava.

"Giles." Lily looked over at the old man. Like Ava, he was surprised to have a job. If he thought his role was to keep the palace fires burning, he was sorely mistaken. "You're with me. I have a special assignment for you."

28

THE LAST FEW hours had been a blur of activity. Lily had been pulled from one task to the next, providing guidance and decisions to the military and Royal Guard about the upcoming battle, giving Naomi direction as she herded civilians from the city, and overseeing the evacuation of the palace. Keeping busy was good, as the severity of the situation hadn't been able to truly sink in.

As she orchestrated the evacuation and battle preparation, Lily's mind drifted to Brigadier James and how she had seamlessly run an entire frontline war effort as well as her own enormous base. The brigadier made it seem so effortless, and clearly had the respect of Jake and her team. Lily wished she had half the woman's skill and presence.

She wondered what had become of the brigadier, and Jake, and everyone on base at DRHQ. Were they alive? Injured? Captured? Sending a silent prayer to the universe for their safety, and an apology to the brigadier and her people, Lily set her mind back to the task at hand, trying to remain stoic.

However, there were moments where Lily sent people off on one job or another and wondered if she'd ever see them again. Would these really be her last hours? Deciding whether the palace art was worth taking the time to save? Lily had been so focussed on the unfairness of Prudence's prophecy, but now that it seemed to have come for her, Lily barely had time to register her impending doom and savour these last moments.

She shook herself from her morbid reverie. She was now seated in the back of a vehicle, driving as fast as was safe through the streets of Burlaron, heading north to the battle-field. A pang of sadness hit her as she realised she had missed seeing half the city one last time while lost in her thoughts.

"How long?" she asked Jason, who, having helped the general identify the battleground, had returned to escort Lily. Forever her bodyguard.

"Not long, Your Majesty," he said quietly.

Lily nodded. That meant the Meridians were advancing at speed. In order to set the conditions for the fight, the general had needed to sacrifice distance and had chosen a location closer to the city than Lily liked. But at least if the Meridians were making a thunder run for the capital, they weren't attacking the small towns along the way.

Yet.

Lily's face was set with steely resolve. No. The Meridians would not attack the towns because the Highacrens would defeat them. They had to win, whether or not Lily would be around to see the results of that victory.

Lily turned her attention back to the chaos outside the vehicle. The sun was setting fast and things would be far worse in the darkness. Sirens were blaring, and a booming voice instructed everyone to remain calm and head to the western city exits. The monotonous voice was at odds with the screaming and panic of the citizens.

Sympathy tugged at Lily's heart, imagining the terror of the families trying to gather everything important to them and get out. She saw people trying to leave in vehicles, packed with everything that would fit inside. But the roads were quickly becoming clogged. Already, people were abandoning their vehicles, adding to the congestion.

She saw rows of people weaving through the stalled traffic on foot, packages strapped to their backs or balanced on heads. She saw children similarly tethered to parents or siblings. Some trailed behind their families, eyes wide, taking in the chaos.

They slowed, entering a street filled with people outside their homes. Lily watched the families embracing and realised that they were separating. Some were fleeing to the mountains, with the others leaving to get brief instruction in weapons and fighting before joining the rest of the ragtag army Lily and her team had cobbled together.

Tears filled Lily's eyes as she watched spouses separate, older children either joining a parent in the queues to mount the army trucks or farewelling both parents, left in charge of their siblings. She wiped her eyes. How the hell was any parent supposed to make decisions like that?

As they approached the end of the street, Lily saw a mother struggling with three small children milling around her, another baby on her hip. The woman dropped her belongings, items spilling across the road, and she gave a cry of frustration.

"Stop the car," Lily ordered, her door open before the vehicle had completely halted.

She had half expected a hand on her arm and Jason advising that they needed to hurry, but she heard a door open and then he was hurrying to help Lily with the woman. Like a slap, she remembered Jason's family. Gwen must be out there somewhere, similarly struggling to get their children and possessions to safety. She couldn't imagine the guilt Jason must be feeling, but she was struck with her own, thinking back to her unspoken promise to Gwen to keep Jason safe. That losing his leg and eye was enough. And here he was, heading to war with her.

Having swept up most of the woman's lost possessions, Lily and Jason returned to the woman, combining the items in one large pile. Jason darted back to the car as the woman began thanking them profusely.

"Thank you so much. I thought I had it all bundled up, but then with the kids, and I just—"

"It's fine. Let's just get you sorted here," Lily said reassuringly.

Jason reappeared with an empty pack, whatever had been inside now lining the trunk of the car, and began packing the items inside.

"Oh my gosh, I can't take your backpack," the woman said, mortified. "You'll need that for yourselves."

"We'll be fine." Jason waved her off, pulling faces at the baby, who giggled as if the world wasn't falling apart around her.

"Okay, there you go," said Lily, adjusting the pack on the woman's back and tightening the straps so it was secure, but she could still wrangle her children.

"I can't thank you enough. You're angels, both of you." The woman beamed at them, looking at them properly for the first time. Her smile slipped as her eyes took in Lily and she saw something familiar. It clicked in her mind and horror filled her face. "Oh my days, Your Majesty."

The woman tried to fall into a low curtsy, but was hampered by the heavy pack and her children. Lily caught her arm before she toppled over.

"No need to worry about that," Lily reassured her as she made sure she was stable.

"But you shouldn't be stopped here helping me, Your Majesty. You need to go. Get out of here. I would have thought you'd already be gone." The woman shot a hard look at Jason as if he should have thrown Lily over his shoulder and run hours ago.

"It's okay, really," Lily said, forcing herself to smile gently. "I'm not evacuating. I'm heading to the battlefield."

The woman looked like she might burst into tears at the idea of Lily heading to danger. But whatever she might have been going to say was lost as tremendous explosions rang out from the direction of the northern city walls.

"Go now," Jason ordered the woman. "Head west, follow the directions from the Royal Guard."

The woman nodded, grabbing at her children's hands and breaking into a slow jog.

Jason ushered Lily to the car and asked the driver about the explosions as they headed off, faster now.

"Meridian scouts," the driver reported. "At least five groups have been reported inside the city limits. Must have been ordered to create havoc here to try and get us to divide our forces."

"They want to slow our advance," Jason mused. "Buy themselves more time to get here and pick their own battlefield."

"Well, it won't work," Lily said firmly. "Tell the Royal Guards overseeing the evacuation to send a small contingent to ensure the Meridians don't interfere with the evacuation itself. If they want to blow up the city, let them have at it. We can rebuild a city. Protect the people."

Jason relayed Lily's orders as the driver diverted from their route to avoid the rubble of the bombs, and soon the city was behind them. It was dark now, and the driver was going as fast as he could while using the fog lights. Lily stared out the window, trying to see beyond her reflection to the landscape as it flew by.

She could make out some trees, some fences in the fields. They passed some large shadows, and she smiled. Giles had followed her orders with an efficiency only Giles could manage.

Too soon, the vehicle slowed and Jason murmured that they had arrived. Lily got out, staring into the darkness back towards the city. She could see the glow on the horizon—lights, fire, or both.

"We're so close," she said.

"We are," Jason replied grimly.

"Can they hit the city from here?"

Jason nodded. "Their rockets and missiles have the range. But they shouldn't get here before the evacuation is complete."

Lily frowned at the city, not wanting to trust that such a large movement of people would go smoothly, and knowing that despite their best efforts, not everyone would get out. She turned, looking at Jason.

"I have one last job for you."

29

THERE WAS an eerie peace in the air as both sides stood on either side of the rolling field that the general had selected for this final battle. The urgency of reaching the position had dissipated. Lily had thought that she would head straight into the battle, practically running from the car into the fray. But she and Jason had arrived in the early hours of the morning to find both sides preparing on opposite sides of the field. Her generals had advised making the most of the unexpected preparation time, despite the fact that this would afford the same to the enemy.

And now it was just waiting.

The wind blew through Lily's hair as she stood on the hill, watching the battle preparation below.

How did it come to this?

She thought about all the people who had already died in this unnecessary war. The war she hoped to end today. No, the war she *would* end today. Images of those she'd known floated through her mind.

Lady Octavia. Richard. Edmund. Austin. Addison. Most likely Claire.

So many lives had been lost. So many friends. And for what?

The sun was shining brightly, but the wind was keeping the temperature down. Lily looked up at the brilliant blue sky, peppered with fluffy white clouds. From this angle it felt like any other normal day. A beautiful day to spend with friends. She closed her eyes, breathing deeply and indulging in the fantasy for a few seconds.

Opening her eyes, Lily looked down onto the open plains below. A whirlwind of activity was beneath her as everyone prepared for the battle. And on the horizon, Meridia. She could see the black wall of their army in the distance. There were so many.

She turned towards the coast, straining to see the Valmeadian forces. But the landscape didn't allow her to see that far.

Returning her eyes to her army, Lily steeled the resolve within.

It was time.

She had a war to win.

By the time Lily reached the bottom of the hill, she was ready. This was happening. No more time for fear or trepidation. She couldn't afford to second-guess herself or think about the fact that she might not survive the day. She would fight and she would succeed, no matter if she lived or not. They had to win. And now she needed to project that confidence for her people.

"There you are." Giles fell into step beside Lily, clearly relieved to have located her. "Really, I don't mean to complain, but this *is* outside my preferred tasking."

Lily halted, smiling warmly at the old man. This was

the closest he'd been to his old self since Addison died. Giles looked at Lily, his frustration melting as he returned her smile.

"Of course, this whole war"—Giles gestured at the soldiers all around them—"is not any of our preferences, so I'll do as required. I live to serve." He gave Lily a little bow. As he straightened up, Giles's attention was caught by something over Lily's shoulder. "No, do *not* put that there." He hurried off.

Lily looked around at what had become Giles's domain. There was already a dirt track that ran through the camp, made by the feet walking its length repeatedly. The separate groups had been given discrete areas along the path's length in which to prepare, and while most stuck to their assigned spots, there was a high level of traffic walking between the sectors, retrieving supplies, delivering goods, and generally helping each other.

Giles had done exceptionally well for the time he had been given. An enormous enclosure had been erected quickly, though it looked thoroughly secure.

She wandered up to the fence and created a telepathic link.

Thank you for indulging the humans' fears and agreeing to stay in the enclosure, she said to the several large beasts within.

A couple nodded, focussing on eating, and one snorted, approaching the fence where Lily was.

You know we'd be out of here in a heartbeat if we wanted to, the fire-eater said, looking disdainfully at the structure. *There's no way this thing would hold us.*

I know that. But they don't, she said, indicating the workers with a nod of her head. *And it makes them feel safer. I need them to only worry about what's out there, not what's in here.*

The fire-eater shrugged. *No flakes off our scales. Just keep the food coming.*

I have my best man on it, Lily said. The fire-eater followed her gaze to Giles, who was ordering a bunch of workers around.

Lily turned back to the fire-eater. *I can't tell you how much I appreciate you all coming. Especially after how you've been treated.*

The fire-eater swallowed a huge mouthful of food and looked right at Lily. *You let me live, and then you got me released from that tiny enclosure into the sanctuary.*

After the Trials, Lily had arranged for land to be put aside as a wildlife sanctuary in which animals, including the fire-eaters, could live unimpeded by humans.

It's alright then? Big enough? Lily asked.

Oh yes. The fire-eater nodded enthusiastically. *It's got room for all of us, and best of all, no humans.*

Perfect, said Lily, relieved.

So we're happy to help. But then we're square.

Absolutely, said Lily. *See you out there.*

As the fire-eater went back to her food, Lily continued walking around the area, nodding at workers as she made her way to a huge, empty enclosure. Leaning on the chest-high fence, Lily scoured the area, looking for any movement.

A high-pitched yip sounded from her right, and Lily vaulted the fence and hurried over. Kevin bounced up to her, slapping her toe to indicate she should pick him up, and she happily obliged. After an appropriate amount of cuddles and tickles, Kevin wiggled to be let down, and when his tiny paws hit the dirt, he ran two tight circles around Lily's feet before bounding off.

Lily followed Kevin, wondering where he was headed. He sprinted the length of the enclosure before zooming in circles again. As Lily approached, she saw he was zooming around a lighter coloured pelotromo. The new pup was slightly smaller than Kevin, and where his face was snub-nosed, hers was more pointed, putting Lily in mind of a fox.

"Oh, Kevin!" Lily said excitedly. "You have a girlfriend!"

The lighter pelotromo growled, a high-pitched, weed-eater sound.

"Oh, sorry. Wife?"

The female pelotromo made a happy sound and nuzzled into Kevin, who had stopped still, panting. Soft squeaks sounded from some bushes in the rear corner of the enclosure, and what looked like three balls of fluff waddled over towards the pelotromos.

"Kevin! You have babies? Holy crap, you're a dad!"

Kevin yipped proudly, nudging the tiny fluffy puppies around.

Lily's chest felt light and full watching them and envisioning them playing in the palace. But then the feeling vanished, replaced by a terrified, nauseated worry.

"Kevin, I appreciate you being here, but I don't want any of you hurt. You have your kids to think of. Maybe you should head back to the palace."

Kevin ran behind Lily, grabbing the hem of her pants in his tiny mouth and pulling with all his might. Lily stood and watched as he yanked, jumping and throwing his entire body weight into it. It felt like she had snagged her hem on a loose twig.

Guessing what he wanted, Lily started moving away from the little family, Kevin still pulling her leg, growling with satisfaction, as if it was his strength making her move. Finally, he stopped and sped back to his family, now some distance from Lily.

She heard a small pop, and suddenly found herself

facing two gigantic fluffy puppies that towered over her. Lily heard a squeal from behind her as the workers froze upon seeing the mammoth-sized pets. Kevin gave a booming yip and a couple of screams sounded off to Lily's right, where the rest of her forces were preparing.

Three quick pops sounded and beside Kevin and his wife were three elephant-sized baby pelotromos. Another quick pop sounded and one of the babies deflated to the loud, squeaking titters of its siblings.

Lily stared at the group, wide-eyed. For the first time, she understood why everyone had always seemed so terrified of little Kevin. Ava had told her once that Kevin could still move at this size as he did in his smaller form. She could not imagine seeing him barrel towards her as big as he was now.

More pops and the family returned to their smaller sizes, and Kevin and his wife bounded up to Lily, who bent down to pat them. Kevin indicated to himself and his wife and licked Lily's hand. He turned to his children and nosed towards the palace. They would go home while he and his wife would fight.

"Thank you, Kevin." She tickled under his chin. "And you." She scratched Kevin's wife's ear. "We'll have to figure out your name when this is all over."

Because they would all survive, she told herself. Lily blinked quickly, refusing to even entertain the possibility that this cute little family would be separated in any way.

"Thank you for coming," she told them, standing again. "I'll see you both soon."

Lily jumped back out of the enclosure and continued down the road, still in Giles's sector. She walked in the middle of the path, head high, knowing the people needed to see her. That they'd take some comfort from knowing she was here, too. That she would fight with them.

A huge roar split the air, causing several people to scream and jump, dropping their items. She noticed the road deviated here, with most of the foot traffic giving the area a wide berth. Lily continued straight, and as she rounded the trees, she saw Jenkins and his dragon.

Geraldine was standing on her hind legs, now a little taller than a light pole, her wings spread and her head stretched to the sky. The very image of a medieval crest. Lily watched as Geraldine snapped twice, roared again, and then let loose a burst of flame.

"Jenkins," Lily said excitedly as she approached. "She's grown since I last saw her."

Jenkins nodded happily. "As expected. Dragons take a long time to hatch, but then—boom! They grow very quickly. Growth here a little faster than her home dimension. Fascinating."

"Is she okay?" Lily asked, watching Geraldine snap at the sky again.

"There's a fly she's trying to catch," Jenkins explained proudly.

"Jenkins!"

The two turned, seeing Juliana calling from the road. She was carrying some rope and was on her way back to her sector.

"I've been meaning to say thanks for the cigarettes. They really helped me out of a tight spot."

Jenkins bobbed his head and gave her a wave, turning back to Geraldine.

"Your Majesty, swing by when you get a chance. The girls would love to see you."

Lily nodded and waved back, and Juliana continued on her way, not once indicating that there was anything out of the ordinary about the enormous dragon behind them.

"Are you okay with this, Jenkins?" Lily asked gently.

She could see the love he had for Geraldine. And she was still so young.

But Jenkins nodded. "Dragons like to fight. Will be good for her to burn off some steam. Also, energy." Jenkins gave a high-pitched giggle, pleased with himself. "Plus, scales like armour. Likelihood of harm is low."

"Are you going to be okay watching her?" Lily asked, hoping he was planning on returning to the safety of the palace.

Jenkins shook his head, leading Lily over to what looked suspiciously like a leather saddle. Lily stared at it for a beat.

"Does she need a rider?"

"Oh no." Jenkins shook his head. "Telepathic," he reminded Lily. "I asked her about the fight. She's happy to help."

"But then..." Lily pointed at the saddle.

Jenkins leant in conspiratorially. "Good excuse. Haven't ridden a dragon before. Lifelong dream."

Lily was caught by a wave of anxiety yet again. She closed her eyes, breathing deeply, and reminded herself once again that she couldn't protect everyone, and they all deserved to make their own choices.

She felt a soft hand on her arm and opened her eyes to see Jenkins looking at her with concern.

"My choice. Have analysed risks. Very low, by the way. Much better than your odds. Way better. Your odds, pretty terrible. But if something happens..." He shrugged, smiling broadly. "What a way to go!"

He patted her arm and returned to Geraldine, who lowered her massive head and licked him, almost knocking Jenkins off his feet. The dragon looked over at Lily, and a woman's voice sounded in Lily's head, letting her know that Geraldine would keep Jenkins safe.

Lily nodded her thanks, turned, and continued on her

way, comforting herself with the notion that Geraldine's presence alone was a massive morale boost for their side and killer for their opponents. If Geraldine needed to fly away to protect Jenkins, she would, and the rest of them would be fine.

We're all going to be fine.

The road stretched for a ways, allowing some distance between all the animals that Giles had gathered and the human component of their army. She joined a ragtag group gathered near a tree. A box had been dumped at its base and standing atop it was Juliana, giving an impassioned speech.

"... until we are no more. Because we are the forward lines. We are the arrow tip. We will destroy the enemy and keep our country safe."

Lily looked around at the faces. They were all captivated by Juliana, though she had the impression that their respect for her was keeping their attention more than her words.

"And we will prevail!" Juliana said, punching a fist into the air. A few people in the crowd called out and a few fists joined hers, but it was clearly not the reaction she was looking for. After a quick calculation and adjustment for her demographic, Juliana tried again. "And we will fuck them all right up!"

"Yeah!" a rousing reply came from the crowd this time as they got to their feet, punching the sky and hooting and hollering. Lily was pretty sure some of them had no idea exactly who would be fucked right up, but neither did they seem to care.

A girl standing next to Lily flicked her long hair back and commented, "Not bad for a prime minister."

Juliana, who had jumped off her box and made her way through the crowd, appeared in front of them. "*Acting* prime minister," she corrected.

The girl shrugged, muttering, "Whatever," as she walked away.

Juliana ushered Lily through the crowd, giving her an impromptu tour of her area.

"We're ready. We have teams or individuals depending on what effect you need. We can be loud, silent, or anything in between. Or everything at once!"

Lily smiled at Juliana's infectious energy. "I think we'll need all of it."

"We're ready," Juliana said again with meaning.

"Congrats on the position, by the way."

"Thanks," said Juliana, waving her away. "It'll mean something when the people vote for me. This is just a party popularity endorsement."

"Still," said Lily, smiling before a thought occurred. "Should you be here? I mean, I need to be, but shouldn't one of us stay out of the fight to lead the country if it all goes wrong?"

"This is the big one, Your Majesty. If we don't succeed, then there is no Highacre. And there's nowhere I'd rather be."

Lily looked into Juliana's eyes, seeing steely resolve and a strong love for her country. Juliana squeezed Lily's shoulders and then walked away.

"Alright ladies, let's fuck up some Meridians."

"Yeah!"

Lily smiled at the cheers as she walked on. The groups of people became steadily more organised as she continued down the road. The chaos of Juliana's team was replaced by a bewildered but determined group of civilians, trying to ensure some order in their camp by casting furtive glances at the next-door section of Royal Guards and copying what they had done.

At the far end, and by a stretch the biggest sector of

humans, was the military. Despite the general's warning that their forces were concentrated up north in the Disputed Region and defending Monkronia, there were a significant number of professional soldiers in the camp. Lily was surprised by the numbers, and heartened.

The soldiers had erected hundreds of tents in straight lines as far as Lily could see. She knew they had spent the night here, getting the grounds ready for the other members of the battle group. They had also erected a large mess tent where they were making food for everyone, as well as a field hospital. When Jason had told her about the camp they were setting up, she had objected to the level of effort being expended. After all, their plan was expansive, but intended to be quick.

"Prepare for the best. Plan for the worst," he had replied. In the event everything went wrong today, the military's camp would enable the Highacren forces to keep fighting, resting some troops before switching them out and handling the injured.

She pushed inside the command tent and found Jason and Naomi in huddled discussion around a table.

"How's it looking?" Jason asked.

"Perfect. You've both done an amazing job," she said with gratitude. Jason and Naomi puffed up at the compliment, having both worked all night to pull the forces together.

"How are we looking here?" Lily asked, peering down at the map on the table that Jason and Naomi had been discussing.

The map showed the battlefield. They had chosen a huge open plain bordered by forests to the west and hills all around. This left the southern approach for Highacre, the north for Meridia, and a small gap to the east for Valmead to enter, if that was their intention. But any approach from

Valmead would be seen, allowing for appropriate preparation.

Lily looked at the figures that had been placed on the map and wasn't surprised by Jason's reply.

"We're outnumbered. Even with our animal friends, they still have the advantage."

"And if Valmead joins in for Meridia, we're screwed," added Naomi. "Of course, if they join for us, Meridia will probably still outnumber our forces."

"We know the Valmeadians have formed up to the east," said Jason. "But we've had no indication where their allegiance lies at this point. We reached out to them, trying to open a line of communication, but all of our runners have had weapons pointed at them until they leave."

"But our guys saw Valmead doing the same to the Meridian runners, so that's something," said Naomi.

Lily frowned, staring at the map, thinking. That bit of intel indicated that Valmead hadn't come at Meridia's behest at least. Unless that was a ruse, intended to make Highacre think they weren't working together. She stifled a sigh. How did anyone plan a war? Anyone could be doing anything and signs could mean whatever you wanted them to. You'd only find out for sure when it was too late to plan anything.

"Alexei will be on our side," Lily said, trying to convince herself as much as Jason and Naomi.

"Did Ava get through to him, then?"

"No, I didn't," said Ava, pushing through the opening to the tent. "And he wouldn't see me either."

"You went over there?" Lily asked, pointless worry coursing through her despite Ava standing right there, clearly fine.

Ava nodded. "Got the same treatment, though. Rifle pointed at me, guards yelling for me to back away."

"He's on our side," Lily said again. Ava nodded at her, though there was doubt in her eyes. "Even if he's not, he won't fight us."

"Then why are they here?" Ava asked gently, Jason and Naomi nodding behind her.

Lily turned back to the map, moving the marker for the Valmead forces closer to the battlefield. They had sent people to observe the Valmead army as it made land and headed further inland. Along with numbers and force constitution, their spies had reported that Alexei was with them. But now Ava said he wouldn't see her.

What did that mean? Was he still mad at Lily for her failure to release him in time to say goodbye to his father? Mad enough to lead his country to war? Or was he still deciding whether to enter the conflict, and if so, on what side?

The tent flaps swished as the rest of the advisors entered, gathering around Lily. She turned, looking at them. At her family.

"Thank you all for everything you've done. For me since I got here, and to get everything ready here today. I couldn't have done this without you. And now, I need you and your people to get me to the centre. To put yourselves in harm's way one more time. Thank you for all showing up. For being willing to risk the dangers of battle to get me where I need to be."

"Always, Your Majesty," Juliana called out, the rest of the group nodding emphatically.

"I'll reiterate again though," she said, looking at each in turn. "If you're having any doubts. A bad feeling. Whatever. You do not have to do this. I will think no less of you if you decide to return to the palace, or simply stay here in the camp."

The advisors shook their heads at Lily, glancing around

at each other, looking to see if anyone would back out. Their collective gaze came to rest on Ava. Noticing their eyes on her, Ava shrugged. "I'm not going to go out of my way to kill my countrymen, but I will protect Lily," she said, her stare broadcasting her resolve.

A swish of the tent flaps drew everyone's attention to the entrance. A young soldier stood there, breathing hard.

"Your Majesty?" his eyes searched the faces staring at him, looking for his sovereign. Finding her, he gave a quick but respectful bow.

"They are coming."

30

Lily's heart was pounding, her adrenaline spiking. Her army was spread out on either side of her as everyone marched to the centre of the battlefield. She had a pistol snug in its holster on her right hip, and a short sword in a sheath on her left. Lily remembered her confusion at having to learn sword fighting when she first arrived. The memory soured as she thought of Austin teaching her and all she now knew about the man he had been.

"What do I need that for?" she had asked Jason as he attached the sword to her belt, ensuring it hung at her side correctly.

"If things go wrong and we wind up going hand-to-hand, you'll need it," said Jason darkly.

"Plus it looks cool," added Naomi.

Lily and Jason turned to look at her, and she shrugged. "What? You know it does. Don't tell me a small reason for her wearing it is not to give the troops a boost."

Jason's cheeks coloured, and he busied himself making minor adjustments, as if to perfect the length.

Now, as they walked towards the advancing Meridian

force, the tip of the sheath banged against her leg with every step. She hoped the morale boost was worth the annoyance.

Lily's eyes scanned the length of the Meridian army. It seemed impossibly large, and she now felt silly standing in front of it with a sword, like a child with a toy taking on a modern military. Feeling exposed, Lily wished she could use the troops' morale to justify wearing full plate armour, but Jason had waved that suggestion away, saying he had something better.

Lily glanced around again, checking that the small woman was still there. Lily was able to maintain a fairly powerful shield thanks to Prudence's training, but it was critical that she preserve her power. The young soldier behind her could make a shield of energy. If she concentrated hard enough, she could extend it to cover herself and Lily for almost a minute. It was her job to ensure Lily could stand at the head of her army without being the first one shot by Meridia.

Lily felt good being at the front. It was where she should be. If she was going to ask all these people to put their lives at risk, she shouldn't be hiding behind them. Of course, as her one job was to make it to the middle of the battlefield without dying, being at the front was also perilous, but once the battle started, her troops would charge around her.

Jason raised a fist, and Lily heard the order to halt being passed through their force. She could feel the ground shake as the Meridians continued to advance.

"Did they bring their whole army?" Lily asked Jason, trying to sound flippant, but growing pale at the solid wall of soldiers facing them.

He grunted. "Our units on the front lines in the DR are reporting a slight reduction in their contacts with the enemy. And they still haven't replaced the level of security at the signal tower. It looks worse than it is," he added in an attempt at reassurance.

Lily worried. The Meridian force looked so much bigger than the Highacren side. Not to mention they were all trained soldiers, not the hodgepodge her advisors had pulled together so quickly. But her side was fighting for their country. Their home. Still, if the fight dragged on, the Highacren forces might be in trouble.

Better do this quickly.

Noise came from her right, and Lily looked over to see the Valmeadian army come to a halt, just off the edge of the battlefield. Her attention was quickly drawn back to the front as the Meridian army halted with a loud crack, thousands of boots all hitting the ground at once. Lily tried not to be intimidated, but it was impossible with so many of them, all dressed in black with helmets that covered their entire head, standing a couple of football fields away, staring at their enemy.

Suddenly, it was quiet. The kind of awkward quiet where a cough stands out. Lily felt like they were cars at an intersection, all politely waiting for the other to go first.

"I didn't think modern war was like this," she commented quietly to Jason. "Marching out and facing each other. I feel like I should have a musket."

He gave a soft snort. "It's not usually like this, ma'am. This battle is very different. But that's because it has to be."

Lily felt the anxiety rising all around her. No one wanted to fight, but if they were going to have to, it was preferable to get it going. The anticipation was awful. She glanced down the line, seeing nervous fidgeting and shifting. But next to her, Jason was still. A veteran, he wasn't jittery like she was, looking around everywhere and checking that her weapons were still there.

"Are you sure you won't head back to the command tent? Run things from there?"

Jason shook his head. "This is it. We can all feel it. If we win today, Meridia will have to agree to a ceasefire. Maybe even peace. But we need to win, and to do that, we all need to help. We need to get you where you need to be."

Lily looked away, her eyes falling back on the mass of troops staring at them from behind their helmets. She was filled with a sense of guilt and dread.

"I promised your wife that you wouldn't fight in the war."

"I promised her I would stay in the command tent," he admitted guiltily.

Lily turned to look at him, one eyebrow raised. "Well, you'd better not die, or your wife will kill me."

A voice sounded off to Lily's left. Juliana was encouraging her girls, getting them pumped up and ready for the battle. Geraldine roared, and Lily saw some of the Meridians flinch, which made her feel better. A booming yip sounded; Kevin getting excited. To her surprise, more people jumped at hearing him than the dragon.

Lily cast her gaze over to the Valmeadians, wondering again what they would do. It could make or break Highacre. As if in answer to her question, a loud thump came from their forces as thousands of warriors came to attention. All eyes from both Highacre and Meridia settled on them, wanting to see what the Valmeadians had come here to do.

As one, the Valmeadian army turned to face their enemy.

Meridia.

A cheer went up through to Highacren forces, spirits buoyed. The additional troops might not be enough to defeat the larger Meridian army, but it certainly helped, and meant they weren't doomed trying to fight both Meridia and Valmead.

In response, a shout came from the Meridian side, and Lily could see their soldiers positioned on high points behind the infantry readying missiles.

"Jason?" Lily asked, trying to keep the worry from her voice.

"We're fine," he said, standing stiffly, staring down the enemy.

A call went out to fire, but after the projectiles left their tubes, they fell harmlessly at the firers' feet. A relieved laughter broke out through the Highacren lines.

"Smart bombs are fancier, but far more vulnerable," Jason observed.

At Lily's direction, Jason had reached out to Hudson, who had hacked the guided missiles they knew Meridia intended to use at the start of the battle.

"Hudson couldn't have made them explode when they hit the ground?" Naomi asked.

Jason shrugged. "He had time to interfere with their trajectory, not the safety systems."

A single crack echoed across the field and a middle-aged Highacren woman, one of the citizen soldiers, fell forwards, dead.

A split second passed as everyone processed what had just happened, and then chaos erupted across the battlefield.

Both sides rushed forwards like a burst dam, running at each other in a terrifying game of chicken. Jason, Naomi, Ava, and some of the Royal Guards moved in around Lily, their job to escort her to the middle of the field. They let some of their troops move in front to buffer the fighting and then set off at a run. The sooner Lily was in place, the sooner she could stop the fighting.

To her left and right, her people fell, picked off by Meridians. Lily hoped that her people were taking out just as many Meridians as they all hurtled towards the middle.

A roar echoed to their right as the fire-eaters met Meridia and trampled the western section of their army. She saw one of the fire-eaters fall; the Meridians were trying to focus fire on one animal at a time. But this enraged the others, and they began rearing up and stomping down viciously, trampling the soldiers into the ground. Lily felt slightly nauseous as she watched two of the fire-eaters using their tails. The spiked balls clubbed hapless Meridian soldiers, some impaled, others bludgeoned to death.

Meridians surged up from the rear, filling gaps as quickly as they were made. It was like watching someone poking holes in water.

She could make out bodies weaving through the carnage. Juliana's girls were using the distraction of the fire-eaters to infiltrate the enemy's lines and wreak havoc from behind.

Screams sounded as Geraldine began strafing the troops, blasting them with waves of fire. Jenkins's cries of glee at flying were at sickening odds with the sheer panic and pain of those on the ground. Lily couldn't see the effects from her position and for that, she was glad. She needed to defeat Meridia, but if she could do that with as little loss of life as possible, that would be best.

A horrible crunching smash echoed as the two forces collided in the middle, each hitting at top speed. Lily wondered how many—if any—of the front line soldiers from each side had been able to survive just that clash.

She was suddenly aware of bullets flying everywhere and bodies falling all around her. She tried to focus her attention forwards, but so much was happening, and her mind went into overdrive alerting her to the millions of threats surrounding her.

Alexei appeared on her left, and behind him she saw Kevin and his wife burst through the Meridian lines from the side. Bodies were thrown, crushed, and trampled as they engaged in the most violent zoomies ever witnessed. Lily felt like she was in a dream. Everything was so surreal.

"You okay?" Alexei yelled in her ear, his face concerned seeing her wide-eyed stare.

Lily nodded, blinking and forcing herself to focus. "Thanks for coming."

"Wouldn't miss it." Alexei grinned at her, letting her know she was forgiven.

"I thought you'd be busy being the ruler of a country."

Alexei shrugged, then threw out an arm, stopping Lily from running into Jason's back as the bodyguard stepped forwards, stabbing his bayonet into a Meridian who had broken through the Highacren lines as Naomi fired her pistol into the necks of two running close behind the first. Alexei pushed Lily to the right as the group altered direction to avoid a particularly scrappy skirmish directly in their path. Lily saw Alexei and Ava fist bump before returning their attention to the battle.

"I was," Alexei said, as if nothing had interrupted their conversation. "But I had to make a deal with my stepmother to secure the spot. She'd support me if I would lead the army heading to the DR. I agreed so long as I could decide who we supported." He shot Lily a quick grin. "She allowed that, so long as her son was in charge while I was gone."

Despite the chaos around her, Lily still felt a spike of anger towards Alexei's stepmother. Though she had to admit, the woman wasn't stupid. In supporting Alexei as Great Leader and allowing him to pick whose side Valmead took, she stood to gain Highacre's support if Alexei was tragically cut down in battle. And with her son already Acting Leader, he'd almost be assured to take Alexei's place. Lily glanced around anxiously, making sure there were no Valmeadian soldiers near her friend. She wouldn't put it past his stepmother to arrange for Alexei to die in the battle.

"And you're okay with that?" Lily asked as Geraldine strafed in front of them, blasting them with hot air but clearing a path.

"I spoke with my brother alone. He's a good person, and he knows what his mother's like. I've asked Sergei to keep an eye on him. He'll make a good leader. But perhaps in a few years." He winked.

Hearing raised voices, Lily turned to see a large group of Meridians rushing at them. She raised her arms, fireballs blasting from her hands, knocking the soldiers to the ground and setting several on fire. Jason and Naomi fired their weapons into the group, killing those still standing, as well as the people rolling on the ground desperately trying to put out the flames.

Without time to think about what she'd done, Lily turned to see another group advancing. She was about to shoot more flames, but stopped just in time as Kevin's wife darted in front of them, bowling over the Meridian soldiers. Those not taken out turned, firing at the huge ball of fluff. She howled as the bullets impacted her rear leg.

A yip of rage echoed, and suddenly Kevin was there. He grabbed the soldiers in his mouth, whipping them from side to side. It was cute when he stole Lily's sock and did it, but Lily watched in horror as limbs went flying and she was sure she could hear bones cracking above the noise of the battle raging around her.

Kevin spat out the bodies, swiping at others with his paw as he made his way to his wife, checking on her. She was licking her back leg, but at his nudge got up, and together they continued their rampage through the Meridian army.

More attackers came, and Lily raised her arms again. Ava's hand landed firmly on her shoulder before she moved in front of Lily and, with precision, gunned the advancing forces down.

"You're meant to be saving your energy, remember?"

"Well, if I die, the conservation would have been rather pointless," Lily called back, frustrated. She had forgotten in the chaos of the fighting. Her instincts were taking over and telling her to kill before she was killed. But she made an effort to restrain herself and let the others do the fighting as they pushed the final few metres. All the while, her heart screamed at letting her friends risk their lives for her.

For the chance at peace.

"Now!" Jason roared.

Lily's friends formed a circle around her, facing out and repelling anyone who came close. Lily reached for her power, remembering the feeling she'd had that first day. The wave of power that had emitted out from her. She pushed it out as far as possible, willing it to cover the battlefield ahead of her and everyone on it.

Drones dropped like rain. Weapons fell silent. Meridian soldiers grabbed at their heads, their implants suddenly failing.

"Cease fire!" Jason shouted. Others took up the cry, and it echoed across the plain.

A hand grabbed Lily's arm, making her jump, but it was just a Highacren soldier assigned to her for this moment.

"Meridian soldiers!" Lily's voice boomed around the battlefield, magically enhanced by the soldier at her side. "We have negated your technology. Your implants will not work. Your weapons will not work. We could wipe you out right now, but we do not want to kill you."

Lily paused, letting her words sink in and ensuring the Meridians were listening.

"Highacre does not want this war. We never wanted this war. I sought peace with your president soon after it was illegally declared by our ex-prime minister. Your president said no. I do not want any more people to die here today. You have seen what we can do. If you wish to continue the war, we will render your technology obsolete at every battle. You can not win without it. Surrender here today and return to your leaders, to your president, and tell them what happened. Tell them what we can do. And explain to them what will happen if they do not seek peace with Highacre."

Lily kept a steely expression on her face as she scanned the battlefield, making sure they were listening and that no one was trying to return to the fight. It felt weird, threatening people into peace. But she was sure that very few people other than the president wanted war. She was simply giving them the means to influence him over to the majority's side.

The Highacren and Valmeadian forces remained tense, watching the Meridians, who had recovered from the initial shock of the pulse and were now looking around, unsure of what to do. Shouts rippled across their side of the battlefield, but Lily couldn't make out the words. Suddenly, a white flag, hastily made by ripping the wall from a tent, was hoisted into the air at the rear of their lines.

A deafening cry went up all around Lily.

They had done it.

They had won.

31

Lily fiddled with the papers in front of her, eyes sliding over the words, not really taking them in. The man standing next to her desk in full military regalia was no doubt briefing her on very important things, but all she heard was a dull, droning noise.

She was exhausted. The days after the battle had been a blur of activity. She met with President Taylor again, virtually. The shift was palpable. Not only had Lily shown that Highacre could completely negate any advantage the Meridian forces had, and also half their weapons, but now she was the one on better terms with the Great Leader of Valmead. Alexei didn't even have to say anything—him sitting next to her was enough.

President Taylor was quick to agree to both an immediate ceasefire and a peace treaty, the terms of which diplomats from both sides were hastily drawing up. That was probably some of what the general to her left was talking about. She needed to focus. The terms would be important, and she needed to make sure there was nothing that would cause her people any further harm as they began to heal.

Lily had addressed the nation the night before, reassuring the people that everything would return to normal and she had a plan to ensure stability as they did so. An election would be held as soon as possible to allow a vote for the new prime minister, and once that person was identified, Lily would work with them to move forwards.

Lily nodded at whatever the briefer was saying, thinking again that she really needed to listen, or just tell the poor guy to leave it for now. Her eyes tracked back to the top of the page she had failed to read.

"Apologies, General."

Lily looked up, hearing the urgency in Alexei's voice. "What's up?" she asked, trying not to feel guilty about her relief at being interrupted.

"We've got him."

Alexei didn't have to say any more. Lily immediately excused herself and the two hurried towards the basement car park.

"Ava's with Naomi preparing the guard," Alexei explained as they strode through the corridor. "They'll meet us in the basement."

"And we're sure we found him?"

"Positive. He was picked up by our scouts and Jason had Hudson check the cameras. There's a perfect shot of him looking right at one."

Lily frowned. She'd had Naomi send scouts to systematically patrol the city looking for Ezra. The scouts were anyone they could find whose magic allowed them to sense implants; some were civilians embedded with groups of guards. Soon her people could return to normal, but while Ezra was still out there, no one was really safe.

The confirmation by the camera bothered her. The cameras were hidden. That Ezra would at once be so careless as to be caught on camera and then look directly at one seemed off.

Sensing her concern, Alexei added, "Naomi had her people surround the building, monitoring who's going in and out. He hasn't left, so either he doesn't know we're coming or—"

"Or he's waiting for us," Lily interrupted, her deep sense of foreboding increasing.

Alexei hesitated before saying, "I was going to say that he's overconfident about the abilities of his implant and assumes he can hack the cameras. But you're right. And that's why we've got the guard coming as backup."

Neither Naomi nor Jason had been thrilled when the three friends had announced that when Ezra was located, they would deal with him personally. And they weren't wrong in pointing out that risking one head of state, let alone two, in the current climate with Meridia was risky. But Lily felt it was a necessary one.

She was the only one who could negate his implant, and Alexei, having been told by Ava about Ezra's desert glass shield, the cube that he had used during their conflict in the Tower, had come armed with an enchanted device that looked to Lily like a fancy slingshot.

Slightly offended by her muted enthusiasm, Alexei had given her a demonstration. "The enchantment enhances the user's ability to aim. I can make impossible shots, even fire it so the projectile curves through the air at the target."

"That is great," Lily had said, trying to make up for her perceived lack of enthusiasm. "But Naomi tried to shoot Ezra when..." Lily faltered. With everything that had happened, she hadn't really had time to process Addison's death. Thinking of that day forced an image of her broken body into Lily's mind, and she had choked back tears as she repressed the memory. There would be time enough to grieve later. Alexei put a reassuring hand on her shoulder and she grasped it. They had all suffered too much loss.

"The partraka—"

"Slingshot."

"*Partraka*," Alexei had insisted, looking mock-annoyed at her belittling the invention. "Its point is to get the projectile to the cube. Its enhanced aim will help us hit the cube and not Ezra, and because it's not powered by technology, it can't be destroyed if you need to use your power. But the key is the projectile. We know from Naomi's attempt that bullets can't get through the shield. But Valmead's research shows that these will."

Alexei had opened his palm, revealing what looked like a bunch of small marbles.

Desert glass.

"But I thought it was all destroyed?" Lily had asked. "And won't they negate the enhanced aim?" Following her encounter with Ezra's impenetrable shield, Lily had been briefed on desert glass. It was only found in Valmead and was rare. Valmead had collected all known samples to provide to Meridia in what would have been a catastrophic exchange for Highacre. Desert glass could block all forms of magic and enchantments.

Fortunately for Highacre, the entire shipment of desert glass had been destroyed in a train accident that occurred shortly before the assassination of the royal family, and so not much had been done to confirm whether any glass remained and if so, how much. A quick investigation following the untimely revelation of Ezra's cube had suggested that no other quantities were available.

"Most of the glass was shattered into dust," Alexei had explained. "Our scientists tried to find a use for it, but as a dust it seems impotent. However, there were some tiny shards. I had them reshaped into these pellets. They should be impervious to Ezra's shield. And this"—he'd tapped the leather strap into which the desert glass would go— "will absorb the desert glass's influence. It's the handle of the partraka that's enchanted."

Lily and Alexei strode into the garage.

"I've got three units en route already," said Naomi by way of greeting as and she fell in beside them. "Two more will follow us there."

"And the shields are with us?" Lily asked.

"Yes ma'am," Naomi confirmed.

Lily agreed the backup was necessary, but all she really cared about was having someone with them who could provide a barrier of their own while she and Alexei brought down Ezra. The rest of the guards would be largely useless until they dealt with his shield.

She sensed Ava on her other side and glanced over. Ava wanted to be there; to be a part of bringing her father down, but she was the most vulnerable. Jenkins had fashioned a blocker for her, a little metal square that emitted a frequency that would prevent Ezra's access to her implant. He was confident that it would work, and Ezra's arrival at the Tower that fateful day told Lily it did. He wouldn't have shown up personally to gather intelligence if he didn't have to.

"I'm fine," said Ava firmly, though not unkindly, as she felt Lily looking at her. "And I know I don't have to be here," she added, correctly predicting Lily's words.

"I'm just worried," Lily said.

"I know. But I have to do this, Lily. I need to see it through."

Lily rubbed Ava's arm to let her know she understood, and then they all piled into an SUV, Naomi behind the wheel.

The trip to the Tower was fast. There was little traffic on the roads and the flashing lights of the Royal Guards' vehicles ensured everyone else got out of their way. Lily saw flashes of the destruction wrought by the Meridian scouts. There were some burned buildings, and some completely destroyed ones. But she was heartened to see the reconstruction efforts had already started. Soon, Burlaron would return to normal.

"We've found a secret door in the hallway on level twelve," Naomi briefed Lily. "A false panel. Looks just like every other panel, but one of our guards has X-ray vision and could see the space behind it."

Lily felt Ava flinch at the mention of one of the abilities she had lost.

"When was it put in?" asked Lily.

"That's the thing, ma'am. No one knows. One of our guys brought up the plans. Nothing. No record of that addition to the building later, either. Jason's putting some people on it. They'll look into how it came to be there, and also how an ex-Meridian spy managed to take up residence in a secret room inside the Highacren parliamentary building."

The Tower was already surrounded when Naomi pulled the SUV to a screeching halt at the entrance to the building. Lily felt relieved when she saw they were already evacuating people.

"Okay." Lily took command as they walked swiftly towards the doors. "Naomi, get your shields and follow us. The rest of the detail can fall in behind, but when we reach him, I don't want anyone else getting in the way. They won't be able to touch him with his barrier."

Naomi nodded, gesturing to three guards who immediately fell in behind the group. Lily entered the building and headed to the elevator. Her group got in one car and she saw two other groups of guards waiting to use the other elevators. A bunch of less lucky guards were already filing into the stairwell at a jog.

Lily stared impatiently at the numbers slowly climbing.

All she cared about right now was dealing with the man behind everything that had befallen Highacre, starting with the death of her parents.

They formed up outside the secret door. Lily, Ava, and Alexei took the front, a shield behind each of them and Naomi bringing up the rear.

"On three," Lily commanded. "One, two, three!"

Alexei thrust open the door and followed Lily and Ava inside. With unnatural speed, the door slammed shut once the three had entered, locking Naomi and their shields outside.

"Oh no," came Ezra's sarcastic drawl. "You found me."

32

Lily looked around the room they were now trapped inside. It was strikingly bare; the walls were metal with pipes and cables running their lengths. She estimated it was maybe double the size of her office back at the palace, and there were four thin pillars, each an equal distance from the corners.

Ezra was on a platform that abutted the back wall. There were two steps leading to it, and it was bordered by desks that held various screens and computers. A glance at one of the monitors showed Lily that Ezra was not only aware of the cameras in the Tower, but had hacked into the feeds. He had watched them arrive and march right up to his door, lured into his trap.

Lily reached out, probing for his implant, and was frustrated but not surprised to find herself blocked by his barrier.

He tsked at her, sensing her attempt. "Now, now. Manners. You've only just arrived and here you are, trying to invade my mind. You know I wouldn't have invited you here without using my shield. Not after last time. You tried to burn me alive! And certainly not now that you've revealed your... special talent. I remember quite well how it knocked me off my feet that day you were training with the late Lady Octavia. Though I didn't know it was you at the time. If I had... well. Perhaps I might have handled things differently."

"You're right, Ezra. How rude of me." Lily matched his sarcasm. "How have you been? Keeping well?" Before Ezra could respond, she called, "Now!" and her friends sprang into action.

Lily and Ava began a barrage of attacks; Ava with bullets and Lily with fire. They knew they couldn't hurt Ezra, but the aim was to keep him focussed on them while Alexei tried to deal with the cube. Lily and Ava would draw fire and Alexei would take aim at each of his pockets, starting with the one inside his jacket from which the cube had tumbled last time.

It was a risk, and the glass pellets were in short supply, but they didn't have any other options. Lily fired off a few more fireballs at Ezra, diving to her left as he fired lazily back at her. He was toying with them—happy to injure, but by no means shooting to kill. Ava, on the other hand, was aiming dead-on for her father's head, but her rate of fire decreased rapidly as her bullets were repelled and rebounded off the metal walls, becoming more shrapnel for them to deal with.

Alexei had dashed to his right and was crouching behind a pillar that offered his bulk very little cover. Taking aim, he fired a glass pellet, hitting Ezra directly in the chest.

Feeling something hit him, Ezra's smug grin faded immediately. He focussed intently on Ava, who froze mid-step. She stood like an awkward statue, her eyes bright in alarm, and then, satisfied his daughter was under his control, he trained his gun on Alexei.

"Ava!" Lily cried, rushing to her girlfriend in alarm.

Ava's eyes followed Lily, but the rest of her remained still as stone.

"She's quite alright," Ezra drawled, his eyes glancing to his daughter and back to Alexei.

The implant.

Lily started rummaging in Ava's pockets for the blocker Jenkins had made. Maybe it had malfunctioned? Or somehow switched off and she could flick it back on?

"Clever idea," came Ezra's voice. "Targeting the frequency. Of course, then all one has to do is pulse that frequency and... poof."

Lily wheeled, glaring at Ezra in time to see him gesture with his free hand, indicating something turning to dust. *How could he have known?* Was there another plant in her team?

Ezra tapped the side of his head. "You're not the only one with mind reading skills, you know."

Lily cursed. She was so sure she'd kept her barriers up in the Tower. But perhaps with everything going on she'd let them slip. Or maybe Ezra's implant was simply more powerful.

"Oh no, not you, Your Majesty. Dear Addison had as much trouble keeping information to herself in her mind as she did through her inane chatter."

Lily's blood boiled at the insult of her dead friend. Addison had been told about the device by Giles when she'd asked about Ava's presence and the danger it posed. It was a cruel irony that her concern for keeping information out of Ezra's reach had handed him exactly what he needed.

Lily's stomach sank. It was over. With no shields of their own, and no real cover, Ezra could pick them off, one at a time. Alexei had had one chance to destroy the cube before Ezra figured out what they were up to and took precautions. And it looked like he'd picked the wrong pocket. For his part, Ezra seemed in no hurry.

"Intriguing," said Ezra, moving to the edge of the platform and looking at Lily and Alexei as though they had surprised him. "You have more glass then?"

His tone told Lily that Ezra had thought there was no more beyond what he himself had, and the evidence that he was wrong infuriated him.

"Yes," said Alexei, omitting to disclose the quantity.

Keeping the pistol trained on Alexei, Ezra looked over at Lily. "You have come a long way, Your Majesty. You've really stepped up into your role. You might even make a good leader. Well, you may have, anyway." An evil smile slid onto his lips. "The girl who first arrived here seemed paralysed by the weight of responsibility. But here you are, in control. Making decisions."

Ezra took a couple of steps towards them, descending the stairs and moving slightly to his left, giving himself a better shot at Alexei, who seemed to consider moving but realised there was nowhere else to go, so he remained in place.

"I have a decision for you. Your lover or your friend."

"What?" asked Lily.

"I'm going to shoot one of your friends," Ezra explained as if he were speaking to a child. "But I'm going to let you pick which one gets to live. Your girlfriend, whom you seem to love, but let's face it, is a Meridian spy and unlikely to be accepted by, well, any Highacren. Or your friend, who as the new leader of Valmead stands to lead his country out of poverty and oppression and save thousands of lives. What will Lily do? Is she truly the queen, or still the scared little girl?"

"You sick bastard," Lily spat. "You'd really shoot your own daughter?"

Ezra's eyes flicked briefly to Ava, a frown ghosting across his expression, but he quickly looked back at Lily. "That, Your Majesty, is entirely up to you."

Lily's mind reeled. Ezra was crazy, and he had already shot two people right in front of her. Could Alexei get another shot off? Perhaps she could rush him. That might distract him enough for Alexei to shoot at another pocket.

Despair threatened to engulf her. She knew there was no way to stop him. They had tried, and they had failed. At best, Alexei might get a shot off, but Ezra would shoot him in return. And even if he hit the right pocket and managed to destroy the cube, Ezra could shoot her before she could access his implant.

And he would shoot her. He hadn't lured her here just for another chat. The only reason she was still alive was that Ezra was a cat, playing with his mouse until he got bored and snapped its neck.

In order for the world to live, you must die.

It hit Lily with resounding clarity. She wasn't going to walk out of this room. This was where it ended for her. But she would take Ezra with her, and she would do everything in her power to save her friends.

"I choose me," she said simply, willing her voice not to waiver.

"No," cried Alexei.

Ava couldn't move, but Lily could sense her panic at Lily offering herself as sacrifice.

Lily took a step towards Ezra. "You want me to choose someone for you to kill. I choose me."

Ezra looked at her in patronising disappointment. "But Your Majesty. You weren't one of the options. It's okay. I'll give you a little more time to mull it over. I know how difficult decisions can be to make. I've been making them for a long time now."

Ezra began a long-winded diatribe about his early days of being director of the Meridian Intelligence Agency and all the difficult decisions he'd had to make.

Lily glanced at Alexei, but like her, he didn't seem to have a plan that might see them survive. He shifted his weight behind the pillar, and Ezra raised his pistol aggressively, though his tone remained the same and he didn't miss a beat as he continued with his story, taking them all the way to his public sacking.

"It was then that I realised the true power was money. I rebranded myself into a businessman and all but selected the next president. But I couldn't fix things with influence over my own country alone. What with you hiding advancements like interdimensional travel from the world. So selfish," he spat. "Technology belongs to all of us. What else have you kept from the world with your secrecy? Medical advancements. Food production. How many have died because you wanted your toys for yourself?"

Ezra was unravelling now, but as if sensing it, he paused, running a hand over his hair and ensuring it was in place.

"Governments keep advances that can benefit us all to themselves. Corporations though; we bring the people what they need. We provide the people with what they want, even before they know they want it. I knew that if I could gain control of Valmead and Highacre, just as I had with Meridia, I could make sure we were all working together for a better world."

"A better world?" Lily couldn't stop herself. "A better world for who? Not for Addison or Austin or Richard or Lady Octavia. Not for the hundreds of Highacren citizens your HSP harassed and detained and beat and killed. Ezra, thousands of people have died in *your* war. How has any of this been about anything other than benefitting yourself?"

Ezra looked at Lily curiously, as if she'd missed the obvious point. "I've run the numbers. Yes, some people had to die while we're implementing the plan. But the lives that will be saved once I have control dwarf this blip in the system."

She gaped at him and he blinked, as if remembering what he was meant to be doing. "But we were talking about decisions. I made the decision to take control of Highacre. First, I needed to get rid of the monarchy. Such an antiquated system. But the prime minister's new ideas for government weren't as popular as they should have been, and it was taking too long at any rate. So I expedited the process. Imagine my surprise when I learned there was one royal left." He smiled coldly at Lily.

"But we adapt, and so upon meeting you and realising how malleable you were, I decided you weren't a fly in the ointment—you were the key! I could use you as I did President Taylor back in Meridia. You were a much better prospect than Toth in the end. More pliable and less prone to getting your own ideas. And far superior longevity. But then you started thinking you *should* be queen. As if anyone *should* be in charge." He spoke with no apparent irony, despite somehow also simultaneously holding the opinion that he should apparently be in charge of literally everything.

"So, once again, I'll need to pivot here. It should be relatively easy. The original plan accounted for the tragic demise of the royal line. Though it would seem that I'll need to find an intermediary now, seeing how you have tarnished my reputation. That complicates things, but is not insurmountable."

Lily blinked. The man was insane. She wasn't sure how he expected to get out of the Tower alive, let alone continue to meddle in Highacren politics, let alone the world's.

Ezra turned his attention to Alexei, gesturing with his pistol as if it were his hand. "Now Valmead, I was never overly worried about. You're always so desperate for trade, it's easy to buy influence. But then your father died, and you took over. Which proved to be another complication, especially when you didn't jump at my initial offer."

Lily's head whipped around, and she stared at Alexei. Initial offer? Had there been a subsequent one? A wave of nausea washed over her as she wondered if they were working together. Maybe this was how their plan had gone so badly wrong so quickly. She felt a sting of betrayal, but then recovered herself. That was not Alexei. Her friend had proven himself time and again beyond reproach. He was on her side.

"But luckily your stepmother is more amenable to offers that benefit her people. And her pocket." He smirked in a theatrical aside. "And, as it turns out, not only is she not opposed to harm befalling her beloved stepson, it appears she views that as an added benefit."

"I'm still considering your offer," said Alexei, grasping for time. Lily could sense his panic at hearing Ezra's infiltration of his country.

"Yes, well." Ezra frowned, cocking his head to the side. He turned, looking at Lily, but still addressing Alexei. "Unfortunately, sometimes when you take too long, the decision is made for you."

Ezra pulled the trigger.

33

Alexei collapsed to the ground, blood pooling around his body.

"Now." Ezra's voice sounded a million miles away as Lily tried to process what had happened and figure out a way to save Ava. "Let's give you another chance."

Lily turned to see Ava moving towards her. But it wasn't Ava in charge. Her eyes were panicked and her body was moving stiffly as she tried to fight Ezra's commands.

"You suggested I kill you, rather than your friends. Let's see if you really are willing to die for the ones you love, or if you wind up killing your girlfriend to save yourself."

Without further warning, Ava launched at Lily, punching her in the stomach and sweeping her legs from under her. Lily crashed to the floor, her breath knocked out of her, and crab-crawled backwards, earning some space before lashing out. Other than shielding herself, the main focus of Lily's lessons with Prudence had been to master her electronic pulse. As an area weapon, it had ended the war, but it was precision that Lily would need to bring down Ezra. She had just never imagined using her power on Ava.

As she had been taught, she reached out with her magic, similarly to when she was reading minds. Locating Ava's implant, Lily hesitated for a beat before allowing the tiniest bit of magic to buzz through the connection. She needed Ava to stop, but she didn't want to hurt her.

Ava stumbled, her implant losing power, severing the connection to Ezra. But almost immediately she stood back up, straight as an arrow, and started advancing again.

"A nice try, Your Majesty," called Ezra, clearly enjoying himself. "But you'd have to destroy it—and her—to win here."

Lily regained her feet before Ava reached her and blocked her next attacks, suddenly grateful for Austin's hand-to-hand training. But Ava was a far superior fighter, having trained longer, and soon she overpowered Lily again, forcing her to the ground.

Lily reached for her implant again and hesitated. She wasn't confident in using more power than she already had. Prudence had warned her that frying someone's implant would likely kill them. She'd been more than happy to test that out on Ezra, but looking up at the woman she loved, Lily realised she wasn't prepared to risk killing her.

Ava grabbed Lily and raised her to her feet before unleashing another string of blows Lily struggled to deflect. She blocked two punches from Ava before temporarily locking their arms, and in the moment of closeness, looked into Ava's eyes. A tear rolled down Ava's cheek, her eyes pleading with Lily to do what she knew she could not.

The moment was broken as Ava pulled free, pivoting and landing a powerful punch that sent Lily flying. Expecting the crack of her head on the concrete, Lily was surprised at landing on something hard, but not as solid. The hand that she'd extended to break her fall slid through something thick and warm.

With horror, Lily realised she'd landed on Alexei. She tried to push herself off him, but slipped and crushed him again. Nose to nose, she saw how pale he was, and her hands moved, searching for the wound to try and stop the bleeding before she remembered her precarious position. Lily heard Ezra's laughter at her scrambling in her friend's blood and knew why Ava hadn't advanced again. Ezra was enjoying Lily's discomfort far too much.

Letting the anger take her, Lily went to push herself up off her friend's body, and jumped as his hand clasped her wrist.

"Take it," Alexei whispered weakly. Lily looked down and saw him pushing the partraka towards her. Though her heart leapt at seeing that Alexei was alive, she knew he wouldn't remain so for long.

Lily scrambled to her feet and squared up to Ava, who was moving towards her again, though this time less quickly. A drop of blood dripped from Ava's nose as she slowed to the speed of a rusty robot. Ava was fighting Ezra's control.

She looked at Lily with fire in her eyes. "Do it," she said with effort. Lily didn't know if she was referring to the sling-shot or to her pulse ability, but either way, Lily hesitated. If she was unwilling to hurt Ava, they would likely all die, anyway. If she did take Ava out, Alexei might have a chance at least.

Lily rushed at Ava, bringing the base of the partraka down on her head hard before she could think about it. As she made contact, Lily was simultaneously worried that she had hit Ava too hard, and not hard enough. But her girl-friend dropped to the floor, unconscious. Her head made a horrible crack as it hit the concrete and Lily cringed, wanting to check on her, but knowing she had no time.

Diving toward Alexei to retrieve the desert glass, she called out to Ezra, "Why didn't you just kill me before?

Would have been much easier." She didn't expect him to answer, but any distraction would help at this point.

"I needed you out of the way, but I also needed war." Lily could hear Ezra's footsteps as he moved to get a better angle. "To kill you after the Trials would have merely focused Highacre on the infighting. But if you were missing..." She glanced up to see him leering at her, clearly pleased with his genius. "Your advisors would be distracted, fighting to get you back. Which left me to keep prodding Toth along unimpeded."

"But then why didn't you kill me in the Tower?" asked Lily, keen to keep the madman talking as she pulled the glass projectiles from Alexei's pocket and scooted behind the pillar. "You had your war, and like you said, you couldn't control me."

"With Toth gone you were the best bet. You're right, I didn't hope to control you as I had him. But you're a very young woman. Who better to lead Highacre to defeat? Had I killed you, it was likely Minister Bellingham would have come to power. She's highly respected, both here and internationally. She would have brought a higher probability of peace. *I* certainly would have put her in charge if that was the outcome I desired."

Lily peered from behind the pillar, fuming at the assumption that her age and gender made her less likely to succeed, as well as the implication that if Lily wanted peace, she should have stood aside. But what caught her eye was the furtive glances he threw at his daughter, who was stirring on the ground. Ava was okay, but Lily would need to move fast before Ezra sent Ava after her again. She hesitated. Something in those dead eyes when Ezra looked at his child niggled at her.

"You kept me alive for her."

Ezra bristled at the accusation, but his chin wobbled,

and the denial he'd been ready to fling died on his lips. "I had hoped she would come home," he said quietly. "Killing you would have closed that door for good."

"You're not my home," Ava spat, now conscious and still struggling against Ezra's hold on her. "Not my father."

The warmth died in Ezra's eyes. "I guess that's that then."

Ezra turned and fired. He missed, but was already moving to get a better shot at Lily. She flinched behind the pillar, then took a deep breath. Lily couldn't use the enchantment to assist her, so she had to concentrate hard on aiming. Leaning out from behind the pillar, she fired at him. And missed.

Ezra was no longer laughing. Finished playing with his prey, he raised the pistol and fired again at Lily. She dove left and rolled, ending the movement on one knee, and quickly took aim before firing and missing again. Ezra trained the gun on her, pulling the trigger as Lily rolled behind the next pillar.

They repeated this dance, Lily eternally grateful that Ezra was using a simple pistol and not one of Meridia's guided weapons like he had last time, presumably to avoid her rendering it useless with her pulse. Eventually, Ezra aimed at Lily, pointed the pistol and pulled the trigger, only to hear a click. He glared at it in frustration, and Lily took her chance, steadying her aim and holding her breath. She fired, and a satisfying tinkle of broken glass came from Ezra's pocket.

The time it took for alarm to appear in Ezra's eyes was all Lily needed.

Seizing control of his implant, Lily let loose with her power, sending a pulse of energy directly into Ezra's head. She felt her energy engulf the implant. It had a metal covering that sought to protect it. Lily increased the intensity. Her pulse penetrated the armour and began to fry the implant, destroying it from within.

The implant, as she found, was wired intricately throughout his entire brain. That was how he had controlled Ava so completely. They were effectively one organism. No longer man and machine, but a blend of the two.

Lily could feel her power burn along the many tendrils of the implant, destroying as it went. Ezra's body began to convulse as the energy wreaked havoc in his brain. Though she had no problem killing the monster before her, feeling his brain dying so intimately made Lily feel sick.

It was over in seconds, though it felt much longer. With a small gasp, Ezra Brown's body dropped to the ground, dead.

It was finally over.

34

THE SETTING SUN burned across the sky, bathing the land in an orange glow. Lily stared out from her seat on her balcony, enjoying the view and absently patting Kevin. His wife, who had allowed Lily to call her Renee, was curled up in a soft basket beside the chair. Her rear leg was bandaged and a plastic cone fixed to her neck to prevent her from licking her wound and disturbing the stitches. Despite her hatred of the cone, Renee had refused to let the healers help her, snapping at any brave enough to approach. She had also taken to growling at anyone who looked in her direction and failed to indicate that they might remove the cone, and Lily wished, not for the first time, that she could communicate with the pelotromos telepathically. But now Renee was sleeping, with her children rolling around in the basket beside her.

Lily heard the door open, but didn't look up. There had been a steady flow of people interrupting her over the last week, needing documents signed or decisions made. She had asked Giles if this was unusual, perhaps owing to the sheer volume of work required to bring Highacre back to its former glory. Giles had hesitated before suggesting that the number of urgent matters was certainly higher, and had said that in the coming months she would likely be interrupted less after hours.

"May I join you?"

Lily looked up to see Cyril standing beside her, also admiring the view. He was completely at ease, as if he visited her on her balcony all the time, rather than never having actually spoken to her.

His eccentricity put Lily in mind of Jenkins, and she smiled and offered him the seat beside her. He sat, and rather than explain why he was there, Cyril simply continued to enjoy the view with Lily. She found the silence comfortable.

"I was hoping to see Prudence," Lily said after a while. "She made such a big fuss about this prophecy. I was supposed to die to save the world and all." Anxiety permeated Lily's voice. A worry that it wasn't over. That the war and the battle and Ezra weren't the big threats the prophecy was talking about.

She looked over to see an embarrassed smile on Cyril's face as he turned his gaze from the view and looked at his hands. "I don't much go in for prophecies," he admitted.

Lily's eyebrow raised in surprise, but Cyril didn't go on. After a beat, she looked back out at the view, assuming he wasn't going to expand on his comment. Addison had mentioned he took a bit of getting used to. Having spent hundreds of years mostly in seclusion, his conversational style was... unique.

"It is odd how some people are happy to read all manner of things into flowery statements, presuming that they couldn't possibly be read literally, but the minute a prophecy suggests someone will die, they can't help but interpret it verbatim." Cyril looked over at Lily. "Why couldn't it be, for instance, referring to the figurative death of your old life? That you had to choose Highacre over your family in order to save the world."

Lily felt relief course through her, her body relaxing for what felt like the first time in weeks. But at the same time, she felt a little disappointed. The prophecies had been built up so much by Prudence, as if they were so important. Literally life or death. And now Cyril made them sound like horoscopes. Kevin started licking her hand, pulling her fingers with his tiny paws to areas of his body she should pat for him.

"The prophecies Prudence told you about are factual, though. And they do require literal death for the world to survive."

Lily's heart sank to the floor, ice filling her veins. She gaped at Cyril, who was still enjoying the view, a bland expression of contentment on his face. As he turned his head, looking over towards the coast, Cyril caught a glimpse of Lily's expression and performed a double take.

"Oh, but they're not about you. No, Lady Octavia wasn't often wrong, but on this occasion, she was slightly off. *Most* of the prophecies she found were about you. But the one that so flagrantly called for death, that one refers to another."

Lily's heart returned to normal. So she wasn't going to die. But a sense of disappointment still washed over her. Much as she didn't want to admit it, she had felt special. *The saviour of the world.*

Cyril turned to Lily, about to say something, but caught the look on her face. "But of course, you did fulfill all the others. With flying colours in fact! This one little prophecy doesn't refer to you, but you did manage to save thousands of people and avert a global conflict that would have devastated the world for decades. That's something to be proud of."

She appreciated the sentiment, but her mind remained fixed on that one prophecy. "Do you know who it is? We'll need to find them. Help them. As much as we can…"

Lily felt for this unknown person. She knew the aching sense of fate. The crushing knowledge that no matter what you did, you would not survive. She understood the effort it took to reach acceptance and simply be glad that others might go on.

"Yes… and no," said Cyril thoughtfully. "I know who it is. Or I should say, who it will be. It is my belief, based on my reading of the prophecies, that the prophecy in question refers to one who is yet to exist."

Lily stared blankly at Cyril.

"This prophecy is to come to pass in a few hundred years from now."

"Oh," said Lily, not expecting that answer.

"So yes, I believe I know to whom it will refer. And no, you don't need to help them. I will take care of that whenever it is that they arrive."

Cyril and Lily sat in silence together, Cyril enjoying the view and Lily processing his words, before Cyril simply stood and exited the balcony back into the Lodge. He was an odd man, but Lily found herself liking him.

She had heard someone pass Cyril on his way out, and so wasn't surprised when Jason took the seat beside her.

"I want to keep the troop numbers high in the DR," Lily started without preamble, assuming, as had been the case for the last few days, that he was here for business. "But anyone we can spare from the front can help with the rebuilding. As things settle, we can draw more back in, but I want to keep a strong presence there, given the tensions between Valmead and Meridia."

"Hopefully that won't be too long," said Jason. "Once Alexei returns home, things should settle down."

"Yes, but the doctor says he'll need to stay here at least another week. And even then, when he returns to Valmead, he'll be weak. I can't imagine his stepmother won't try to take advantage of that. I've offered to send some guards with him, just so he has some people he knows he can trust. But he wasn't too keen on that. Understandably."

The euphoria Lily had felt once the doctors told her Alexei would survive was diminishing the closer it came to his return to Valmead. She missed their time in her home dimension, where the three friends were together and obligations weren't driving them apart. Not to mention, given the political situation her own country had just endured, she couldn't shrug off a deep sense of foreboding. A fear for Alexei's safety.

"He's being quite open about not wanting to retain the leadership for life," Jason said reasonably. "Surely that will help keep the stepmother at bay."

"True," agreed Lily. "And if he won't accept the guards, I'll have a plan in place to make sure he's got a way out, if he needs one."

Lily already had Jenkins working on such an escape plan. When Alexei regained consciousness, he had told her he'd awakened with a new sense of what was important to him. And while that still included his country and his brother, it also included a drive to live his own life. He had already asked Lily if it might be possible for him to visit Elaine, and they had discussed the pros and cons of him moving there, or Elaine joining them here. She was half-Highacren, after all.

She hadn't mentioned it to Alexei yet, not wanting to get his hopes up, but she had approached Jenkins to see if he could build a similar device to the one her mother,

Belinda, had kept hidden. The device that had brought her home to Highacre. She told the scientist that she didn't care if it transported him to the other dimension or to Highacre—it just needed to transport him away from Valmead instantly, if required.

Lily hoped he could use it to visit Elaine. To give them a chance to develop their relationship before making such a momentous decision as moving to another dimension. But either way, it gave her a sense of comfort to think he could disappear if his stepmother sought to move up the timeline of her son's succession.

Jason placed a rough hand on Lily's soft one. "How are you, Your Majesty?"

Lily hesitated. She knew he meant now that she'd had time to process everything that happened. But she didn't want to think about any of it. It was all too much. Too overwhelming. She lowered her eyes, focussing on patting Kevin. "I'm fine."

"How is Ava?" Jason tried.

"She's good. Back in Meridia for a bit." Lily saw Jason's surprise and added, "There's a lot for her to sort out. Her job, house, life. Burying her father. But she'll be back."

The two sat quietly before Lily said softly, "She just needs some time. Losing Ezra, no matter how much of a megalomaniacal arsehole he turned out to be, well, it's a lot to process. And our fight when Ezra took control of her, not to mention that I'm the one who killed him…"

"But she understands," Jason said confidently. "You had no choice. Ezra forced your hand. There was no other way."

"And she gets that," said Lily. *I hope she gets that.* "But understanding doesn't help the heartbreak. She so desperately wanted a family."

Jason nodded. "I think we've all had enough heartbreak."

They drifted into silence, each lost in their thoughts. Thoughts of the fallen, both friends and the sheer numbers overall. So many dead. All for one man's need for control. And they were only just starting to realise the full extent of the damage done by the HSP. Between people dead, missing, and just simply now distrustful of authority, it was going to take years to fix.

"Any word on Claire?" Lily asked quietly. Every time she asked, dread gripped her heart, waiting for an answer she didn't want.

"Still nothing," Jason said sadly. "Which is probably a good thing. I'd imagine if Ezra killed her, he'd want her body found. He'd want to hurt us."

Lily nodded. It made sense. But where was she? Records found in the old HIA building showed that Ezra had discovered her duplicity. If he hadn't killed her, what had he done? Lily's mind drifted to images of Claire held captive in some secretive Meridian facility. Or maybe he had brainwashed her again, and she was now working for the Meridian Intelligence Agency. Or lying in wait as some kind of twisted failsafe to kill Lily if Ezra fell.

Maybe she was simply hurt with some kind of brain injury that had stolen her memories, and she was wandering, lost and alone. Lily forced her mind to stop spiralling. If history was anything to go by, Claire was more than capable of taking care of herself. Though, that didn't stop Lily from scouring the reports of the latest casualties uncovered each day.

A joyous whoop sounded overhead, drawing them from their thoughts and breaking the dour mood that had settled on them. Jason and Lily looked up, smiling to see Jenkins riding Geraldine, streaking across the sky, Geraldine sending happy bursts of flame up to match the burning sunset.

"It's not all bad." Jason grinned at Lily.

"No." She smiled, watching Jenkins. "And we'll all need some joy as we start to rebuild."

"Does that mean you've decided to stay? For good?"

Lily knew there had been some anxiety about that. A feeling that now the crisis was over, she may want to go home. Be with her family. Relinquish the burdensome responsibility.

She nodded. "This is my home. My country. My people. It's my place to lead them out of this mess and into something better. I do need to visit the other dimension though, once the first shipment of felixium is delivered. I want to see my family and make sure they're okay."

Jason squeezed her hand. "I'd be happy to go with you, if you'd like. And obviously, if your family wanted to move here, we can make that happen."

Lily nodded, sniffing. "I'll certainly ask. And Elaine might, at least for a bit. But if they do want to stay there, I want to help them do that. Make sure they have enough money and a decent place to live."

Jason gave her hand another squeeze and after sitting with her a while, he excused himself to get a start on the tasks Lily had outlined.

As she heard the door close behind him, Lily returned to patting Kevin and gazing out at the country that had become home. The sun was almost gone now, the light beginning to fade.

Jenkins flew back across the sky, closer this time, causing Kevin to yip at him and spooking the birds in the trees, who all took to the sky in the opposite direction of Geraldine, reminding Lily of Edmund.

She smiled, wiping a tear.

So many lost, but all heroes who gave their lives for others. She hoped she truly would have been willing, had

the choice been presented to her, and her thoughts turned
briefly to the one in the future who would have to make that
sacrifice.

Lily took a deep breath and looked at Kevin and his
family. It was not going to be easy, but for the first time in a
long time, it was going to be okay.

The Highacren Prophecy

Regent (free prequel novella)

Royal

Return

Reign

Rogue (free bonus chapter)

The City Chronicles

Rise of the Divvinium (free prequel novella)

City of Stone

City of Shadows

Echoes of the Divvinium (free bonus novella)

City of Sorrow

ACKNOWLEDGMENTS

So many people have helped me along the way in getting this series written, beaten into shape, and put out into the world.

A huge thanks to the crew over at GetCovers for doing such an amazing job on all the covers for this series! I can't believe you came up with such amazing designs so quickly and thank you for being patient with my little changes along the way.

This series wouldn't be what it is without the incredible support of my editor, Courtney over at Elevation Editorial. Courtney, thank you so much for your amazing guidance and support in making these books what they are - the story wouldn't be what it is without you!

I need to give a shout out to my writing companions, Ducky, Biggie and Butters. Ducky sticks with me while I write, snuggled and snoring in his bed. Biggie reminds me to eat. Well, that he needs to eat and since I'm fixing him something I should get a snack too. And Butters helps get me out of the chair and moving periodically by generously allowing me to throw his ball for him.

The hugest of thank you's to my incredible wife. Thank you for your unwavering support and encouragement. And thank you for re-reading this series more than anyone should ever have to. For someone who doesn't re-read often, I really appreciate your willingness to dive back into High-acre again and again. Most of all I appreciate your feedback. This story is so much better thanks to your ideas and input and you're the best writing, and life partner I could have ever hoped for.

And last, but definitely not least - a massive thank you to you! Thank you for reading my stories! I hope you enjoyed them as much as I loved writing them for you.

If you did enjoy Reign, please consider leaving a review on Amazon or Goodreads, or really anywhere you like! They really can make a difference, especially in helping other people find my books, and it'll go a long way to letting me keep writing stories for you.

Feel free to to head over to my website (www.kthold er.com) where you can sign up to hear about book releases and other fun things! If you sign up, you get Regent, an exclusive prequel novella, for free!

You can also get updates by following me on Facebook and Instagram, and I'm also on Goodreads and BookBub!

Thanks again!